Slashed Beauties

Slashed Beauties

A. Rushby

BERKLEY
NEW YORK

BERKLEY
An imprint of Penguin Random House LLC
1745 Broadway, New York, NY 10019
penguinrandomhouse.com

Copyright © 2025 by Allison Rushby
Penguin Random House values and supports copyright. Copyright fuels creativity, encourages diverse voices, promotes free speech, and creates a vibrant culture. Thank you for buying an authorized edition of this book and for complying with copyright laws by not reproducing, scanning, or distributing any part of it in any form without permission. You are supporting writers and allowing Penguin Random House to continue to publish books for every reader. Please note that no part of this book may be used or reproduced in any manner for the purpose of training artificial intelligence technologies or systems.

BERKLEY and the BERKLEY & B colophon are registered trademarks of
Penguin Random House LLC.

Book design by George Towne
Interior art: Ripped texture background © Street Boutique / Shutterstock

Library of Congress Cataloging-in-Publication Data
Names: Rushby, Allison, author.
Title: Slashed beauties / A. Rushby.
Description: New York : Berkley, 2025.
Identifiers: LCCN 2025000977 (print) | LCCN 2025000978 (ebook) |
ISBN 9780593954645 (hardcover) | ISBN 9780593954652 (ebook)
Classification: LCC PR9619.4.R87 S53 2025 (print) |
LCC PR9619.4.R87 (ebook) | DDC 823/.92--dc23/eng/20250113
LC record available at https://lccn.loc.gov/2025000977
LC ebook record available at https://lccn.loc.gov/2025000978

Printed in the United States of America
1st Printing

The authorized representative in the EU for product safety and compliance is
Penguin Random House Ireland, Morrison Chambers, 32 Nassau Street,
Dublin D02 YH68, Ireland, https://eu-contact.penguin.ie.

For men to be instructed, they must be seduced
by aesthetics, but how can anyone render the
image of death agreeable?

Arnaud-Éloi Gautier d'Agoty (1741–80)

Slashed Beauties

T*HE KNIVES ARE freshly sharpened for us by day, ready for each night's pleasure.*

Small, light, mother-of-pearl handled, they are weapons fit for ladies—though, of course, we are not ladies. Far from it. Ladies do not rise each evening at the devil's bidding. Ladies do not murder.

You might think it would be difficult to take the life of another, undetected. Of a man. One who is larger. Stronger. But it is not. It is surprisingly easy.

I am never questioned as I haunt the darkened streets of London Town, sniffing out my prey. Why would I be? Women such as I have found themselves upon these streets as long as men have trodden them. It is generally a simple task to extricate my target from his friends. To find a darkened corner.

To do what I am called upon to do is not challenging either. For I have no will in this. My hand is forced by another. There is no choice in the matter.

Evil guides the blade to the exact place where it must go.

Malevolent witchcraft ensures that the assault is accurate. Merciless. Swift.

There is often surprise on his part at the realization that he is being attacked. Astonishment floods his countenance. Then there is a pitiable attempt to grasp at the fast-fraying strands of life before he slumps. Perhaps a few final choked words, the gurgle of blood in his throat, bubbling at his lips.

And then . . . stillness.

The city does not even blink, draw breath.

My evening's work accomplished, I am turned about on my heel by that selfsame hand that drew me here, am compelled now to make my hurried escape. The knowledge of what I have done steals my breath away.

It is never really an escape, for I know full well that there will be no reprieve. There is no end to this. No freedom for me. I will be called upon to do the same again the following night. And the night after that . . .

ALYS

SEOUL, PRESENT DAY

The text, when it finally comes, arrives at three twenty-three a.m. Wanting to be kept in the loop, I'd provided one of the hospital nurses with a burner phone and a large wad of cash a week ago. And then I'd waited.

X

This one simple letter tells me all I need to know. Mr. Yoon is dead.

Hours on from that text, as I sit on a hard subway seat on my way to visit a client, I wait again. My heart beats out the theme tune of anxiety in my chest, as it's done since the early hours of the morning. Now I wait for another message, this one from Mrs. Yoon's solicitor.

The first in a long line of dominoes is teetering.

Feeling nauseous, I pop a ginger chew into my mouth and check my phone for what must be the hundredth time today. Still nothing.

I'm about to tuck it back into my satchel when the hairs on my arms rise.

A man, somewhere in this carriage, is watching me. I'm sure of it.

With my silvery violet pixie cut, my tattoo-dotted arms and the tank top I'm wearing on this hot summer's day, I'd expected a few stares. I know I'm an outlier. An oddity. Other. What was I thinking, attracting attention to myself? But I knew the truth of it. It wasn't other people's attention I was attempting to attract. It was my own. My new look was a deal. A deal I had made with myself. The hair, the tattoos—I was readying myself to become someone new. Someone different. Someone who . . . *could*. Or at least *was going to*. Once I'd signed the paperwork Mrs. Yoon's solicitor would provide, there would be no turning back for me.

Still, I must admit, now that I'm on full display in the subway, I regret not taking up my client's offer of sending a car.

Why, just once, couldn't I have said yes?

I don't know Seoul. I've never been to Hannam-dong before. I'm carrying something precious.

But I was never going to agree to that car, was I? I didn't want to owe anyone any favors.

Ugh. I can still feel his eyes on me.

It's nothing, I tell myself. *Nothing*.

Unable to concentrate, I shove my phone into my satchel and my gaze falls upon my upturned wrist and my latest ink—a likeness of a brooch I'd sold months back and couldn't seem to get out of my mind. Victorian, 1864. I let my finger trace the circular frame of the outside—pearls and gold—and then the woven crisscross of flaxen hair encased in the center. I hadn't thought I'd grown attached—until it was gone.

This happened now and again. Sometimes I'd dream about

pieces after I sold them. Sometimes I'd dream about them while they were still in my care. Sometimes they gave me nightmares. There had once been a necklace of bog oak that I couldn't rid myself of fast enough.

My finger starts to move up to the tattoo above this one, a twist of braided hair open at one end. This one is a permanent mark not only on my skin but in my heart. Just as I'm about to settle my attention upon it, I feel that gaze once more.

I look up.

There he is. Standing. Leaning. He's younger than I'd expected, though I'm not entirely sure what I'd expected. Something middle-aged and leering in an ill-fitting suit, perhaps. When our eyes meet, he startles, his attention darting to the phone in his hand. There is no challenge here. I have stepped on a twig in the forest, and he has bolted.

I'm about to glance away when a small flicker of a smile crosses his face.

He stretches. Shrugs. The sleeve of his T-shirt lifts.

And a tattoo peeks out from under the hem.

Oh.

I see then that I've read this whole thing wrong.

He doesn't think I'm an oddity. He was—is—sharing.

And this I don't know what to do with.

I am never comfortable around men. I am always wary. Fearful of what might happen. What I might do. Being looked at is never good. But being seen is worse.

I move my gaze to the floor and try to pull myself together. I think of my therapist. What would she say about this? I still can't believe I have one (a friend made me find one), but I have to admit that she's been . . . helpful. Which is surprising, considering the lies I've told her about myself. The half-truths. The fabrications.

As the train rocks along, I return to a talk the two of us had a while ago, about control. About feeling like *I* have control of my life, and things do not just happen to me. I am capable and have agency. I am the mistress of my own fate.

Her words resonated with me that day.

The mistress of my own fate.

I'd repeated the phrase for weeks. Could I ever be the mistress of my own fate? Whenever I thought back, I couldn't remember a time when any sort of control was my reality. A time when I called the shots.

Not that I think back often. I've learned the hard way that there is nothing to be gained by revisiting what can never be changed.

But once Mrs. Yoon signs that paperwork, it will all be up to me. The choices . . . mine.

That's what I need to focus on now.

The train stops. I don't look up, but I see his feet move. He departs.

See? There was no need to panic. He was simply a walk-on part. The smallest of characters in my story. There was never any threat.

The subway carriage moves forward with a lurch, and I look down at a different tattoo on my arm, a simple phrase in a fine, sloping hand.

I am the mistress of my own fate.

The domino continues to teeter, and I hold my breath, waiting for it to fall.

I FOLLOW THE DIRECTIONS on my phone; they lead me up a long, steep hill. On my way, I stop at a café and order two matcha lattes before continuing.

When I get to the house with one window, I halt. Veronique had told me I'd know it when I saw it.

She was right.

A double garage at the bottom, the house looms above, an austere concrete tower with one small square window.

Veronique's partner is an architect.

I press the buzzer next to the glass front door.

There's a pause, and then I see movement inside. Veronique is coming down the glass-sided stairs. She wrenches the door open.

"You're here! Come in. It's so good to have you visit."

We usually meet when we're both in London.

I step inside, onto the polished concrete floor, and take my sandals off. "Well, I have to see this room of yours I've heard so much about. I brought you a matcha latte. I know it's your favorite."

"You're an angel. Let's go upstairs." Veronique's eyes move to my satchel.

I'm not offended by the absence of small talk. My clients usually eschew unnecessary conversation—a reflection of their gnawing hunger for whatever object of mine they're looking to acquire.

The door snaps closed behind us, and we head up some wide wooden stairs. We exit the concrete tower and enter the building proper, walking into a room that is vast and open-plan and ... sparse.

"I know," Veronique says. "It looks like a morgue."

"Not a morgue," I reply. I look around, further taking in the polished concrete floor, the huge slab-of-marble bench in the kitchen. "A mortuary, maybe. A nice one. Expensive." Then I laugh. "Not really. The wood saves it."

Veronique rolls her eyes. "That's exactly what Richard says. It 'adds warmth.'"

"Perhaps that's the attraction between you two? He designs places that look like expensive mortuaries, and you fill them with your beloved collection of..." I don't how to put it. I probably should have just stopped at "beloved collection."

"Dead people's hair and eyes?" Veronique tries.

"I was searching for a slightly more eloquent turn of phrase."

"I'm not sure there is one."

I walk over to the marble bench and place my satchel gently on top. The bag with the matcha lattes, I set down beside it. I lift one out and pass it to Veronique.

"Thanks. I adore that café."

She pulls out two stools that were tucked out of sight under the bench.

We both sit.

I don't waste any more time. I grab my satchel and bring out a small metal case. I flick the latches on it.

Veronique leans in and I open the case.

Her breath catches. "Oh, Alys, it's even more exquisite than I thought."

"It really is lovely," I agree. And it is. The Georgian brooch is surrounded by twelve cranberry-colored flat-cut garnets and a ring of tiny seed pearls, which set off the dark chestnut hair swirled in its center.

"I had to have it." Veronique's eyes never leave the piece.

"I can see why," I say. But I don't ask her *exactly* why. I never ask why. With this kind of person—a person like me, like Veronique—there is always a why. And the truth is, you're better off not knowing. Why would someone alive be so fascinated with death? I've found that if you dig deep enough, there is always a reason. But it doesn't really matter. Veronique wants the brooch. I want to sell her the brooch. That's all either of us needs to know.

Veronique looks to me and I nod. She brings the brooch out to cradle it in the palm of her hand.

"Oh, you lovely thing," she croons.

I give her a moment. When she finally glances at me again, it's with narrowed eyes. "Wait. Why come all this way to deliver it? I'll be in London again in just a few weeks. Do you have something else to tempt me with? Something . . . better?"

"Well, that was quick. So you're not happy with the brooch now? Because I have someone else who's looking for—"

"Stop it. I love the brooch. You know I do."

I smile. "Sorry. I don't have anything else for you. Not today."

There's a pause. Veronique's eyes remain narrowed. "So why Seoul, then? Are you delivering to someone else? Or are you buying?"

"It's just a work trip," I reply coolly.

A longer pause.

Veronique stills. "No. It's true? One of the Venuses is really here? I heard a rumor, but I thought it was just ridiculous gossip."

I don't answer.

"Is one of them for sale?" Her breath catches. "Is it Elizabeth? I've seen photos of her. She's absolutely stunning."

I get off my stool.

"Sorry." Veronique holds up her hands. "Stupid of me. I totally forgot. You're related to one of the Venuses, aren't you? The original models, I mean. It's personal for you."

Again, I don't answer. I don't discuss the Venuses. Ever. And I would especially not discuss them with someone as indiscreet as Veronique.

"I might not have much time." I move the conversation along. "Do you mind if we . . ."

"Of course! This way." Veronique almost tips her stool over in her haste to round the bench. "I hope you don't think I meant anything by it. It's just that the Venuses are so fascinating. You know, I did a Jack the Ripper tour once, and the whole time I was on it, I thought the tour company should offer one based on the Venuses."

I force myself not to grimace. Those Jack the Ripper tours make me sick to my stomach. I think it's abhorrent how people relish the tale of the throat slitting and gutting of five poverty-stricken, vulnerable women stuck in horribly grim existences. Even now they're seen as "just prostitutes," these human beings who deserved so much better in life and in death. It truly amazes me how they continue to be served up on a platter for our entertainment. But this is neither the time nor the place to get into that. "It's fine," I tell Veronique. "We're fine."

I follow her past the kitchen and down a short corridor. She slides open a door and flicks on some lights. "Here we are," she says.

"Oh." I exhale, taking in the room, which is far more impressive in actuality than in the pictures I've seen. "It's really something."

Veronique's collection is encased in custom-built floor-to-ceiling recessed glass cases with overhead lighting. The pieces have been thoughtfully and carefully mounted on a backdrop of black slubbed silk. I walk over to the closest wall, dotted with eye miniatures. At least a hundred single eyes stare back at me—painted likenesses of eyes that were once alive but now exist only in this form, forever unblinking. The eyes are surrounded by heavenly clouds and have been fashioned into brooches and snuffboxes, pendants and toothpick cases, cherished reminders of loved ones who have passed away. A bit of a fad, they were made for only around one hundred years, from the 1770s onward. When I get to the very bottom row, I spot something and laugh. A real false eye sits, unblinking, set in a gold ring.

"Veronique, that's macabre, even for you."

"I know. I couldn't help myself, though. Who would do that? Do you think someone actually wore it?"

"Unfortunately, yes." I resume moving, wanting to take in the delicious room. Necklaces of heavy jet, some polished to a high sheen, some matte, call to me. And then, of course, there is the hair. So. Much. Hair. Braided, woven. Fashioned into rings and bracelets, watch fobs and brooches. Simple strands tied with a ribbon and encased in glass, or intricately weaved into fancy wreaths and lace. White. Gray. Black. Lush waves. Wiry strands. Wisps of baby curls. So much love. So much pain. So many memories. This is the answer to *Why?*

Mourning jewelry is my specialty—hairwork in particular.

I hover over one piece I know intimately. An oval locket made of gold, it is commonplace. Not an expensive or rare piece. Not at all. But there is something about the finely woven hair encased inside it, two shades bound together for all eternity—one fair, one dark. There is love there. Longing. Regret. I know it. Can feel it. I might not have known the deceased but there's no denying it. Some pieces stand out. Some pieces hold an energy that others do not.

I look down at a spot on my forearm, and there is the locket, tattooed upon me.

"If you ever want to buy it back . . ." Veronique says.

"That's kind of you, but I don't need to own it," I tell her. "I just need to remember it. And this way, I do."

"Is the braid-of-hair tattoo significant? I've always wanted to ask."

Where would I even start? "Mm . . ." I reply, and, not wanting to discuss it any further, I move on to the next case and see something that makes me suck my breath in. "What. Is. That?" I tap the glass, my gaze fixed.

"Damn. I knew it." Veronique steps forward and clicks open the glass case. She reaches in and brings out the brooch.

A fake.

"How can you tell from that far away?"

"It's my job to tell."

She gives me a look. "Come on. How long have you been doing this? How old are you really? Twenty? You've got to be under twenty-five."

"It's in my bones." I know this will be enough for her. Everyone interested in these sorts of goods knows my family has been in this business for hundreds of years.

Veronique sighs. "I should have known. I'm going to stop. I'll only buy from you from now on."

"You won't. You know you won't. And you don't have to. You know you can always call me for advice."

"That's kind of you."

"I mean it." And I do. Veronique is a very good customer. I see something I know she'll like, and then I sell it to her at a price that works for both of us. No haggling. No arguments. Everyone's happy. I love working with customers like Veronique.

My phone vibrates.

Mrs. Yoon will see you now. Please provide an address and a car will be sent for you.

And just like that, the first domino has toppled.

This car I accept without question.

There's no time to waste.

THE SLEEK BLACK car arrives within twenty minutes. Two men are inside. Neither introduces himself, but the one in the passenger seat gets out and opens a back door for me. I slide in and we are on our way.

A fifteen-minute drive sees me back where I started from, in Gangnam. I'm escorted into a shiny glass office building and into a lift, where I throw on the linen jacket I've brought with me in the hope of looking a little more presentable. We exit on the sixteenth floor.

The lawyer's office has moved since the last time I visited, but it's the same lawyer—Ms. Han, who is waiting for me in the doorway of the glass-walled boardroom.

She greets me, shaking my hand. "Please take a seat. Mrs. Yoon is already here."

I enter the boardroom. Mrs. Yoon is seated at the opposite side of the long table, wearing a beautifully fitted suit and upswept hair. Her face is pale and slightly puffy behind her chic clear-rimmed glasses. If it seems odd that she's meeting with me only hours after her husband's death, well, that's because it is. Our situation is . . . unusual, for want of a better word.

"I'm sorry for your loss, Mrs. Yoon," I say.

Ms. Han looks to Mrs. Yoon to see if she would like her to translate.

Mrs. Yoon only taps the polished tabletop with one finger. Business.

"I'm afraid Mrs. Yoon has much to do," Ms. Han says.

"Of course." I slide into the chair that has been pulled out for me, my heart already beating rapidly at the thought of what's to come. "It must be a difficult time."

"Water? Coffee? Tea?" Ms. Han offers.

I shake my head. "No, thank you."

"Then we shall begin."

And so we begin. A small pile of paperwork sits neatly before me, waiting to be signed. As agreed, upon Mr. Yoon's death, the goods in question will be transferred to my ownership.

And then I will destroy them. It. Her.

Elizabeth.

I'm sweating. Can they tell? I hope not.

Ms. Han clicks her pen closed. "There is one small issue."

My eyes had been locked on the contract. Now I look up, wary. This should be straightforward. The terms had been set. "Oh? And what's that?"

Ms. Han glances at Mrs. Yoon. "It has to do with Mrs. Yoon's son, Geon."

I'd met Geon only once. The Yoons had been in London and had invited me to some sort of business event they'd been hosting. Mr. Yoon had mentioned several times that I must meet his son, but Mrs. Yoon had expertly prevented any such meeting. That evening, she couldn't prevent our coming together.

I'll admit it: Even before meeting Geon Yoon, I hated him as much as I hated his father. I knew what he would be—another lecherous, salivating male. As I was led toward him I saw exactly what I thought I would see. He was tall. Handsome. Well turned out with a beautiful suit (naturally).

And then, as I closed in, I caught sight of his expression.

I'll never forget it. As his father brought us together, nudging his son in the small of his back, Geon came to stand before me reluctantly. His gaze flicked over me, and then he immediately looked away. In that flicker, I saw distrust. Distrust and fear. He did not want to meet me. He did not want to be in my presence. And I knew then that Mrs. Yoon had warned her son thoroughly. About Elizabeth.

And about me.

Geon Yoon wanted nothing to do with either of us.

A wave of guilt washed over me as I shook hands with Geon that night. I knew it wasn't my fault that the Yoons had been caught in the web of the Venuses, just as I knew it wasn't my fault that I had been either. But I also knew that, while Geon Yoon was currently a free man, he would shortly not be.

This was because he hadn't yet noticed the transparent silver threads of web that I had woven around him. I would soon snap those threads tight. And I would not release him until his mother had finally given me what I wanted. Elizabeth.

Across the boardroom table, Ms. Han clears her throat, returning me to the present. "Master Yoon has become . . . interested in the item. Mrs. Yoon desires that the item be taken from the country immediately. She would prefer her son not know its future whereabouts."

Oh no. I attempt to remain calm. I'd warned both Mr. and Mrs. Yoon. Clearly. "How did this happen?" I ask.

Ms. Han hesitates for a moment before continuing. "Unfortunately, Master Yoon was taken to the storage facility without my client's knowledge. The situation has progressed, and Mrs. Yoon does not wish it to progress any further. Thus, she would like the item to be destroyed within a week's time."

I almost bark out a laugh. A week! This is completely unreasonable. And yet they hold the line. Ms. Han shifts in her seat, silent. Mrs. Yoon's jaw is tight. She does not look me in the eye but stares fixedly at a point somewhere around my chin. But she's sweating too. I can sense it.

This is a standoff.

I think hard.

A week. It's an initial offer, a starting point for negotiation. I hold all the cards here.

I take a deep breath, sit back in my chair.

"That isn't the time frame we discussed," I tell Ms. Han. "We'd agreed upon six months."

"That is correct."

"It's really not my problem if Mr. Yoon let his son get . . . involved."

"That is true. But unfortunately, it has happened, and now Mrs. Yoon would like to expedite the proceedings."

A week. It's ludicrous. And yet, I'm torn. Maybe it would be better to rip the Band-Aid off quickly? Everything has been leading up to this moment for so long—for, in fact, hundreds of years.

For the reunion of the three Venuses—Elizabeth, Eleanor and Emily.

For their combined destruction.

Anyone interested in the backstory of the Venuses has heard rumors that they are connected to my family. They will have heard the gossip that we are related to—and in possession of—Eleanor; that Emily was destroyed long ago. And then there is Elizabeth. There have been whispers for many years that we have tried, and failed, to acquire Elizabeth. Well, wait until everyone hears that I've finally done it.

I'd sensed an opportunity when the Yoons came along. Elizabeth had been held by an elderly Austrian businessman for some time. When he'd passed away, she was sold very quickly by his family. As soon as I had found out who the highest bidder was, I'd started to make inquiries. I'd heard whispers that the acquisition of Elizabeth had caused some marital tension in the Yoon household. That's when I learned that the Yoons had a son. A son, I was betting, the mother might very well want to protect. Not only this, but Mr. Yoon was significantly older than Mrs. Yoon. I knew I might not get such an opportunity again.

So I decided I would exploit the family's weaknesses to their full potential. Unbeknownst to Mr. Yoon, I approached Mrs. Yoon. I cut her a deal. I let her know that, as soon as it was possible, I would be happy to take Elizabeth off their hands. And, more importantly, that, on taking ownership of her, I would destroy her.

This would, of course, leave her son forever free of the strange, bewitching, breathing creature that had possessed his father.

Mrs. Yoon enlisted her solicitor's help. We drew up the terms of our agreement. And then we bided our time. Mrs. Yoon, as it turned out, was a smart woman. Still keeping her husband in the dark about our deal, she managed to casually insert me into their lives. She had a third party introduce me to Mr. Yoon, who then brought me on as a consultant, thrilled about my family's long connection with the Venuses and about the fact that I was in possession of Eleanor. Elizabeth's previous captor had embarked on a no-expense-spared restoration, and Mr. Yoon built the princess a castle to live in, which Mrs. Yoon (the dragon?) made sure was a good distance from the family home. During the planning of this repository's construction, I played up the danger aspect. Special safeguards were built into the design. I reminded the Yoons of the stroke Elizabeth's previous owner had suffered (a strong family history, apparently) and the heart attack the owner before had died from (supposedly drug related).

And then Mr. Yoon's own health worsened. A coincidence? Who could say? In any case, Mrs. Yoon sensed that her chance was coming. I did too. I would have paid Mrs. Yoon to take

Elizabeth off her hands. But here, now, in Ms. Han's office, I sense another opportunity. Mrs. Yoon is desperate. Her husband has been stupid enough to mix her beloved son up in this abhorrence. No one else will destroy Elizabeth, and she's scared to do it herself. There are too many tales of swirling, shadowy magic surrounding the Venuses.

Mrs. Yoon wants Elizabeth destroyed. *Needs* her destroyed. As do I.

And I know a coven of good witches who will help me to incinerate her.

I tap my pen on the table and attempt to look like I'm weighing my options. "One week is out of the question . . ."

Mrs. Yoon understands enough to know that I'm stalling. She speaks a few crisp Korean words to Ms. Han.

"Mrs. Yoon is happy to pay a generous fee to make this happen," Ms. Han says. She writes down a figure on a small notepad and pushes it across the table. "An incentive, to leave the country this evening. We will arrange everything, of course."

£150,000

I hesitate upon seeing the sum. She really *is* desperate. No money was meant to be changing hands. Transportation was meant to be arranged on Mrs. Yoon's end, but that was all. It seemed an extremely generous deal, considering what Mr. Yoon paid for Elizabeth. I didn't know the exact amount, but I guessed it was somewhere between fifteen and twenty-five million dollars. It seemed ludicrous to give her away, but no one else would destroy her.

No one but me.

I stare at the notepad and wonder, How much time has Geon Yoon spent with Elizabeth? Where is he at this very moment?

Does Mrs. Yoon have a family member watching over him while he scratches at the walls, trying to get to her? Has she sent him out of the country?

I certainly hope she's changed the codes to the repository.

But none of this is my problem.

"If you accept this offer, you must leave for London tonight. The item must never return. Master Yoon must never be informed of its whereabouts. And it must be destroyed within a week's time."

I pick up the pen that is placed neatly before me at the table. I don't need the money, but I know someone who will benefit from it. I write down a different figure on Ms. Han's notepad and push it back toward her.

£250,000

"Two weeks."

Breathe.

Don't think about what's to come.

Do I feel guilty about shaking Mrs. Yoon down? Not as much as I'd like. The last time I checked, the Yoons' net worth was roughly 2.5 billion US dollars. Mrs. Yoon is going to be okay. But her son may very well not be, thanks to his father, and she knows this. Two hundred fifty thousand pounds is an investment for Mrs. Yoon, an investment in her son's well-being and future.

And my future? Well, let's not go there.

Ms. Han looks to her client. Mrs. Yoon stares at me for a moment, then turns and speaks to Ms. Han again. This time, her words rush out in a river of bile. She keeps going and going, becoming more and more animated. Some spittle flies from her mouth and lands upon the beautifully polished tabletop. I've opened my mouth, ready to accept a lesser amount—anything to leave this place—when a commotion outside the boardroom sees our attention shift.

Outside the boardroom, something is going on.

Ms. Han stands, her brow furrowed.

The glass closest to us is clear, facing a corridor. Farther along, nearer the reception area, it is smoked. On the other side of that translucent span, there is a flurry of movement. Dark suits. Voices calling out.

A screech.

And then a figure appears. Wild-eyed. Disheveled. Desperate.

Geon Yoon.

He spies his mother. And then me.

His eyes brighten as they take me in.

Smoothly, Ms. Han moves to the door, and locks it—just as Geon lunges for the handle.

He yells something. Moves to the glass. And begins to bang on it.

He says something in Korean I can't understand.

I see that things are much worse than I have been led to believe.

I look to Mrs. Yoon and see that her expression has changed. Where moments ago there was only hate for me, now there is only fear for her son.

Mrs. Yoon stands. Smoothly buttons her jacket. Collects her handbag. And, ignoring me, her expression cold as steel, she gives a final instruction to Ms. Han as she walks to the door, unlocks it and exits.

Only her hands give her away—her hands are shaking.

By the time she reaches Geon, two security guards have arrived. Master Yoon is escorted from the building, his mother following close behind, grim faced.

Ms. Han and I look at each other. I don't have to ask what Mrs. Yoon's instruction was. In that moment, she would have agreed to anything.

We spend only a few minutes tidying up the details. I will be taken from here to my hotel to pack up my things, then to the storage facility where Elizabeth is being held. From there, we will leave for our nine p.m. flight. It is already eleven a.m. The timing will be tight. I note that my preferred art-removal company has been booked and is ready to go. As has a seat on my preferred airline.

I rise from my seat and shake Ms. Han's hand for the last time. As I push my chair in, I find that I have to ask, "What did Mrs. Yoon say? Before her son arrived. She was saying something."

Ms. Han hesitates.

"No, really, I'd rather know."

Ms. Han looks away. "It was very rude. She says you . . . sicken her, that you are a monster."

If only Mrs. Yoon knew the truth of all of this. Of Elizabeth. Of me. Our situation has the form of an iceberg, and Mrs. Yoon has viewed only the very tip. If she could see the horrors that lurk below the waterline, she would not have entered into a contract with me. Or perhaps she would have anyway. What choice did she have? None of us have much choice in any of this. Not Mrs. Yoon, not Geon Yoon, not me. I've often wondered myself if I'm a monster. Maybe I am. But this isn't about me. It's about Geon Yoon. Mrs. Yoon is simply afraid for her son. Afraid that his father's fate will befall him. Entranced. Enamored. Bewitched. How many hours did Mr. Yoon spend with Elizabeth?

Did he neglect his family to be with her? Neglect his health? Did his obsession with her lead him to an early grave?

No. I don't blame Mrs. Yoon for her anger. If I were in her position, I'd be angry at me too.

Ms. Han accompanies me all the way to the car waiting downstairs. "Thank you for agreeing to expedite the proceedings," she says as the door is opened for me. "I do think it will be for the best."

It would be the best for Geon Yoon, I think. But for me? I'm not so sure. "It's always been a pleasure to work with you, Ms. Han."

"Thank you. The feeling is reciprocated." Ms. Han hesitates. "So, she is to be destroyed. I wish I had seen her in real life. This Elizabeth. I only ever saw the photo that was on file."

I sit back in the car, and my gaze rises to meet hers. "Best be careful what you wish for, Ms. Han. Especially where Elizabeth is concerned."

THE DRIVER AND escort take me to my hotel. There, I quickly pack up my things and settle the bill. Then it's back into the car. We drive farther now, to the edges of what looks like an industrial area. I flick through the paperwork as we travel. Everything is exactly as I would have arranged it myself. Mrs. Yoon wants to make my—and Elizabeth's—exit as quick and as seamless as possible.

Get out. Go, the paperwork screams at me. *Leave us.*

My phone vibrates, and I see that the money has already hit my bank account, care of Ms. Han.

When we pull up at the small, purpose-built brick building, I vaguely recognize it from the pictures I've been shown previously. It stands on its own, squat and nondescript. Anything could be inside. A large removal van is parked outside, waiting for us. Four men alight when our car pulls up.

I open the car door before the escort can reach it. "Everyone must wait here," I tell him as I get out.

He nods.

I make my way up to the thick wooden door and punch the first eight-digit code from the paperwork into the electronic lock. The door clicks open. I slide in and close it behind me, shutting out the world.

The air inside is wonderfully cool and devoid of humidity amid the heat of the Seoul summer. The foyer has been decorated with warm, honey-toned woods, and a small lit alcove holds a pretty ceramic bowl. There's something about the space that makes me wrinkle my nose, something sterile and lifeless. I think about the hundreds of times Mr. Yoon must have entered this space, eagerly awaiting his visit with Elizabeth. And then, one day, he decided to bring his son along for the ride. I shake my head in disbelief. How could he? Did he not realize he was setting his son up for a life of misery? Of withering away, staring at . . . an object? How could he even consider passing on the baton? Or the poisoned chalice, more like. Leaving his son behind to drink from that bejeweled but deadly cup. Poor Geon Yoon. I see him in my mind's eye, violently banging against the boardroom glass. In his sweatshirt, his hair mussed, expression frenzied. He deserved better. He didn't want to be like the others. Like his father. I truly believe that. I'd felt it when I met him.

I walk over to the next door. But here I hesitate before I punch in the next eight-digit code. I haven't seen Elizabeth for . . . some time. This is beginning to feel all too real.

I tell myself to push on. I have a plane to catch, and the past is a dangerous place for me. Whenever I drift back into it, I can find myself lost for days—weeks sometimes—in a sea of melancholy, of remembrance.

I take a deep breath and punch in the numbers before I can think any harder about what I'm doing.

Click.

The door opens.

The room is larger than I expected. Darker too. I can just about make out the perimeter. Something about this makes me nervous. The room feels like an endless ocean. Anything could be out there, lurking in its depths. I turn to see an alcove dimly lit just inside the doorway to my right.

The earphones.

Installed at my suggestion, they weren't necessary, I knew. But with so many rumors surrounding Elizabeth, about how dangerous she was, I needed to look like I was offering Mr. Yoon some form of protection from the creature in its cage.

Give the punters what they want.

I pick up the earphones and put them on, thinking of Mr. Yoon as I do so, of all the times he had slipped on that headset and closed the world out.

As several phrases repeat calmly in Korean, I listen, trying to remember the exact phrasing I had requested be played every five minutes. Something like:

This is not real.
This is but a dream.
Feel your feet on the floor.
Stretch your arms.
Move your fingers.
Only you exist in this space.

Every cell in my body tells me to flee, even though I know I'm perfectly safe.

I put the earphones back in the alcove.

And then, slowly but surely, I let my eyes wander over to the star of the show, spotlighted to great effect in the middle of the room.

To Elizabeth.

Elizabeth.

I take a step over.

Then another.

Her beauty, as always, is a small thrill, a breathtaking jolt.

Just to be allowed to exist in her presence is something.

Elizabeth reclines on a forest green velvet chaise longue. One arm tucked behind her head, lustrous waves of thick red-gold hair fan out upon a fat silken cushion. Her eyes closed, her expression is one of rapture, making me wonder what it is she dreams of. An expanse of radiant skin is displayed along her neck, highlighted by a set of dazzling pearls—real, of course. Her décolletage is thrust upward and pushes against the golden tucks and ruffles of her dress, the smallest of dainty seed pearls painstakingly sewn on, the bodice dotted with miniature ribbon roses.

Her chest rises and falls, rises and falls.

See? she says. *I am real. I am only sleeping. Believe in me. Want me. I can be yours forever. And you will be mine.*

She is an enchantress. A clockwork enchantress.

I stand and watch her for some time, willing my heart to calm itself.

"You look good, Elizabeth," I finally say, my tone far too breezy. "Not a day over two hundred seventy-six."

Elizabeth is actually 277 years old.

After her grand restoration, I must admit that she looks

more beautiful than ever. It seems almost wasteful that she has been kept in this room, hidden away, to be viewed only by Mr. Yoon, who sat here and dreamed of... I probably don't want to know what.

I try to imagine how Mr. Yoon initially explained to his wife his acquisition of Elizabeth. Had he played it all down? *Mr. Yoon: Honey, I'm buying a medical model. Mrs. Yoon: Sounds fascinating, darling. Go for it!* How had he described this object he desperately coveted? Had he told her Elizabeth was nothing more than a wax figure, originally intended to teach medical students the anatomy of the lungs? This much is true; if you undress Elizabeth's waxen torso, you can take her apart in layers in order to gain a basic understanding of thoracic anatomy. But why the milky breast? The luscious hair? The pearls? Well, it was believed that these "delights" were the only way of capturing and sustaining the attention of the male medical students. Then again, maybe Mr. Yoon didn't need to say anything. Maybe he just did whatever the hell he wanted.

He certainly had the last time I'd seen him. It had been at that event where I'd met Geon Yoon. After his wife and son had melted off to some place where I wasn't, Mr. Yoon had lingered. His English was limited, and my Korean was nonexistent. When we'd met before, there had been an interpreter. It turned out that we didn't need one this time. Before I could say anything at all, his hand darted out and ran through my hair.

"Beautiful," he'd said.

I'd recoiled in horror, pulling back sharply, to leave several long strands of hair trailing from his hand. My stomach lurched. I knew of the repulsive men who had kept Elizabeth before him—I had researched them in depth—but I'd never met one of her keepers in the flesh before.

And I swore I never would again after that night.

I'd left the event immediately, cutting my hair short the following day. And I'd sworn Elizabeth would be mine through Mrs. Yoon.

And that I would finish this.

Once and for all.

I take a deep breath. "Come on, Elizabeth," I say. "We're going home."

ELEANOR

LONDON, SEPTEMBER 1769

I WANT TO GO home.

I no longer have a home.

The thought of running away had been so thrilling. A new life in bustling London, a husband by my side. Together, we would carve out a better existence for ourselves, bigger and brighter than the lives we had been living out in the dowdy little villages we hailed from. The son of a baker, my sweetheart swore he didn't want his father's existence—lifting backbreaking sacks of flour, baking half the night and then tending shop by day. And me? All my future held was years of unpaid labor, teaching the few dim-witted students my stepmother had been able to keep on as boarders since my father's sudden demise. An educated man, he had attended university before his family fell on hard times due to his father's gambling debts. He had become a tutor, married and then eventually taken students into his own home. He had taught me to read. To write. To think.

But now, as I pause under a lamp and look about myself uncertainly in the Vauxhall Pleasure Gardens, I wonder if my father forgot to teach me some other, equally important, lessons, the sort that do not come from books.

Yes, the thought of running away had been thrilling. The act of it, less so.

I had begun to doubt my choices even before I left the warmth of my own bed. I hadn't dared rest that evening lest I sleep the whole night through. When everyone in the house had finally fallen asleep, I grabbed the few things I'd prepared and ran.

Only to trip and fall, twisting an ankle and muddying my best dress, not ten steps from the front door.

I'd hesitated. Should I return and change?

But no. There was no time.

I had to meet Nicholas.

And he'd been there, waiting for me, at the church lych-gate, just as he'd said he would be.

Nicholas.

He'd taken my hand, and we'd run together, our entwined hearts fairly bursting from our chests, breathless as we were from exertion and the thrill of escape.

Nicholas had arranged for us a ride with a friend who had borrowed a wagon in order to deliver some goods to London. That part of our journey I'd enjoyed. I had barely noticed how uncomfortable I was for the sheer joy of lying down in the cart, pressed up against Nicholas. I had even managed to doze off. When I awoke, dawn was breaking. I had sat up then and looked on, wide-eyed, as the city closed in around us until we reached our destination—Covent Garden.

I'd imagined a glorious place full of riotous color and life.

Instead, the place was gray and grimy.

Everywhere I looked was a putrid sight, the streets a

wretched cesspool of filth and despair. Emaciated and disease-ridden cats and dogs haunted the shadows, and the members of the public who braved the early hours had faces twisted into surly masks of grim desolation as they went about their business.

And, oh, the stench of it! My nose was assaulted by smells that I struggled to pick out, each one making me gag as I realized its source: rotting vegetables and fruit, horse droppings, wood smoke, coal smoke, even the puddles underfoot, which had formed not by rain from the heavens but from sewage that reeked.

The noise too! The yelling from men drunk from the night before, and from Londoners crying out their wares for sale on this new day. The bawling of babies, the clatter of hooves, the whinnying of horses, the laughter of a toothless old woman.

I'd longed for home—the home I hated.

But there would be no turning back. My stepmother would have discovered my disappearance by now, read the note that I had left.

It was too late to return.

So I'd kept going. I'd let Nicholas lead me to our lodging.

I'd imagined it as a small but presentable room.

It was small. Presentable, however, it was not.

Even in the dim morning light that was filtering through the broken shutters, I could see that the room was filthy.

Nicholas saw it, too, but he did not seem to mind as much. And he soon found a way to distract me from the grime.

For some time our attention was diverted by other things—more... pressing needs.

When I'd awoken, Nicholas was gone. There was a moment's panic before I saw the small pie he'd left for me. He must have gone out and come back to leave it, knowing I'd be hungry. I supposed he'd gone in search of his friend—the one who had promised him work on his arrival in London.

He was away for what seemed like forever. In the cold light of day, the foulness of the room became even more apparent. The dirt halfway up every wall. The soiled linen. The scrabbling that could only mean vermin under the floor.

As I picked at my pie, I longed for home, familiarity. But the home I once knew was no longer, my father gone from this world. It was not possible for me to return. Going back would mean more than a lashing from my stepmother's tongue. It would mean the embarrassment of her barring the door to me. My short absence would be her excuse to be rid of me forever, as she'd always wanted. I imagined the gleeful look that would have fallen upon her face as she read that note of mine, how she would have rushed to tell her daughters the good news of my disgrace. Our neighbors. The whole village. She would have put on quite the show. Oh, how she would have sobbed. Her husband—gone! And now this!

The pie eaten, I had paced the room and stewed. When Nicholas finally returned, hours later, he was worse for wear and in almost as foul a temper as I. The friend who had promised him work now had none. This, apparently, was my fault. I'd dithered regarding leaving. And now the work was gone.

With Nicholas in a rage, I'd had to forget my demands—for better lodgings, for answers to my questions about when we were to be married. We'd gone to bed hungry that night. But we hadn't managed to stay angry for long. And our other activities soon made me forget the rumbling in my stomach. Night after night, day after day, we proceeded like this.

Now, two weeks on, in the middle of Vauxhall Pleasure Gardens' Grand South Walk, I turn about on the gravel path, my eyes searching for him.

Nicholas.

Where is he? Will he come tonight? I need him to come tonight. To rescue me.

I scan the men and women promenading up and down the wide pathway, the freshly lighted lamps illuminating their excited expressions. There are all sorts here—ladies and gentlemen, shopkeepers and merchants, pickpockets and ne'er-do-wells. We have all paid our shilling to enter and rub shoulders in the famous pleasure gardens.

I turn to my left and start toward the Triumphal Arches. Maybe I'll see Nicholas there? I had marveled at those arches as we'd walked under them on our first visit together—wondrous constructions that tower overhead and lead the viewer's eye toward a huge painted canvas of a Chinese pagoda, a deceptively real mirage of a faraway land.

Nicholas had been by my side then, my willing guide. He had been to the pleasure gardens twice before, on visiting the city, so he considered himself to be quite the expert. As we entered through the proprietor's house, he had explained the gardens to me via a small printed map.

"Here are the main walks." He had pointed. "Here are the supper-boxes, for refreshment." A tap with his finger. "The pavilion houses the orchestra. And then there are the arches, the statues and the cascade, which is a sight such as you have never seen before, a waterfall that is not a waterfall but glittering tin sheets that give the illusion of one. Can you believe such a thing exists?"

Slow down, I had wanted to say. *Explain all these wonders to me in detail.*

But he was already tugging my hand, pulling me inside—my husband-to-be.

And then ... oh, then.

We had taken a few steps and he had spread his arms wide, stepping aside to present a whole new world. My mouth opened in wonder as I took in the vast grounds, the spacious tree-lined avenues, a place so unlike anything else I had seen in the city—so unlike the putrid, jail-like confines of Covent Garden—that I could barely believe my eyes.

I was about to turn to Nicholas and attempt to speak when I was grabbed by the waist, spun around. A man's laughter filled the air. I was released, and I stumbled, giddy. A man in a patterned silk suit did a little jig in front of me before running away with a group of gentlemen.

"Enjoy, lovers!" he called out as he went.

"Who was that?" I asked Nicholas, thinking it must be someone known to him.

Nicholas chuckled. "No one. Everyone. He is the embodiment of the pleasure gardens. Anything might happen here and sometimes does." His expression turned suddenly serious. "That reminds me." He fumbled with the map, opening it once more. He pointed to yet another spot. "This place here is not for you."

"'Druid's Walk.'" I read the printed words aloud.

"Mind what I say. Nothing good can come of going there. It's full of cutpurses, women of the night—and worse."

"Worse?" I wondered what might be worse.

Nicholas leaned in. His voice fell to a whisper. "Evil magic—so they say."

I pulled back with a laugh.

But Nicholas's expression was serious. "It is no laughing matter, Eleanor. You must stay away. Such magic is real."

I ceased my laughter. "Really?" I'd wanted to know more.

But Nicholas only shook his head, as if reluctant to discuss the matter. "As long as you have me for protection, all will be well. Come on, then." He tugged at my hand once more. "Come and see the delights."

Recalling Nicholas's words now, I look up to view the spacious tree-lined avenue and those same beautiful arches he pointed out to me on that evening that now feels so long ago. I continue on my way, but I am careful not to stray as far as Druid's Walk, for I am on my own, without protection of any kind, and fearful of each dark shadow I spy in this unfamiliar city. I turn on my heel before I reach that dissolute place, and I make my way back to the Grand Walk. Looking. Always looking.

Caught up in remembrance, I think back yet again. Yes, our first trip here had been magical. The ride across the Thames in the little boat, along with all the other excited folk, had been wondrous. We had all been so jolly in anticipation of our evening's fun, and one of the party was a musician who played upon his French horn for us. And then the thrill of entering the pleasure gardens themselves, that faerie land of illuminations, music and paintings, of pavilions and grottoes and temples. Oh, it was what I imagined heaven must be like. It was everything I dreamed London would be, and more.

I turn again on the path, starting to feel dizzy from my constant change of direction, my lack of sustenance and my panic. Everything seems different this evening. Now I don't notice the lanterns. I don't hear the fine music, see the people dancing, marvel at the artificial waterfall. There is no pleasure to be found in these pleasure gardens anymore.

It is my second night here without Nicholas, searching for him to no avail. He left our lodgings three days ago, after yet another argument. He said he wasn't coming back.

At the time I hadn't believed him.

Now I believe him.

Nicholas is not coming back, and I am a fool.

A fool with dwindling funds, and fear rising in her chest.

And then, just as I have given up all hope, I spy him in the distance.

Relief floods my body, and then I am off. I run as fast as my legs will carry me, people staring at me as I go.

It has all been a terrible misunderstanding.

"Nicholas!" I tug upon his arm.

He turns.

"Madam." The arm pulls away.

It is not Nicholas. Of course it is not. It is only wistful thinking on my part that it might be him. This man is older. It is only his curly hair that makes him at all similar. My imagination has been playing tricks on me.

As he departs, I stand on my own, overwhelmed by a tumult of emotions that pull me in different directions. I am embarrassed. Ashamed. Frightened. And full of rage. How could Nicholas do this to me? How could he entice me from my home only to desert me? Didn't he realize I am not like him? I do not have the choices available to me that he has as a man. My options in life have been restricted by the very chance of my birth.

It is as people push past me, laughing, chatting, enjoying their evening, that I notice her again. The lady. I saw her last night, when I came here searching for Nicholas. She was here the first time I attended the pleasure gardens as well. Nicholas had noticed her too (every man had noticed her). Tonight, my gaze follows her as she breezes toward me on the Grand Walk. It is as if she owns this place. The crowd parts for her, everyone watching as she goes. This evening, she wears a stunning dress of midnight blue silk. A necklace of sapphires twinkles at her neck and draws the eye to her chest and the globes of her breasts. Her skin is flawless, unmarked by the pox, with a flush at the lips and cheeks that looks like natural exertion rather than the vermilion of rouge. And her hair—oh, it is truly glorious, a red-gold cascade so bright, so brilliant, it is hard to believe it is real. However, it is not any of these attributes that I truly covet. No, it is her confidence that I envy most, for she seems as if she understands through and through this foreign land I find myself in. She is comfortable here. She would know what to do in any situation. In *my* situation.

Striding along this evening, she looks to be on a mission. Perhaps she is on her way to dine in a supper-box? To spend an evening enjoying the company of friends? For a clandestine meeting with a lover?

Only her eyes give her away. They dart here and there, as mine do.

I realize she is looking for someone.

I tilt my head to the side as she passes, and our eyes meet. There is a flicker of recognition, and I am surprised to see that she remembers me, that she has also noticed me these past few nights.

With a rustle of silk, she is gone.

Or perhaps not. She turns.

"I would hazard a guess that we are both here for the same thing," she calls out, walking back to meet me.

At first I think she means Nicholas, but then my tired mind catches up.

"We are both far too pretty to be kept waiting. Men should be falling at our very feet!" she continues.

My cheeks become hot. How can she be calling me pretty? Me in my muslin gown, even if it is my best.

"Ah, you should blush more often! It is very becoming. Now, what is your name? Mine is Elizabeth."

A grand name for a grand lady. "Eleanor," I say.

"Very pretty. And who is it you are searching for, Eleanor? A sweetheart?"

My eyes scan the Grand Walk once more. "His name is Nicholas. He..." And I can't help myself. The whole sorry tale tumbles out, along with some hot, salty tears.

After some time, Elizabeth stops me. "I think we both know neither of our friends will be joining us tonight. So we shall be each other's company. Come, let us find a vacant supper-box and have something to eat."

"Oh," I start. "No. I can't. I don't have—"

But Elizabeth only waves a hand. "Come, now. I will pay. This way. We shall dine, and you shall entertain me with the tale of the dastardly Nicholas."

WE SLIP INTO one of the supper-boxes, and Elizabeth summons a liveried waiter. She immediately orders all sorts of delicacies—champagne and chicken, thinly sliced ham, bread and butter, tarts and arrack punch.

"We shall make a feast of it," she says. "We deserve no less."

I keep an eye out for Nicholas until Elizabeth leans forward and covers my hand with hers.

"My dear, he is not coming. Best forget him and turn your mind to new thoughts."

She stares directly into my eyes—hers the same sparkling blue as her dress.

I nod. Her comment finally makes me see sense. Elizabeth is right. Nicholas isn't coming. He hasn't had an accident. He hasn't been called home because a family member has fallen ill. Nicholas isn't coming because he has gotten what he wanted out of me, and now that he has had it, we are done. We will not be married. Ever.

I reach across the table, take my glass and polish off the champagne in it.

Elizabeth pushes the plate of chicken toward me. And the ham. And the tarts. She signals to the waiter for more champagne.

"So, now you understand. It is a hard lesson to learn. Especially the first time."

"I feel like a fool."

"No. *He* is the fool. You seem a smart, willing girl. And beautiful too. I have never seen eyes such a green as yours. It is his loss, and he will realize it in time." Elizabeth leans back in her seat and takes a sip from her glass of champagne. "So, what is the plan now that there is no more Nicholas? You mentioned that there is no going home."

"I suppose . . . I'll have to find work. Perhaps in a milliner's shop."

Elizabeth shrugs. "I expect you believe it involves little more than trimming bonnets and toying with ribbons, fashioning pretty bows. I'm sorry to say it's not as it seems. I know many a girl who has worked in a milliner's shop, and it is terrible work. Their eyesight begins to fail within a year or two."

I take in Elizabeth's fine gown, her sparkling jewels. "I suppose you don't have to work."

Elizabeth laughs heartily at this. "Why, I've worked every day of my life since I was four years old! I began by working in my father's tavern. And then, when I was thirteen, I changed my line of work entirely."

"Really? What is it you do now?"

Elizabeth smiles at me. "You haven't guessed?"

I shake my head.

She chuckles. "My dear, I'm a member of the Cyprian Corps. A Thaïs. A devotee of Venus."

I frown, not understanding.

"I'm a fallen woman. A harlot."

I startle. "But . . . but you look like a fine lady."

"I am a fine lady!"

"I didn't think . . . I didn't think they looked like—"

"Let me guess. You thought we all look like miserable, toothless old hags riddled with disease, rutting against lecherous fools in dark corners of Covent Garden?"

"Well, yes."

Elizabeth shrugs. "To be fair, some of us have little more to offer than a threepenny upright. But many others could not be further from your imaginings. Here. Let me show you what *Harris's List* says about me." She reaches down, into her pocket, and pulls out something that looks like a pamphlet. "Can you read?"

"I can read," I tell her.

She opens the pamphlet to a particular page and passes it to me. "I always carry it on myself, as it is quite the charming review! How can I explain it? *Harris's List* is like a catalog in which one might see what services of the flesh are on offer in Covent Garden, and go straight to the supplier. Clever, no?"

I take the pamphlet, which is full of names and addresses, with some writing under each listing.

"This is me." Elizabeth reaches over and taps the page.

I begin to read.

The celebrated Elizabeth, Queen of Covent Garden, has been of service since her thirteenth year, with Mother Wallace. Now about twenty-three, this enchanting creature is unknown to few. What is there to say? Each limb and feature is a delight. Her entire being is so transportingly charming as to fill the beholder with rapture. Slim and tall, with eyes as clear and fine colored as the azure blue, flowing tresses of flaming golden silk and skin of polished ivory. A witty, convivial and engaging soul, she has, little wonder, been kept for two years by the captain of an East India ship. We hear she is soon to strike out on her own, and we wait in anticipation of this day.

"There is not a finer review in there," she says when I am done. "And many of them are not pleasant. Harris can be terribly cruel. Just listen to what he says about Anne at Mother Grayson's." She takes the pamphlet from me, flicks forward a few pages and begins to read. "'She is not pretty, and in all her actions she shows the lewdness of a monkey and the wantonness of a goat.'"

"Goodness," I say.

"A little unfair to monkeys and goats, I feel, knowing Anne as I do." Elizabeth pockets the pamphlet. She assesses me for a moment or two. "Eleanor, we are both women of the world. Let us speak freely. You ran away with this boy—am I correct?"

I nod.

"It would be my guess that much passed between you even before you'd left home."

"I..." I feel my cheeks begin to heat up again, and not from the champagne.

"And those activities most definitely continued when you arrived in London." She pauses. "Come, there is no need to be coy with me of all people."

I see no judgment in her eyes. "There were... activities, yes."

Elizabeth looks at me in an assessing manner. "I would presume that you enjoyed these activities."

I glance around me. No one is paying us any heed. Feeling bold, I toss my head. "Perhaps I did."

"Ah, there is fire in you. I like it. And let me just say, there should be no shame in admitting it—no shame whatsoever—for it is the most natural thing in the world."

I listen closely, taking her words in. I am shocked to admit she is right. When I was lying with Nicholas, it *had* felt like the most natural thing in the world.

"I can see I have your attention! Now, what would you say if I told you that all those things you did with that silly boy you could have earned one hundred pounds for if you had done them not with him but with a lord, or an earl, or a viscount, or some such?"

"One hundred pounds? Why, I wouldn't believe you."

"Well, it is quite true. My maidenhead was sold for just that sum, to a lord. Actually, it was sold for that sum and then also sold to two other gentlemen for almost the same amount again."

I frown. "That's not possible. Not the money, I mean, but—"

Elizabeth smiles. "Selling a maidenhood thrice—yes, it was a small untruth, though easily accomplished. As my friend Charlotte likes to say, a virginity is as easily made as a pudding! And the gentlemen were perfectly happy just the same, so what does it really matter? Now, I must add that I didn't see all of that money. A great deal of it went to Mother Wallace, the woman who ran the establishment I worked in. It helped to pay for my gowns, my paste jewelry and so on. But within only a few weeks I had paid her back and was earning a very tidy sum for myself. I worked for Mother Wallace for some time, and now I have set out on my own. I am about to open up my own establishment—a *sérail*, no less." She says the word with a French accent.

"*Je ne connais pas ce mot.*" I tell her I'm not familiar with the word.

Now it's Elizabeth who is taken aback. "You speak French?"

"Yes. My father was a scholar."

"Italian?"

"Not very well. A little."

"And can you play the pianoforte? Sing? Dance?"

"Yes. My stepmother has two daughters. She insisted that they take lessons."

Elizabeth gives me a long look, her eyes skating over my hair, my face, down to my chest. "How very accomplished you are, my dear. But to answer your question about the *sérail*—it is a sort of establishment new to Paris. I visited one there myself."

"You went to Paris?"

"One of my gentlemen friends took me to Paris. It was he who bought me this lovely necklace and dress. It was he I was looking for tonight. Sadly, to no avail, which means I must focus entirely on my *sérail* now. It is a place that offers a genteel evening of entertainment and fine company. Never dull, but of the first order—sophisticated, witty, charming and fresh."

"It sounds lovely."

"It will be lovely. Are you finished with your meal?"

"Oh, yes. Thank you very much."

"I take it you don't have anywhere to stay?"

I dip my head. "I do for tonight. But after that . . ." Panic floods my body once more, despite the champagne and good food.

Elizabeth stands. "It's decided, then. I can't have you wandering the streets like a penniless waif. You must come with me. We will send for your possessions in the morning."

"Oh, but I . . . I couldn't!" I stammer.

Elizabeth looks down at me. Clear-eyed, confident, she is a woman who knows what she wants and has no trouble asking for it—demanding it, even. I remember what I thought on first seeing her. She and this city have an understanding.

Perhaps she could help me to speak its language too?

She gives me a small smile. "I must insist that you accompany me, for I require you to give me your thoughts on the rooms I have rented for my *sérail*. And you must meet my new friend Emily. She has been living with me these past two weeks. She is in need of a companion, and you will adore her—I just know it. So, you see, I need your assistance just as much as you need mine."

I stand, a little unsteady from the drink. "Well, if you need my assistance, how could I refuse?"

"How could you refuse indeed?" Elizabeth chuckles. "Come, my dear. Let us depart."

"HERE WE ARE," Elizabeth says as our carriage draws to a halt. "King Street. Note how close we are to St. James's Park. And Almack's is right next door. The location could not be more perfect."

"Almack's?"

"A club. There is dancing, supper, cards. It is becoming quite fashionable. All the important people in society are going there of an evening."

Elizabeth alights from the carriage first, and I come to stand beside her. She looks up at the towering terrace house with Doric columns that glow white in the moonlight. "It is fine, is it not?"

"You've rented all of this?" The terrace house is of aristocratic proportions.

"I have. I have been here a month already, decorating and

making preparations for my grand opening. The kitchen and scullery are downstairs, there are two drawing rooms, three bedchambers upstairs and the servants' quarters are in the attic. Come. You shall see for yourself."

Elizabeth has us enter via the glossy black front door, and we are standing upon the marble floor inside the entrance within moments.

"Ah, I see Emily has not yet retired for the night. How fortunate." Elizabeth turns left, into a room that is well lit despite the late hour. "You must give me your honest opinion of the large drawing room, Eleanor."

I follow her, and I gasp as soon as I see the room itself.

I step onto a parquet floor in what is truly the most beautiful room I have ever seen. Everywhere I look there is a feast for my eyes, from the high sash windows, with their waterfalls of gold drapes, to the rust-red Turkey rug, to the lacquered cabinets filled with fine teapots, teacups and figurines, to the elegant matching gilt chairs and chaise longue. But the highlight is the wallpaper. What a spectacle it is to behold. A rich, deep blue, it is covered all over with trees that stretch from floor to ceiling. The branches hold brilliant birds with feathers of carnelian and peridot, citrine and topaz—along with similarly vivid leaves and dazzling flowers.

"It's wonderful," I breathe. I turn about on the spot, drinking the room in. It's like seeing inside an aviary in an exotic faraway land. "Oh!" I reel back as I see that there is a living, breathing bird in a corner of the room. For a moment I had thought it was the wallpaper come to life. Scarlet in color, with long tail feathers, it rests upon a gilded perch and eyes me with disdain.

"This is Polly." Elizabeth goes over to the bird, who butts up against her arm. I move to greet the animal, but Elizabeth shakes her head. "Best not. She's been passed around from pillar to post, the poor thing. She detests everyone but me, for some reason."

I stay where I am.

"I'm so glad you like the room," Elizabeth says, the bird now nuzzling her hand. "I chose everything myself—with some help from my new friend Emily, of course."

"Did I hear my name mentioned?"

I turn to see framed in the doorway a creature whose beauty far eclipses that of the bright birds upon the walls. Her skin is of a dark hue, highlighted by the dusky pink of her silk gown. It is not her physical beauty, however, that captivates me, but something else. Something more profound. Something . . . innate. This girl radiates life itself, her deep brown eyes sparkling with inquisitiveness, her head cocked in the most beguiling manner as she inspects me, sizing me up, measuring me as if I have been placed upon this earth for her exclusive amusement. I find that I can do naught in her presence but blink.

"Emily, this is Eleanor."

"Our first visitor! And what a pretty one she is!" Emily steps forward to greet me. I note that one tight curl has escaped its pinned constraints, bouncing playfully, and for some reason this pleases me very much. She is perfectly imperfect. "I much prefer you to that sour old macaw." She pulls a face at it before turning back to me. "Do avoid it. It bites."

As if to show its displeasure, the bird ruffles its feathers and relieves itself upon the floor.

"Disgusting," Emily says.

"No one is asking you to clean the mess up, Emily," Elizabeth says. "Polly will be of great amusement to the gentlemen—I am sure of it."

"Who will, hopefully, leave with all their appendages intact."

"So dramatic," Elizabeth says with a smile. "Emily, I met Eleanor at the pleasure gardens this evening. We enjoyed a delightful supper together."

As I gape rudely at her, Emily approaches me. "I see many questions in your eyes, which I will attempt to answer for you, for I find it is the best way. My mother was my father's mistress in Barbados, a beautiful creature he stored away for his personal use only. With my father often in England, she managed to hide my existence until I was born, then presented me to my father as a fait accompli and squeezed as much money as she could out of him. When he decided to cut off her funds, she paid someone to write to my father's devout wife, who immediately sent for me. My mother was happy for me to go, for it would have been difficult to continue to make a living in her trade with a squalling brat at her feet. Thus, I found myself in the arms of a wet nurse who escorted me to my father's estate in cold, rainy Surrey. There, I was brought up alongside my five sisters, and served as a constant reminder to my father of his infidelities. Goodness, what fun we had!"

"Ah..." I am not sure what to say.

"Emily jests, Eleanor." Elizabeth smiles kindly at me as she moves toward a drinks cabinet. She soon crosses the parquet floor back toward me, holding a glass. "Here. A small glass of ratafia wine may be in order while you collect your thoughts."

I take the glass from her and sip. The wine is sweet and spicy. I remind myself that I must say something or appear a fool. "Are you... are you to be employed here, Emily?"

Emily twirls, her skirt fanning out. "I most certainly am."

Elizabeth passes a glass of wine to Emily, and then returns to the cabinet to pour one for herself. "Some advice for you." She looks up to meet my eyes. "Never play Emily at cards. I believe she cheats."

"Is it truly cheating if you do not get caught?"

"Yes" is Elizabeth's dry reply.

"But it cannot *truly* be cheating, for I am young and naïve and simply have a limited understanding of the rules," Emily returns.

"A persuasive argument," Elizabeth says with a nod, "and one I am sure the gentlemen will believe as you flutter your eyelashes at them. And then they will return home and realize you have taken them for all they are worth."

"Isn't that what gentlemen are for?" Emily twirls again.

Elizabeth chuckles in agreement.

Emily smiles at me. "I'm afraid I've always been quite wild. It was the only way to get any attention in that dreary old place where I lived."

"Emily can dance, sing and generally run rings around any man," Elizabeth tells me.

Emily finishes off her glass of wine and twirls once more. I note that she makes quite sure to avoid Polly, who squawks at her. "Ah, not any man, it would seem. That first one made me look a fool, and I swore I would never be taken for one again. Elizabeth saved me, you see."

"She did?"

She comes to a stop. "Yes, she did."

"May I ask what happened?"

"Emily will tell you even if you do not ask," Elizabeth replies.

"And can you blame me? For it is quite the story!" Emily replies.

"It *is* quite the story," Elizabeth agrees. "And you had best get on with telling it before poor Eleanor dies of boredom."

"Well"—Emily turns back to me, her eyes wide—"it all began when I met a handsome man at an assembly. He was with friends, and several of them asked me to dance. Days later, I was on one of my walks to the local village when I ran into him once more, quite by chance—or, as it turns out, perhaps not. I was with two of my sisters and thought nothing of it. But I began to run into him more and more, and we then began to meet in secret. He told me he would take me away from that horrible house and we would be married immediately. And he was true to his word. I ran away, and we were married that very evening. He then whisked me away to an inn where he had secured a large room. We ate a private supper, and then he blew out all the candles and ravished me."

"Oh," I say, not entirely knowing where to look.

"Ah, but that is not the end of the tale," Elizabeth says.

"It most certainly is not," Emily continues, "for the next morning, he was gone, nowhere to be found!"

I gasp.

"The marriage was a sham. It had been set up so that my maidenhead could be stolen from me. As it turned out, this man was already married!"

My mouth opens and shuts. "But . . . you mentioned that someone had married you."

Emily toys with her empty glass. "A friend of his, apparently, masquerading as a clergyman, both of them using assumed names."

I cannot believe my ears. "Emily, that is a terrible tale! What did your father do when he found out?"

"My father had always wanted me to return to Barbados, but his wife would never allow it. She enjoyed my presence, as I served as a constant reminder of the vows he had broken. However, when they found out what had happened to me, even she did not want me in her house. She sent me to the city, to stay in a lodging house. Elizabeth heard of my tale of woe and came to my rescue. She found the man who was behind the scheme and told him she would have him charged with kidnapping, his pretend-clergyman friend too."

I look over at Elizabeth, who is watching our exchange with a small smile on her rosy lips.

"And did you?" I ask her.

Elizabeth gives me a look. "Of course not! What good would that serve? No, that was simply a threat. They decided to pay me in order that I might keep quiet. And the money I took from them has provided this fine roof over our heads, and new furnishings."

"Ah," I say. "That was clever of you." I am shocked at what I've heard. I had no idea gentlemen were capable of such terrible schemes. "I'm sorry if I seem so ... unworldly. I am not used to a life of such happenings. I thought things like this only occurred in novels."

"And yet they have now happened to you," Elizabeth says. She turns to Emily. "Eleanor was also the victim of a ruse, you see. A ridiculous boy named Nicholas whisked her away, but soon tired of her when they'd reached the city."

"A sad but familiar tale when it comes to matters of the heart," Emily says. "I suppose that is why we are all here in this room."

Elizabeth chuckles. "I'll have you know it was my decision to create this *sérail*, and nothing to do with my sea captain. Still, it is kind of you to believe that I have a heart!"

"It is kind of me!" Emily laughs.

I look from one to the other, not entirely understanding. Elizabeth had saved Emily. She had come to her aid when her family deserted her. And she had saved me too. She had seen that I needed assistance. She had provided supper, a place to sleep. I would think she had a very large heart indeed.

Emily starts toward the drinks cabinet, but Elizabeth intercepts her on the way and deftly takes her glass from her.

"Eleanor speaks French and a smattering of Italian," Elizabeth says.

"As refined as she is pretty, then!"

"She also plays the pianoforte and dances."

Emily comes back over to me, takes my hands in her two soft, warm ones and twirls me about until I find that I am quite out of breath. I do not think it is entirely from the dancing.

"I love to dance!" Emily says. "How wonderful to have a brand-new partner. She is light on her feet too!"

Elizabeth eyes us for a moment or two. "And what a pretty pair you make. But you will wear poor Eleanor out. Come, ladies. Sit." She takes a seat upon a fine cream and gold chaise longue and gestures for us to take the two matching gilt chairs, which we do.

Elizabeth waits until we are seated, and then smiles kindly at me. "Now, Eleanor, I have a proposition for you. If I taught you a thing or two—how to present yourself, what to say, how to act—and if I gave you somewhere to live, food to eat, fine clothes, paste jewelry, what would you say to giving me half of what you make?"

I glance at Emily, but her gaze does not shift from Elizabeth, so gives nothing away.

I turn back. "What would I . . . what would I be doing? That is, I believe I already know. What I want to know is what that would mean . . . *exactly*."

Elizabeth smiles brightly and smooths the silk of her skirt with one hand. "Whatever the situation calls for, I find. And every situation is different."

"It's only . . . I'm not like those women we spoke of. I don't know if I could—"

Elizabeth leans forward. "Ah, but it's as I told you. The trick is to be unlike those women. Remember that this is a different style of establishment. Refined. Elegant. Everything will be very proper."

"You mean, until we retire for the evening, and then it will be very *im*proper." Emily laughs.

"Emily," Elizabeth says sharply.

"Well, 'tis true! Never fear, Eleanor. If you remain here, Elizabeth will teach you everything you need to know. I know I've learned more in the past two weeks than I had in my whole life!"

There is something in the way she says this, a sort of . . . false bravado to her levity. I am also beginning to see that she has had more to drink than I thought.

"Come, Emily. You and your sisters had the finest of governesses."

"Yes, but what they taught me wasn't half as entertaining as what I've learned here."

"I shall take that as a compliment," Elizabeth says dryly.

Emily reaches over and grasps one of my hands. "You must think of it as make-believe. Acting! Gentlemen will like to believe you're naïve, fresh off the farm. They will like to think you were wholesomely milking cows just this morning."

"I've never milked a cow," I say, "wholesomely or otherwise."

Emily titters. "The gentlemen are unlikely to produce one for you. It is but a small untruth."

I remember Elizabeth using the same phrase. It would seem that London is a place built on small untruths, one stacked haphazardly on top of another.

The clock chimes, and Elizabeth claps her hands together, making the macaw flap its wings.

"Well, I do believe we would make a fine trio, but you need not give me your answer this very minute, Eleanor. It is an important decision to make and should not be rushed at this late hour. It is time to rest, and you are our very welcome guest. Let us retire, and we shall discuss this further over breakfast. Emily will show you up to your bedchamber."

THE FOLLOWING MORNING, I push myself up on my elbows in the beautiful four-poster bed I was given for the night, and I see a girl standing near the washstand.

"Oh! Hello."

"Sorry, miss. Didn't mean to wake you, miss. I won't be a minute."

With my bleary eyes, I watch the girl as she scuttles about the room. I didn't rest well at all. While the bed was extremely comfortable, I only tossed and turned in it, my mind full of Elizabeth's proposition.

"Have you worked here long?" I ask the maid after a while.

"Me, miss? No, miss. Miss Elizabeth only took on this place a month ago."

"But you've worked for her for some time?"

"Less than a year, miss."

"That's long enough. Have you been happy in your employment? You've been paid fairly?"

She pauses, the water jug in her hands. "Yes, miss. Miss Elizabeth has her ways, but she's fair. She wouldn't cheat you, miss, not when it comes to money. She has strong feelings about money, does Miss Elizabeth."

"I see. That is good to know. And can you tell me, is there much work to be had in London?"

"Not decent work, miss. Plenty of work in the new factories, though."

I have heard of some of these places—brick kilns and soap factories and so on. There are many accidents, and the wages are low.

"I must get on, miss." She exits the room before I can ask her name.

I drop back into the soft folds of the bed and ponder my situation. I cannot return home. Nicholas has abandoned me. I have nowhere else to go. Emily seems happy here. The maid believes Elizabeth to be a fair mistress.

Awake now, I rise and wash.

I dress, and then pull the curtains to see that it is a fine day outside. Heartened, I head downstairs to see if Emily and Elizabeth are also awake.

"Eleanor!" Elizabeth calls out as she hears my footstep upon the stairs. "Do join us."

I crane my neck to see that Emily and Elizabeth are seated in a small dining room that adjoins a drawing room. Polly is there as well, perched on the back of Elizabeth's chair, happily accepting small pieces of toast. I make my way over to the mahogany table.

"Do sit." Elizabeth gestures. "Toast? Bath cake? Tea?"

"Tea, thank you." I select a Bath cake from a pretty porcelain plate Emily offers me. It has gilt edges and is decorated with mazarine blue and birds to match the wallpaper in the nearby drawing room.

"Emily has had a wonderful idea," Elizabeth tells me.

Emily swallows a piece of toast. "I have! I couldn't help but notice last night that we are almost exactly the same size. My gowns should fit you perfectly. It being such a wonderfully fine day today, I thought we might get dressed and go out for a stroll."

"Everyone will be in St. James's Park today," Elizabeth says. "I am sure of it."

As I eat my Bath cake and drink my tea, I listen to the pair chatter about who they might see in the park. They speak of lords and viscounts, earls and marquesses. It all sounds very exciting.

"Eleanor will look exquisite in my light blue taffeta," Emily says.

"It will bring out her eyes," Elizabeth agrees.

Only minutes later, Emily is dragging me up the stairs to her bedchamber, Polly squawking noisily at us as we go. When we get there, Emily calls the maid, whose name is apparently Sarah. They begin to fuss over my hair, and then they dress me in a combination of my clothes and Emily's. I blush at the thought of disrobing in front of Emily—I never even deigned to undress in front of my stepsisters—but Emily thinks nothing of it, helping Sarah until I wear only my own shift. I am then dressed in Emily's stockings, hoop petticoat and stays, and my cheeks warm at the intimacy of it. I balk when I see the fine fabric of the stomacher, the silk petticoat and, of course, the dress—a stunning confection of light blue taffeta embroidered with tiny rosebuds.

"Oh, Emily, no. It is too beautiful. What if I dirty it in the park?"

"Then it will be made clean."

The dress is slipped around me from behind and tied to the petticoat at the front. I stroke one of the lace cuffs. I have never worn anything quite so beautiful before.

"We truly are the same size. How fortuitous." Emily is thrilled to find that even her shoes fit me perfectly.

When Sarah is finished with me, Emily is dressed next, in

an equally gorgeous gown of sage green, embroidered with leaves.

I reach out and stroke the exquisite material. "Elizabeth bought you this?" My eyes lift to meet Emily's.

"She bought me everything. And I will have to repay her. Her books are kept impeccably. She will happily show you every receipt."

"It must be terribly expensive."

Emily's gaze flicks to Sarah. "Yes, but you wait. Wait until you see the admiring looks you receive today, and you will understand how it might be paid back quickly." Half-dressed, with one stocking on and with her stays unlaced, she runs to the window and peeps out of the shutter, making sure the weather is still clear.

"Hurry!" She rushes back in order that Sarah may lace her up.

I smile at her excitement. "You must have enjoyed your other visits out."

"Elizabeth has taken me to St. James's Park several times now, and there is always a flurry of messages sent to the house afterward. I adore it. You see, I'd never been wanted before. Asked about. Included. Now everyone wants me. And I am going to lap up every second of it!"

Sarah leaves the room to find some pins. As soon as she's out of earshot, Emily turns to me and her entire countenance changes, her eyes narrowing, sharpening.

"I must play my part. I could not say anything in front of Elizabeth, or Sarah—they cannot suspect that I would speak to you of this—but do you not have anywhere else to go?" Her eyes do not leave mine for a second. "No family?"

I'm surprised at her sudden change of demeanor, but I answer her question, thinking of my stepmother as I do so. "No."

"No willing brothers, sisters, aunts, uncles?"

I shake my head. "Why do you ask?"

Emily bites her lip momentarily. "It's only"—she lowers her voice—"at this moment, you are relatively free. She has not purchased anything for you, has she?"

"Elizabeth? No." But then I remember. "Oh, there was supper, at the pleasure gardens."

"I mean gowns, jewelry."

"Oh, no. Nothing like that."

"Then you are still free to go. That is, she would not be happy about it, and you could never work here, in London, in the same capacity, but she would not bother to pursue you."

"But why would I want to go? You seem happy enough."

Emily's expression darkens. "Eleanor, do not be so naïve. We are not the same, you and I. Our pasts are not the same."

"No, but—"

She grabs my wrist and pulls me closer to her. My breath catches as I breathe in her scent. She smells like lavender water. She begins to whisper. "I am only saying, if you would care to leave, now is the time. Not later. *Now*. It would not be in your best interest to cross Elizabeth. She—" Emily stops hastily, drawing back as Sarah returns with the pins.

Sarah flies through her tasks, and Emily is soon bustling me back downstairs. There we find Elizabeth in the drawing room, in a stunning bronze gown that sets off her pale skin and glorious hair perfectly. She rises when she sees us. "What a pretty sight!" She walks over and comes to stand in front of me, taking me in. "Here. You must wear my pearls."

"I couldn't."

"I insist." She comes behind me and fastens them around my neck.

They are still warm from her body.

"Emily always wears her pearls. Perhaps you could have some, too—if you decide to stay with us, of course." She moves back in front of me. "Lovely. Very fresh."

Emily joins her, eyeing the pearls only momentarily. "I agree. The gentlemen will swoon when they see you." It is as if our conversation before never happened. She has returned to her former, giddy self.

"Which is how it should be!" Elizabeth says. "Come look at us together, all three." She takes my arm in hers, and then Emily's loops through my other arm. She guides us over to the gilt-framed looking glass above the fireplace. "What a wonderful sight we make."

I stare at myself. With my fine clothes, with Elizabeth's string of pearls about my neck and with my hair swept up expertly, I hardly recognize myself—not to mention that I am flanked by two creatures who may as well be from a fairy tale with their fine gowns, dazzling visages and magnificent hair.

"We must go straight to St. James's Park and show off our plumage," Elizabeth says.

My throat catches as I remember what I am to do. "Will I…"

Elizabeth pats my arm. "Eleanor, you must not fear. We have weeks of training ahead of us yet. You must understand that what I am trying to create here is everything I did not have. I was taken advantage of, used. What I want to create is something entirely different. I want to bring together women who can rely on one another. I want to strive for fairness, openness. Mother Wallace gave me none of that, you see. She screwed every last shilling she could out of me. And all the time I watched her do it, I knew that there was a better way, that if she had only believed we could work together, we might have been unstoppable. That is what I want to create here—an unstoppable force. We may already have done it. Look. You may view it yourself. Turn. Turn and look at yourself, Eleanor." Elizabeth swivels me about to face the looking glass once more. "Your star is ascendant. No longer shall the Nicholases of the world be allowed to keep you down. Come, Emily. Draw closer."

Emily comes to stand beside us.

"We three are strong, capable, independent women. Our new lives begin in this moment. And we decide what they shall be, for we are young and beautiful and in one of the grandest cities in the world. No man shall dictate how we live. We will make our own rules, and everyone else shall bend to them. Now, let us go. Let us go to St. James's Park and *let them look*."

ALYS

LONDON, PRESENT DAY

By the time I get to my apartment in Bloomsbury, it's midafternoon on Wednesday. No, wait, Thursday. I think. As I close the door behind me, I breathe a sigh of relief. I've made it. Not to Whitby, where I currently live, but to London, at least. I scan the quiet apartment, taking in the beautifully restored Georgian fireplace, the high sash windows with their painted shutters, the worn wooden floor.

Home. Or my old home, at least.

It looks like Ro is out. She's been staying here for a week or so while she has business in London. Evidence of her presence is dotted about. A phone charger. Her laptop. A short shopping list in her familiar, messy hand.

I drag my suitcase into the bedroom and eye the bed longingly. The flight was thirteen hours long, and while I had a very nice seat (thank you, Mrs. Yoon), I'd managed only to doze on and off, adrenaline running high. I pull out my phone and text Ro.

Thanks for making my bed. I'm getting in and I'm never coming out.

While I wait for her reply, I zip open my bag. I've got to brush my teeth, and then I'm slipping in between those sheets, clothes and all. Maybe I'll take my jeans off. I don't know. I make no promises.

Have a nap and I'll be back by 6 pm. I'll cook. Also, I bought you something.

She sends me a picture of a two-headed fetal pig in a specimen jar, and I recoil—an involuntary shudder coursing through me when I see the beast suspended, forever lifeless, in that sepia sea. I know it's not so much the fetal pig that disturbs me but the sudden haunting remembrance of another time and place, shelves of other specimen jars—row upon row. But Ro is oblivious to that. Of course she is. She's simply winding me up, because the fetal pig is not actually a gift for me. I know exactly which one of her clients it's for. I delete the image from our trail, so I never have to see it again, then text her back.

Usually houseguests opt for flowers. Or chocolates.

Her reply zings.

Boring.

It probably says a lot about us that there are plenty of people in our lives who would far prefer a two-headed fetal pig as a hostess gift to flowers or chocolates.

I send back a sleeping emoji, and then I put my phone on silent, brush my teeth and slip between the deliciously fresh sheets.

When I wake, I roll over with a groan and check the time on my phone. Six thirty. I hear movement outside my bedroom door and push myself up on my elbows. *Elizabeth.* She's always at the forefront of my mind. But then I remember where I am. Elizabeth is safely in her crate. It's Ro I can hear. I go to the bathroom, and then head out to the kitchen.

"That smells amazing, Ro," I say, sniffing as I go.

"Linguine with chili, crab and watercress," she says. "Your favorite."

I pull out a kitchen stool and sit down. "I've missed watercress."

"You say that so wistfully every time I make this. We had it less than two weeks ago."

I shrug. "Watercress used to be a thing."

"You also say that every time I make this. I'm continually astounded by your ability to make watercress sound exciting. Oh, and before I forget . . ." Ro ducks around the counter, retrieves her satchel and digs around in it. "I was passing by a health store and saw this. Here—catch." She throws me a packet.

I turn it over in my hands, reading the label. "Ginger hard candies. Thanks. I haven't tried these ones." I've tried just about everything else for the ever-present low-lying nausea that has plagued me for so long. Ginger chews. Ginger tea. Ginger cordial. Crystallized ginger, uncrystallized ginger. All the gingers.

I watch as Ro returns to the kitchen, fills a glass with water from the fridge-door dispenser, brings it over and pushes it toward me. "Hydrate. Then wine. For me, that is, because you don't drink, but I do. So my gift to you is, as it turns out, all mine. I made sure to get you something I'd like."

She gestures toward a bottle of Chenin Blanc that she's just opened. I also notice a bunch of flowers and a box of chocolates.

"That's big of you. I hope you didn't spend too much."

"Are you saying I'm not worth it?"

"You're hysterical. You know, on the plane, I was thinking we should eat out. But why would I want to go out when I've got my own personal one-woman dinner and show right here?" I take a sip of my water. Normally I'd find a way to surreptitiously tip it down the sink. I don't like drinking things other people have poured for me, but Ro is different. Also, I just watched the water come directly from the fridge door, so there's that.

Only a few minutes later, Ro has plated up dinner and we're sitting at the small, round dining table.

"Cheers." Ro touches her wineglass against my water glass.

"Cheers. And thanks for cooking. So, what was your week here like?"

"Not bad. I went to a couple of auctions. Standard bits and pieces. Brooches. Rings. I lost out on the necklace that I really wanted."

"Ugh, sorry."

We both shrug it off. That's the nature of this game. You win some; you lose some.

There's a long pause, in which I can sense what's coming.

"So"—Ro winds some pasta around her fork—"Elizabeth's finally here. In London."

"And Mrs. Yoon paid me two hundred fifty thousand pounds to make that happen."

Ro's eyes widen. "What?"

"I know. On one condition."

"Which is . . . ?"

I take a deep breath. "That I destroy her. Within the next two weeks."

Ro puts her fork down. She's silent for a moment. "Oh."

"I know it's quick. I should have checked with you to see that it was all right." The thing is, to destroy Elizabeth, I'm going to require some expert help. This is where Ro comes in. It's not by chance that we're living together. We've been living together in Whitby for a while, waiting for this day to arrive. The thing is, Ro is a witch. A good witch. She is my point of contact with the coven that will help me destroy Elizabeth once and for all, because destroying Elizabeth is not as simple as it might seem. She is no ordinary wax model.

Ro starts. "No! I didn't mean that it was inconvenient. I just mean it's a lot. For you."

"It's better this way," I reply. I take a sip of my water, my mouth suddenly dry. "It turns out, Mrs. Yoon's worried about her son, Geon, wanting to carry on his father's legacy. He was taking him for visits to Elizabeth, unbeknownst to his wife."

"Oh no."

I nod.

Another long pause, which neither of us moves to fill. Not that we need to speak. The news I've just dropped like a bomb fills the space.

"How do you want to play this?" Ro asks after a while. "How fast do you actually want to move?"

I wish I knew. "Well, Elizabeth is going into storage tomorrow."

"Alongside Eleanor."

I nod again.

All the questions Veronique had been dying to ask float in the air—the same ones that always float about in the air, mostly unanswered by me, whenever the topic of the Venuses arises. *When will they reunite? What will happen when they reunite?*

Will they magically come to life and start murdering the unsuspecting men of London by night?

Because that's how the legend goes. If the conditions are right, the three anatomical Venuses have the ability to take human form by night. When they do, they're rumored to spend the evening hours hunting and killing any man who has dared to look at them lustfully. And yet, so beautiful are they, and such is their siren song, that men like Mr. Yoon will pay ridiculous money for their exclusive company. Or Elizabeth's, anyway. As Ro mentioned, Eleanor is in storage. And Emily's wax model no longer exists.

It's long been rumored in the antiques business that my family is connected with the Venuses and has been in possession of Eleanor for many, many years. I'm forever being quizzed about the threesome by curious dealers and clients alike. The basic facts are well-known. The anatomical Venuses were modeled on three real women—beauties who worked in London's sex trade. Their likenesses were made into wax models, commissioned by an anatomist in 1769, so that fee-paying medical students might be enticed through the anatomist's studio door. This also meant the anatomist didn't need to acquire real bodies, which were hard to come by and decomposed quickly. After the wax models were made, the real women mysteriously disappeared. There are no further records of them and there were no definitive sightings. Around this time, a number of men were murdered in London, all of whom were connected to both the anatomist and the women, in various ways. But the anatomist had solid alibis, and the women the wax figures were modeled on had vanished. The murderer was never exposed. These facts are all well-documented. It's the theories that stem from these facts that can get a little ... wild.

Some believe the women did not disappear at all but went

into hiding and did the murderous bidding of an underworld figure. One student of the anatomist spoke of strange goings-on in the anatomist's studio. He swore one of the wax models had attacked him, and he claimed that the anatomist himself had admitted it was bewitched. He went on to tour the country with a knife that he claimed was used in the attack (earning a fortune in the process, of course). Others are sure that the tale of the Venuses was nothing but a clever cover-up, that the models were scapegoats used by the real murderer to get away with their killing spree scot-free.

There are some who think that I know the truth and I simply don't want to speak about it, either because I want to create mystery or because I'm ashamed of the connection. But the truth, I have found, is not what people want anyway. The truth is often too ugly to be spoken aloud. There is no glamour to be found in it. Take Mr. Yoon, for example. Had he needed those headphones, with their five-minute reminder of the truth—that Elizabeth was not alive? Debatable. The bottom line was, Elizabeth couldn't rise up and kill him, however much of a "presence" she had. But Mr. Yoon had found the thought that she might be able to do so intoxicating, hadn't he? He had desperately wanted to believe that Elizabeth was dangerous. That she was capable of harm. That he was in constant danger.

Still—I think back to Geon Yoon, bashing upon the boardroom glass. Maybe Mr. Yoon had been a little bit right.

So, Elizabeth has been traveling the world and living with men like Mr. Yoon, receiving a glam makeover in the process. Meanwhile, Eleanor has been kept carefully in storage. And Emily? Sadly, Emily was lost to a fire back in 1769. All that was left was some of Emily's hair, which was recovered from the ashes of the anatomist's studio, where the anatomical Venuses had been kept. That hair is part of a necklace that has been stored away for me by Ro's coven; it's resting safely in an antique crystal jewelry box. Since I learned that Mr. Yoon was ill, the necklace has been recurring in my dreams, calling to me. I stare down at the tattoo on my forearm—the one Veronique pointed out. Its tightly woven strands are always part of me.

Ro's gaze takes in my tattoo as well. There's a moment or two of silence before she speaks. "Why now, Alys?" she finally says. "You know, if you're not sure, we can find a way out of that contract."

I say nothing—because, in my heart, I know Ro is asking only because she truly cares. I open my mouth and find I have no words. "I . . . don't know why now," I finally say, doubting what I've done. I look up from the table to see Ro staring at me intently. "I've been trying to answer that myself. There are so many reasons. It all seems to have come together at once—someone finally willing to release Elizabeth to me, but also . . . Emily. I've been dreaming about her more and more. And . . ." My eyes well up.

Ro's hand darts across the table now and grabs mine. "Hey. You okay?"

I nod, taking a deep breath. This is a safe space. "I don't know if I can even explain it. There's just something in me that's so tired—of this legacy, I mean. I can't carry it with me anymore. I feel like it's all I am, all anyone thinks about when they look at me." Where has all this spilled from? I *never* open up like this.

Ro only nods, as if she understands. "It's a lot." She's quiet, waiting for me to continue.

But I've already said too much.

I pull my hand away from hers, and wipe my eyes. "Sorry. I'm being silly. I'm probably just tired from the flight. Time zones, you know."

"It's not silly. It makes perfect sense. I just want you to know that I see you. That I'm here for you. When I look at you, I don't see anything but you, Alys. I don't think about the Venuses, about your past. There's no . . . baggage."

I nod. I know that. I know she's telling me the truth.

"I want to do this," I say firmly. "I do. I'm going to follow through."

"Okay. Well, I've got you. All the way."

"Thanks. How do we . . . get moving?"

"I'll talk to the others."

"Okay."

Ro twists some pasta around her fork. "I have to say, though, you're a terrible liar."

I jolt, but then Ro continues, explaining herself.

"I mean, come on. You can't be tired from the flight. I saw the photo you sent me of your seat."

I laugh. Ro always makes me laugh. "I got lucky. I don't think Mrs. Yoon knows there are other classes on planes."

"Elizabeth would have been livid down there, in the hold, you up top, sipping champagne—not that you did, but you know . . . you could have."

"Ah, there, you're wrong. Elizabeth would never have flown first-class. Elizabeth would have demanded her own private jet. And she wouldn't have paid for it either."

"That sounds about right." Ro chuckles. "But listen . . ."

I meet her gaze again.

"Whatever you need, you know you only have to ask. Everyone's here for you, Alys. We always have been."

W E SET OFF at nine the next morning for the art-storage facility, Ro behind the wheel of her van. It's about a forty-minute drive, and the text comes in when we've been on the road for only fifteen minutes.

"Elizabeth's going to get there before us," I tell Ro.

"Maybe Sorrel will get there before we do?" She glances over at me.

Sorrel was my previous point of contact with the coven. She's an antiques dealer, and one of the people who—as Ro mentioned last night—have always been there for me.

"I'll text her."

Sorrel's reply is with me in seconds. "She's already there," I tell Ro. "She says she'll get them to load Elizabeth inside." I text her my unit entry code, which I'll change after our visit. No one has that code except for me and my solicitor.

Sorrel is part owner of a massive art-storage facility, and she has been kind enough to let me store Eleanor in one of her storage rooms. Now Elizabeth will join her.

I turn and stare out the window. *What have I done? What was I thinking? Is storing them together sheer madness?*

"All good?" Ro asks.

I glance over. "Yep. Sure. Have you told Sorrel about the contract? About the two weeks?"

"I have."

"Good." That makes me wonder what's been going on behind the scenes. But I don't ask. I can't yet. I need to get through today first. The arrangements settled, I throw Ro a look. "Also, stop being so polite, and formal. It's weird."

"I'm being polite? And formal?"

"Yes."

"Well, sorry. I'll try to be ruder. Ruder and more informal. Where should I start? Dirty limericks, maybe? 'There once was a man from Nantucket—'"

"That's better."

When we pull up at the facility, I can see Sorrel standing in the waiting area. It's not difficult to spot her. In a sharp green velvet suit, and with a wild mane of salt-and-pepper corkscrew hair, she is unmistakable. She waves, and I wave back.

"Alys! It's so good to see you," Sorrel says when I get into the waiting area. "Let me look at you." She takes both my arms and gives me a good once-over. "You look great. I'm loving the hair. Now, how are you feeling about everything?"

"Surprisingly okay, all things considered."

"Good. Well, let's get moving and have you signed in. Now, where's Ro got to? Ah, here she is."

Ro opens the glass door and enters. "Hi, Sorrel."

Sorrel gives her a look. "I'm not sure if I should be talking to you after our little disagreement the other day. How did things turn out for you?"

Ro grins sheepishly. "You were right. There was nothing good in that stupid box."

I sigh. "Have you been buying mystery boxes again?"

"Um, no? I would never do something stupid like that."

I groan. Every so often, bits and pieces will be sold at auction that the seller doesn't think include anything of intrinsic value and thus can't be bothered to sift through. They're typically from estate sales. Usually the seller is right, and there's nothing of great worth in there, but sometimes—*sometimes*—there is an amazing find.

Ro hasn't yet unearthed an amazing find. But Sorrel has. She sometimes has a hunch about things, and she once found a little velvet drawstring bag full of Roman coins in a nondescript box of costume jewelry.

So Ro lives in hope, despite the fact that her own hunches are rarely correct.

"You're just no fun," Ro tells me.

"And richer for it."

Sorrel laughs. "Quit bickering. Sign in, and I'll walk you through. As discussed, we've moved you into a larger unit."

Ro and I sign in with the security guards, and the three of us are buzzed in through the steel door.

Sorrel ushers us down a short hallway that opens up to the building proper on both sides, where there are all sorts of different storage facilities for all sorts of different art and artifacts. All polished concrete and steel, the midsection of the building is cavernous. If you didn't know any better, you'd think you were in an art gallery. "Everything went seamlessly. Of course it did. This is a fine facility."

"You have to say that," Ro says. "You're a part owner. I mean, I'm not saying it's not a fine facility. It *is* a fine facility."

"Time to stop talking," I say.

Ro sighs dramatically. "It usually is."

I take a quick step forward so I'm next to Sorrel. "Speaking of fine facilities, you have to let me pay you more for this. The rates you're giving me are far too low."

Sorrel shakes her head. "It's fine. Really. I have different rates for friends. Anyway, you're always letting me put people up in your apartment. Free accommodation in Bloomsbury? I'm sure I'm getting the better deal."

"It's too generous of you."

"It isn't at all. Now. We're getting close. Right, and then the second room on the left."

We turn right, into another wide hallway, and stop in front of a door.

"After you," Sorrel says.

I step forward and punch the code into the lock. The door retracts to reveal two huge wooden crates sitting on top of wooden pallets.

"Oh" is all I can say. Elizabeth and Eleanor are together

again. For the first time in—I take a moment to do the maths—254 years.

"Don't feel you need to rush in, Alys," Sorrel says.

I can't stop staring at the two rectangular wooden crates that look like oversized coffins. I take my time, as suggested, because I have to. I feel faint just looking at the two of them, side by side.

Dread preventing me from entering the storage unit, a good minute passes before I dare put one foot in front of the other. When I finally cross the threshold, a wave of nausea hits me. The thought of the door closing on me, leaving me trapped... I'm that person who is always facing the door in a room. Looking for an escape route. Asking to be seated in the exit row of life.

"All right?" Ro says.

I glance behind me and see that she and Sorrel are here, still with me. *I'm okay. I can do this. Nothing is going to happen.* I turn back around and force myself onward, approaching the crates. Coming to stand in between them, I reach one hand out gingerly and touch Elizabeth's box first. And then, slowly, I reach for Eleanor's with my other hand, my fingertips hesitating just before they hit the pine surface.

Forward, I tell myself. *Not back, forward.*

I push myself to close that minuscule gap, and my fingertips finally skate over the rough wood. I'm surprised to find that I feel... nothing. No sign of Eleanor. Why I thought I would feel something, I have no idea. It was only... the two of them together again...

Then, in the silence, I think I hear a sigh, a stirring.

The whispering of my name.

Sorrel puts a hand on my shoulder, and I jump.

"Sorry," she says. "I didn't mean to startle you."

"Did you hear that?" I ask, looking from her to Ro, and back again.

"Hear what?" Ro says.

"I heard some of the staff talking outside, if that's what you mean," Sorrel says.

I shake my head. It wasn't that. It wasn't... of this realm. I listen for a moment.

The room is still. Still and silent apart from the living.

"It was nothing," I finally say. "My imagination. This is just... a lot." I'm being ridiculous. Elizabeth is nothing but a wax model without the necklace of hair, and the necklace has a spell upon it—a strong spell that the coven has assured me a hundred times can't be broken unless they decide, as a group, to break it. It's impossible for either Elizabeth or Eleanor to stir. It simply can't happen. And yet...

"Would you like us to open the crates?" Sorrel asks.

I shake my head quickly. "Definitely not."

"Is there anything you need?" Sorrel continues, a weight to her words.

I think for a moment. *Is there anything I need?*

There are so many things I need that I don't even know where to begin.

Two weeks.

I've got to move forward now. And I've got to do it fast.

ELEANOR

LONDON, OCTOBER 1769

I PEER OUT THE carriage window as we bounce along. It feels strange to be back in Covent Garden. It has been two weeks since I was here last, and that somehow seems like a lifetime ago. Since then, my days have been filled with dress fittings, shopping and strolling in St. James's Park. Elizabeth times our outings carefully, attempting to "bump" into this gentleman and that gentleman—she names so many earls and lords, and even a duke, that my head spins. The gentlemen make my head spin, too, with their handsome faces and finely tailored suits. They smell of linen and spice and soap. Nicholas did not smell like that. Not at all. I see now that he was naught but a boy.

"Stay close behind me," Elizabeth says as our carriage pulls to a stop.

I crane my neck, attempting to glimpse the theater—our destination for the evening.

Elizabeth exits, and Emily and I do as we are told, following in her wake like two little ducklings as she pummels and pushes through the crowd. We're almost at the theater entrance when Elizabeth stops suddenly. She has spotted someone. At first I think it might be someone of importance, for she is always aware that she must be seen at her best by the right people—but when I follow her gaze, I see that she is actually looking at a group of women in the distance who are touting for business. Her eyes narrow as she inspects one woman in particular, who is older than the rest and half propped up against a wall. She is obviously drunk. Elizabeth makes a soft snort of recognition, and then takes off once more. I go to follow her, but Emily doesn't move, her eyes fixed upon the woman Elizabeth showed interest in.

"Who is that?" I ask Emily. She gives me a sharp look and shakes her head. Realizing Elizabeth has moved on, Emily grabs my arm and we scramble to catch up with her.

By the time we finally get to our box, I am exhausted.

The three of us sit, examining the playbill for a moment while we catch our breath.

It is a mixed bill this evening, which means there will be a play followed by some lighter fare, including a short farce, a strong man and, of all things, a ropewalker. Fanning my face with the playbill, I lean forward to look at the swarm of people below. I thought the theater would be a genteel place, and it seems I was wrong. It is noisy and chaotic, workingmen and women squeezed in tight. Right in front of the stage, several young males are drinking and throwing peanuts at one another, while others make their way up and down the aisle, flirting and greeting friends. I inspect the boxes too. I'm surprised to see that the ladies next to us have set up a small card table to play during the performances.

Emily occupies the space beside me, whispering amusing things in my ear and making me laugh all the while. She is so at ease in this place, so poised in her resplendent attire. I feel dull as ditchwater beside her, but if she thinks I am, she veils her thoughts masterfully. She seems to enjoy my presence, and I wonder—hopefully, longingly—if I finally have a true friend. I have never really had one before. There were girls in my village who I would pass the time with, but I never cared for their company. Not like this. Despite my lush surroundings, my gaze is drawn to Emily again and again. I cannot help myself. Can such a treasure be real?

Emily sighs. "Will it ever start?"

"The performance? Why do you ask?" There is so much to look at. The audience seems to be putting on its own performance, just for me. Unless . . . A terrible thought crosses my mind. "Am I boring you?" I say, worried that I might be.

Emily nudges me. "Do not be ridiculous. As if you could ever bore me. You are endlessly entertaining!"

I cannot help it. I grin back at her like a fool.

"No, I only want the performance to start because then perhaps people will stare at the stage and not at me. I often try to tell myself they're ogling me because they are enraptured by my sheer beauty, and not because of the color of my skin. I attempt to make a game of it. It rarely works."

"I daresay that . . ." Elizabeth starts, but her words trail off as her attention is caught by a party that has entered a box across the way. She quickly looks away, shifting in her seat to angle herself toward us. "Emily. Eleanor. Quickly. We must laugh and look as if we are having a wonderful time."

"Oh. Are we not having a wonderful time?" Emily says.

"Quiet. Titter. Be merry!" Elizabeth insists.

"Which is it to be, then?" Emily asks. But before Elizabeth can pinch her by way of reply, Emily breaks out into peals of laughter, as if one of us has uttered something very amusing indeed. "La, la, la. Merry! So merry!"

I join in, my hand fluttering to my breast as I laugh along with them.

"How long do we need to do this for?" Emily asks.

"Are any of them looking? Eleanor, you may check."

I glance over at the box. A handsome gentleman is seated next to a small, rather plain-looking woman in a fine gown of plum silk. While the man talks to someone else in their party, the woman stares straight across the theater at Elizabeth. Perhaps sensing my interest, she turns her attention to me. Her gaze is filled with such loathing that I pull back in my seat.

"The woman in the plum gown is looking our way. She does not seem . . . pleased."

Elizabeth looks like the cat that got the cream. "Excellent news. She knows who I am."

"Of course she does," Emily says. "You have made sure of it."

Elizabeth chuckles at this.

"But who is she?" I ask.

"Here. Let us inspect the playbill together," Elizabeth says. "We must look as if we have not a care in the world."

Our three heads move in to inspect the one playbill.

Emily finally answers my question. "The woman in the plum gown is the betrothed of Elizabeth's sea captain, Sir William Kettering. He is the gentleman who had Elizabeth in high keeping for two years."

"I'll have you know that that is a *very* long time to be in high keeping," Elizabeth adds. I'm surprised to find in her voice a strange note that I haven't heard before. A crack. I wonder—did she care for this sea captain?

"She is not nearly as beautiful as you," I tell her.

"Of course not." Elizabeth's jaw hardens. "But she has something else to recommend her. Money. Lots and lots of money. That is the attraction." She looks across the theater now, and pretends for all the world that she has only just seen the captain. She gives the pair both a gesture of acknowledgment and a smile, as if they are old friends.

They turn away—from both Elizabeth and each other.

"Not very friendly," Elizabeth says, with a brittle laugh. "Silly little bitch. She thinks she has won, but she hasn't bothered to think ahead. He behaves himself now, but the moment they are married, her money will all be his and he will do exactly as he pleases. He will attend my *sérail* with renewed funds. *Her* funds. If anything, I should go over and thank her. Goodness knows I thoroughly depleted his."

"Do you . . . miss him?" I ask her. I haven't seen her this way before, and something inside me warns me to be careful of what I say.

"What a funny question!"

"Is it, though?" Emily goads.

"Well, I suppose I do miss him in a way. He was a cull, but he was *my* cull. I had the perfect existence. A place to live, funds. Steady work. And as the captain of a ship, he was rarely there to tell me how I should live my life and spend his money. All of that, I miss very much."

She says this flippantly, but as I watch her, I am not sure I believe her. She is like a wounded animal lashing out. Her eyes meet mine and I look away, pretending to be interested in the stage, for I get the feeling that if I am not careful, those claws of Elizabeth's may come for *me*.

T HE PLAY IS the Shakespearean tragedy *Coriolanus*, and the actors, sets and costumes are all magnificent.

However, I notice that Elizabeth has her eye trained on something else. At first I believe it is her captain, but before long it becomes clear that she has turned her interest to a man in the box two to her captain's right. After a time, I realize that I recognize his features. Elizabeth rises and comes to sit beside me.

"It is the gentleman you pointed out to me once in St. James's Park," I say, nodding in his direction. "The one with the fine bay stallion."

"Very observant of you." Elizabeth seems pleased with me. "His name is Lord Levehurst."

"Is that his wife?"

"It is."

As if she senses us talking about her, the woman looks over. Immediately she turns to her husband and engages him in conversation.

"I always find it entertaining to note how these women are not interested in their husbands in daily life, but when I am around they suddenly become very interested indeed. It is miraculous what I can do for a marriage, really!" Then her countenance turns thoughtful. "Lord Levehurst could be worth pursuing for you, Eleanor. I know for a fact that he has paid handsomely for other maidenheads. A cousin of his frequented Covent Garden a little too often as a student, and it ended in disease. He is a careful man in that regard." Then she pauses. Hesitates.

"What is it?" I sense that there is something else.

"On his own, he is agreeable, but I do not care much for the company he keeps. Oh, look now! They're getting up. Perhaps for a walk, or refreshments. This is our chance. Eleanor, you are to come with me. Emily, remain here for the time being."

Outside the box, it is even busier than before.

"It is half the price if you enter to see the second half of the performance," Elizabeth explains, seeing my surprise. "Quickly, this way. We must catch Lord Levehurst. When we reach him, make sure not to speak. Simply parade past and give him no heed."

As we make our way through the crowd, I am impressed to see how many people Elizabeth knows. There is a nod here, a smile there. It has been the same during all our visits to St. James's Park. In fact, it is like this wherever we go. Everyone seems to know Elizabeth, and yet I have also noticed that no one really stops to speak to her. Instead, they ogle, watch, whisper. Only the gentlemen on their own acknowledge her properly, or say a passing word. And yet she makes this all look natural. Her brisk pace says *I cannot stop, for I have a pressing engagement,* as if this is how *she* wants things to be.

And perhaps it is? I do not know her well enough yet to say.

On our return journeys from St. James's Park, she always tells Emily and me the same thing. "Let them talk about us. Let them wonder. Soon, they will leave their wives at home and come calling, so many that we will have to turn them away night after night, as the *sérail* will surely be full."

"Ah, there he is." Elizabeth stops and pulls me close to her. She pinches my cheeks for color and adjusts my pearls. Before I know what is happening, she turns, her back blocking my view of the crowd. Her hand slips down my bodice and adjusts my bust, making me gasp.

"Oh, do not be so coy," she tells me. "You must show the gentlemen your wares. Otherwise how will they know what delights their money might buy? Now, listen carefully. As I said before, we will walk close by him, but do not meet his eye. Look sweet. Innocent. Fresh. How did Emily put it? As if you were wholesomely milking cows just this morning. Now, follow me, but leave space in order that he might view you in your entirety."

Elizabeth sets off at a leisurely pace, and I follow a few steps behind. The moment Lord Levehurst notices us, I demurely look away and adopt what I hope is a sweet smile. But there is a moment when our eyes meet, and I can see immediately that there is something in the glance. He is interested in me, I can tell. I envisage being bedded by such a man, who is so entirely unlike Nicholas that I can barely imagine what it might be like. And while part of me is fearful of such an encounter, I must admit that there is another part of me that is ashamed to wonder if I might enjoy it. Or maybe I'm not ashamed at all? Maybe I am more like Elizabeth than I thought.

Elizabeth moves me along, and the moment we are out of Lord Levehurst's line of sight, she halts. She pulls me over to one side, out of the flow of people.

"Now we pause a moment, and then we shall retrace our steps in order that he might have a second viewing," Elizabeth says.

And this is what we do.

Now, however, we walk all the way back to our box.

"Very nicely done," Elizabeth tells me before we rejoin Emily. "He noticed you. And tomorrow I will send him a note that will remind him of this fact."

WHEN WE ARRIVE back at King Street the hour is late, but I am not tired. In my stepmother's house I rose early and went to bed early. Here it is the exact opposite. We rise late and go to bed late. That is, we go to bed in the early hours of the morning.

"There are more parcels, madam. And a letter," Sarah, the maid, says, passing a letter to Elizabeth.

Elizabeth goes over to release Polly from her cage, and Polly butts happily at her hand.

"Yes, yes," Elizabeth croons. "Mama is here. Tea, please, Sarah."

"Yes, madam."

Emily and I take seats in the two gilt chairs. We begin to peel off gloves and take off our shoes. Elizabeth reclines on the chaise longue, reading her letter. When she's done, she sits up.

"A gentleman is interested in you, Eleanor," she says, turning to me. "Another lord. Perhaps an even better choice for you than Lord Levehurst."

"Better how?" Emily says.

"He has a son, currently at university, who is timid with the ladies. He is hoping to encourage him and is looking for a pretty girl with a good head on her shoulders. Most importantly, a clean girl."

"The perfect first cull," Emily says.

"Don't call them culls," Elizabeth says.

"But you yourself . . ." Emily begins to argue, trailing off when she sees Elizabeth's expression. With a huff, she gets up and goes over to pour herself a glass of ratafia wine, for which Elizabeth gives her another look before returning her attention to me. I must admit I have noticed that Emily has already had much to drink this evening.

"The boy is young and pliable and will cause you no trouble," Elizabeth tells me. "If you play your cards right, he could even become quite attached to you. Lord Levehurst would not have you in high keeping, but this boy's father might consider it if he thinks you a good practice piece for his son."

"And what have you found for me to practice my skills upon?" Emily polishes off her wine. She moves as if to pour another glass.

"Do sit down, Emily," Elizabeth says, a warning note in her voice.

With a sigh, Emily returns to her seat, her glass empty. As I look at her, I wonder if it is her past that causes her to drink so much.

"I have someone in mind. Unfortunately, he has been in the country, but I hear that he returns tomorrow, and I am devising a plan in order that we might tempt him. He is a... collector, of sorts."

Emily's face contorts. "I think I would prefer someone young and pliable, too, thank you."

Elizabeth guffaws. "Well, you might practice your milkmaid act. Never fear. A man will pay a tidy sum for you. I am sure of it. It will simply be a different sort of man. Now, let us see to these parcels. And bills."

As we wait for the tea, we open the few parcels that have arrived, and Elizabeth sits at her writing desk and makes entries in the ledger, noting down what everything has cost.

All three of us have access to the ledger and can see bills and receipts for what Elizabeth has purchased.

She looks up to see me inspecting her work.

"It was not like this for me," she says. "The ledger was hidden away and kept under lock and key. I was swindled—out of hundreds of pounds. I swore that, one day, I would run my own establishment and things would be different. I did not want to run a place where the girls would find they had only sixpence in their pockets come Sunday. I wanted a place of companionship, of protection. I wanted—want—something more like... a family, I suppose."

For the second time this evening, I find myself surprised to see a different side to her. This time, a softer one. I pull my chair closer to the writing desk.

"May I ask what happened? To your family?" I look over at Emily, to see if she is listening, but she is engrossed in a novel.

Elizabeth puts her quill down on the writing desk. "Do you really want to know my story?"

I nod.

"All right, then. I told you my father owned a tavern, yes?"

I nod again.

"Well, that is where my story begins. My mother died giving birth to me in that same tavern. My father had, of course, wanted a boy. A girl was not much good to him in a tavern. And my father had a tendency to get what he wanted, so when I wasn't a boy, he simply pretended that I was. Everyone believed me to be so. Why should they not? I was long and lean, and he saw to it that I was dressed like a boy and that my hair was cropped short. When I was able, I started working as a potboy, ferrying drinks, shadowing my father, then assisting at the tap and counting profits. When I was older, I became a waiter and began to learn how to gratify the customers' less legitimate requests. To be honest, I almost forgot I was not a boy. I got to the age of thirteen before anyone discovered the truth."

"How did they find out?"

There is a brief pause as Sarah enters with the tea. Elizabeth gestures for her to pour.

Elizabeth takes a cup before she continues with her tale. "How did they find out? That is a story within itself." She focuses on her steaming tea for a moment before taking a deep breath. "There were rooms above the tavern. Men would have meetings in there. Drunken meetings. Extremely drunken meetings. I would often have to bring food to them. More drink. Women. Whatever they wanted. One night I was going back and forth on the dark stairs when two of them grabbed me. I was shuffled into an empty room. And raped."

I gasp. "But... how did they know you weren't a boy?"

"They didn't. I don't think they cared what I was. I was just... there, a body to be used and discarded. Someone found me... after. They fetched my father. And not being an understanding sort of man, he stabbed the two men who had attacked me. They both died. As did he, for he was hanged for it."

I cover my mouth with my hand and set my teacup and saucer down shakily.

"After that, I was left with no father, no mother. And so I went to work for Mother Wallace."

Emily closes her book, and I look over to see her watching us closely.

"I had known Mother Wallace all my life, through the tavern. She was happy to have me now that I was a girl. She could see my potential. And so she should have been happy to have me. The thief." Elizabeth gives me a quick smile. "But don't worry. I got my own back. In time. Oh, that reminds me..." She brightens, as if all she has just told me is a mess that might be brushed swiftly and neatly under a rug. She pats her pocket and brings out the letter she was reading before. "I am arranging a visit from a physician. His name is Dr. Chidworth. He will want to inspect you. This will happen every week once the *sérail* is up and running. It will give the gentlemen peace of mind."

"So, he shall look us over as if we are livestock," Emily says, "in order to see that we are not diseased."

"Precisely!" Elizabeth says. "Dr. Chidworth will want to take liberties with you, of course, but I have told him that under no circumstances will this be possible until your maidenheads have been sold. Now it is time for bed. If the doctor is coming in the morning, you will need to look your best. I will finish up here, and come up to bed myself momentarily." With a flick of her hand, she shoos us away.

Emily rises, and I stand myself and follow her from the room. Side by side, we start up the stairs for our respective bedchambers.

"It is all coming together for us!" Elizabeth's voice trails after us.

"It is all coming together for *someone*." Emily takes my arm on the stairs, whispering to me as we go. "I've heard about Dr. Chidworth. Sarah told me his hands creep. But I believe he will do what Elizabeth tells him to—for now, anyway."

The tea has unsettled my belly, making me feel nauseated. Or perhaps it is the talk of Dr. Chidworth that has done it. I say nothing more, and trudge up the few final stairs as if I'm headed to the gallows. We reach Emily's door first. I go to continue up the hallway, but she catches my hand.

"Come with me," she says, pulling me into her chamber with a grin. She closes the door firmly behind us. "We will leave all talk of lords, and sons of lords, and physicians. Their lobcocks and twiddle-diddles will be left outside, in the hall."

I burst out laughing. Lobcocks and twiddle-diddles!

Emily laughs along with me, and then goes to flop down on the bed.

"I'm so glad you've come," she says, pushing herself up on her elbows to look at me. "There was another girl. Elizabeth found her at the pleasure gardens as well. She thought better of the situation and absconded to an aunt's house in the middle of the night."

"Oh," I say, wondering if I should have done the same after Emily's warning. But there had been nowhere to go and no one to turn to.

"Here." Emily pats the bed beside her. She shuffles over. "Do not fret. It will be all right."

Shyly, I go over to lie beside her. Her arm, warm, presses close to mine.

Emily turns her head to look at me.

"I forgot to tell you—do you remember, outside the theater, that woman?" Her voice lowers to a conspiratorial whisper.

I think back. "Do you mean the drunken one? Older? Propped up against the wall?"

Emily nods. "That was Mother Wallace."

"Mother Wallace? Are you sure? From what Elizabeth said, it sounded as if she was the owner of a prosperous establishment not so long ago. How can she be down on her luck so quickly?"

Emily leans in. "I've heard that Elizabeth made it so. Apparently Elizabeth's sea captain was paying a fine sum to Mother Wallace when he had her in high keeping, but Mother Wallace lied about the sum to Elizabeth. She was cheating her. Elizabeth was out hundreds of pounds. When she found out, she turned on Mother Wallace."

"What did she do?" My fingers grip Emily's arm tightly.

"I do not know, but it must be true, for I've heard the same from several people. It is common knowledge around Covent Garden, and Elizabeth does nothing to stop the rumors. She likes people to be afraid of her. She wants us to be afraid of her too. But I'm not. I'm not afraid of anyone."

"But . . ." I think on Elizabeth's words. "Surely she would never do something like that to us. She said she wanted a place of companionship. Of protection. A family."

"Elizabeth says many things, I have found."

"Oh." I draw back a little.

But Emily squeezes my hand. "Take heart. I think there is some truth to her wanting to run her establishment differently, fairly, but it would be a mistake to stand in her way when it comes to the *sérail*. I did try to warn you that this life is not for you. This world is not what it seems, Eleanor. People are people, no matter their funds. They are base and ugly and cruel. It is only their exterior that is gilded in this world."

I think about this for a moment before turning to look her in the eye once more. "But you're not base and ugly and cruel," I tell Emily. She is anything but these things.

She smiles at me. "I should hope not. And neither are you. *We* will never be so." She lifts her head and darts forward to give me a kiss on the cheek. "So deliciously plump!" She sighs and flops back, making me laugh at her antics.

We lie in silence for a moment or two, during which worries begin to build inside me.

Perhaps Emily senses this, because she turns her head. "Oh dear. It has come out all wrong, and now I have worried you! But I would do you a grave disservice if I said nothing. Elizabeth may bestow her praise upon you, weave the tragic tale of her childhood to make your heart break and look for all the world as if she is watching out for us, but at the end of the day Elizabeth looks out for herself. Mark my words. If you stand in her path, she will cut you down, and another one just like you will pop up in your place."

"But there is nothing to be done now," I say, "for Elizabeth has paid for gowns and jewelry and all sorts."

Emily shifts onto her side, and her eyes meet mine in a deep gaze. "It will be all right," she says. "Your little pliable student sounds ideal. It will not be so bad. Perhaps your debts will be paid after that, if his father bids high enough."

"Yes, perhaps." I close my eyes, as if I am tired, but I am not. The questions simply will not stop swirling in my head. *What if there are no bids? What if there are, but they are too low? What if none come in for Emily?* What if, what if, what if . . .

But no. Here, in the safety of Emily's bed, all is well.

We have each other. And I am content with this, for it feels like more than I have ever had before.

ALYS

WHITBY, PRESENT DAY

I RUN AS FAST as I can, but I can't reach her.
  I can never reach her.
On and on we go. On and on and on.
Her hand stretches back toward me, making me believe I can bridge the distance after all. Hope surges in my chest.
But she doesn't turn. Doesn't stop.
"Emily!" I cry out. "Emily, wait!"
She presses on, her voluminous ice-blue silk skirt jolting as she goes. I have to reach her. I run faster. And faster. I get closer. But never close enough. Sometimes I think I might actually make it, that our fingertips are about to touch.
Close now. So close!
But then, somehow, I realize I'm not close at all. I'm farther away than ever before.
I slow to a stop.
I feel something in the palm of my hand and look down. I hold a necklace of braided hair. There are three strands, of different

colors—burnished gold, hazelnut and ebony. I trace the darkest strand with one finger as it twists and weaves.
  Emily's hair.
  When I look up again, she is far, far away, in the distance.
  So I begin to run again.
  On and on we go. On and on and on.

LESS THAN TWENTY-FOUR hours after reuniting Elizabeth and Eleanor, I awaken in the dark, sweating, the sheets and blanket flung to the floor. My right hand is clenched, and in it I half expect to find the necklace of hair.

There's no necklace in my hand, of course.

Slowly, one by one, I release my fingers from their death grip.

And breathe.

I stare at a crack in the ceiling for a while, wondering *Now what?*

I'd been so focused on reaching this point. On acquiring Elizabeth. Bringing her home. When Mr. Yoon had become ill, I moved to Whitby to be closer to Ro for support, knowing the time was coming when I would need the coven's help. Then there was the waiting for Mr. Yoon to pass away, the transportation of Elizabeth. Storing her. I was so busy. It wasn't . . . real, as such.

Well, it's real now. All too real. Elizabeth's here. In storage. Beside Eleanor. And I have less than two weeks before I must destroy her. I'm also aware of the fact that people with an interest in the Venuses will somehow find out I've brought Elizabeth home. They'll begin to gossip. Someone will tell a journalist friend, and the media will become interested. Or, worse, they'll tell Catherine. A journalist who has a connection to the Venuses herself, she's hounded me for years as she works on writing a book about them.

Still, I'm not changing my mind. I know that it's time to enact the plan I've had all along, to finally break the connection between the Venuses. And there *is* a connection—not that I would ever admit that to anyone out loud, and certainly not to Catherine. I know everyone enjoys the delicious thought of three beautiful anatomical wax models coming to life by night to murder men who have wronged them, but the reality of their being able to do so—their being truly dangerous—is something else entirely. It opens up a world beyond ours. Of evil magic. Of terrible, wicked deeds. A second world, running alongside this one, that is so wrong and cruel, so full of pain and suffering, that it is best kept as far as possible from the one most of us enjoy living in. Very few people understand this.

But I understand it. It is my reality. My burden.

One I will soon no longer need to carry.

To be honest, I'm surprised I haven't heard from Catherine yet. She's usually the first to know anything about the Venuses. Sometimes I wonder if she knows things before I do. Any new piece of information that comes to light will see her contacting me, attempting to dig a little deeper, to uncover even the smallest trace of something so that she can add it to that wretched book of hers. She's cornered Ro on the street. Tried to sit down with Sorrel at a table in a restaurant while she was having a business meeting. She even traveled to Seoul and tried to get in touch with Ms. Han, wanting to speak to the Yoons. She's clever. And dangerous—not to others so much, but to me. I need to somehow let Catherine know that I've acquired Elizabeth and she's off somewhere new. Maybe . . . Kyoto. But that doesn't make sense, does it? Would Catherine believe I would rent Elizabeth out when I've never done so with Eleanor? Perhaps I could say they're both off somewhere. With a new master. No, wait. A new mistress. Catherine would *love* that. Maybe someone in Madrid? *Ugh, I'm overthinking this.* It doesn't matter where. I just need people (Catherine in particular) to believe the Venuses are . . . elsewhere. Gone. And then, in time, hopefully everyone will forget they ever existed. Thankfully, I know the coven will help with this. They have skills in persuasion. In making people remember things in a foggy sort of way.

Anyway, that's the basic plan.

Now I just need to enact it.

I take a deep breath and sit up so I can see out of the window. On the second floor of this Victorian building there is little to see, as Church Street is narrow, crammed on either side with shops that sell antiques and plum bread and teas and jet. So much jet. It's the jet that drew me here, to Whitby. Well, the jet and Ro, who is, hopefully, still asleep downstairs, one floor below me and one floor above the shop. Ro is from a family of jet specialists. Dense and black, jet is basically coal—fossilized wood that's somewhere around two hundred million years old. When the shop is quiet, I like to rescue the brooding black necklaces and brooches from the confines of their glass cabinets and hold them in wonder.

Two hundred million years. Amazing, really.

I get up and open the sash window as wide as it will go. I stick my head outside and see the first signs of light—it looks like dawn is just about to break. May as well make the most of it. Especially as I can't sleep after the dream. I never can. I throw on jeans, a T-shirt and a jacket and shove my phone in my back pocket. Time for a walk. For some fresh air. And being a seaside town, Whitby does fresh air well. In some ways, I wish I'd moved here sooner. There are fewer memories here.

The sea air seems to sweep old ones away, making space for new ones.

Making as little noise as possible, I pad down the creaky old stairs and make my way out the back, through the mudroom, slipping on some shoes as I go. I head outside, into the cool air, and close the mudroom door quietly. It's only a few steps from there to the large wrought iron gate that leads to the street. I let myself out, and then carefully lock the gate behind me.

It's quiet outside, the only signs of life the lights that are on in a few of the businesses I pass by—the fishmonger, the bakery, the florist—but it won't be long before Church Street comes to life. Postcard racks will appear; stands with bags and hats will be placed outside shops, as well as A-frame signs advertising ice creams and teas and cakes and fish-and-chips. Seagulls will begin to squawk endlessly overhead and cars will honk, their drivers fussing about backing up and moving onto the pavement so they can pass one another by. I pause to look at the pictures displayed in one of the art galleries, then move on, reaching out to touch one of the dollhouse-like front doors that you have to bend your head to enter through. Well, most people do. Being short, I'm fine. That's why I love it here. This place was made for me. Church Street makes me feel like I'm home somehow. And living with Ro makes me feel like I have a family, of sorts.

I can't believe my luck. Marco, the owner of my favorite coffee shop, has the door to his fine establishment propped open and is hauling in some milk. "Tell me the machine's ready to go," I call out.

Marco spots me limping to the caffeine finish line. "Ah! You're back. And up early. Jet lag?"

"Something like that."

"A coffee for each hand?"

"You know me too well. But I don't want to look greedy. I'll take one now and stop by for a refill on the way back." I'm such a regular, I have my own stash of reusable travel cups here. And a tab. I pick up a crate of milk and follow Marco inside.

"You opening today?" he asks as he makes his way over to his beautiful lime-green coffee machine—his pride and joy.

"Mm . . . not sure. That might be up to Ro—and how good your coffee is."

Marco snorts at the insult. His coffee is always good.

"Oh, I'm only joking. You know you have the best coffee in town."

"In Yorkshire."

I pull a face. "Hmm. I don't know. There's this little place . . ." I trail off. Marco looks worried for a moment, then realizes I'm joking again.

"You had me going for a second." He ducks behind the counter. "Hey, I'm going to toast myself a ham, cheese and tomato chutney. Do you fancy one?"

"No, just coffee, thanks. Lashings of coffee."

"Not a problem." Marco begins to work his magic on Esmerelda, the machine.

We chat as he pulls shots and steams milk. He pauses at one point to open a jar of tomato chutney, and he struggles.

I click my fingers and he passes it over.

I open the jar easily, and when Marco gives me a look, I shrug. "I've always had a knack," I say as I pass it back.

It's an easy exchange, and I'm glad to note that things feel normal between us once more, because for a while there, they didn't. About six months ago, Marco asked me out. We were standing in exactly the same spot.

I hadn't expected it, and I'd wanted to turn and run. What

had I done to make him believe... How had he got the impression that I... we...

"Um, I..." I hadn't known what to say. "I don't... can't..."

Marco had pulled back as if he'd realized something. "Oh, sorry. I didn't realize. Are you and Ro...?"

"Ro? Oh, no. No, we're just friends." I had no idea how to explain. Not that I had to, of course, but he needed to know. It wasn't him. It was me. It was most definitely me. And men. And... life. Men weren't for me. I mean, neither were women. People, even. Well, that's not entirely true. There was one person. Once.

It's complicated.

Marco had waved his hands. "It's all good. No explanation needed. I hope it's not going to be weird. Between us, I mean—that I asked."

"No, of course not. I'm flattered."

But things *were* weird for some time. I made sure I still picked up my coffee, of course. I certainly didn't avoid him. But I did avoid the familiarity we'd once had.

So I'm glad to see we've got over it—or I have. Marco was probably well-adjusted and fine with everything all along.

I lean against the counter. "Is there a reason you wanted to know if we're opening up today? Are you in the market for a jet necklace? An Edwardian locket? A pretty bauble of some description?"

Marco laughs. "No. Just curious."

We don't open up the shop every day, because we don't have to. Church Street Antiques isn't really somewhere tourists are going to pop into and spend their money. Who buys a couple postcards, a bag of fudge and a three-thousand-pound Georgian brooch? No one—that's who. We shouldn't really be on

Church Street at all, because we simply don't need a shop front. But when I was looking for somewhere to live, the place was for sale and it felt right, like home.

"You going up the abbey?" Marco asks over the noise of frothing milk.

I nod. "I figure, with the coffee and the climb, I'll be awake after that."

"Should be nice up there. Supposed to be a beautiful day."

"I hope so."

"Here you go, then. Enjoy the walk!" Marco passes me my double-walled glass cup of awake.

"I'll see you in an hour for a refill," I tell him.

After only a short walk up the cobbled street, I'm at the bottom of 199 steps. I take my first sip of coffee, brace myself and start the climb.

As I walk the wide, winding steps, the sky begins to lighten slowly and the seagulls start their day's squawking. I leave behind the tight alleyways and terrace houses and float above the rooftops and the chimneys of the town.

Along the way, there are benches on which to sit and take a break, but I don't stop to rest.

Instead, I sip my coffee and huff and puff my way right to the top. There, St. Mary's sits solidly, in the middle of a vast churchyard on a cliff top. The grass is dotted with headstones, each one tilted by time. Behind the church is the derelict abbey, open to the elements, its arches gaping. And on the other side, the spectacular view. As a few more people find their way to the summit, I take it all in—the River Esk, the little boats, the rows of houses, the piers, the seafront.

It's beautiful here in the daytime, but my favorite time to come is at dusk.

Then, the tourists retreat. The abbey is spotlighted, bats fly overhead instead of seagulls and all is silent and eerie. That's when the busy world stills and there is space to think. Whitby is famous for being an inspiration for Bram Stoker's *Dracula*. He had already started writing the novel when he visited Whitby, and that visit changed the story forever. The pages of the novel are dripping with this place.

I'm strolling along the path, thinking about Bram's trip (we're on a first-name basis), when a cat darts out and surprises me. It stops to give me a good hiss just as my phone begins to ring.

"Yes, thanks so much for your opinion," I say to the cat as I fumble for my phone in my pocket.

I look at the screen. *Speak of the devil.* It's Catherine calling. I decide to take the call. If I don't, she'll just call me again. And again. And again. Until I finally take the call. She. Is. Relentless.

"Hello, Catherine," I say. "I take it you've heard."

"Hi, Alys. How exciting for you to have acquired Elizabeth. And to have her back in the country. You must be so pleased."

I wouldn't say "pleased" is the word I would use. "She's not staying," I say quickly.

"Oh? She's off on another adventure?"

You could say that. "Mm." I give nothing away.

"And you've stored her with Eleanor?"

Catherine guessed a long time ago that Eleanor was in Sorrel's storage facility. She even tricked a staff member into confirming this. I say nothing.

"Well, I think that's exciting," Catherine continues. "Two of the Venuses reunited, rooming together cozily. Maybe I should supply them with my knife? Anything could happen! I definitely think we should get together to discuss it."

It takes everything in me not to hang up on her. Catherine's obsession with the Venuses and with the knife that has been in her family for hundreds of years is tiresome. As she'll tell you in her first breath on meeting you, Catherine is distantly related to a man—a student of anatomy—who was almost murdered in 1769. He was set upon by a woman in a tavern—a chophouse, actually. During the attack, he wrested the knife from his fiendishly strong assailant before she ran away. He then very quickly approached the newspapers, and he swore until his dying day that it was one of the Venuses that had attacked him. He spun such a fascinating tale about the wax models being bewitched that the public couldn't get enough of it.

That knife has been passed down within Catherine's family for generations, as has the bewitchment rumor.

Which is, of course, true.

Catherine just doesn't know that.

Time to nip this in the bud.

"Catherine, I'm sorry. It's still a no. It's as I've told you before. I don't have any further information to give you for your book." I feel bad for her. It's a fascinating story, I know. And she's worked so hard. She's uncovered every little detail she might have been able to without my help. But she's also guessed that I know more, and she wants that information. Badly.

Catherine being Catherine, of course she doesn't take my no as a *hard* no. "If you don't have time, perhaps I could speak to your mother."

I stiffen. "I'm just going to stop you there. I thought I told you that she's in care now. She has early-onset dementia. Visiting her won't be possible. Now, I really have to go. I've got a lot going on today."

"Sorry. You did tell me about your mother. It slipped my mind somehow. She's in Surrey, isn't she? But are you still in London? It really would be great to catch up." Catherine just keeps on going. You've got to hand it to her—she's got stamina.

I hesitate, not knowing how to reply. There's no right answer. If I tell her I'm in London, she'll hunt me down. If I tell her I'm in Whitby, she'll know Elizabeth will probably remain in storage for a while and wonder if she can badger me into viewing her—and Eleanor. "I'm afraid I've got to run," I say, and I hang up. I stick my phone back in my pocket. Poor Catherine. She deserves to tell the story of the Venuses. She really does.

I sigh and go to take another sip of my coffee. It's mostly gone now. And cold.

Ugh. Another reason to dislike Catherine.

Time to make my way back down to my good friend Marco.

And then I suppose I'll have to check in with Ro.

I'll definitely need to be well caffeinated for that.

RO, BLEARY-EYED, TURNS to look at me as I enter the kitchen. The kettle is singing and she's hovering over it, waiting impatiently.

"Not so jolly now, are you?"

She waves a hand. "*Mmpf.* No talking. Tea first."

She's never much good until the second cup.

"I'll just have to talk for both of us. I've got a lot of energy to give, considering this is not my first." I hold up Marco's finest.

"That stuff will give you a heart attack."

"I seriously doubt that."

Ro is a firm believer in tea, and lots of it. I sit down at the worn, familiar kitchen table and watch as she goes through her morning ritual. She hums as she warms the pot and opens tins, deciding which tea to have. When the tea is finally drawing upon the table, she sits down.

We sit in silence until she pours her first cup, takes a sip.

"You're up early," she finally says. There's a pause. "I heard you. Last night. You had your dream again."

The downside of living with other people is that there are other people. "Catherine called me." I change the subject.

Ro sighs. "Of course. Will she ever let up?"

I think we both know the answer to that question.

Ro is quiet as she pours more tea into her favorite fine bone china teacup, decorated with ivy, but I hear the question she's not asking as clearly as if she's speaking it.

What now, Alys?

I take a sip of coffee that I really don't need, given my current level of anxiety. Something's wrong. I thought I was so sorted. But now . . . something's off.

I glance up from my cup, and Ro's green eyes meet mine. "I spoke to the others. Everything's ready in the New Forest."

"At Jennet's," I say. Jennet is the coven leader. I don't know what you call a coven leader. Head witch? This side of things—bewitchment, magic—is not something I like to discuss, because it brings up painful memories for me. So we skate along the top of things, pretending we're friends. Flatmates. Workmates. Plain and simple. Not that we aren't those things, but the truth is, nothing about our situation is plain and simple.

"Yes. At Jennet's. Everything's ready. Including the hair necklace. The entire coven is on standby."

The necklace. Emily. My heart picks up pace. It begins to race faster than it had when I was climbing the 199 steps, because of a combination of caffeine and anxiety and an always-weak stomach. I'd been so brave back in Seoul. In London, even. With my plans. With my pressing on. Moving forward. Now all I seem able to think about is the past.

I *hate* thinking about the past. I am the queen of living in the moment. Not because I'm some self-actualized wonder but because it's the only way I can survive, get through my days.

Ro clears her throat. "Maybe . . . maybe it would be best if you visited Jennet by yourself first? No pressure. Her cottage is amazing, so peaceful. It's a wonderful haven. You could spend a few days there if you wanted. There's time."

"No, I should just . . ." I pause. I can't say the words.

Something's off again.

But what?

What the hell is wrong with me? I know this is the right time. I signed Mrs. Yoon's contract. I agreed to her terms when it came to haste. And I know what needs to be done.

Why am I hesitating?

I'd thought my early-morning walk might clear my head, give me some perspective. But my doubt remains. And I don't understand it. Why can't I just move swiftly along? Destroy what must be destroyed? That whisper I heard in the storage unit—surely that was simply my subconscious reminding me what I needed to do. And fast. The Venuses must be banished from this earth forever. Why? Because they should never have been here in the first place. Just look at poor Geon. People suffer because of them. And I know I can end the suffering. It's my duty to end it.

And then?

And then I can rest.

"Alys?" Ro looks up from pouring her tea.

I stand and take my cup to the sink, rinse it out.

"You know, I think I'm going to make a quick trip to Hampshire. I have a . . . few ends to tie up." I gloss over the details. Ro knows why I go to Hampshire.

"Do you want me to come?" Ro asks.

"No, that's okay. I'll only stay one night. I'm not running away, if that's what you're thinking."

Ro gives me a look. "There's all the time in the world, Alys—if you want it."

I return her look. "I know."

"Really. If you need to break the contract with Mrs. Yoon—"

"No," I say quickly. "We're going ahead. I just need a couple days to sort myself out—that's all."

There's a pause. A long pause, in which I busy myself putting my cup in the dishwasher. "So, what are you going to get up to here?"

Ro shrugs. "Oh, um . . . a couple phone calls, I guess. Leads."

"You going to open the shop?"

"I don't think so. When I do that, people tend to come inside it."

I laugh. "How rude of them," I say. "Anyway, I'm off to pack a few things." I start for the stairs. The wall next to the stairs is lined with antique mirrors, and as I head up, I take the opportunity to inspect my bloodshot eyes in one of them. There's only so much coffee can do. I'm about halfway up when Ro calls out. I turn to look down at her, and her expression is serious, which is unlike her.

"Hey, if you need anything, just call, okay? I can meet you. Anywhere. Anytime. Trust me on that."

I nod, wishing I had the luxury of trust.

That I could truly trust anyone. Ever again.

ELEANOR

LONDON, OCTOBER 1769

THE DAYS FLY by, and my new life is like a dream. Some mornings, on awakening, I am surprised to find myself in my opulent chamber, Emily often slumbering peacefully beside me. Her presence is a balm to me, and I lie still in the quiet of the dawn, staring up at the fine fabric canopy of my bed and thinking back. To my beginnings in London. To Nicholas. To the room with the filthy walls. To the fear when he was nowhere to be found. None of it seems quite real now. In many ways, the time I have spent with Elizabeth and Emily does not seem quite real either. I have a new wardrobe of beautiful gowns, and glittering paste jewelry, all the better to show off my figure. And I *am* shown. Paraded. Elizabeth leads us in a daily stroll through St. James's Park. I am proud to walk along beside them, every onlooker's gaze fixed upon us. Often, Emily's arm is to be found entwined in mine. She has become more than a friend over the past few weeks. She is a cherished confidante, the dear sister my heart has always yearned for.

In the evenings, Emily and I ready ourselves, dressing and fussing with our hair, drinking wine and laughing. Our nights are spent at Almack's, or the theater. Elizabeth reminds the gentlemen of the *sérail*'s address. Provides them with cards. Tells them that bidding for our maidenheads will begin shortly.

I try not to think too much on my situation. Who I was. What I am about to become.

I concentrate diligently on Elizabeth's lessons. Each day, we practice. She informs us how the hours will pass in the *sérail*. Tells us stories of gentlemen she has serviced. Imparts many an amusing tale. Nothing seems to touch her, worry her. She glides smoothly forward through life, like a beautiful figurehead on a majestic ship, navigating her course effortlessly, letting nothing stand in her path.

I drink her experiences in, hoping the knowledge will save me. If I know what to do, how to behave, what to expect, then all will be well.

Elizabeth certainly seems to believe all will be well. As is her plan, the more we are seen, the more we are noticed. Letters begin to arrive, letters of interest that inquire delicately as to when bidding might open. Elizabeth is pleased. She spends more money. On wigs. More jewelry. And then the pièce de résistance. A mantua-maker fits us for three stunning gowns of Spitalfields silk. The fabrics are of a quality I have never encountered before. Elizabeth selects a bolt of ice-blue silk for Emily, and a rose pink for me. But the fabric Elizabeth chooses for herself—oh, it is the most beautiful silk I have ever seen. It is an elaborate, shimmering mix of gold. Autumn has come and the leaves have turned to warm shades, floating down from the plane trees above in the cooling breeze. I know Elizabeth has considered this, as well as the shade of her red-gold hair, and will use all of this to great effect.

She is exquisite, at the very peak of her beauty. And she knows it.

Her sea captain knows it too.

Emily and I see his eyes on her. At Almack's. In St. James's Park. And tonight, when we are again at the theater.

But this evening, as I look at her, I wonder... does it prey on her mind, what comes after? After autumn comes winter. After a peak, a descent. Is this why she races to open the *sérail*? To shore up her fate for what comes after Sir William?

"Do you think he will return to her?" Emily asks me, her mind obviously on Sir William as well.

Interestingly, he is alone at the theater tonight. The sentimental comedy on offer is dull, but Elizabeth and the sea captain proceed to make their own entertainment from their requisite boxes, exchanging many a meaningful glance. Now she has disappeared. As has he, coincidentally. To find a dark corner, I expect. I consider Emily's question. I know Elizabeth must have spent a staggering amount of money lately, much of which Emily and I now owe her, as it has been jotted down in her ledger—down to the very last farthing, which would be fair if there were ever any consultation as to her expenditure.

"I suppose that—" I'm cut off as Emily elbows me firmly in the ribs.

Elizabeth sweeps back into her seat. Her face is flushed, her expression triumphant. "Well, that was a success," she says.

"In what way?" Emily replies, her tone droll.

But Elizabeth will not be brought down from the clouds. "In all the ways one might expect," she quips. "Also, Sir William would like to visit the *sérail*. He is keen to view my macaw."

"That's a name I've not heard it called before," Emily replies, and I can't help but laugh.

Thankfully, Elizabeth is in such a good mood that she laughs along with us. "Sir William mentioned that my little establishment sounds a fine business investment. I expect he will stop by in a day or two. Perhaps even tomorrow, now that he's been reminded of what he's been missing. Who knows? He may even be interested in investing in my business."

THE FOLLOWING MORNING, Elizabeth is no longer in good spirits. She sighs loudly. "Honestly, Eleanor, Polly could do a better job," she tells me, crossing the drawing room to let the doting macaw nuzzle her hand.

Emily has just this moment finished playing the part of a gentleman arriving at the *sérail*. I have greeted him, led him to the drawing room, offered him a glass of French claret, suggested that he might join us in a game of cards—all the things I have been told to do, in the order I have been instructed to do them in.

But it is not enough.

Apparently I have not done them with the correct *feeling*. My manner is unnatural, forced.

"Be merry, Eleanor! Goodness, it is as if you are at a funeral. We are meant to be enjoying ourselves! The evening is but young, and we will be spending it here, in fine company, in this wonderful *sérail*. Along with all our funds."

"Yes, let us not forget that last bit." Emily twirls toward me, deftly takes the glass of claret from my hand and downs it in one gulp.

"Emily!" Elizabeth exclaims, again displeased. Polly squawks loudly, as if in agreement. Elizabeth comes over to wrench the glass from her apprentice's hand. "You have only just finished breakfast, my girl. Pace yourself."

Emily pouts. "The evening is but young! You said so yourself."

"Quick-witted as ever, I see." Elizabeth points the now-empty glass at Emily, then at me. "You could learn much from her, Eleanor—as Emily could learn from you to drink less, lest she soon find herself in the gutter, squabbling with Mother Wallace over the dregs of a bottle of gin."

My gaze shifts between them. The truth is, Emily has been drinking more and more. I wonder if Elizabeth even knows how much, for I have been begging Sarah to secrete away the empty bottles I have found in Emily's chamber. I have attempted to quiz her on her habits, wanting to understand her—to help her—but my inquiries seem only to cause her to retreat from me. She becomes less her true self when she partakes, and more the frivolous creature she believes the world wants her to be. When I attempt to lure her back to me, she grows angry and drinks yet more, leaving me on constant tenterhooks.

Perhaps sensing my uncertainty, Elizabeth places the glass on a small side table and comes over to take my hands. "Let me give you some advice, Eleanor." In a motherly fashion, she leads me over to sit on the chaise longue. "You must be sure of yourself. It is the only way. It is as Emily told you the first night you arrived here. You must learn to pretend you are an actress on the stage and that this is simply a role you are fulfilling. As you grow older, you'll find that women fulfill many roles in one lifetime, in order to survive. Satisfy yourself that at least this role will be paid. Handsomely. And you will be in control of how you play it."

"You do seem to enjoy playing your role," I say doubtfully.

Elizabeth laughs heartily at my words. "Oh, I like the money, Eleanor, but that is where my enjoyment ends. Men are despicable creatures. I hate them all with a passion. But I am very willing to part them from their funds. Every. Last. Shilling."

"You hate them all? Your sea captain too?" I ask boldly.

Elizabeth doesn't flinch. "Of course," she says, with a toss of her head.

Her reply is quick and easy, but I do not believe her, for I have noticed how she looks at Sir William. She wants more from him than his money. She wants his ... devotion. She wants him to want her and only her. To choose her above all others. Despite money. Despite her past. Despite everything.

Sarah enters the room. "A letter, madam."

Elizabeth rises from the chaise longue. "Thank you, Sarah." She pauses when she sees the writing. Rips the letter open quickly. Her eyes fly down the paper, and when they lift again, they are glittering.

"Sir William is coming. We must make haste, for I will have to change. And you will both have to go out."

"THANK YOU, SIR." Emily bobs as she takes the lead and accepts the guinea very generously proffered by Sir William. Elizabeth has had Sarah invite the *sérail*'s first proper caller into the drawing room. He is tall and sturdy. Up close, his face is weathered for his age, but there is an air about him—a quiet decisiveness. I can see why Elizabeth is so taken with him. As he takes a turn of the drawing room, inspecting it with an assessing eye, I can see he is astonished with what has been achieved (Elizabeth has been wise enough to put Polly in her cage, and it rattles wildly with the bird's fury). It is obvious that Sir William did not expect the *sérail* to be quite so first-rate. Elizabeth watches him closely, looking like the cat that got the cream. Moments ago, she informed him that her new friends were just about to depart, adding that they might, perhaps, require some funds for their entertainment. Thus the guinea he has just pressed into Emily's palm. We all know it is too much. He is attempting to impress—not us, but Elizabeth. He may not have her in high keeping anymore, but he still desires her approval.

"Sir William has a generous nature," Elizabeth says, her eyes moving from Sir William to me and back again, suggestively.

"Yes, well..." He does not look quite so decisive in this moment, but rather trapped. And yet he finds it within himself to locate another guinea. He passes this to me, and I bob as well.

"*Most* generous," I agree, half-scandalized that Elizabeth is comfortable with being so brazen (Sir William had obviously meant that initial guinea to be for both of us) and half-thrilled to have a whole guinea in my palm. I wonder if, one day, I might have the ability to conjure money out of gentlemen in such a fashion. Imagine having such a skill!

Emily trots over, tugs upon my arm and pulls me, stunned, from the room. As directed, we have both readied ourselves to depart and are out the door in but a moment, attempting to stem our laughter as we go. We manage to hold it in until we are away from the town house, and then pause to clutch at each other.

"A full guinea!" I say. "Each! What are we to spend it on, do you think?"

"Ourselves. All of it on ourselves. And quickly, too, before Elizabeth can take it from us."

"Elizabeth would not do that," I reply.

Emily gives me a look, then lets my comment go with a shrug. "That poor man. What a fool he is for her."

"A fool in love, perhaps?" I say.

Emily wrinkles her nose. "In lust, more like."

"I suppose it is also that. But Elizabeth loves him deeply, I believe."

A snort. "Elizabeth loves only what he can provide for her."

I am not so sure she is correct. "She certainly did not seem to enjoy losing him."

Emily catches my arm, this time not in jest. Her expression darkens. "That was not about him. Elizabeth cannot bear to lose anything. Why you persist in seeing so much good in her, I truly have no idea. Trust me. She is no savior to you. That evening she brought you home from the pleasure gardens? She was actively searching for other girls. For the *sérail*. You must know that."

I pull my arm away. Of course I know this. Elizabeth did not bring me home like a stray pup out of the goodness of her heart. I was not special. Fate had not brought us together. I remember how I had seen Elizabeth talking to other young women at the pleasure gardens on the night I was there with Nicholas too. "You think me as foolish as Sir William," I say.

Emily sighs. "I do not think you foolish."

"You wanted me to leave as soon as Elizabeth brought me to the town house. You told me to go."

I expect Emily to deny this, but she does not. Instead, she does quite the opposite.

"I would hope so. Had I not, I would have been cut from the same cloth as Elizabeth. This is no life for you, Eleanor. You are not like Elizabeth. Or me."

"So you are always saying." I turn away from her, tired of being thought of as a child.

Emily catches my arm once more. "Come, let us not quarrel. We have two fat guineas and most of the day to spend at our leisure. Now that Elizabeth has ensnared Sir William in her web, she will take her time with him—you can trust me on that—so let us start over. We will take a stroll in the park to clear the air."

It does not take long for me to forgive Emily, for she is an easy person to forgive. The day is fine and we are free from our lessons. Within moments we are chatting easily again, as if not a sour word has passed between us.

"Oh, look." I slow to view the offerings of a bookseller who has set up a table on which to display his wares. "Isn't it odd? There is not a single book in Elizabeth's town house." I realize how much I miss the smell of books, being able to select one, sit in an armchair by the fireplace and idly flick through.

"There is the ledger to read," Emily points out. "As if we could forget that. Did your house have many books? My father's did. There was a library full of them, but they weren't to be touched. They were for collecting and admiring, not for reading."

"My father's books were the opposite. He adored books and would read until his eyes were tired each day." I turn to look at her. "Here, let me select one that we might both enjoy."

Emily seems doubtful. I know it must be a book that will pique her interest. And I know just such a book. I laugh and whisper a few words to the bookseller. He pulls back.

"You sure, miss?"

"Quite sure," I tell him.

He crouches down to rummage around under the table, and finally stands to pass me a book.

I turn it back and forth. "It is a little worse for wear," I tell him, getting ready to bargain.

We finally settle upon a fair price, and Emily and I are soon on our way toward the park again. "I think you'll find it a fascinating tale," I tell her.

"How so? What is it about?"

"It is about a girl called Fanny Hill, who comes to the city."

"It sounds a tad dull."

I laugh. "It is anything but dull, for Fanny is a very interesting girl. The title is *Memoirs of a Woman of Pleasure*. I tried to read the book once, but my father found out. He kept the book locked up after that, but I managed to pick the lock."

Emily's eyebrows shoot up. "And now *I* am intrigued. Perhaps I will find this book interesting after all."

The day is unusually warm as we make our way through St. James's Park. We pause to purchase fresh milk, which we drink from tin cups. When we finally get to Rosamond's Pond, Emily reveals that the spot is known as a place of assignation.

"Who knows what we might see?" She laughs. "And who we might see doing it?"

As it turns out, there is nothing to see but a small amount of water and some ducks.

"Still, they are quite handsome ducks," I say, and Emily laughs, pushing me down onto the grass. Feeling drowsy after our milky feast, we loll about in the sunshine, Emily's head resting on my stomach. Her fingers toy with the fabric of my dress, lightly beating out a tune she has heard somewhere—perhaps at Almack's.

It is lovely, just for a few moments, to feel as if I have not a care in the world.

Elizabeth is far away, Nicholas long forgotten. It is just us two. Together. In the quiet.

"Read to me," Emily says after a while. "I do so love to be read to."

I bring out the book and begin to read aloud. We are soon ensconced in the world of Fanny, who moves to London at the age of fourteen, after both her parents die of smallpox. She finds employment as a maid, or so she believes. It turns out that her employer has other plans for her, which mainly involve selling her maidenhead. Fanny is soon seduced and begins a life of sexual adventure.

"Give me that." Emily sits up, grabbing the book from my hand. She lies back down on the soft green carpet beneath us, holding up the book to block the sun, and begins to flip through it, reading bits and pieces as she goes, her eyes ever widening. "Goodness. Is there anything this girl has not seen?"

"It would seem not," I reply. "There is not much she does not seem to delight in either."

Emily dives into the book again. She is certainly captivated now. "Listen to this," she says. "Fanny and her friend have been watching a man and a woman through a peephole."

She glances up briefly, and I raise my eyebrows. "Go on..."

Emily begins to read. "'She lifted up my petticoats, and with her busy fingers fell to visit, and explore that part of me, where now the heat, and irritations were so violent, that I was perfectly sick and ready to die with desire.'" The book lowers and Emily stares at me, her eyes wide. "Eleanor, I do believe I am having... feelings."

A sudden flush heats my cheeks, and it is not the sun's doing. I laugh nervously, not entirely sure how to reply, or whether to admit the surge of desire I felt as she read to me under the sun's embrace. It is strange how being with Emily causes me to question my time with Nicholas, to look back and view our relationship through different eyes. I see now that the pleasure I took in Nicholas's company was not my own. It was in only the giving. My happiness was not true. It had stemmed only from seeing *him* pleased at my gratifying his every desire. It is not like this with Emily. Emily sees me for myself. She is interested in *me*. In my thoughts. My desires. Nicholas saw me only for what

I could provide him. And when I had provided it, he discarded me.

But Emily . . . I believe Emily and I care for each other's pleasure. Or we would, given the chance.

Perhaps this is my chance? Here. Now.

I will myself to speak, to say something. But I cannot find the words. What I feel is weak and has no shape or definition—it struggles to make itself known, as small and as helpless as a fledgling bird. I must wait. Give it sustenance. Care for it. Study it. Understand it.

Emily abandons the book beside her and closes her eyes, lazily bringing one arm up to rest behind her head. "If only all our days could be spent like this," she says. "We could live here, in the park, just the two of us. We have sunshine. All the milk we could ever drink. A filthy text to entertain ourselves with. The remainder of two guineas."

"Yes."

"We could build a cottage. Right here. With a gate to keep everyone out. There would be no one to tell us what to do. What to be. And inside, there would be only happiness. And safety. And freedom. And us two. And there would be roses climbing around the front door. There always are. We could call our abode Rose Cottage accordingly."

Speak, Eleanor, I will myself. *Say something.*

"What else might two young ladies need?" Emily encourages me to join in.

Pleasure, I think. "Our good health, I suppose" is my actual answer. "Which we have."

There is a slight pause. "Yes. I suppose so." Emily abandons her daydream, and rolls over onto her front and begins to pluck at blades of grass with her fingers. "What do you want, though? Really? What's your heart's desire, Eleanor?"

Now is your chance, I tell myself. Emily is rarely serious, but I sense that in this moment she is seeking a thoughtful response from me, not frivolous talk of cottages. But I do not know how to answer. My heart's desire is not something I have ever stopped to consider. I'd thought it was Nicholas. But now I see it wasn't Nicholas at all that I had truly craved, but the promise of a different life. Of being loved. Being wanted. "I am not sure," I finally reply, fearful of giving the wrong answer and ruining the moment. "Do you know?" I ask. "For yourself?"

Emily considers my question. "I suppose I do. I want . . . just one person. One person to stand beside me."

Oh. My heart plummets when I hear this. She means to find at the *sérail* a gentleman who will have her in high keeping. Or perhaps even a husband, if such a thing is possible.

"Of course you will find a gentleman," I tell her.

Beside me, Emily stills. And I know instantly that I *have* given the wrong answer and that I have failed her terribly. I have not understood what she is saying at all. My heart quickens. Could it be true? Could she possibly want the same thing I do? A deeper connection? I long to take back my words, but it is too late. I reach out and touch her arm, and after a moment or two, she turns to me.

"My mother loved me. I think," she continues, her eyes a little too bright. "At least, I would like to remember it that way. I was very small when I was brought to England. Still, I believe I recall her face close to mine, her singing to me. Unless that is something I simply imagined . . ." She trails off.

"I am sure she loved you, Emily."

"Do you remember your mother?" Emily asks.

I shake my head. "I was too young. But my father . . . I miss him very much."

If my father had still been alive, there would have been no

running away with Nicholas. No London. No meeting Elizabeth. No *sérail*. My father would have found someone suitable for me to marry by now. I would have a happy home. Children, perhaps.

Emily's gaze meets mine, and I guess that she is thinking the same thing. If she had remained with her mother, perhaps she would have made sure that Emily's life was different to her own. Fought for her daughter not to enter the same line of work. Or maybe that is what she believed herself to be doing when she sent Emily to England?

"I am so afraid," I blurt out, finally giving voice to some of my feelings. "You were right. You were right all along. I am not sure I can do this—be what Elizabeth wants me to be." I shudder as I think of all the gentlemen who are about to pass through the *sérail*'s door. Leading them upstairs. Having to satisfy their every whim, whatever it might entail.

Emily grasps my hand. "It need not be forever. And I think it is a good thing to know—that this is not the life for you."

I cock my head. "What do you mean?"

Emily thinks for a moment, drawing a deep breath. "I was reminded of something just this morning—when Elizabeth was talking of actresses, and how you must strive to be like one on the stage. I realized that's not what Elizabeth is at all. What she reminds me of is an automaton. Have you ever seen one?"

I shake my head.

"My father took the family to see one once. It was like a doll. A moving doll. It was a lady, sitting at a dulcimer, striking the strings with her little hammers. She could play eight songs. It was most impressive. But the whole time she played for us, I could not stop looking at her eyes. She was moving, but her eyes were so . . . dull. There was something horrifying about it. And that is Elizabeth. She can perform many a superlative song and dance, but there is nothing behind it. No life. No feeling. Just motion. Does that make any sense?"

I stare at Emily in wonder, my mouth agape. It is *exactly* that. Elizabeth is like a very fine doll. Beautiful to look at. A joy to behold. But she is fashioned out of porcelain and is hard and cold to the touch.

"Now you are shocked. Pay me no heed. All I am saying is that I would be very sad if you were to become a soulless beast such as her. If you were to lose all hope for something else. Something better. If you were to lose the light in your eyes." She reaches out and clasps one of my hands. "To see you lose your love for others, to think only of yourself. I could not bear to see that. And yet at the same time, I worry about what will happen if you cannot harden your heart to survive this world that we find ourselves in." Emily has shifted nearer to me, and her face is now close to mine. For a moment, I think . . . But then Emily's eye catches some movement behind me. She is up in a moment, dragging me along with her. "Quickly, up. Gather yourself."

My head spins from the sun and from rising so fast. It takes me a moment to see that two men are approaching us. In the distance, another two men watch them, waiting in curricles.

"They have recognized us. That is Lord Levehurst back there." Emily nods toward the second curricle. "Now we must be on our guard."

I dredge up from the bottom of my mind something Elizabeth said about Lord Levehurst, that he pays handsomely for maidenheads but she does not care for the company he keeps, the company that is approaching us now.

"Should we run?" I whisper.

Emily gives me a look. "No. We must stand fast. It will be worse if we run. Their kind love nothing more than the thrill of the hunt."

It is too late to run anyway. The men are upon us.

"You are easily spotted, miss," one of them says to Emily.

"All part of my cunning plan, sir." Emily bobs. "A lady must have a point of difference."

"A lady, eh?" The second man guffaws.

"Yes," Emily says. "A lady. *Two* ladies, in fact."

"What a coincidence," the second man continues. "For we have been on the hunt for exactly that number of ladies in order to have a little sport today. A small race around the park is in order." He grabs my arm forcefully, and his friend takes Emily's. "Do join us. *Ladies*."

He says this as if he is giving us a choice in the matter.

I begin to panic. My heart hurling itself at my breast, I go to wrench my arm away, to flee. But when I look over at Emily, she only smiles broadly at her captor, as if this is the happiest of chance meetings. "Why, is that Lord Levehurst I spy over there? How wonderful! Of course we would love to join you in your thrilling race."

Amazingly, the man's grip on me loosens slightly on his hearing this—which is when I come to see that Emily knows exactly what she is doing, and that, if I want to escape this situation, I must follow her lead.

"How . . . lovely!" I join in, a terrible squeak to my voice.

"And fortuitous," Emily adds, "for I have a secret to share with Lord Levehurst."

"A secret?" the oaf dragging me along roughly says. His breath reeks of whatever he was drinking into the early hours of this morning. Or perhaps he has not stopped drinking at all.

"A scandalous secret?" Emily's gentleman "friend" asks.

"Oh, I only collect scandalous secrets," Emily jokes, "for they are the only kind worth sharing."

We have reached the two curricles now. The gentleman in

the first one looks at us with little interest. "Do hurry up, Henry," he says to the man who still has a grip upon me. "Your endless antics bore me half to death." His gaze never meets mine. My plight is of no consequence to him.

Henry ignores his friend, pausing beside a tree, which he pushes me against.

Emily glances over at me for a moment, her eyes saying much, willing me to stay upright, to stay strong. "Now, I must whisper my secret to his lordship," she says, "for you can't all hear it. Really, it is not even fit for the horses!"

The men all look at one another and laugh. Emily is guided over to Lord Levehurst's curricle. She beckons him down, and at the same time, her jailer boosts her up, groping as much of her as he can in the process.

I try very, very hard to calm myself, and to take charge of the situation, such as Emily is doing. "I . . . I wonder what the secret might be." I must engage the beast upon me in conversation. I want him to remember that I am here. Living. Breathing.

"I wonder what secrets *you* keep." He leans into me heavily. Despite the warmth of the day, my entire body chills, the sweat at the nape of my neck and the top of my lip like ice. I am frozen as Emily whispers into Lord Levehurst's ear, while Henry's awful, clammy hand fumbles at my dress.

The other men avert their eyes. They do not want to know. There is nothing to see here, for, just as I feared, I am nothing. If events go awry here, it is of no consequence. Any small scandal will be smoothed over by the gentlemen's families, by Elizabeth. All will be forgiven. Especially if money changes hands, for the inconvenience.

I attempt to speak once more, but I find I cannot. Someone has stuffed my head with horsehair. I am a doll, twisted here and there as Henry tugs at my clothing. I am reminded of

Emily's dull-eyed automaton. Perhaps it is better to be like that. Unfeeling. Unknowing. Perhaps I can simply pretend to be an automaton for these few moments in order to survive. I will strike my dulcimer and think of nothing, be nothing.

Then Lord Levehurst's head turns from Emily's. His gaze moves to me then, and he looks me over, assessing me. "Get off her, Henry, you oaf," he finally bellows. "Go on. Get off her now. You've had your fun."

This voice of authority Henry listens to. He retreats with a grunt. I hurriedly straighten my gown, attempting to hide the trembling of my limbs. Henry straightens himself, too, then ambles over to the curricle. Emily jumps down nimbly, and Henry shoves her aside with his hip before clambering aboard. The two curricles pull away, the gentlemen giving nary a backward glance, as if nothing has happened.

I burst into tears.

"Come, now," Emily says, patting my arms. She turns her back on the curricles so the gentlemen might not see my distress. "You are not hurt?"

I shake my head. I am not hurt, but shocked. It is difficult to fathom how one happy moment might be turned about so violently to become the exact opposite. "What . . . whatever did you say to him that made them leave?"

"I simply reminded him that he might find himself with a distinct lack of superior maidenheads if he displeases Elizabeth. Also, I promised that he would be first to hear when bidding opens."

My belly heaves. I bend over and spill its milky contents onto the gravel path below.

"Oh dear," Emily says. "Come. Let us walk off this unpleasantness. Never fear. We will inform Elizabeth of this Henry. I very much doubt he will be welcome at the *sérail* at all if this is how he behaves. And I suspect Elizabeth will not think much of Lord Levehurst after what has occurred today."

I am quiet as we walk away from the park, Emily chattering away as if naught has happened, trying to bolster my spirits. Back in Covent Garden, she purchases two pies. "For you must be hungry now," she says.

But I am not. And the pie and Covent Garden serve only to remind me of Nicholas and different, equally unhappy times. I begin to look around for him as I did at the pleasure gardens. Perhaps he has been searching for me. He will appear now, and we ...

"Eleanor!" Emily says, breaking my spell. She gestures toward the pie in my hand, uneaten.

"I cannot," I say.

"Then I will." Someone snatches the pie from my hand. A woman. A woman who looks as if she has been in her line of work for some years. I recoil as she shoves the pie into her mouth almost whole. Her appearance is close to the description of the woman Elizabeth told me about in *Harris's List,* the woman who was as lewd as a monkey and wanton as a goat. "Not polite to stare," she tells me, her mouth full.

"What do you want?" Emily snaps at her. "Away with you."

"Ooh, aren't we all high-and-mighty?" The woman curtsies. "Think you're right ladies, don't you? I thought I'd come across you sooner or later, for I've heard all about this *sérail* business." She laughs. "Fancy word for what you can find anywhere around these parts—for cheaper, too, I'm sure."

"What. Do. You. Want?" Emily says again.

"To do you a favor, my dear. That's why I've been keeping an eye out. I'd watch out if I was you. I was with that Elizabeth of yours at Mother Wallace's."

"You were at Mother Wallace's?" Emily says quickly. "What happened there?"

I remember Emily telling me something had happened, but she did not entirely know what.

The woman grins, showing one blackened tooth. "Ah, I wondered if anyone had told you, for I wouldn't work for her knowing what I do."

"Elizabeth told us that Mother Wallace cheated her," I say. "Is that not true?"

The woman swallows and nods. "Aye, that's true enough. Mother Wallace cheated Elizabeth. And Mother Wallace paid for her deception. Elizabeth made sure of that. But others paid for it too. Three others. She's the devil, she is, that Elizabeth. And you best watch out for her, or she'll have you too."

"What do you mean?" Emily says. "What did Elizabeth do? What do you mean, three others paid for it?"

The woman pauses. "You want to know what really happened? Well, I'll tell you, because it's not right what she did. Innocent girls, they was. Good-hearted girls. And it's not as if they saw a penny of Elizabeth's funds. So, here it is, plain as day. Elizabeth got that doctor of hers, that Chidworth fellow, to find a man with the pox. And then she paid him to bring the pox into Mother Wallace's house, to ruin her business. And ruin it she did, for three of the girls in the house—girls Elizabeth knew well—died. So, that's my warning to you. You keep an eye on each other—and the other one on that Elizabeth, if you know what's good for you."

ALYS

HAMPSHIRE, PRESENT DAY

I SEND A QUICK text to my contact in Hampshire. Then I throw some things into a bag and head off before Ro can change her mind about going on a road trip with me. It's not that I don't enjoy her company, but she's trying so hard to be... bolstering. Her cheeriness will probably kick in again after two cups of tea, and I just need a bit of space to get my head around what I've signed up for here.

It's a five-and-a-half-hour drive to Hampshire, which turns into six and a half hours with traffic.

Unfortunately for me, that's a little more thinking time than I was looking for.

I spend the drive working my way steadily through Ro's bag of ginger candies and considering my situation.

What's stopping me from taking the next step forward?

I end up concluding that maybe all I need is to connect with Emily one last time. I need to look her in the eye, and to feel that what I'm about to do is right. I'd felt the need to see her—to travel to Hampshire and view the portrait of her that resides there. Maybe that really is all I need? To meet her gaze. To sense her approval. To feel that she's behind me in this, that it's what she wants too.

I hope so.

It's so strange. There wasn't a doubt in my mind about bringing Elizabeth back, about whether destroying her is the right thing to do. I thought it was right for Eleanor and Emily as well. Why something has changed for me now—shifted—I'm not sure.

I can't pinpoint what's wrong.

All I come up with is a general feeling of unease. A feeling that something's not right. That I've forgotten something, overlooked something.

Back in the storage facility. Seeing the two crates side by side. That moment when I thought I'd heard my name whispered...

But no, I couldn't have.

Being in that room with Eleanor, all so silent and still. I know destroying her is the right thing to do.

I know it is what Elizabeth would *not* want.

But Emily? Emily is forever running away from me in my dreams. Elusive. Always close, but also farther away than ever.

As I close in on my destination—a stately home called Poulston Park—I take a quick detour through the village of Chawton so I can drive by Jane Austen's house. It's summer, and Hampshire is green and heaving with tourists. The house is a beautiful redbrick, and the garden is looking lush. The little shop at the back, which sells everything Jane—from mugs, to tea towels, to magnets—is busy with visitors. It's a delightful museum, with so much to look at—from her writing desk to some of her letters, and first editions of her books.

But there's no time today.

From here it's only a fifteen-minute drive to Poulston Park.

There's a lovely florist shop in a nearby village, and I stop and buy a large bunch of yellow roses for Mrs. Owen, the stately home's housekeeper. I know they're her favorite. By the time I turn into the private tree-lined avenue that leads toward the manor house, the day has clouded over, turning gloomy and oppressive.

I pull up beside the gatehouse, with its amazing stonework and its architectural quirks, exposed beams and portholes. This is where Mrs. Owen lives. Her family has lived and worked at Poulston Park for generations. The manor house is now owned by a Greek family who reside in Switzerland, and I believe they've visited only twice. I think Mrs. Owen secretly quite likes having the place to herself.

Mrs. Owen likes to remind me of our long-standing connection. "Your mother, Bridget—always such a breath of fresh air around here. How I miss her visits. And so lovely that my own mother knew your grandmother Gwen too." She never fails to mention both Bridget and Gwen—when she can remember their names, that is. Mrs. Owen is so very kind to me, always happy to let me stay in one of Poulston Park's little purple-wisteria-covered barn conversions. The previous owners used to rent these buildings out, but the current owners aren't interested in doing so. Thus, I'm now able to visit Emily's portrait—and Mrs. Owen—whenever I like.

Mrs. Owen must hear my car tires crunch upon the gravel, because she appears from the back of the gatehouse to give me a wave, two oven mitts on her hands.

"Perfect timing, Alys!" she calls out when I pull up. "I've made some little quiches for afternoon tea, as I wasn't sure if you'd have had lunch. I'll pop them in a container, and we can head up to the house before it gets dark."

"Sounds perfect," I reply.

"I've unlocked the first barn. Why don't you put your things inside, and then meet me back here?"

As Mrs. Owen disappears, I do exactly that. I grab my belongings from the car, and walk them briskly to the first little barn. Inside, everything is perfectly made up. Of course it is. Mrs. Owen is the best. She admitted to me a while back that she had been headhunted for one of the royal palaces, which didn't surprise me at all. It also didn't surprise me that she couldn't leave Poulston Park. Of course she couldn't. Poulston Park is in her blood.

A few minutes later, I hear the crunch of tires on gravel again and head outside, carrying Mrs. Owen's flowers. She's pulled up the little golf cart she tootles around the estate in.

"I should have given you your flowers to take inside," I tell her. "Do you want me to run them in for you?"

"Let's take them up to the house," she says. "I can put them in the kitchen there, a little treat for me to admire when I'm working." She waves me into the buggy, taking the flowers from me. "They're beautiful." Once I'm seated, she passes them back to me, along with a tin that is warm to the touch. "You hold the quiches. I'm looking forward to those, and a pot of tea and a catch-up."

"Been busy?" I ask her as we set off up the long drive.

"Too busy. I had my three grandchildren here for the weekend and needed to lie down for most of Monday. How about you?"

"The same. Well, without the grandchildren. Busy, I mean. I just got back from Seoul."

"Seoul! Fancy that! And you're down here already. Can't keep you at home." Mrs. Owen's expression shifts, and for a moment I think she's left something back at the gatehouse, but then I realize what the problem is.

She glances over at me. "And how's your dear mother? How is that home working out? Where was it, again? I can't, for the life of me, remember."

This is because Ro came to Poulston Park with me once, and Ro has the ability to make people . . . not forget things as such, but to make the remembering of them difficult and hazy. I'm surprised Mrs. Owen even remembers about the care home. Magic makes me very uneasy—that's why I've not met all the members of Ro and Sorrel's coven. But I do know that Ro's "help" has had varying degrees of success, depending on the person involved. For example, both Ro and Sorrel have met Catherine and cast the exact same spell upon her that they told me they used on Mrs. Owen. But Catherine—sharp as a tack, and thirsty for knowledge—has always been able to find her way out of the murky memory maze.

"It's in Surrey," I tell Mrs. Owen.

"Of course! Of course it's Surrey. Silly me. What's her name, again, dear? I had it on the tip of my tongue a minute ago."

"Bridget," I tell her.

"That's it! Bridget! How is Bridget finding it?"

"Oh, she's very happy there." I shift uncomfortably in the buggy's seat. I don't like lying to Mrs. Owen.

"Are you able to visit her often?"

"All the time." I lie again.

Mrs. Owen squints. "Have you changed your hair?"

"Yes." I touch my head, with its short, silvery stubble.

"Well, I approve. It suits you. Very fashionable."

"Thank you."

"You can only stay tonight?" Mrs. Owen asks as we finally pull up to the back of the manor house.

"Unfortunately, yes. Just passing through. It's lovely of you to have me."

"I adore having you, and you know it."

I smile. I do know it. And, equally, I love my visits with Mrs. Owen. I exit the buggy and go to make my way through the walled kitchen garden, to the back entrance.

"I don't think so, young lady. You go around to the front door, and I'll meet you there," Mrs. Owen says, taking the tin and the flowers from my hands.

Young lady. I almost laugh. "All right, then." Mrs. Owen likes to give me the full Poulston Park experience. The house isn't open to tourists, and with the owners visiting so rarely, I think she enjoys having the opportunity to show the house off to someone who truly appreciates it.

I make my way to the entrance of the stunning Tudor manor house, which, with its heavy gabled bays and dormers, has been fundamentally unchanged since the sixteenth century. There was a wing that was added on—only to burn down later, so the house stands as it was meant to from the beginning.

Mrs. Owen greets me at the front, opening the heavy double doors wide. "Now, should we admire the fireplace first?" she says as she closes the doors behind us, shutting out the increasingly darkening skies.

"Definitely."

I follow her through the south wing to the drawing room.

As if the wood paneling in the room, carved with the symbols of Henry VIII and Catherine Parr, isn't enough to make my head spin, there, in the center, is the fireplace.

Huge and ornate, spanning from the floor to the high, gilded ceiling (commissioned for a visit from James I), the fireplace is carved from a single monumental block of chalk to a design by Holbein. With its intricate curls and scrolls, columns and crests, it literally takes my breath away every time I see it.

I stare at it for some time before turning to Mrs. Owen. "I can't believe you get to look at this every single day."

"I know. I'm very lucky." And there's that frown again. Confused. Bewildered. "I think... your mother loved it—didn't she?"

I nod. "She did. Very much."

"It's too hard to get her back here to see it?"

"Yes, impossible now."

"Such a shame." Mrs. Owen sighs. "Now, portrait before lunch?"

"You read my mind."

Poulston Park's art collection, including one of the only portraits of Anne Boleyn in existence, is something else. Usually I'd want to admire every single painting, every single tapestry. But today I have eyes only for one portrait at Poulston Park, and as we enter the dark reaches of the great hall, we both turn our faces up to look at it.

The portrait is of the entire family: Emily's bewigged father; his wife, staring down eternity in a fine gown of silvery gray silk; their five fair-haired children; two cavorting spaniels... and Emily. What's heartbreaking is how the family is positioned in the portrait. The five fair-haired children stand on one side of their seated mother, light from a nearby window shining down upon the angelic-looking group. Their father stands on the other side of his wife, his hand resting on the back of her chair. And then there is Emily, receding into the shadows in an unattractive olive green gown on the dark side of the portrait. A good arm's length from her father, she blends into the vegetation in the background. The portrait tells you all you need to know about how Emily lived her life in the house. Always the outsider, she was wanted as a reminder of infidelity, and nothing more.

Mrs. Owen sighs again. "You know, every time I pass by this portrait, I think of her. After many years of working here, your eye becomes lazy. You tend to stop noticing many of the house's features. But I don't think I'll ever stop noticing this appalling portrait. Poor Emily. Imagine being dragged away from your mother and brought here to be gawked at. She really did have a proper wicked stepmother, didn't she? Such cruelty from a supposedly devout woman. I know Emily ran away, and I know about her disappearance after that, of course. And sometimes, as I pass by, I make a little wish that she really did make it out of London, that she got away and created a new life for herself somewhere. Maybe she even made it back to Barbados. Maybe she was finally happy."

I turn from the portrait. "I don't think many Georgian sex workers went to Barbados and lived happily ever after. They simply died. Of the pox. Of infection. In childbirth. Sorry. Not that I want to burst your bubble, but that's the historical reality."

Mrs. Owen sighs. "I suppose you're right. So unfair." Her stomach grumbles, distracting us. "Excuse me. I forgot to have lunch. I'll go and put the kettle on and leave you to it . . ." She moves over, takes one of the chairs from the long dining table and places it in front of the portrait. Mrs. Owen believes I'm doing some research on the portrait. The details here are murky to her too. "You come down to the kitchen when you're ready."

"Thank you," I say as she bustles off.

I take a seat, and I sit in silence for a minute or two, staring upward.

Tell me it's all right, Emily, I think. *Give me your blessing to move forward.*

All is quiet. Silent. The family stares ahead for all time, immovable.

I close my eyes.

Tell me I'm on the right path, that this is what you want. And then I can go. I can move on and do what I have to do.

I breathe. Focus. Imagine Emily not in the green monstrosity of the gown in the portrait but in the ice blue she wears in my dream.

In my mind's eye she comes to life, running once more. Again, away. Always away.

Emily, I call out silently. *Emily!*

On and on.

Her hand stretches back.

Just one word. Anything.

Please.

And then... then... like magic—and perhaps it is?—she begins to turn. My heart skips a beat. She's finally going to do it. She's going to give me her blessing.

Relief floods my body. My eyes still closed, I reach out, here in my chair, lean forward. My arm stretches, strains. Just a little more...

She turns farther, and I smile. She's really going to do it this time. This is all I need. Just this. And then I can gather all three Venuses, end it all.

"Emily!" I call out, our fingers about to finally—finally—connect.

And then she whirls about.

I gasp.

For it's not Emily's visage I'm met with but Elizabeth's. Her face appears in front of mine—in front of Emily's—a wry grin mocking me, taunting me. I am frozen in time as the specter contorts into a disfiguring, grotesque expression, no longer beautiful but terrifying in its malevolence.

I am here, her expression says.

I am returned.

And I will be victorious.

My eyes snap open and the vision vanishes. Horrified by what I've just seen, I jerk violently from my chair, which tips backward onto the floor with a crack.

A trembling hand reaches up to cover my mouth as I gather the courage to look up at Emily's portrait once more. Still, silent, her gaze transfixed. She is staring outward for all eternity. Alone.

I don't understand. What is this? What does it mean?

I've never had a vision of Elizabeth like this before. She's never appeared to me other than in my nightmares. This is a glimpse into a realm of terror I didn't know was possible. She's here. Close. I can sense her.

I came here to put myself at ease, to remind myself that I was doing the right thing, what Emily would want. I'd wanted her to finally—*finally*—turn in my dream; to bestow her blessing, tell me that all was good, that it was time to gather the Venuses, to put them to rest.

Instead, I got this.

Why didn't I listen to my gut? I'd known something didn't feel right. My name—I'd thought I heard my name whispered in the storage facility. I'd told myself no, it wasn't possible. It couldn't happen—not while the Venuses were separated.

There were *rules*. At least, that's what the coven had always told me. They'd assured me that every possible safeguard had been put in place.

I frown, something else coming to mind. Geon Yoon banging against the glass of the boardroom. His eyes, both wild and glazed. Was it only his father who had worked him into that frenzy? Or had someone else had a hand in it?

"Alys?" Mrs. Owen's head pops around the door, and I jump again. She sees the chair on the floor. "Are you all right?"

"Sorry! I'm so sorry." I move into action, bending down to pick up the chair. "I stood too quickly. So clumsy of me." I replace the chair, attempting to pull myself together as I do so. My hands are shaking.

"Ready for lunch?" Mrs. Owen asks.

"Yes. Thank you."

I follow her from the room, trying to hide my pale face, my breath that comes too fast.

How can this be?

It can't be.

And yet, it is.

I'm going to have to find out what's going on.

But I know what's going on, don't I? I knew it would come to this. Somehow.

Elizabeth's here. Back. Returned. *Connected*. And while that might be impossible, that's Elizabeth all over, isn't it? How did I think it could be simple? That such a beast could be contained? Somehow, she's managed it, found a way. There might be rules, but rules never applied to Elizabeth in life. Why would they in death? Now she's figured out what my plan is for her and can't let it happen. Won't let it happen.

She has to stop me from destroying the Venuses.

And I know she'll do whatever it takes.

ELEANOR

LONDON, OCTOBER 1769

ELIZABETH IS NOT in the finest of moods when we return from our outing in the park.

"You certainly took your time." She looks up from her ledger.

I glance at Emily. I am still shaken from our encounter with Lord Levehurst and his detestable friends, from our chance meeting in Covent Garden, where we were informed of just what sort of treachery Elizabeth is capable of.

"We were under the impression that the entire point of the exercise was to take our time," Emily replies, biting back. "Did Sir William not stay long?"

Elizabeth eyes Emily with a cold stare. "He stayed long enough," she answers. "However, he is a busy man and has matters of business to attend to, just as we do, for Dr. Chidworth will be here momentarily." Elizabeth looks from one of us to the other. "Eleanor, he shall see to you first."

Emily loses her defiant demeanor. She steps forward. "I will accompany Eleanor when the time comes."

I nod quickly. "Yes, please. I would prefer it."

Elizabeth rises with a chuckle. She comes over to take my chin in her hand. "Emily is not your mama, dear. There is no reason to be afraid. I have laid down the law where Dr. Chidworth is concerned, and he knows better than to cross me. He will inspect you. Nothing more."

Sarah appears in the doorway. "Dr. Chidworth has arrived, madam." She ushers him into the room.

"Ladies!" A gentleman of middling height strides across the drawing room carrying a leather case. He looks about himself as he goes. "What a charming establishment you have created. Ah, and what do we have here?"

"No, sir, do not—!" Emily starts.

I watch in horror as Dr. Chidworth bears down upon Polly, his free hand outstretched.

The moment he is within striking distance, the bird darts forward and delivers a nasty nip in a flurry of scarlet plumage.

Dr. Chidworth squawks himself, and draws back, dropping his leather case. It lands with a thump and a tinkling of glass.

"Polly does not care for gentlemen," Elizabeth drawls.

Dr. Chidworth stares at Elizabeth for a moment, then begins to laugh.

"She takes after her mistress, I see," he says, inspecting his finger. When it begins to weep crimson drops of blood, he whips a handkerchief from the pocket of his coat and holds the finger tight.

"I'll thank you not to bleed upon the Turkey rug," Elizabeth tells him. "Now, we have a busy day before us. We must make haste. This is Miss Eleanor, and Miss Emily." Elizabeth herds the two of us closer to Dr. Chidworth with a firm push on the smalls of our backs.

"What fine specimens. And new to London, for I have not seen them before. Where did you find them?"

"Why, Elizabeth found us in St. James's Park. Under a bush." Emily waves a hand.

"Emily," Elizabeth chides.

Dr. Chidworth only tosses his head back and laughs that laugh of his again, as if Emily is a true wit.

I begin to wonder if he has been drinking. I notice the beads of perspiration clinging to his forehead, and the stain upon his coat. It would be my guess that he is not the most well-regarded doctor in town.

Elizabeth throws me a look. "Eleanor, please show Dr. Chidworth upstairs. You may use my chamber, in order that you might have more space."

I falter, looking to Emily for guidance.

"Come! We do not have all day." Elizabeth hurries me along.

I cross the room and exit through the door, Dr. Chidworth and his bag following. Elizabeth catches his arm as he leaves the room. She inclines her head to whisper something in his ear as he goes.

"Of course," he says, wrenching his arm back. "You have made yourself perfectly clear."

He joins me on the stairs then, flashing me a smile that makes my skin crawl. We pass Sarah, busy about her work. She avoids catching my eye and scuttles away.

I open the door to Elizabeth's chamber and allow Dr. Chidworth to enter. He gives me a sickening, simpering smirk, and I see a hunger in his gaze—he is thinking of all the things he might be able to do to me in the future. I wipe my hands on my skirts, enter and close the door behind me.

"A fine room." He places his bag upon the rich mahogany dressing table, taking in the stunning screen painted with exotic birds, and the beautiful four-poster bed with its harrateen hangings. He removes his coat and throws it upon the counterpane, leaving him in only his shirt and waistcoat. "Your mistress has done well. The gentlemen are all clamoring for bidding to begin, and for this *sérail* of hers to finally be open. Now, you may undress to your chemise."

"Here?"

Dr. Chidworth looks at me as if I am a fool. "Unless you can suggest somewhere better?"

I begin to disrobe, placing each item slowly and carefully upon Elizabeth's bed as I remove it.

Dr. Chidworth watches me as I do so, and he does not hurry me along. When I realize he may actually be enjoying my slow pace, I quicken my movements until I am left finally in nothing but my thin chemise.

"Good, good. Now, let me inspect you in your entirety."

Dr. Chidworth approaches me. He takes my head in his hands and tilts it forward. His fingers begin to work their way roughly through my hair.

"No lice?"

"No, sir."

He grunts. "Can't see any." He releases my head, grasps my chin in his hands. "Open," he commands.

I open my mouth and he inspects my teeth, squinting as he does so.

"A fine set."

He moves on then to inspect my skin, peering closely.

"You do not use rouge, or powder?"

"No, sir."

"Good. I am convinced that it is bad for your health. I have warned Elizabeth. Best to protect her investment."

"Yes, sir," I say, beginning to feel slightly more at ease. Perhaps this is a simple medical examination after all.

"Arms out," Dr. Chidworth instructs.

I do as I'm told. He begins to inspect both limbs closely, right down to my fingertips. I'm reminded of Emily's comment regarding livestock.

"Not a mark on you, is there?" His eyes move up to my bosom. "A shame you do not entirely fill out your bodice. Still, though they are small, they are firm."

I do not reply.

He gets down on his knees and inspects what he can see of my legs. "No sores?"

"No, sir."

"*Anywhere?*"

"No, sir. Honestly," I say quickly.

He holds my gaze for a moment. "Good."

He rises from the floor, and moves over to the bed, pushing my pile of clothes roughly to one side. My entire body tenses.

Dr. Chidworth sits himself down upon the counterpane and pats the place beside him. "Come sit beside me."

I hesitate, then go over to sit as far away from him as I can without seeming rude.

He pats the spot beside him again. "There is nothing to be afraid of."

I shift imperceptibly closer.

"And might there be anything else I need to know about? Any concerns for your health?"

I think for a moment. "My stomach, sir. It has been unsettled."

Dr. Chidworth nods. "Elizabeth's rich food, no doubt. You would be used to simpler fare. I would chance that you will adapt. But if you do not, let me know. There is a draft that may help. It contains ginger."

"Thank you, sir."

Dr. Chidworth smiles a smile that does not quite reach his

eyes. "Now, Elizabeth tells me that you might need some help with something else."

"Help, sir?"

"In persuading gentlemen of your intact maidenhead."

"Oh." I straighten. I'm not sure what to say, or how to say it. "I haven't . . . many times, sir," I mumble.

"Well, it is as if it never happened, then. There are things we can do. A concoction of herbs will make everything . . . more believable."

"Herbs, sir? To drink?"

"No, it will be a lotion. Dock, plantain, roots of caperbush, oak bark, bistort. It is all boiled in wine to produce a concoction that will tighten everything up. We can also have you insert a small bladder of animal blood that will rupture. The gentlemen will be none the wiser as to your previous encounters. And lucky fellows they will be, too, for you are a fine, clean specimen, Miss Eleanor. A fine, clean specimen indeed."

His hand creeps onto my thigh, and a cold flash runs through my body.

After a moment or two, he removes it and I think we are done—until it darts out to cup my groin.

"And definitely no sores." He squeezes.

"No, sir." I stand quickly from the bed and his hand is pushed away. "Elizabeth will be wanting me back, sir. If you are done, it is time for our next lesson."

Dr. Chidworth clears his throat. He spends a moment adjusting his breeches before rising himself. "Teaching you all her tricks? She has a few."

I do not answer him, instead going to move toward the door. But Dr. Chidworth grabs my wrist, his nails digging into my flesh. "Run to your mistress, but I'll have you know I am not done. Far from it. I will be looking forward to a lengthier examination in future, Miss Eleanor. I will be looking forward to it very much indeed."

BACK IN THE drawing room, Emily passes close by as she leaves to meet Dr. Chidworth.

She gives me a look that asks if all is right with me.

I nod.

"Elizabeth has news," she says as she makes her way to the stairs.

"You do?" I turn my attention to Elizabeth, who is sitting at her escritoire, penning a letter.

She sits back in her chair, assessing me. "You are not diseased, I hope?"

"Of course not."

"Good. Then yes, I do have news. I have had a note from Lord Levehurst. He has put in a bid—a fine bid—before bidding has even opened. How you must have caught his eye, Eleanor! He mentions that he wishes to know immediately if anyone betters it when bidding commences."

With this, my stomach begins to churn again. "And what of the student you spoke of?" I ask.

"We shall see. But this is a very good start. In his letter, his lordship mentions an encounter in St. James's Park."

I nod, biting the inside of my lip.

"Why did you not mention it to me?"

"I did not think it important," I lie.

Elizabeth huffs. "Of course it was important, you silly goose! Still, it has given me the most brilliant idea. I will need to call in some favors. But I can make it happen—I'm sure of it."

"Make what happen?" I ask.

Elizabeth wrinkles her nose, delighting in keeping me

guessing. "Something so daring, it will mean your name will soon be on the tip of every rake's tongue in the city! But now we must prepare for this evening."

"Where are we going this evening?"

"To the pleasure gardens. And for this visit, we must look our absolute best, for I will let every gentleman who lays eyes on us know that tomorrow the bidding will open in earnest."

ELIZABETH MAKES SURE extra care is taken with our appearance ahead of our evening at the pleasure gardens. And I must admit that the three of us have never looked more beautiful. She personally attends to the final touches herself, dabbing a touch of powder here and a dab of rouge there, despite Dr. Chidworth's advice. I think about challenging her and decide it best to say nothing.

"You must look, of all things, natural, healthy. Never look as if you are attempting to hide anything. It puts the gentlemen on their guard. Now, come along. And remember, you must shine brighter than any other star in attendance tonight, even the ones in the sky. Come, see how radiant you are."

Elizabeth hustles us downstairs, to the large glass in the drawing room.

As we stare at all three of our reflections together, I see that she is correct.

We are glorious in our new gowns of Spitalfields silk.

Emily is grace personified in shimmering ice blue embroidered intricately with silvery fruits and leaves. She is almost luminous. The rose-pink confection I am garbed in is exquisite, the stomacher an enchantment of pink and green, embroidered delicately with winding ribbon. And Elizabeth's gown? It is something no mere mortal should be allowed to own, let alone wear. It is a creation fit for a goddess. As expected, it complements her striking red-gold hair, the tucks and ruffles of the stomacher sitting flush against her creamy skin. The smallest of dainty seed pearls provide a constellation of celestial beauty, and the miniature gold-ribbon roses add to the opulence.

Elizabeth has Sarah polish our pearls to a high luster, and they sit snugly against our throats.

We are about to leave when Elizabeth halts in the hall. "The evening is cooler than I expected. Sarah, fetch my swansdown muff."

Sarah rushes off, but after several minutes pass, she seems unable to locate the item.

With a sigh, Elizabeth heads upstairs to locate it herself, leaving Emily and me alone. It is then that I remember something I have been meaning to ask Emily in a quiet moment.

"Emily, did something occur between you and Dr. Chidworth today?" I ask.

His examination had taken longer with Emily than it had with me. But it was something else I had noticed that gave me pause. Elizabeth had remained at her writing desk as Dr. Chidworth departed. He had bidden her good day from across the room, wary, I supposed, of approaching Polly. But then, as he had taken his leave, he passed by Emily and I saw a look shared between them, a knowing look. I saw that they had a secret, a secret that was not being shared with Elizabeth.

"Occur?" Emily repeats the word. She looks down, fussing with her skirt. "Whatever do you mean?"

"Emily . . ." I say slowly, waiting for her to look up. She knows what I mean, for she had caught my inquisitive gaze as Dr. Chidworth left the room.

Several moments pass before her eyes meet mine. "If you

are asking, did he grab and poke at me, then yes, of course he did," Emily replies.

"That is not what I mean at all."

"Then nothing of consequence occurred," she says brightly. Her gaze turns upward, refusing to meet mine. "Goodness, whatever can they be doing? How difficult can it be to locate a swansdown muff?"

So it would seem it was a secret that was also not to be shared with me.

"Emily," I say quickly, "you worry me."

But then Elizabeth comes hurrying down the stairs. "Can you believe my muff was exactly where I said it would be found? Incredible!"

And then we are off.

We do not make our way immediately to the pleasure gardens. Elizabeth parades us closer to home first. She links her arms with ours, and we stroll. She wants everyone to see us. *Everyone.* She has been clever enough to have some discreet cards printed with the address of the *sérail*. These she hands out so that gentlemen may write and place their bids at their leisure, in private. The gentlemen eye us openly and Elizabeth discusses our maidenheads freely, vouching for our health. "For they have been examined by the esteemed Dr. Chidworth just this morning."

Some of the gentlemen take the cards. Some do not. One of them snorts at the mention of the "esteemed" Dr. Chidworth.

And then we are at the pleasure gardens. The weather has been fine for days, and the pleasure gardens are almost as alive and radiant as we are, lanterns twinkling, everyone merry.

Everywhere we go, we draw attention. We walk and walk and walk. Elizabeth marches us up and down and up and down as if we are soldiers being drilled. And I suppose we are, in a way. How had Elizabeth put it during our first meeting here at the pleasure gardens? She had said she was a member of the Cyprian Corps. And now Emily and I are the new recruits under her command, obeying her every order.

At one point, we near Druid's Walk—that place of disrepute that Nicholas warned me of. Only then does my step falter. "Elizabeth," I say nervously, "I fear we have gone too far."

Elizabeth follows my gaze down the darkened pathway. "You think I am frightened of Druid's Walk? If I am on Druid's Walk, *I* am the thing to be feared."

"That I would believe," Emily says, "but I am tired. And thirsty. Can we not pause for refreshment?"

I look at her gratefully.

Elizabeth sighs. "How you dote upon each other. It is either charming or sickening. I cannot quite decide which."

We return to the supper-boxes. Even before we order, a bottle of champagne is delivered to us, purchased by a nearby table of gentlemen. Elizabeth has us lift our glasses to them and asks the liveried waiter to deliver her cards in return. We drink our fill, laughing and talking all the while. When a little bell rings, Elizabeth hustles us off into the night.

"Quickly," she says. "It is the signal for the cascade."

She directs us to the woodland area near the Center Cross Walk, where the cascade is situated. I saw the cascade before, of course, with Nicholas, in that time that seems so long ago, but I marvel at it again now, the tin sheets that give the appearance of real water, shimmering and shining. I know all is not as it seems. It is no magic spell, but an illusion. I know the tin sheets are moved by a simple mechanism, but the effect is beautiful in the flickering light of the lanterns. That is all that matters. I grasp Emily's arm, and we allow ourselves to *ooh* and *aah* at the spectacle, along with all the other young ladies. Our antics catch the eye of several more gentlemen, and Elizabeth passes out more cards.

When the display is complete, we make our way along the Grand Walk once more. It is there that Elizabeth's step falters, her sharp eyes spotting something. Emily and I follow her gaze through a crowd of people milling about, enjoying the orchestra over by the Grove. Her jaw sets in a line.

"It is Sir William," Emily whispers. "And his betrothed."

I finally spot Sir William, with the woman from the theater on his arm. I recall that she had been wearing a dull plum gown that evening; her gown this evening is equally dreary.

"She must be very rich indeed," Emily says, eyeing her doubtfully.

"She is," Elizabeth replies. "She is also a bore."

Elizabeth pauses, as if about to cut her losses and stalk off, but at that very moment Sir William says something. The woman looks up and laughs, her head tipping back gaily. Sir William laughs as well.

They look, for all the world, as if they are ... happy.

This is Elizabeth's undoing.

"Come," she says, with a toss of her head. "We must go and greet them. It would be rude not to."

"Elizabeth!" Emily grabs her arm. "No. That would be unwise." To do so would be to cross one of Elizabeth's most important instructions; she has told us we must never approach or acknowledge a gentleman in public, that he must always approach or acknowledge us first.

But it is too late. Elizabeth refuses to heed Emily's warning. She pulls her arm away and strides, a golden blur beneath the lanterns, toward the pair. Emily and I look on in horror. No good can come of this.

Elizabeth is with them in a moment. She pulls to a halt. It is Sir William's betrothed who notices her first. Her eyes widen as Elizabeth speaks, and she takes a step backward, unsure—frightened. She knows who Elizabeth is. She knew that evening at the theater. She was bolder then, with her disparaging looks. She is less bold now that the viper is close enough to strike. As for Sir William, his happy visage turns to an expression of thunder. He links arms with his beloved and turns sharply away, speaking not a word to his former lover.

Elizabeth is left standing on her own.

After a moment or two, Emily and I approach her. Cautiously.

Her color is heightened. Her breast rises and falls. She has been in a heated argument that eventuated only in her mind, for nary a word passed Sir William's lips.

"Well," she huffs. "No matter. It is his loss."

She tries to cover it, but there is a wounded tone to her words.

Sir William has stabbed her in the heart. He prefers another to her.

I glance at Emily. It is obvious that Sir William's sudden departure is more than a simple public snub. It is over between the two of them. Elizabeth's hopes of resurrecting anything they shared in the past have now been dashed with one fell blow. He will not come to her again, will not invest in her *sérail*.

As if finally realizing this truth herself, she turns sharply and stalks off in the direction opposite to Sir William. She walks quickly, Emily and I struggling to keep up with her.

"Perhaps some wine?" Emily suggests.

"Wine is not always the answer, Emily," Elizabeth retorts.

"Champagne, then."

We walk. And walk. And walk. But I know Elizabeth cannot outwalk Sir William's slight, or her bruised heart.

The evening wears on, the gardens now illuminated but charmless to our eyes. They have lost their luster.

"Perhaps we might retire?" I suggest to Elizabeth, who has finally slowed. "We have been sighted. We have accomplished what we came for."

"Not while I have more cards to hand out."

Emily and I soon tire. We link arms, and we stare drowsily at our feet as we are forced to take one step and then another.

I am not sure how long we walk, but eventually I notice that the gardens have darkened considerably and the grounds are quiet. We are alone.

We are alone and on Druid's Walk.

"Emily," I whisper as the darkness nips at our heels.

But before Emily can reply, the three of us are approached. A figure glides from the shadows. It is a woman. She is dressed tidily and plainly, her hair scraped back into a low knot. Her eyes are bright and quick.

"Ah, my three beauties," she says. "I spied you at the cascade and have been meaning to catch you all evening. How fortuitous that we have crossed paths."

"Fortuitous?" Elizabeth replies. "Is that so?"

"Yes, for I believe you might care to see the model I am showing."

"For a fee, I gather?" Elizabeth eyes her shrewdly.

The woman inclines her head. "I have been showing her for a fee to some, to others for free. And to three such beauties, I would happily show her for free."

"Nothing in this world comes for free," Elizabeth retorts.

"There you are correct," the woman says with a chuckle, "for I come with a proposition."

Elizabeth sighs. "This is nothing new. I find I am often propositioned."

"You are very droll, madam. But it is a proposition of a different nature, I suspect."

"Is that so?"

"Quite so. I show the model for free in the hope of finding *new* models. She is an anatomical model, you see, made of wax. And I have been entrusted with finding new beauties upon whom further models may be based. I work alongside an esteemed anatomist. He pays those who sit for him most handsomely."

At the mention of a handsome fee, I note how Elizabeth's eyes focus in on the woman. She has caught her attention now. "An anatomical model, you say?" Elizabeth clarifies.

"Yes. Used to educate students of medicine. I am sure you will find it most interesting. She is quite the wonder."

Elizabeth's eyebrows lift. "Well, then, come, Emily, Eleanor. We must end the evening on a high note by viewing a wonder. Let us hope this woman can supply one, for you will find many a gentleman promises you a wonder and leaves you sorely disappointed."

"You will not be disappointed," the woman says. "Your name, madam?"

"Elizabeth."

Now the woman's eyebrows lift. "Elizabeth. Emily. Eleanor. Three *E*s. There is something to this; I am sure of it. Fate has brought you together."

"I have always believed so," Elizabeth replies. "And *your* name?"

"You may call me Briar," she says. "Now, this way, please."

We follow the woman to a small, ornate stone building. I am wary, remembering Nicholas's words of warning concerning Druid's Walk. But then I realize, perhaps it was Nicholas I should have been wary of. I glance at Elizabeth and Emily. I will be all right. I have them by my side. And Briar is an old woman. What harm can she do to us?

Briar unlocks the door to the building with an iron key and opens it for us, ushering us inside. "This way," she repeats. She lifts her arm, and I notice that she wears upon her wrist a strange bracelet fashioned of braided hair—the hair of a departed loved one, perhaps. A daughter. A sister. She has loved, has been loved.

Surely there is nothing to fear.

Elizabeth strides forth, Emily and I in her wake.

But only a step or two inside, both Emily and I falter.

For in the suddenly suffocating confines of the small chamber is a wax model of a woman. Her lifeless form reclines on a bed swathed with the deepest midnight blue velvet, her arms restful as she slumbers. A pillow cradles her head, her neck tilted back for all eternity as if to display the creamy pearls nestled there. There is a cascade of lush ebony hair fanned over the pillow—dark and shiny as a raven's wing. Luminous skin is lit by flickering lamplight, while flushed, plump cheeks and slightly parted lips tell tales of desire. She is at peace, enjoying, it would seem, erotic dreams. But then . . . oh, then . . .

Down, down the eye goes, and her body tells another tale. The soft skin is suddenly, viciously, ripped apart, revealing abominable, unspeakable secrets—a ghastly maw. In this nightmarish cavity entrails splay themselves, fanning out with malevolent intent, beckoning the living to inspect the macabre scene.

The thing is a horrifying mix of intimacy and science. Here the boundary between life and death is grotesquely, confusingly blurred.

I clutch Emily's arm as I turn from the scene in disgust. I do not know what to make of it.

Briar rounds the waxen figure. "Do not be alarmed, miss. She is merely a dissected grace, a slashed beauty," she says. She begins to remove some organs, placing them on the velvet drape. "She is for teaching, as I mentioned. Learning."

I turn the phrases over in my mind, for I have not heard them before, not even in my father's books. *A dissected grace. A slashed beauty.* They are strange terms. I turn back to see Briar stroke the model's hair in a familiar, motherly way that makes me shiver and wish I had not turned at all.

"Is she not a delight to behold?" she continues. "The models must be beautiful, you see. If the students are to be attentive, the models must be pleasing to the eye."

Emily scoffs, viewing the model doubtfully. "Men cannot learn to cut off a limb unless they have studied upon anatomical models wearing pearls? Surely this will be problematic at war." She affects a low, manly voice. "Sorry, sir. I cannot possibly saw your leg off today, for you have lice upon your head and a face marked by the pox. Also, you do not wear your pearls."

The woman laughs. "I see you are not simply three pretty faces but great wits. The anatomist will enjoy your humor very much. And what think you, madam?"

Elizabeth has been quiet, inspecting the model up close. But now she speaks.

"I know her," she says.

Briar pauses, those bright eyes of hers studying Elizabeth intently. "You are acquainted with the woman she is modeled upon?"

Elizabeth nods. "Yes. Her name is Lavender. I believe she moved to Bath not long ago." She rounds the table, her eyes drinking in the sight before her. "Lavender was always beautiful, but this . . . here she is truly exquisite, resplendent."

Briar continues to watch Elizabeth closely. "We are able to

heighten each model's beauty, perfect small imperfections. The models are produced with the help of an Italian master and ... others."

Emily and I exchange glances. Briar is a strange piece. Why so secretive? Does she honestly believe we will steal her master's business and begin to produce wax models ourselves? I find there is something in her manner that makes my skin crawl, rather like Dr. Chidworth.

Elizabeth, however, is entranced. She glides a finger along the model's arm and traces her skin all the way down her body to her finely turned ankle, quite obviously captivated by her. "Her beauty has most definitely been heightened, admirably. Just imagine—beauty that will never age, never dull with time. Here she is the ripest peach, just aching to be plucked. There will be no spoiling, no rot or decay. She is perfection. Forevermore. It is truly masterful craftsmanship." Only then does she glance up.

"I think it is macabre," I blurt out. I find I cannot help but voice my thoughts, unable to restrain myself for a moment longer. To me, Lavender does not resemble the ripest peach, yearning to be plucked. Lavender, in my eyes, bears no such semblance. She is no earthly thing, but the antithesis of such innocence. I see her as a ... feeling. A sensation. She is fear. Dread. The nameless sensation that begins in girlhood, when the eyes of men suddenly change and become predatory. The unsettling realization that a place is too quiet, the night too ominously dark. There, laid out on that table for all to see, is the truth that lies unspoken between the sexes.

Elizabeth snorts. "You think this is macabre? No. I have seen worse things." Her eyes return to Lavender's open belly. "Far worse things."

"Did she fare well in Bath, do you know?" Briar changes the subject.

"I have not heard," Elizabeth says. "I am sure she did, for she was a great favorite with the gentlemen. But she felt she had exhausted Covent Garden, and she had often spoken of Bath as an alternative."

Briar nods and goes over to proffer a card, which Elizabeth takes. "All three of you would be ideal candidates for the anatomist. As I mentioned previously, he would pay a handsome fee. In fact, for three such as yourselves, I believe he would be willing to send a carriage and pay a fee for you simply to attend his rooms, to view his other models and learn of the process. Would tomorrow evening suit?" As her hand retracts, she plucks a stray hair from Elizabeth's dress.

The familiarity of the gesture makes me recoil, and my stomach turns.

Elizabeth waves a hand. "We are busy at the moment. Perhaps in a week or two . . ."

"I could arrange—"

"I have the address." Elizabeth cuts Briar off, tapping the card she has been given. "I will write when it is convenient."

"Of course." Briar nods. "But I must note that the anatomist is most generous."

"How generous?" Elizabeth is not one to dance a minuet around the topic of money. "What did he pay Lavender?"

Briar licks her lips, considering her answer. "Not enough," she finally admits.

Elizabeth eyes her for a moment. "Is that so? Lavender never did have a head for business—I'll give you that much. What if I were to ask for double that amount and then give you a share of the profits?"

Briar grins at this. "We are both of us women of business. Never fear. I will ensure that you are adequately compensated, madam."

Elizabeth takes a final look at Lavender, inspecting her closely from her unlined brow to her milky white entwined feet. "I must admit, I am tempted, for Lavender has never looked better. But for now, I have your address." She taps the card in her hand.

And with that, she sweeps from the room.

WE ARE QUIET on the journey back to the town house, all three of us tired. Emily leans her head upon my shoulder, and I stay as still as possible in order that she will not move it. But before long, the carriage jolts.

Emily rises with a yawn, glancing out the window at the comings and goings of London Town. "Do you really not mean to go?" she asks Elizabeth, and it takes me a moment to realize she is speaking of Briar's invitation to the anatomist's studio.

"Oh, we will attend," Elizabeth replies. "But it would be foolish to seem too keen, or as if we require the funds. This way we may ask for more. Did you not catch her expression? She wants us to model for that anatomist of hers—very much."

Emily peers out the window once more as we turn and start down King Street. Something catches her attention. She is suddenly alert upon her seat. Her breath sucks in. "Elizabeth," she says, "the debt collectors have come."

Elizabeth springs forward, treading on one of my feet. She pushes Emily aside to look out of the window.

She grunts. "I had been hoping to delay them."

"What is this?" I look from Elizabeth to Emily, and back again.

Elizabeth reaches up and thumps on the roof of the carriage, which then pulls to a halt. She gives me a withering glance. "Don't look so shocked, Eleanor. I might not have paid some of my bills as promptly as I should have. All the best people have small pecuniary embarrassments. I will call in some favors and recover my possessions by tomorrow." She swings the carriage door open and is out in a moment. Emily goes to depart also, but I grab her arm, detaining her.

She turns to me. "It is all right, Eleanor. Elizabeth has simply not been paying her bills. I did suspect she was delaying."

She alights then, and I follow quickly behind. We exit into a sea of confusion—of escritoires and chairs and chaise longues and silverware.

And Sarah wringing her hands in the middle of it all.

"They forced their way in, madam. I could not stop them," she says.

"Yes, Sarah. I am familiar with their kind." Elizabeth weaves her way through the detritus.

As men ferry items from the house and into their waiting cart, one of them pauses to thrust some papers at Elizabeth.

"Got to *pay* for your furniture, you see," he says with a smirk. "Thought you'd have known how it works by now. Way you're going, you'll end up in the Fleet if you're not careful. Master's Side if you're lucky, though not many women there."

I don't understand, and I look to Emily to explain.

She leans in close to me so that Elizabeth can't hear. "The Master's Side of the debtors' prison is far more genteel."

Elizabeth ignores his gibes. "Quickly, quickly," she hisses, looking up and down the street. "Take what you must and get out. But you are wasting your time. I will only pay my debts, and you will have to return it all here tomorrow."

The man shrugs, as if he does not care either way. He looks over the items in the cart, and then up at the door, where a commotion is brewing. One of his men is carrying out a squawking Polly in her cage.

"Not that thing," he calls out. "That bloody bird will take your hand off as soon as look at you."

Elizabeth has been surveying the items taken from the house, and now she grabs at his papers and looks through them. "This will not do. Take the bird. Leave the chaise longue."

I stare at Polly in her cage, flapping her wings. She is utterly distraught.

"Elizabeth." I step forward. "No."

She turns on me in a second, her eyes flashing dangerously. "Not another word."

Emily pulls me back.

"The bird is worth more than the chaise," Elizabeth continues. "Take it."

The man sighs, and waves a hand at his employee. "Go on, then, Joe. Take the bird as she says. But if it bites any of us, I'll—"

Elizabeth steps up to him. "Just remember that I bite too," she hisses.

"Does that cost extra?" one of the men calls out, with a laugh.

Elizabeth throws him a look that makes him stop.

But Polly does not stop. She continues to flap and squawk, becoming louder, and louder again. It is a terrible, fearful sound.

"Can't take it anywhere in the state it's in. Make it quiet down, or it stays here."

Elizabeth strides purposefully over to the man who is struggling with the flapping, screeching Polly in her cage. I anticipate words of comfort, a touch that will calm the frantic bird's nerves.

But instead of offering solace, Elizabeth begins to shake the cage violently. "Quiet," she says. "Quiet!"

My fingers grip Emily's arm, my blood running cold as I watch the cruel spectacle. I look on in horror as Elizabeth rattles the cage again and again, the animal crying out in terror.

Polly.

I can't quite comprehend what I'm seeing. I'd thought—imagined—that Elizabeth and Polly . . . I'd thought Polly was almost like a child to her. The way Polly would nuzzle her hand, she trusted Elizabeth above all others. They shared a deep bond; I had been so sure of it.

Another rattle of the cage sees Polly finally fall silent. But her eyes, the way she looks about herself . . . For a moment, I do not understand what she is looking for. And then I realize—she is searching for her person. She had thought it was Elizabeth, and now she knows she is on her own. Adrift. Abandoned. Yet again, she has no one, can rely on no one. I cannot bear to watch. I turn and bury my head in Emily's shoulder with a sob.

After that, I hear only Elizabeth's voice. "There. She's quiet enough now. If you know what is good for you, you'll keep the cage latched tight," she says. "I'll come and pay in the morning."

EMILY AND I retire to bed, but Elizabeth does not sleep. Instead, with no escritoire, she sits at the dining room table and pens letters at a feverish pace. They pile up, waiting to be sent out first thing.

In the middle of the night, I rise and creep downstairs. I watch Elizabeth for a few moments, and then return to Emily's bed.

Emily shifts and sighs.

"She is still going," I say. "She has the energy of ten women."

"Or the devil himself," Emily replies, then groans. She reaches under the covers and rubs at her belly.

"What is the matter?"

"Nothing, nothing," she says. "I have eaten something, I expect."

"Oh! Dr. Chidworth offered me a draft for my uneasy stomach. I will ask Elizabeth if we might send Sarah for it."

"I do not need a draft," Emily replies. "Do not fuss."

I stare at the canopy above us in silence for a minute or two, thinking of the debt collectors' visit. "Emily, I understand Elizabeth has overspent, but where did the money come from in the first place? To establish the *sérail*. Was it from Sir William?"

Emily rolls over to face me. "No. Do you not remember? I told you when you first arrived. Elizabeth blackmailed the man who debauched me. She told him she would have him charged with kidnapping, and he paid up—a thousand pounds."

I push myself up onto my elbows. "No. You cannot be serious. A thousand pounds? You did not say that. I would have remembered."

"Perhaps we did not discuss the exact amount," Emily agrees.

I shake my head in disbelief. A thousand pounds. It is an astonishing, appalling amount. In my small village, it would be enough for a family to live on for years and years. I recall my father and stepmother once arguing terribly over a pair of smart walking boots my stepmother had purchased for a shocking one whole pound. But a thousand pounds...

"He must have taken her threat very seriously," I say.

Emily nods. "She could have had him hanged. And he knew it."

I frown. "But I still don't understand. Where has all the money gone?"

"Why, it is all around you. It has gone on gowns. Jewelry. Lodgings. Trips to the theater. The pleasure gardens. Almack's. On champagne and good food. On Sarah. Cook. Dr. Chidworth..."

"But is it not *your* money?"

Emily's mouth twists into a wry smile. "I did not demand it.

Or know how to demand it. Or that I might demand it at all. So no. And anyway, now it is gone. If you would like to see it accounted for, I am sure she would show it to you in her ledger."

The ledger. Elizabeth forever pores over it, adding in this, annotating that, totting up the numbers that bind me to her. I cannot bring myself to look at the ledger, so I can only imagine the sum that I owe her if she has managed to run through a thousand pounds already.

Thinking about the things I will have to do to recover the money, I sink into the bed once more and turn onto my side.

"Do not fret, Eleanor," Emily says, her hand stroking my back. "It will all work out. Somehow."

But she does not sound convinced.

I nestle closer to her, my eyes closed.

I want to believe her, and here, in Emily's bed, her warmth beside me, it feels a little more possible.

Yes. It will all work out. Somehow.

Despite the ledger.

Despite the debt collectors.

Despite Polly's wild eyes.

WHEN I AWAKEN, still in Emily's bed, it is morning, daylight peeping through the drapes. I look this way and that, but Emily is nowhere to be seen.

I rise, and dress in my chamber, then make my way downstairs.

Elizabeth has not changed, but she is no longer at her letter writing. The pile of letters has disappeared; I suppose they have already been dispatched. She now sits at the dining room table drinking tea and eating toast and honey. Her cheeks are flushed.

"Ah! There you are, Eleanor. You will never guess. My idea has come to fruition."

"Your idea?"

Elizabeth sighs. "Do you not remember that I spoke of a brilliant idea? Of favors I needed to call in?"

"Oh yes." I do remember. It was after Dr. Chidworth's visit. She had spoken of us doing something daring, of ensuring that our names would be on the tip of every rake's tongue in the city.

I did not like the sound of it much then, and I believe I like it even less now.

"Now that the key players have been informed by letter that bidding has commenced, we need some frenzied bidding. And for that, we need excitement. Talk. Chatter!"

I nod as I glance around. The remaining furniture has been artfully rearranged to fill the gaps, some pieces stolen away from upstairs. There is the small table from the hall, a chair from Elizabeth's chamber. Polly's cage is noticeably absent, as is her squawk of disgust on sighting me.

"Will this idea pay for the furniture?" *And Polly?* I leave the final part of my question unasked. I do not know why I am so worried for this bird, but I am. How frightened she must be, away from her mistress. How dreadfully alone she must feel.

"The funds will come from the bidding, Eleanor. The more attention we can garner, the more bidders I am sure there will be, and the higher the bidding will go. We also need an initial bid for Emily. Thus, you must both make an impression."

Sarah enters. "Two letters for you, madam." She brings them over to Elizabeth.

Elizabeth takes them from her. "Notice the speed with which everyone replies?" She is obviously pleased. "Now, let me see if we can turn my idea into a reality this very morning." Her eye passes quickly over both messages. "Aha! It seems we can." She looks up. "We, my dear, are to have a curricle race."

I remember the meeting Emily and I had with Lord Levehurst and his cronies in the park just yesterday. I stiffen. "A curricle race."

"Yes. It will be our last chance to attract attention and force the bidding higher. You will both bed your gentlemen within days. I now have someone in mind for Emily, too, who I shall make sure attends the race. Oh! And this evening, we will visit the anatomist's studio. I have written to let him know we have miraculously created time in which we might attend, if he is so inclined to send a carriage and pay the fee I requested of him. Perhaps he is as generous as this Briar woman suggested he is."

I recall Briar mentioning a fee for simply meeting with the anatomist.

"But enough chitchat. We must ready ourselves for our exciting day. Where is Emily?"

I pause. When I dressed in my chamber, I had thought Emily must be downstairs. Now I realize she is not. Nor is she in her own chamber. I recall something now. I have a dreamy remembrance of her whispering to me in the early hours, telling me she would return shortly.

And now she is nowhere to be seen.

I feel suddenly lightheaded, as if I had too much to drink at the pleasure gardens last night.

"Eleanor," Elizabeth says, her eyes narrowing, "where is Emily?"

OVER THE NEXT hour, Elizabeth flies wildly from one state to another, going from quizzing and cajoling me ("Just tell me where Emily has gone, Eleanor, for I know she must have told you. Tell me now, and I will not be angry") to tugging at my hair and pinching my arms ("Tell me where she is, right this moment. I insist. Has she fled? If so, you must tell me, for your own sake").

"I don't know, I don't know, I don't know" is all I can answer, my face streaked with tears, for it is the truth—I do not know where she is. And I am not sure if I am worried more for Emily or for me. Has some terrible fate befallen her? Or has she abandoned me? Run?

When Emily finally appears in the doorway to the drawing room, her face is grave and ashen, her eyes frightened. She knows she has been missed. "I am sorry," she says. "I took an early-morning walk and lost track of the time."

Elizabeth streaks across the room and barrels into Emily, pushing her into the doorframe. Her head knocks into the hard wood with a terrible thud. There is a pause, and then Emily gasps and raises a trembling hand to her head. Her fingers come back with blood on them.

I stand from the seat Elizabeth has had me pinned to. "Emily!"

"Stay. There," Elizabeth growls. She does not turn to look at me.

You would think she might be shocked at her action, but if she is, she hides it well. "Where have you been?" Elizabeth thrusts Emily into the doorframe again.

"I . . ." Emily looks about, as if trying to right herself. "I couldn't sleep. And so I went for a walk."

"What sort of fool do you take me for?" Elizabeth pats at Emily's dress, attempting to locate anything that might be secreted on her person.

"I have nothing." A thin stream of blood trickles down Emily's face.

Elizabeth scoffs. "What rot. You have been somewhere. Seen someone. Sold something. And when I find out what you have been doing, you will pay for it."

"I haven't, I—"

"Of course you have! Now get upstairs." Elizabeth pushes her out the door. "Clean yourself up. Get changed. You are to be the star attraction in a curricle race shortly. Eleanor, go and help her—quickly, for we cannot be late."

AS MUCH AS I try to engage with Emily as I ready her for the curricle race, she will not engage with me. She simply shakes her head and will not reply as I pepper her with questions about where she has been.

"Do not fuss so, Eleanor. It is as I said. I went for a stroll. And that is all."

I know this is not true, but Sarah is also in the room, and I wonder if Emily cannot tell me where she has really been until we find ourselves alone.

I dab at her head with some warm water and a muslin cloth, the basin of water swirling with blood as I go.

"You cannot go out in this state," I tell her.

"It is not so bad." Emily touches her forehead. "I am only a little dizzy. It is nothing."

The bleeding has stopped, and the wound is small, but it is not nothing. I am scared for her. For us. Elizabeth was like . . . a wild thing, a thing possessed.

"Anyway, I have had worse," Emily continues.

She has had worse? "What do you mean by that?" I stop dabbing and look at her.

She glances up at me. "Worse beatings. From my stepmother. An uncle. One of my sisters. A governess who detested me."

"*Emily.*" I place a hand on her shoulder.

She shrugs my hand away. "Hurry now, before it happens again. Once it begins, it only ever gets worse, you know."

I hasten my movements.

As Elizabeth said, we cannot be late.

WHEN EMILY AND I reenter the drawing room, Elizabeth acts for all the world as if nothing has passed. She simply casts an eye over us, one hand hovering over her inkpot. She nods, then returns to the letter she is writing.

I lead a still-slightly-shaky Emily to a chair and ask if I can fetch her anything.

"A glass of wine, please, Eleanor," she says.

I pause, waiting for Elizabeth to pass comment, but she does not. She does not look up from her letter writing again either, instead waving a disinterested hand in the general direction of the wine decanter.

I pour a glass of wine for Emily and bring it over to her. She has taken only a sip or two when there is a commotion outside—the sound of a carriage and voices.

"Ah, that must be our friends now." Elizabeth abandons her letter and stands.

I run to the window and peer outside. Two high-sprung curricles sit outside, each drawn by two sleek stallions. The driver of the first curricle, his back to me, pulls out a flask and drinks from it. As he does so, he turns to look at the town house.

I take a step back.

It is Henry. Horrible, loathsome Henry, from the park. Bile

rises in my throat, my stomach seemingly remembering the emptying of its contents after the last encounter with him.

"What is it, Eleanor?" Emily joins me at the window. "Oh," she says, recognizing Lord Levehurst's crony also. She turns to look at Elizabeth. "This is not a good idea, Elizabeth. He is wild. And already drinking."

"Then he is in good company." Elizabeth eyes the glass in Emily's hand, which she has emptied in one fell swoop without my noticing.

"You are a fool," Emily retorts. "He would have had Eleanor in the park if I had not stepped in and threatened Lord Levehurst, telling him his access to the best maidenheads in town might be cut off."

I grab at Emily's arm, fearing Elizabeth will strike her again. "Emily . . ."

Once again, Emily loosens herself from my grasp.

As for Elizabeth, she simply laughs as she hustles us from the room. "You need not fear his driving. Henry is used to driving in such a state. In fact, it would be more dangerous were he sober, for he is not used to driving in that state at all."

We are out the door in but moments, Sarah shutting it firmly behind us.

"A fine day for it, ladies!" the second gentleman calls out from his perch above. I have not seen him before. He was not one of the party at the park yesterday. For a moment I hope that he is a cut above the other gentlemen I have been introduced to, but then I see a silver flask sticking out of his waistcoat pocket, and my heart sinks.

"It *is* a fine day for it, Edward," Elizabeth replies. "And here I have Eleanor and Emily to race with you."

"I'll take that one." Henry points at me rudely.

Elizabeth ignores him, and gives Emily a hand up into Henry's curricle.

"I shall have to squeeze in until we are at the park," Elizabeth says.

"You can sit on my lap," Henry offers.

"Sadly, you could not afford it," Elizabeth replies. She pushes me inelegantly up into Edward's curricle, and then takes his hand and is hoisted up herself. It is a tight fit.

With a jolt, we set off in the direction of St. James's Park, Edward taking sips from his flask as we go.

"Now." Elizabeth nudges me to attention. She leans in close to my ear. "You must remember to look lively, vivacious. And yet, do not forget you are still that naïve milkmaid, in awe of your new surroundings, the bustling city streets and the novelty of racing in the park."

I begin to wonder if Elizabeth has been drinking herself. Her eyes are too bright, her voice too animated. But then I remember that she has not slept.

"You must not seem scared," she continues. "But appear to be thrilled with the new world you find yourself in, and the gentlemen players within it. Overawed."

"Yes. Overawed." I nod, to placate her more than anything else. I only want this day to be over.

"Slow, Edward!" Elizabeth says, spying something. Edward pulls on the reins. We slow, and Elizabeth boldly salutes a gentleman strolling on his own. He startles and looks away.

"Odd," she chuckles. "For I am sure he must remember me after the evening we shared together. Perhaps if I were to disrobe..."

"Go on, then," Edward says with a laugh.

"I would not discount it, Edward. I have done stranger things in a curricle."

"I'd wager it," Edward replies, quickening our pace again.

I look from one of them to the other. How she is behaving—it is not like her. To draw attention to a gentleman in the street in such a way! She is throwing caution to the wind these days.

"Now"—Elizabeth turns to me once more—"I have made sure that the gentleman who is interested in Emily will be in attendance at the race, so you must both make a good show of the proceedings today."

Within minutes we are at the park, and joining a small crowd of sporting gentlemen. There are several curricles, and a few gentlemen on horseback.

"I shall leave you to it. Take care with my charge, Edward. It is in your best interest to win today." A look passes between Elizabeth and Edward as Elizabeth alights from the curricle.

Another swig from the flask, which is then raised. "I haven't been beaten yet, madam!" Edward calls out, to many a cheer from the crowd that has gathered.

"Oh, but today you will be!" Henry retorts, standing in his seat.

The cheering rises.

"What has Elizabeth offered you?" I ask Edward. "For racing today." It cannot be money, for it seems she has none.

He gives me a quick sideways glance. "Why, you, of course. The winner gets to bed both of you—after all this initial business with Lord Levehurst is over."

I feel a fool for asking the question. Of course that is what she has offered him. What else would it be? What does she have but us? How can I forget at every turn what I am? What I have been reduced to? As his eyes scrutinize me, traversing up and down my person, I have to avert my gaze.

How did it all come to this?

If only I could go back and warn myself, shake my own shoulders. *Run, girl, run,* I would like to say to that morose, gullible creature who roamed the pleasure gardens searching for her beloved after he abandoned her, who was drawn in to sup with her tormentor-to-be. If only I could go back, whisper in my own ear that this was no chance meeting. No, it was all by design, and the creature across the table from me had been observing me all evening. Lying in wait, ready to pounce. Just as I had been waiting for someone to save me. Just as I had waited for Nicholas to save me from my stepmother. And just as I am now waiting for Emily to save me, too, just as she saved me from Henry in the park. Do I have no original thought of my own? It would seem not. I am just like Polly, wild-eyed and caged, at the mercy of my captor. And yet, what are my alternatives? Run? Where? With what? Anywhere I might flee to would be no better than this life. The only benefit, I suppose, would be that my downfall would be on my own terms; my soul would be my own to bargain away, instead of being jotted down in Elizabeth's ledger.

In the curricle, Emily turns in her seat.

Hold on, she mouths. Her hand again reaches to her head for a moment, making me wonder if it pains her, or if she is still dizzy.

I nod by way of reply, and I move about, seeing where it might be safest to get a firm grip on the seat.

Edward and Henry settle themselves as fear begins to constrict my chest. It is bad enough to be forced to race with Edward, but Henry ... I do not trust his judgment for a second, and I am worried for Emily's safety.

"The horses are a new match," Edward says, adjusting his hands upon the reins. "This will be a good test of their disposition. Now steady yourself. We must ready ourselves for the signal. We are to travel three times around the park."

The small crowd of gentlemen—Elizabeth in their midst—quiets. I push myself back in the seat, bracing myself. One gentleman steps forward, everyone expecting him to give the signal to begin. But then another gentleman unexpectedly steps out from behind a tree and blows a horn. The horses are spooked, and they set off at a breakneck speed, Henry's immediately pulling out in front.

"Oh, no, you don't." Edward urges his two horses on. Faster and faster he makes them go, until they seem as quick as lightning and I imagine we must appear as a blur. I have never traveled at such a pace. Gripped by fear, I cannot cry out, but simply attempt to hold on to this and that, grabbing at anything, including Edward's leg. "That's the spirit!" He tilts his head back and laughs at my desperate actions. "Grab whatever you like!"

Edward seems the more masterful driver, catching up to Henry in no time, and overtaking him easily. I catch sight of Emily's face as we pass her and Henry. It is drained of color, and her eyes, expressionless, meet mine. I can see she wants this to be over as much as I do.

When my gaze returns to the path stretching before us, I see that a bend is fast approaching. We hurtle toward it at an incredible speed, and I have no idea how it will be possible to negotiate it. Surely we will tip?

I cry out in fear for my very life.

There is a whoop in the distance, a cheer, the gentlemen urging Edward on just as he urges the horses on even faster.

"Come on! Come on now!" Edward does not seem to see a need to slow down.

I squeeze my eyes shut tight, bracing myself for the inevitable, fear coursing through every fiber of my being. Just as we approach the treacherous curve that promises to be our doom, there is a sound—an earsplitting crack. The sound shatters the air, and my eyes open in sheer terror as there is a wrenching, a tearing and then . . . air.

A void. Falling.

A horse's whinny.

A terrible, awful slam into the ground. My back! I gasp for air, but I cannot breathe! And then . . .

Nothing.

"Eleanor? Eleanor!" is the next thing I hear.

My eyes flicker, then close again.

"Stop fussing, Emily," Elizabeth's voice says. "She will be all right. See? She is already rousing."

I turn my head toward the voices, confused. My eyes open again. I blink. I get the feeling that time has moved on. Passed.

There is Emily. Elizabeth. A gentleman who seems to be . . . sketching me?

A cold breeze upon my legs alerts me that my dress is pulled up, my petticoats showing.

"My dress . . ." I manage to say, my chest strangely tight. My back is aflame. I cough, and the pain is so bad that I wonder if I will be sick.

Emily moves forward.

"Leave the dress, Emily. The gentlemen enjoy a glimpse of a finely turned leg," Elizabeth says, leaning in so others cannot hear. "It will make a wonderful sketch in the newspapers, and that will garner far more attention than the curricle race would have."

Above me, Emily stares Elizabeth down. Their gazes locked, Emily smooths down my dress, restoring the little dignity I have left.

The artist waves the concern away. "It is no matter. I have it already."

"Emily . . ." I say weakly, worried that Elizabeth will strike her once more.

She bends down to grasp my hand—the only part of me that does not hurt. I want to thank her for standing by me, but my eyes close again as the pain throbs inside me like a second heartbeat. Emily squeezes my fingers as if she understands.

"I am here," she says. "Never fear. I will watch over you."

I nod as best I can. Polly may have lost her person, but mine stands steadfastly by me.

I drift off again then, but I jolt when a voice calls out loudly, cutting through the fog of pain.

"Do not move him, damn it! You'll do more harm than good," a man says.

Henry's voice. Only then do I realize I have not yet seen Edward. My eyes flicker open once more.

"May as well. No harm can come to him now, sir," another man replies.

"Oh, and are you a physician? No, I did not think so," Henry argues, panic in his voice.

I turn my head in the direction of the arguing voices, wincing as I do so. But Emily steps to the side, blocking my view.

"Do not look. It is not a pretty sight," Emily tells me.

My wool-filled head finally catches up, understanding what has happened. "Edward is dead?"

"Good news for you, I suppose," Elizabeth says. "You will not need to service him now."

I DO NOT RECALL much of the next few hours. I remember only snippets. Being bundled into a carriage, then out of it and into the town house, up the stairs and into bed. A wet cloth on my forehead. Emily's soothing voice. And then, after some hours, I think, waking to see Emily beside me on my bed. She is groaning. Has she been hurt too? I attempt to sit up and groan myself, pain flashing across my back.

"Eleanor!" Emily looks over at me. "How do you feel?"

"What happened?" I reply. "I remember a noise. A cracking noise. And then falling. A man sketching me. Learning that Edward had died. But not much else. It is all hazy. Like a dream."

Emily sighs. "I do not know the ins and outs of it, but something on the carriage gave way, some sort of fitting. That led to another part splintering, I believe. And you landing upon the path. And most of the carriage landing on Edward."

I recall Elizabeth's words. She had not seemed particularly shaken by the event. Had she been hiding her shock? Or was she truly that callous? She did not seem to care one whit. I attempt to right myself yet again and fail. "Oh!" I start. "My back."

"Yes, you have quite the bruise. But I do not believe anything is broken."

I frown. "But were you also hurt?"

"Me? No."

"I heard you. Just now. Groaning."

"Oh, that. It is nothing. Just a small headache. The sun, I expect. Rest now, for apparently we must still visit this strange anatomist later."

I close my eyes, but there is no rest to be found. Instead, awful visions dance behind my closed lids—visions of the curricle hurtling down the path, of Emily's head connecting with the doorframe, of Polly flapping wildly in her cage.

My stepmother's hateful tongue is nothing now, I see. What I would give to go home. But doing so would mean leaving Emily behind, and that I could not bear to do. A sob catches in my throat.

"Come, come," Emily says. "You are all right now. I am here with you."

My tears well over. "I do not understand it. Why is Elizabeth behaving so? She said she wanted a place of companionship, of protection. She said she wanted to create something akin to a family. Was that all lies?"

Emily reaches up and plucks a tendril of hair from my cheek. She smooths it back as she listens to me.

"We are trapped," I whisper. "Trapped and easily discarded, just like Edward. She will use us and cast us out when she is done." I think also of that woman who approached us in Covent Garden, the unfortunate creature from Mother Wallace's who stole my pie. I am no different from her. My fate will be the same. I cover my face with one hand. "You tried to warn me. You did. It was only through luck that I did not end up under the wheels of that carriage today. Your knock to the head might have been far worse. She would find others to replace us in no time. I see it now. I see how she operates. We are nothing to her. And it's as you said. It will only get worse. What will tomorrow bring, Emily? What danger will we find ourselves in next?"

"Stop." Emily takes my hand. "Calm yourself." She brings my fingers to her lips and kisses them one at a time. "There, now. A little better?" She releases my hand.

I nod, although I am not feeling calmer at all. In fact, my heart races. I stare into her eyes. Does she know? Does she feel the same way I do?

"Good. Now, we must be logical about this. Do not forget that Elizabeth must recoup her losses. It's that she is interested in. And so we may be trapped, but we are not yet so easily discarded."

I am not so sure of this. "Look at what she did to you this morning, Emily, when she thought you had run. It could easily have been the end of you had she pushed you any harder. Or one of us could have been Edward under that carriage."

"I know," Emily replies. She takes a deep breath. "Now I must tell you something."

My breathing stills as she takes my hand again. This time her fingers entwine with mine.

Oh, if only we could stay here for eternity. Safe. Warm.

Alone. Together.

I am sure I am blushing. My cheeks feel as if they are on fire.

"And you must promise me you will not be shocked, that you will listen."

Silently, I nod.

"I have been thinking. And I think, perhaps, you should leave," Emily whispers, her face close to mine.

I pull away. "Leave? What do you mean?" Of all things, I was not expecting this.

"Shh . . . Quietly. Yes. Leave."

I am heartbroken. I had thought . . . maybe . . . I lift my chin, embarrassed by what was obviously only a girlish daydream. "I cannot leave. I owe Elizabeth too much. She would never let me leave now. She would hunt me down, as you said, to the ends of the very earth."

"She will have to let you go, because we will send you somewhere where she will never find you. And I will offer to pay your debt," Emily says. "I will pay both our shares. I can do it. And then, when I am done, I will join you, wherever you are."

"No," I say flatly. It is a ridiculous plan. Emily has not had the offers I have had. It would take an age for her to recoup the money that has been spent on us. She would be bound to Elizabeth forevermore.

"Eleanor . . ."

"*No!* I could never ask you to do such a thing. It is impossible.

With the amount she spends—there will be no end to the debt. No. We will stay. We will work. Together. And *then* we will go. And we will be free. Free of her. Free of this life."

Tears well in Emily's eyes, mirroring my own. As I gaze at her, I recognize beside me the true Emily, stripped of artifice and playful veneer. She is easy and calm, and I can see that she speaks from the depths of her soul, with sincerity. Her hand reaches out to touch my cheek. "You are good, Eleanor. True and good," she murmurs, her voice weighted with feeling. "You and I, we must care for each other. Whatever comes. No matter what. We must be our own family, until the very end."

"Yes," I say. "Oh yes." My heart swells. I think... I believe... I have not been imagining it after all. There *is* something there. There is. And I may not fully comprehend the nature of this connection that exists between us—what Emily wants, what I want, what we might become—but whatever it is, or might be, I know the beginnings of it are true. True and good. And that is all I need to know for now. I might not have a name for what we have—what we are—but I am eager to find out what it could be. To discover what it might become. What it might grow to be. Who we are.

"Yes," I reply softly, again, with a nod, and a wince at the pain that shoots through my back. I shuffle carefully over to rest my head upon her chest. "We will be our own family, until the very end."

ALYS

HAMPSHIRE, PRESENT DAY

I PULL MYSELF TOGETHER as much as I can, and I join Mrs. Owen in the kitchen at Poulston Park. At the scrubbed wooden table, I toy with the mini quiches that are pushed upon me and I drink tea and make idle chitchat. And all the time, I see Elizabeth's fearsome face in my mind's eye and doubt everything—everything I've ever known about the Venuses.

I had told the coven from the start that I wanted to know only the bottom line, what needed to be done. The manner of the Venuses' bewitchment—how it all . . . operated—that wasn't something I could talk about. It was a source of deep trauma for me that went way back, and that was a place I didn't want to revisit. I left the ins and outs of it—the minute details—to the coven, but I knew what needed to be done. I knew that the spell that controlled the Venuses could be reversed by the witch who had cast it (now long gone). Or it could be cleansed, with fire.

We wash up. Lock up the house. Mrs. Owen navigates the

buggy back to the gatehouse, my hands clammy as they grip her now-empty tin. I still can't get Elizabeth's face out of my mind. Was it real? Was the voice I'd heard in the art-storage facility real too? Or am I losing my mind? What should I do? Should I hurry things along? Move even faster? Gather everyone—everything—in the New Forest?

I'm working myself into a frenzy when my phone vibrates, a text stopping me in my tracks.

It's from Catherine. Of course it is. She always has impeccable timing. I glance at Mrs. Owen and wish Catherine were as willing to forget as she is. I know Ro and Sorrel have the capability to use a stronger spell, but I also know they don't like to do so. Not unless it's truly necessary.

We need to meet.

My fingers fly as I type a speedy reply to Catherine's text. But before I can send it, she sends me a selfie. This is weird, and at first, I think it must be a mistake. But then I recognize the setting. She's sitting at a table for two outside my favorite coffee shop in the village closest to Poulston Park—the coffee shop with the pretty pink front door and the climbing pink roses that trail the wall beside it, framing the window.

She's *here*.

I can come to you, or you can come to me. Your choice.

Unbelievable.

But what choice do I have? I'm not letting that sociopath come to Poulston Park. I reply as fast as I'm able.

I'll be there in ten.

Mrs. Owen pulls the buggy to a stop under its little shelter.

"A friend of mine is in the village. I'm going to run up there and meet her for a quick drink." Seriously, I almost gag on the word "friend."

"Lovely!"

"Is there anything you need while I'm out?" I ask.

Mrs. Owen shakes her head. "I'm all stocked up, thank you. Remember I told you I'm out this evening, so pick up something for your dinner if you need it."

"Thanks. I will."

"Feel free to invite your friend here if you'd care to."

Not likely, I think to myself. "That's so kind of you, but she's just passing through." I hop out of the buggy, passing Mrs. Owen her tin. "Thank you so much for your time this afternoon. And the quiches."

"You're always so welcome, Bridget," Mrs. Owen replies, looking a little vague.

I don't correct her.

"CATHERINE." SHE'S STILL sitting at the cute green-painted cast-iron table at the coffee shop, the fragrant pink roses climbing the wall behind her, the people beside her tucking into a shared slice of Victoria sponge. It seems a strangely twee setting in which to discuss the Venuses. I know it's them she'll want to discuss, because they're all she ever discusses.

This is not a social call.

"Alys!" she replies, as if we're two old friends catching up, as if I should be pleased to see her. Before her sits a scone with strawberry jam and clotted cream, which she is halfway through enjoying. There's even a pot of tea. Honestly, she is diabolical.

"I'll order you a coffee." She gestures to the other chair at the table. "Take a seat."

"I don't want a seat, Catherine. Or a coffee."

"You might want to take a seat," she says. "We have a few things to discuss."

There's something in her tone that's not... threatening, but not far off it either.

Now I really don't want to sit down.

I take a step back from the table. "Who told you I was here?"

"Does it matter?"

"It matters to me."

Catherine simply blinks as she looks up at me like butter wouldn't melt.

"Look, what do you want?" I say. "I thought I made myself pretty clear on the phone. Turning up here like some kind of stalker isn't going to make me change my mind about anything."

Catherine wipes her fingers on her napkin. It takes her a moment or two to look at me again. "I really wish you'd reconsider your position, Alys. You seem to see me as the enemy, and I'm not. My manuscript is almost complete, and it's good. In fact, it's really good. My agent's very excited. She's talking about a big publishing deal. Movie rights. The works. I can sell it as it is, but I know it will be even better if you're on board, if I can gather and examine every last piece of information about the Venuses that's available. I just don't see why you're being so obstructive."

"Just because you're not getting what you want doesn't mean I'm being obstructive. It only means you're not getting what you want. I've told you before that I don't want to be involved, which is my right."

Catherine takes a breath before she continues. "You know,

I've spent a lot of time going over this. Attempting to understand your motives. Why you behave the way you do. At first I thought you were simply one of those intensely private people. Your family has been caretaker for Eleanor for generations. And you're related to her original model, which makes things more personal. You have skin in the game. And you know it's the same for me. It's personal for me, too, considering I'm related to the medical student who was attacked by someone most likely connected to the Venuses, if not by one of the original models herself. But Alys, the more I learn about the Venuses, and the more I learn about you, the more things don't add up. Why keep Eleanor under lock and key? Why acquire Elizabeth only to lock her up as well? Why so tight-lipped about the Venuses' backstory? Over the years, I've started to think there's a lot more to it than you let on. I've started to think your family knows what really happened back in 1769. I think you and your mother know how things truly played out. About the sex workers who disappeared. The murders. The fire."

I snort. "You sound as if you think we're covering something up."

"Are you? Because to me it looks like your family has been doing exactly that for generations. So many births and deaths abroad. Always so evasive."

"Lots of people live abroad, Catherine."

"Mm. But your lot made sure they never quite cut ties. Always managed to keep in touch, asking to buy the ledger, the knife."

I attempt to look bored by her little speech when I'm anything but, my heart racing to beat my thoughts, which sprint ahead this way and that. I wonder where she's going with this. "Well, your family sold us the ledger, so I guess it was worth asking."

She sniffs. "For far too low a price, in my opinion."

"Ledgers are boring, Catherine."

She stares at me for a moment. "You're the first one who's really lived here in a long time, been based here."

"I don't know what you're getting at."

She pauses. Takes a sip of her tea. And I see that she doesn't know what she's getting at either. I think she's just poking. Prodding. Hoping I'll accidentally give something away.

I've got to wind this up before I slip and say something I shouldn't. "Why does it matter, Catherine? Why does any of this matter now? It was all so long ago."

"Because it's a mystery. Why is there an endless parade of shows on every single streaming service about unsolved murders and elusive serial killers? Why are people still hunting down the ghost of Jack the Ripper, almost one hundred and fifty years on? Because people love the thrill of the unknown—that's why. They want to know the truth about what happened to those women the models were based on. They want to know who murdered those men."

I snort. "So, if people want a mystery, go write a mystery!"

"I want to write *this* mystery. I have written it. But I think it can be better—with your input."

This woman and her tunnel vision. "I don't know what you want me to say. I'm an antiques dealer. I own two anatomical wax figures. That's it. That's all there is."

Catherine leans forward. "Is it all there is, though? Because, like I said, I think there might be a little bit more to it than you're letting on. I think you might be in ownership of more than just the two anatomical wax figures. I think you might also have a diary. Letters. Jewelry. Or something similar."

I still, trying very hard to give nothing away. "I don't have a diary. There are no letters, or any sparkling jewels." This is true.

Catherine stares at me. Hard. *"Or something similar."*

I roll my eyes—and cross my arms so my braided-hair tattoo is not in sight.

"Aha! I've hit the nail on the head. You do, don't you? You do have something. What is it?"

"You're putting words in my mouth. Even if I did, so what? Even if I had a diary, a huge sack of letters or a mound of glittering jewels, it's as I said before. It's still none of your business, isn't it? I don't *owe* you anything, Catherine."

Catherine shakes her head, disagreeing with me. "Maybe you do, though. Just because you have ownership of Elizabeth and Eleanor, why should their story live and die with you? What about the truth? Isn't my family owed that? What about the truth about the women whom the wax models were fashioned upon and who disappeared? If they truly were only models, how did they become scapegoats for a spate of murders occurring in the city? And what about the men who were murdered? The murderer was never uncovered. What if you're withholding information that might point to the real killer?"

I close my eyes for a moment. I'd like to just walk away, but Catherine is trouble. She's a bloodhound that has sniffed something out. And now she'll follow me. Forever, it would seem. Right to the ends of the earth. We need to have this out, here and now. I open my eyes. "And? So?" I finally say when I've collected my thoughts. "What if I could tell you who the real murderer was right now? What if I knew? It was roughly two hundred fifty years ago, Catherine. There won't be any justice for anyone involved."

"But there would be in a way, because that's the kind of book I'd write. So I'll ask you again. Can you?"

"Can I what?"

"Tell me right now who the murderer was. Tell me the true story of the Venuses."

I stare at her incredulously. "You're actually serious."

"I'm deadly serious. Because the thing is, I know you're lying to me."

Her comment is as good as a slap in the face. "I'm lying to you," I say slowly. "How so?"

"Your mother isn't in the care home you've told people she's in, Alys."

My stomach plummets. "You've gone to my mother's care home? What is the matter with you?"

"This is my job—remember? I'm an investigative journalist by trade. I check everything. *Everything*. Especially when I'm left with very few avenues to check. Which is how I know about your family's sketchy paperwork, and that you lied about your mother. What I don't understand is *why* you would lie about that. That's what I'm set on investigating."

I choose my next words carefully. Very carefully. "Really? You've followed me to Hampshire, and you really can't see why I wouldn't want you to know where my mother is?"

"Oh, no, I can see that quite easily. But the thing is, you didn't just lie to me about where she is, did you? You also lied to other people. People you trust more than me. Like your friend Marco, the café owner. I was chatting to him this morning. Why would you lie about your mother to the charming Marco, Alys? It makes me question everything you've told people. It makes me think you're *really* hiding something, something much larger and more important than just where your mother is situated."

With a shake of my head, I turn on my heel. I have to get out of here. "You couldn't be more wrong," I tell her, leaving with a wave of one hand.

And that's true enough, because Catherine *is* wrong. I'm not hiding something about the Venuses.

I'm hiding *everything*.

I STALK AWAY FROM Catherine's afternoon intervention, resisting the urge to run. Within moments, my phone starts ringing.

Catherine, of course.

I consider blocking her. But unfortunately, I don't think I can do that. I need to know what she's up to, because I'm scared of what she might uncover about the Venuses, about me—of what she *will* uncover, knowing Catherine.

I switch my phone to silent.

Within moments I'm back at Poulston Park and packing up my things. I sweep through the bathroom and bedroom, stuffing items haphazardly into my bag as I go. I just have to get out of here.

Now.

Ignoring yet another call from Catherine, I book a spot in a parking garage near my apartment in London. Not the one I usually use, in case she knows about that too. I'm officially on the run. Not that I can run from this—from the Venuses—but I can run from Catherine, at least for a while. Until she catches up with me again. And perhaps by then, my plans will have been executed.

Done. Spot reserved, I turn my phone off, ignoring the shaking of my hands. And then I'm out the door.

I put my suitcase into the boot of my black Audi, and as the hatch of the car clicks shut, I feel as if I'm closing more than just one door.

This is goodbye.

I go and locate Mrs. Owen, who comes out of the gatehouse's back door wiping her hands on a tea towel.

"I'm so sorry, Mrs. Owen, but I have to go. My friend..." More lies. I will my gathering tears away.

"Oh no. I hope everything's all right. That is, I don't mean to pry..."

I know she's not prying. Mrs. Owen is just awfully kind. And she's worried about me.

"Everything's fine." I lie yet again. "It's just... work." And then it seems I can't stop myself. I step forward and hug her, surprising myself. I'm not a hugger, and we have never hugged before. I'm not sure how she'll take it. But Mrs. Owen is a surprisingly receptive and skilled hugger. She even manages to envelop me in a way that doesn't make me feel trapped. "Thank you," I say to her, drawing back. "For everything. You've always been so good to me."

"You're so very welcome. It's always a pleasure to have my favorite visitor here. You'll be back soon, I hope?" I can see she's struggling to find my name again.

"Of course." I keep right on lying. But it's better this way.

Mrs. Owen pauses for a moment, and then her gaze sharpens. "You know, I've been meaning to say to you, Alys, that if you're ever lonely, or need anyone, I'm always here. Feel free to call. Or visit. My door is always open. I do worry about you. You're so young to be out on your own."

I can't take any more kindness. I can't. I garble something or other and make my escape.

As I drive away from the house, I raise my hand and wave, telling myself not to look back.

But I may as well have looked, for my days of not looking

back are over. From here on in, that's all I'll be doing. Looking back. Combing through the past. Remembering. Constantly looking in the rearview mirror.

I'm going to have to if I want to move forward.

Forward to the end.

ELEANOR

LONDON, OCTOBER 1769

BY THE TIME the carriage arrives to deliver us to the anatomist's studio, I am feeling a little more myself. I have had time to rest. To think. To ponder Emily's words. I take heart from what she said about Elizabeth needing us in order to recoup her losses. It is true. For now, Elizabeth requires us to be safe and well, for the two of us are how her funds—which she needs so desperately—will be replenished. But as to Emily's plan of remaining with Elizabeth while I run? No. I cannot consider it, however much Emily cajoles me to do so. I saw what Elizabeth did to her when riled, violently knocking her head against the doorframe, leaving her dizzy and bleeding. I can only imagine Elizabeth's wrath were she to learn that I was gone for good and that Emily was party to the scheme. We simply must find a better way—a way to escape this life together and be free.

Elizabeth peers out the carriage window as we make our way through the dark streets to Holborn. "I have made inquiries into this anatomist," she says. "He sounds a tad... eccentric. Apparently, he is quite famous in some circles. Students flock to his studio, as his wax models are second to none—imported from Italy at vast expense, they say."

"Why does he require more models, then?" Emily asks.

"I do not know. Perhaps he wishes to expand his business? He must be quite serious about having us sit for him to pay the fee I asked for. Briar did seem to think we were ideal."

I say nothing, and stare out the opposite window.

"Still sulking, Eleanor?" Elizabeth says eventually.

"Elizabeth!" Emily protests. "Eleanor does not feel well. She has been in an accident."

"As have you, Emily," I say, continuing to stare out the window.

Elizabeth sighs, which turns into a cough. "If only you both knew what easy lives you have had." She coughs again. "How annoying this cold is. I do not have time to be unwell."

I turn to see Emily inspecting Elizabeth closely. "You are flushed." She holds a hand to one of Elizabeth's undeniably blotchy cheeks. "You have a fever."

"Never! I have the constitution of an ox." She bats Emily's hand away.

But I cannot help but notice that Elizabeth coughs again, trying to cover the sound by clearing her throat.

We alight in a dim passage in Holborn to see Briar waiting for us, holding aloft a lamp that casts eerie shadows. As she was at the pleasure gardens, she is plainly dressed, her hair scraped back. Again, I notice her eyes, so quick and bright, always moving from one of us to another. Seeing everything. Missing nothing. She guides us into one of the street's black-and-white half-timber houses, and up some timeworn wooden stairs that creak and groan, protesting under our collective weight. Nervous, I turn to look at Emily as we make our way along a shadow-draped hallway. Briar opens a door, and we enter a cavernous room that displays a grim assembly of long tables, each one veiled in a shroud-like cloth, the ghostly form of a body lying underneath—a wax model like Lavender, I suppose. The room is deathly cold, and in the air there is a sharp smell of alcohol, and something rich and rancid underneath that—the stench of... death. I shiver and instinctively take a step closer to Emily, rubbing at my arms as icy tendrils find their way through my clothes and pinch at my skin.

Briar moves swiftly around the room, lighting several lamps. "Wait here, ladies, while I summon the anatomist," she says. She pauses in the doorway. "Do mind the lamps, for there is much here that is highly flammable."

She departs the room, leaving us to look around ourselves, now that there is more light to see by.

I pivot, absorbing the peculiar sights about me.

The walls of the room are covered in shelves—so many shelves. They are adorned with glass jars of every conceivable size, from miniature to large. The jars nearest the lamps exude a spectral glow—an uncanny hue, the flickering light conjuring the illusion of animation, of life. I squint, attempting to make out what is encased in these glass prisons. Braver now—curious—I step forward. Beside me is a menagerie—a rat, a snake, a piglet, a frog, a kitten and, I think... I bend down for a closer look, my eyes widening in astonishment.

"It is a fetal elephant. Extraordinary, isn't it?" a voice says as a presence enters the room.

I startle, standing to see a small man with eyeglasses and delicate features approaching. He wears a shirt with the sleeves rolled up, and a thin leather apron that has seen better days.

The anatomist.

When he comes to a halt, my gaze is drawn to something altogether different on the shelf beside him. There lies a macabre procession. It is a line of human fetuses, each one bigger than the next—no larger than a finger to fully formed babies. I find that I desperately want to look away but cannot, my gaze ensnared. "Oh . . ." I say. "I . . ."

"Yes, it is discomforting," the anatomist says, seeing my expression. "But life is discomforting. And cruel. And unfair."

I glance at Emily beside me.

Truer words were never spoken.

My attention turns to the shelf below. Brains. Hearts. Lungs. A hand that surely once worked, cared for a child or an elderly parent, held the hand of another, is now cruelly stripped of its skin. Everywhere one looks, there is a jar housing a life snuffed out, extinguished—or, perhaps even more sadly, never fully ignited—and preserved eternally for study, emanating a silent, ominous presence.

I hear a dripping noise and turn my head to see a bucket next to my foot. It catches drops from a drain in the table above.

The anatomist sees my gaze. "Ice. We must cool the bodies to prevent decomposition."

I take a step back in horror, but of course that is why the room is so deathly cold. "I thought they were wax models."

"I would like them to be, for bodies are difficult to come by, and troublesome to preserve."

Briar speaks up. "Sir, these are my friends from the pleasure gardens, whom I told you about. Elizabeth, Emily and Eleanor. Elizabeth here is familiar with Lavender."

"Ah yes. You did say."

Elizabeth did not cease her tour of the room on the anatomist's arrival. She continues to pick up this, touch that. Now she lifts the edge of a sheet and peers underneath. One eyebrow raises. She lowers the sheet. "It is as I told Briar. I did not know her well, but I knew her well enough as my competition. I believe she is now in Bath."

"So I hear. Now, you must have many questions for me. Briar did pass on your comments pertaining to your surprise at Lavender's pearls—your comments, I believe, miss?" The anatomist's gaze moves between us, then fixes on Emily.

Emily tosses her head in true Emily fashion. "It makes little sense to me. Why the pretty face? Why the string of pearls?"

The anatomist nods. "A fair question. You may well have noticed by now that young men can be dullards. Many of them require such delights in order to pay any heed to the anatomical models that lie before them. Some young men are serious about their studies, and are here to learn, to drink in their anatomy. But many others are little more than drunken fools. However, they are drunken fools with ready money, so I attempt to instruct them just the same. To maintain their interest, I require pearls and pretty faces. Since commissioning Lavender, I have had more students under my tutelage than ever before. I brought a wax artisan over from Italy in order to produce her, and soon I will have him return."

"Which is why you are seeking models such as us," Elizabeth says.

"Precisely."

"And your part in this, madam . . . ?" Elizabeth's gaze narrows as it moves to Briar.

"Briar has been at the pleasure gardens hunting for beauties as fair as Lavender," the anatomist answers for her.

Interesting. Now it is Elizabeth who is the hunted.

"And what beauties I have found." Briar gestures, and once again I notice the bracelet of braided hair at her wrist.

Elizabeth tilts her head to one side, considering what she has been told. "Why send Briar? Did you not wish to attend yourself? Choose your own models?"

The anatomist laughs. "The pleasure gardens are not somewhere I would feel at home." He sweeps an arm. "This is my life. This is my pleasure."

I glance around at the jars once more. It is a curious business to take pleasure in. Having stood for some time now, I shift, and pain flares in my back, making me wince. My head begins to throb. Feeling nauseated, as I have so many times of late, I lift my hand to my mouth and am noticed.

"Excuse us," Elizabeth says. "Eleanor is feeling unwell. She was involved in a carriage accident today. Emily, take Eleanor for a stroll while I discuss matters of business." She shoos us away with one hand.

Briar comes over to give us her lamp, and we depart.

"I need air." I gasp as I leave the room.

Emily guides me firmly by the arm. We are halfway down the stairs when I begin to feel faint. By the time we reach the bottom, I feel I can go no farther, and my legs fail me.

"Here. Rest," Emily says, helping me to sit upon the stairs.

I sink, and after a quiet moment or two of leaning my head against the baluster, I feel much recovered.

Emily places the lamp upon the stair next to her and looks up at me from her lower perch.

"That anatomist..." she whispers. "Something is not right with him."

"Apart from his pleasure in his room full of dead creatures?" I whisper back.

Emily shakes her head. "It is not that. It is more that it makes no sense. Why pay for a carriage for us? A fee simply for coming to meet him? It is too good to be true. I am surprised that Elizabeth is not more skeptical of his motives."

"Do you really think it so strange? I expect he needs the perfect models. The wax figures must be extremely expensive to produce."

Emily looks doubtful. "Briar . . ." Her voice lowers again. "Displaying Lavender at the pleasure gardens—to me it all seems most odd."

"But imagine if there had been no display, if she had approached us at the pleasure gardens and asked us to become beautiful wax models that could be taken apart by students. We would surely have run away at the very mention of it."

"Perhaps." Emily does not look convinced. She shifts on the step, as if uncomfortable. And it is then that I notice the perspiration upon her lip.

"Emily? Is everything all right? You cannot possibly be overheated after being in that icy room." I reach out to touch her face, and she pulls away, wiping her lip.

"Did I not just drag you down the hallway and help you down the stairs? It is the exertion! Did you notice how Elizabeth's cheeks burned in the carriage?" She changes the topic of conversation. "She is ill."

"She did look flushed," I reply. "I thought she seemed feverish this morning, actually. But she had had so little sleep that I dismissed the thought . . ."

Emily shakes her head. "It is not from lack of sleep. She coughs."

I lower my voice again. "You do not think it is . . . the pox?"

"Well, we can only hope so." Emily does not miss a beat. But then she sighs. "It is not the pox."

I nod. "The cough."

As if sensing that we are discussing her, Elizabeth appears at the landing, and we draw apart guiltily. "Let us depart," she says. "There shall be no sitting this evening—not for such a low fee." She sweeps down the stairs, forcing Emily and me to stand. Emily almost tips the lamp over, righting it at the last moment.

"For goodness' sake, Emily, you have just been warned to be careful." Elizabeth kicks out at her with one foot, as if Emily is no better than a stray dog in a gutter.

The pair of us are bustled toward the front door and the waiting carriage. "If I change my mind, I will let you know." Elizabeth turns to look up at Briar and the anatomist, who have appeared at the top of the stairs. "Good evening to you both," she calls out.

And with that, we are gone.

Only in the carriage does Elizabeth show her hand. "We will sit for him, of course. But I will make him wait. We do not want to seem too eager. Goodness, what a strange pair they make. I suspect there is more to it all than they say, for the money is too generous for there not to be. Still, time will tell, I suppose." This said, she coughs yet again and rests her head back, closing her eyes.

"MISS ELEANOR." I'M awoken by Sarah in the dark of the night. "Miss Emily."

For a moment, I forget where I am. I believe I am home and my stepmother is rousing me. But then I see Sarah's face behind the lamp she holds, and I remember where I am, what I am now. I recall returning to the town house from the anatomist's studio, and making my way to my chamber to undress. As I did so, I heard a sound—a sharp cry—and realized that it was from Emily. Half-undressed, I ran to her room, where the door was closed.

"Emily?" I had rapped upon the door urgently.

I was met with silence.

"Emily, is all well?" When I could wait no longer, I opened the door and entered.

In her chamber, Emily was in naught but her petticoat, curled up in bed, her knees drawn to her chest. "Oh, but it burns," she said. "It burns!"

I rushed over. "Emily? What burns? What is wrong?"

She sat up then. "Nothing. It is only . . . my stomach."

"You have eaten something bad? I will ask Elizabeth if we might have that ginger draft. I will go and ask her now." I rose from my position beside her.

But Emily reached out then, snatched at my wrist. "No. No more Dr. Chidworth." And I saw then that there were tears in her eyes. "No. I will be better shortly. It is nothing."

Now, I push myself up onto my elbows. "What is it, Sarah?" I whisper the words, for Emily is slumbering beside me, her knees again drawn to her chest. Best to let her sleep the pain away.

But Emily is awake now also. "What is the matter?"

"Madam is unwell," Sarah says. "I fear you should send for a doctor. I have never seen such a fever. She is burning up."

Emily and I exchange glances. We rise and swiftly make our way to Elizabeth's chamber. There we find her lying in bed, the bedclothes disheveled and thrust aside. She is dressed in nothing but a sodden cotton nightshirt that clings to her form.

"Elizabeth?" I attempt to rouse her, but she only gives a feeble moan.

"She called for me several hours ago," Sarah tells us. "I attended to her as best I could, but she has worsened quickly."

"She is soaked through," Emily says. "Perhaps this means the fever has broken?"

"I had Cook make her a broth, but she would not take any. I also tried a mustard poultice upon her chest. I thought the doctor next . . . ?"

Emily's mouth twists as she stares at Elizabeth. She goes over to place her hand on Elizabeth's cheek. "The fever remains, but perhaps it will depart as quickly as it came on. I think it best to wait until morning to call for the doctor. Sleep now, Sarah. We shall watch over her."

Sarah bobs, and leaves the room, closing the door behind her.

Emily and I stand over Elizabeth in silence as she mutters. Tosses. Turns.

"What do you believe ails her?" I whisper to Emily.

"I do not know, but it is now quite clear that it is no simple cold," she replies. "This is a serious fever, and she is in grave danger." She goes over to the basin of water that Sarah has brought up, wrings out the muslin cloth floating within and places the cool compress on Elizabeth's forehead. She steps back. "Now, let us return to sleep too."

I pause. "And leave her? Should we not stay?" I say, looking from Elizabeth to Emily, and back again.

"And do what?" Emily says. "Dab her brow with muslin cloths all night long?"

"I suppose so."

"Muslin cloths will do little. Anyway, Elizabeth has the constitution of an ox. She said so herself, so there can be nothing to fear."

"Emily..." I remonstrate. "Should we not fetch a doctor?"

"With what funds?"

"Surely the anatomist gave Elizabeth some money. She mentioned a fee simply for attending—remember? And we have the remainder of the money from Sir William."

Emily is quiet for a moment.

"If we do nothing, she will surely die."

Now Emily looks me straight in the eye. "But don't you see, Eleanor? That is exactly what I am hopeful of. Elizabeth's dying this very night would be an answer to all of our problems."

EMILY RETURNS TO her bed, but I cannot sleep. Whatever Elizabeth has done, or said, I could not wish for such a thing as Emily has wished for. I make a bed for myself on the floor of Elizabeth's chamber, and I check on her many times. Her skin continues to burn, and she tosses and turns like a thing possessed. I replace the damp muslin again and again and begin to fear that her fate may be as Emily suggests—there is a chance she will not make it through the night. As the hours pass, I consider fetching a doctor myself. I take a candle and make my way downstairs. I locate Elizabeth's ledger and open it to the last page of entries, marked with a scarlet ribbon. My finger makes its way down her spidery writing.

And there it is, upon the page. Three pounds. I almost knock over the inkpot in surprise. The anatomist handed over three whole pounds simply for the pleasure of meeting us! It is as Elizabeth said—he is serious about having us sit for him. And now, just as she is doing with the bidding, Elizabeth is playing games with this gentleman, attempting to push his fee higher.

Some correspondence has been hastily placed underneath the ledger—letters that Elizabeth was reading before we left for the anatomist's studio. Curious, I bring them out and begin to read. One discusses Emily. Slowly but surely, I learn that there is much information that Elizabeth has not disclosed to us. The author of the letter makes an offer of sixty pounds for Emily's maidenhead. Ten pounds more than previously offered, apparently. The letter writer goes on to say that he does, perhaps, not believe there are other offers on the table, that they have been fabricated by Elizabeth. Thus, this will be his final offer. I wonder if this man is the "collector" Elizabeth spoke of. As there are only initials to go by, I cannot tell.

Another letter, this one anonymous, reveals that Elizabeth has offered both of us to a nameless gentleman for one hundred and fifty pounds. Lord Levehurst? I do not know. All I know is that it is not enough.

I turn the pages of the ledger back then, taking in all I owe. It is a frightening amount, accounted for in minute detail. My rose-pink gown alone came to a sum of ninety pounds.

Ninety pounds!

I replace the two letters, thinking perhaps Emily was right. Perhaps there is not enough money for a doctor after all. Perhaps Elizabeth's ill health is . . . an opportunity for us, as Emily said.

I cover my face with my hands, ashamed of my thoughts. Is this who I have become? A person who wishes others dead for her own convenience? I must leave this place, for I do not recognize myself anymore.

I begin walking back upstairs, and I have just reached the landing when I hear a groan. At first I think it is Elizabeth, but it is not. It is Emily again.

I run to her bed to see her roll over with another groan, clutching her belly.

"Emily? The pain has not abated?"

"Oh!" Her eyelids flutter open. "I did not know you were there. Yes, it is gone. It is only a bad dream."

I am glad to hear it. "I have learned something. The anatomist gave Elizabeth three pounds to have us visit," I whisper. "We will locate the money in the morning. She must have a hiding place."

"Yes, in the morning," Emily replies, her legs tucking into her chest again. "Come, rest beside me. You comfort me."

WE ARE ROUSED by Sarah in the morning.

"Miss Emily, Miss Eleanor." She hovers nervously, wringing her hands.

"What is it, Sarah?"

"It is Cook. She has gone."

"Gone to the market?" I say, not understanding. Usually she sends Sarah.

"No. Departed, miss. Left. She said she's worried it's the pox that Madam has. She asked that I request her pay. Said that her brother will call for it next week."

"She hasn't been paid?" I say. "For how long?"

"For several weeks, miss."

There is something in Sarah's voice.

"You have not been paid either?"

"No, miss."

I sigh. "I will make it right, Sarah. How does Elizabeth fare this morning?"

"The same, miss. I will heat up some more broth, but I do not think she will be able to take it."

"I will go and see to her now," I reply.

"Yes, miss." Sarah bobs and departs.

I turn to Emily, surprised she has not awoken. The bedclothes are pulled up to her chin, as if she is cold.

"Emily," I say.

She groans as she did last night.

I reach out and touch her cheek.

She is burning up.

"Emily," I say, panicked. "Emily!"

She startles, waking. "What is it?"

"You're unwell. You have a fever."

She shakes her head, sits up. "No. No, there is nothing wrong with me. I have simply overheated."

The sweat at her brow and her feverish eyes say differently.

"Do you think it is Elizabeth's sickness?" I bite my lip. *No. Not now.* Not when we might . . .

"Eleanor! There is nothing wrong with me. See?" She is up and out of the bed. She begins to dress.

I do not believe her, but I rise and dress also. We will locate the anatomist's three pounds. And then we will call for a doctor.

WE SEARCH HIGH and low for the place where Elizabeth has stashed her money.

"I know she must have a secret place," I say as we check her chamber yet again. But, of course, Elizabeth is Elizabeth. She is smarter, stronger, more wily than both of us put together. If there is a hiding spot, it will never be found.

In her bed, Elizabeth has stilled now, and fallen into a deep slumber. A terrible rattle emanates from her chest, reminiscent of the unsettling noise my father produced a year ago. It had worsened over the span of a day or two—a dreadful sound that drew the very life from him, as if it were a part of his soul leaving his body. Finally, we located a doctor who attempted to bleed him. But alas, it was too late. Within a matter of hours, he departed this world. He did not even have the strength to bid me farewell.

Emily sits down on the edge of Elizabeth's bed. She has tried valiantly to disguise feeling unwell all morning.

"You both require a doctor," I say firmly. "We will simply have to use the money Sir William gave us." Emily had put it away for safekeeping, and now I am glad of it.

Emily hunches over, her head falling into her hands. "Eleanor, there is no money."

I stop searching the room and look over at her. "What do you mean?"

Her gaze lifts to meet mine. "It is gone. All of it."

"But . . . where?" I don't understand. We did not spend much at all—the milk, the book.

"I spent it."

"You spent it? On what?"

She only shakes her head and looks away.

"Oh," I reply. I remember her absence and guess at where the money has gone.

Emily sighs. "You think I have spent the money on drink."

I pause. "No," I lie. I give her the chance to elaborate, but she does not. "I . . . It is as you said. It matters not." I come to sit down next to her on the bed. She is simply ashamed and cannot admit it. "Perhaps Dr. Chidworth . . . ?"

Emily shakes her head. "*Never.* The man is a fool. He does more harm than good. I will not see him again."

I have an idea, and I turn to Emily to share it. But then I think better of it. She will only disagree, or want to accompany me. And despite what she says, she is too unwell.

"You return to bed," I tell her. "I will have Sarah bring up some broth for you, and I will continue my hunt for Elizabeth's money." I help Emily up.

"Perhaps I will rest for a short while," she says, starting for her chamber.

She is obviously even more ill than I had thought.

I DO NOT SEARCH for the funds at all. Instead, I inform Sarah that I will return shortly, and I walk quickly to my destination. Elizabeth had pointed out the town house on one of our many strolls, so I know exactly where I must go. I do not know how my visit will be received, for it is the sea captain—Sir William—whose feet I am to throw myself at. In my mind, I see his expression at the pleasure gardens. Surely it was over between him and Elizabeth when she had crossed that line, once she had approached him in public—when he was with his betrothed, enjoying his evening, no less.

I know enough not to knock upon the front door. Instead, I make my way down the steep steps to the servants' entrance and knock upon the door there. A woman opens the door almost immediately. She pulls a face in surprise, for I am not what she expects to see, not in my fine dress.

"I must speak with Sir William," I say before she can get a word in. "It is a delicate matter, regarding Miss Elizabeth. He will want to know."

The servant's eyebrows shoot up in recognition. She knows who Elizabeth is. And thus, she knows what I am.

"You'd best come in." She opens the door wider and allows me to pass through, but there is no welcome in her manner. Her expression suggests that she would rather admit vermin into her kitchen. Other servants stare at me, wide-eyed, as she hustles me through the kitchen, to a small room containing a desk strewn with papers, and some shelving that contains household odds and ends. "Wait here," she says, closing the door behind me. It swiftly opens again, and her head appears to give me a look with narrowed eyes. "Don't touch anything."

I wait as directed.

After some time, I hear footsteps upon nearby stairs. Finally, the door opens again.

"Out of my way." Sir William barges into the room. The servant goes to close the door behind him. "No. Leave it open," he says. "There will be talk enough among the servants as it is."

And then we are left alone.

"What do you want?" He glowers.

"It is Elizabeth, sir. She is unwell. Gravely ill."

He looks at me as if I have lost my mind. "And what is that to me? There is nothing between us now. It is over. She knows this. She should never have approached me at the pleasure gardens. Whatever was she thinking?"

I had expected this response. At first I had considered simply throwing myself at his feet, hoping he might have some lasting feelings for Elizabeth. But then I remembered his expression of disgust at the pleasure gardens. I knew this was not a good enough plan if I wanted to make sure that Sir William's physician attend our house. That was when I decided upon a different approach, one that would be sure to work. I clear my throat. "It is only, sir, that after your *recent visit* to our abode, I thought you might care to send your own doctor."

Now Sir William stills, understanding the implications. "You believe it to be the pox that ails her?"

"Perhaps, sir. I thought you might care to send your own physician, in order to ease your mind."

It is not the pox—I am sure of it—or any venereal distemper, but Sir William does not know this. All he knows is that he has had a recent tryst with Elizabeth. Now she is ill, and he may soon be ill also. It is better that he learn what she suffers from. His physician will be far superior to the repulsive Dr. Chidworth. Hopefully I can convince him to see Emily at the same time as Elizabeth.

In front of me, Sir William hesitates. "Are there sores? A rash?"

"A rash, sir," I lie. Elizabeth is flushed. I will tell the physician I believed the flush to be a rash.

"Then I will send for him immediately."

I bob. "Thank you, sir." An idea comes to me. "And if you wouldn't mind, sir, something for my trouble?" I am surprised to find that I am not even embarrassed to beg for money. Only weeks ago, I would have died rather than do such a thing, but I have learned from Elizabeth that it matters not. Sir William has money. We have none. We require food, medicine.

Sir William huffs. "You will bleed me dry," he says. But he reaches into his coat pocket and gives me a few shillings. He retreats from the room then, turning back to look at me before he departs. "You are never to return here. Do you understand? Elizabeth and I are to have no further connection, and there is no more money to be had at my door."

I bob again. "Yes, sir."

"Good." He produces a few more shillings. "That is the last of it."

I hear the footsteps on the stairs once more, and the servant reappears to usher me out.

I push past her before she can spew any of her bile at me. I have gotten what I came here for, and more.

And as my shoulder hits hers, sending her stumbling backward into the doorframe, I see that I have learned more than one lesson from Elizabeth after all.

SIR WILLIAM'S PHYSICIAN attends promptly. Sarah ushers him into the drawing room, and I see him cast an eye around the room, staring at the sparse, oddly placed furniture.

It is clear that debt collectors have been here.

I think of Polly, and I wonder what has become of her now that Elizabeth has not acted with haste upon her vow to retrieve her furniture and other belongings. Has Polly been sold to someone else? Surely not, for who would have her in such an unsettled state?

I direct the physician to Elizabeth's bedchamber. She is no better, her chest rattling away still, but she has not worsened either. The physician peppers me with questions as to Elizabeth's health. *When did she first become sick? When did she begin coughing? What did the cough sound like? When did the fever set in? When did it break?* and so on. I answer him as best I can, remembering to tell him about the poultice, and that we offered her broth but she could take none. Eventually he has me leave him with Elizabeth in order that he might examine her. I go to see how Emily is faring.

In her bed, Emily rests. Her countenance is calm.

"Emily," I say quietly, sitting myself down on the edge of her bed, "the physician has come."

Her eyes flicker open immediately, and there is fear in her gaze. "Dr. Chidworth?"

I shake my head. "No. Sir William's physician. I went to him, told him that I suspected Elizabeth had the pox."

Emily pushes herself up, wincing as she does so. "The pox? But it is not the pox."

My mouth twists. "You know that and I know that, but Sir William does not know that."

"Ah, I see. That was clever of you."

I stand. "It would seem I am learning all sorts of tricks lately. I will have him come and see you momentarily. I expect he will resist, but I will find a way."

Emily opens her mouth as if to protest, then changes her mind. "Thank you."

I give her a look. "You do not need to thank me. You would have done the same."

I make my way back to Elizabeth's chamber. The physician looks up from Elizabeth's bedside.

"Whatever made you believe this might be the pox?" he says.

"She had a rash, sir. Or perhaps I mistook her flushed cheeks and chest for a rash."

He gives me a look that says I may as well have wool in my head. "I believe this to be a simple cold that has gone to her chest. I would normally suggest getting some milk into her—always good for the lungs—but it is too late for that now. You might consider blistering, or bleeding, of course, but that would require further visits, and I do not believe Sir William will be willing..." He pauses, his cheeks coloring. "You understand."

What he means is that Sir William is interested in funding only this initial attendance, to see if Elizabeth has the pox.

I nod. "I understand, sir."

"If she rouses, she may need willow bark for the pain. Though I doubt that she will rouse. She is too far gone now. There are, of course, the free hospitals..." He makes as if to leave.

"Yes, I am aware." Elizabeth would never stoop to the free hospitals. She would rather die. "Please, sir, before you depart, if you could also see to my friend..."

He shakes his head immediately. "I have other business to attend to."

I bar his exit. "Please, sir," I beg. "It will only take a moment of your time. I do not want to have to call for Dr. Chidworth."

"Chidworth!" He pulls a face.

"Precisely, sir. I cannot—not while a fine physician such as yourself is present."

He sighs, gives me another look. "Ah, I see now that this is a ruse. You were never under the impression that your mistress had the pox, were you?"

"But the rash, sir . . ."

"You and I both know there was no rash. Come, now. Show me this friend of yours quickly, so I can be on my way. It is most likely the same problem as your mistress's. If she is lucky, it will not take to her chest so severely."

"Yes, sir. Thank you, sir." I show him quickly into Emily's chamber.

While Emily seems happy enough to entertain any physician who is not Dr. Chidworth, she is surprisingly reluctant to do so in my presence.

I leave her chamber, closing the door behind me.

It is quite some time before the door opens again. When the physician exits, his eyes meet mine and he shakes his head. "That Chidworth has much to answer for . . . I have left a powder for the young lady, and detailed a preparation the maid may make up. Now come. Step aside, for I am late already."

And with that, he sweeps past me and makes his way down the stairs.

"Thank you, sir," I call out. He mutters a reply as he goes, waving a hand.

Mulling over his words, I watch him take his leave. What had Dr. Chidworth done to Emily? What did he have to answer for? But then I recall something—that look that passed between Chidworth and Emily on his departure from the town house. Emily had said it was naught, but it was clear she was not telling me the truth. I had known there was a secret they were both keeping from Elizabeth—and from me.

When I finally enter the room, Emily is sitting up in her bed.

"Is it Elizabeth's illness that you have?" I say. "Will the powder help? The preparation?"

Emily sits up farther, wincing in pain. She smooths the bedclothes. "Yes, I suppose so," she says, not quite looking at me. "Come." She pats the bed. "Sit. I have been thinking."

"Thinking?" I take a seat on her bed as instructed.

Emily takes a deep breath, and her eyes finally move to meet mine. "Yes. Thinking further on my words from the other day. Thinking . . . well, thinking that this is your chance to leave, Eleanor. You must take what you can from the town house and run. Run far, far away from here."

I begin to protest, but Emily holds up a hand, stopping me. "No. Listen to me closely. The debt collectors will be back shortly. They will take everything this time, Eleanor. *Everything*. If you take what you can now and run, you will have enough money to start a life somewhere else, free of all of this—free of us."

I reach out and grab her hand. "No. You are unwell. I cannot leave you in such a state. We will both go. We will take what we can and leave. Tonight."

Emily shakes her head. "I am too weak."

"But you are not as ill as Elizabeth," I argue.

"I am too ill to travel. It is better this way. If Elizabeth recovers, it will take some time for her to gather her strength. She will not be well enough to hunt you down, and she has no funds with which to pay someone to do so. If she rouses, she will be weak. I can say you have gone on this errand and that errand, and by the time she exits her chamber and realizes you are no longer here, you will be far away. Then, when . . ." She pauses here. "Well, when I recover, I suppose, you can send word to me. Somehow. And I will join you. Surely you see that this plan makes far more sense."

No. I want to scream. *No.* I cannot. What of our plan to be our own family, to look out for each other?

"If you remain here, we will both be left with nothing," Emily beseeches me. "And you may become sick also. I could not bear to see that."

"I feel perfectly well." This is untrue. My stomach has been churning for days now—whether from lack of food, or from fear, or sickness, I am unsure—but I must stay strong for us both. "If I leave, who will care for you? What if you worsen, as Elizabeth has done?"

Emily pulls her hand from mine. She wipes her eyes, looking tired and drawn. "Eleanor"—her tone turns harsh now—"I want you to go, to leave. I do not want you here."

"But I—"

"You must take what you can, and go. Take the pearls, all three sets. Sell them, and flee."

I stand. "No. I will not. You are feverish. You do not know what you are saying. We made a pact, and—"

Emily shifts in the bed and gasps. Her hands move to her belly, as they did the other night. And there is that groan again.

"What is it?" I take a step forward. It is not her chest that troubles her; that much is clear. "What is wrong? You must tell me."

She shakes her head. "Go now. I need to rest."

"But—"

"Eleanor"—she closes her eyes and turns from me—"please. I beg you, leave me in peace."

S ARAH AND I are kept busy over the coming days, tending to our two patients and the house. I avoid Emily, who continues to exhort me to flee. Her sickness takes a turn. She begins to vomit. Again and again and again. She will not allow me to enter her room. She allows only Sarah. If I slip inside the door to check on her, she turns from me, asking me why I am still here or begging me to go. Sir William's money is quickly exhausted, and I resort to selling my string of pearls for funds, not caring what Elizabeth, or the debt collectors, will say or do. I send Sarah to purchase willow bark for Emily's fever. Miraculously, she brightens a little on taking it. Meanwhile, Elizabeth's chest continues to wheeze and crackle. But on the third day, she manages to respond to us, and that evening she is able to sit, supported, in bed. She takes a small amount of broth and some willow bark also, before having to rest again.

After sponging Elizabeth's limbs clean, I begin to comb her hair, and I am shocked to see how much hair comes away with the comb, no matter how gentle I am. While she rests once more, I make my way to the kitchen to help Sarah prepare some more broth. Sarah is hard at work. She seems to be making a poultice.

"Is that for Elizabeth's chest?" I ask. All kinds of ingredients are laid out on the table before her. Pennyroyal. Savin. Soap. Lemon.

Sarah is busy measuring some honey and does not look up. "It is a pessary for Miss Emily." Having uttered the words, she jolts. Her hands still. She looks up slowly, knowing she has been caught out. "That is—I did not mean... It is not for me to speak of. Oh, but I don't want you to think me a gossip, miss."

"Of course I do not think you a gossip, Sarah. I know you are fond of Emily. But I need to know, what did the physician say was wrong with her? What was the powder he left for?"

Sarah licks her lips. "I believe it may be... venereal distemper, miss. But then..."

"What, Sarah? You must tell me."

Sarah looks away. "Dr. Chidworth had her purchase some sort of treatment, miss. It made her insides rot. It made everything worse."

"Oh." So that was their secret. It all makes sense now. Emily's tender belly. Her fever. The stinging. Her fear that I might send for Dr. Chidworth. Her wish to see Sir William's physician alone. Sarah's words are like wounds to my very chest. How could Emily have told Sarah these things and not me? How long has Emily been suffering in silence? If only I had known, I might have helped her somehow.

But then, perhaps she is not the only one of us with secrets.

Something has been on my mind since I spoke to Emily of the ginger draft.

It is not only my stomach that has been problematic of late. I have missed my courses. Usually I am not overly concerned when this happens, as it has happened many a time when I have been sick or worried. What frightens me is that it has happened alongside other changes. I have lost weight, yet my bodice strains. Before I can follow this line of thought, there is a loud rapping noise.

"Should I get the door, miss?" Sarah wipes her hands on her apron, her expression concerned. "It could be the debt collectors once more. Miss Elizabeth thought they might return."

"I will go," I tell her. I make my way quickly from the kitchen to the front door upstairs. I look out of the peephole to see a man I do not recognize. My heart lightens when I see that he carries with him a cloaked but familiar shape—Polly's cage—and then it sinks as I realize he must be connected with the debt collectors after all. Has he come for everything else in the town house? I begin to question opening the door to him at all when he shifts, revealing a second man—unfortunately, one I do recognize. It is the odious Dr. Chidworth. Anger flares inside me when I see him. Can it be true? Can he have worsened Emily's health?

What to do? I hesitate, then decide to open up. The gentleman is obviously returning Polly as a gift, and Dr. Chidworth might be questioned as to what he gave Emily. Perhaps there is some remedy?

"Ah, they survive the plague house yet," Dr. Chidworth says by way of greeting. "The rumors cannot be entirely true. In fact, you seem to have thrived, miss." He eyes my bosom lasciviously. "I do not remember you being so . . ." he begins, but then he pauses, his gaze narrowing as he takes in my entirety. His forehead wrinkles. "Hmm. Anyway, this gentleman is here to see your mistress. He is an old friend of hers."

He does indeed have a look about him that says he might well be an acquaintance of Elizabeth's. He has the appearance of a gentleman, but there is also a cunning sharpness about him that suggests he has seen things, done things.

"Elizabeth is still unwell," I say doubtfully. But then I spy the cage once more. I believe she will brighten on seeing Polly. "I will ask if she is taking visitors." I open the door farther, in order that they may gain admittance. "Please wait here."

I leave them standing in the hall and make my way upstairs to Elizabeth's chamber. She is sitting up in bed, pale and still struggling for breath, but alive.

"Dr. Chidworth is here, though I did not call for him," I tell her. "He brings with him a gentleman he says is an old friend of yours."

Upon the pillows, Elizabeth turns her head to look at me. She coughs and spits into a basin Sarah has provided for her. "What is his name?" she croaks.

"I am not sure of his name," I answer her. "I did not think to ask."

Elizabeth sighs. "Of course you did not."

"He seems to have Polly with him."

Her eyebrows raise at this. "Put my cap on. Then show them up," she says.

I locate her nightcap—the pretty one with the French lace—and help her to put it on. She nods, and I depart the room. The gentlemen have not waited downstairs as requested, but are already halfway up the stairs.

"We would not have taken no for an answer," the nameless gentleman says rudely, heaving Polly's cage up with him. Perhaps she remains frightened, for she is quiet within.

Dr. Chidworth follows close behind him. "That room." He points to Elizabeth's chamber.

Elizabeth coughs more now—deep, racking coughs, more spitting. This makes the gentlemen stop in their tracks.

"Do you believe it to be catching?" the man asks Dr. Chidworth.

"From what I have heard of Elizabeth's illness, perhaps. The other one—not unless you climb into bed with her again," Chidworth says.

Again? What does he mean? Does he speak of Emily?

"What are you talking about?" I say. Their manner is making me nervous. I go over to step in front of them, barring their way. "Sir William's physician suggested that your treatment has harmed Emily. She has been in terrible pain."

Dr. Chidworth only ignores me, as does his friend, who pushes past me with Polly's cage. "Get out of our way, you stupid girl."

I am thrust aside and must grasp the newel to stop myself from falling. As I right myself, I catch a glimpse of movement in Emily's chamber. She has left her bed and is peering around the corner. Once the gentlemen have disappeared into Elizabeth's chamber, Emily beckons to me.

"Eleanor," she says. "Quickly."

I race to her room. There, I find her supporting herself with a chair, her face screwed up in pain. I wrinkle my nose, as within her room is a noisome smell.

"Here—sit," I tell her.

She shakes her head. "Sitting only makes it worse," she says, breathing deeply, her fingers tightening on the chair back. "That man, the one with Dr. Chidworth—it is the man who debauched me. Mr. Corbyn. The one Elizabeth blackmailed."

I gasp. "The one who had to pay her a thousand pounds?"

Emily nods. "The very same. We must find out what is happening. Let us listen at the door. Here—help me."

I give Emily my arm to steady her. We make our way slowly to Elizabeth's chamber, Emily wincing as we go. I have many questions to ask her about the news Sarah has imparted, but I know that now is not the time. We must listen in quietly. Luckily, the door remains partially open.

"Back to arrange another seduction? Another sham marriage?" Elizabeth wheezes between words. "Or perhaps you would like to bid on one of our fine maidenheads?"

The man laughs. "Come, come. There is not a maidenhead

to be seen around these parts. And I doubt very much that there will be any bidding at all after I am done. No. I am here to have you return my thousand pounds."

There is a pause.

I crane my neck so I might see inside the room. Polly's cage has been left upon the floor as Mr. Corbyn paces up and down Elizabeth's chamber. And Dr. Chidworth sits upon Elizabeth's very bed, in far too familiar a fashion, viewing the proceedings with interest.

"And why would I do that?" Elizabeth asks, before coughing once more.

"Why, because you have the pox and one of your girls is diseased."

With this, Emily's fingers grip my arm. I remember the smell, the one in her room.

Elizabeth scoffs. "I do not have the pox. And my girls are clean. Chidworth here saw them himself."

"As did Sir William's physician," Mr. Corbyn says. "Luckily for me, I was witness to his accosting Dr. Chidworth on the street and berating him for his lack of curative skill. When he described the patient in question, whereabouts she resided and with whom, I knew exactly whom he spoke of. But it was when he began to discuss the putrid, decaying state of her nethers that I became truly interested, for this did not seem at all compatible with gentlemen bidding for a maidenhead. So I thought I would stop by and quietly ask that you return, by the morn, the thousand pounds you took from me."

Elizabeth barks out a laugh at this.

Mr. Corbyn continues smoothly. "If you cannot find it within yourself to do so, I will submit a new review to *Harris's List*, saying you have the pox and your girl is diseased."

Elizabeth ceases laughing now, her lips setting in a thin line.

"Chidworth informs me that the other girl has no maidenhead either. This is where his interest lies, for you have now told everyone who has been bidding on their maidenheads that he has inspected them. Thus, he has come to discuss why you are cheapening his name, and he demands recompense also."

There is a snort at this. "Chidworth needs no help in cheapening his name. And if Emily is diseased, it is direct from your own nethers, for I have kept a close eye on her while she has been with me. Also, you and I both know I do not have any money to offer either of you, let alone a thousand pounds."

"That may well be true, but we both know you are a clever woman of many ways and means. I am sure you can recover the sum. But I did not come to discuss the matter, only to inform you. My money returned by the morn, or I write my review. I have brought you a gift to show that I mean business. Chidworth, you may do the honors."

"Yes. Yes, of course." Chidworth stands. He goes over to pull the velvet cover from Polly's cage.

And it is revealed why Polly has been so quiet.

She is there, in her cage, still for all time.

Taxidermized, she is a grotesque mockery of her former, temperamental self. A glassy eye stares at me from across the room. It is cold and soulless, accusatory. Her feathers, once resplendent, are now dull and matte, and one wing is at an odd angle, contorted in a way that makes me think she suffered—truly suffered—before a wretched death.

I stagger back from the door in abject horror, clutching at Emily, our gasps of revulsion echoing in the hallway.

Polly.

How could anyone perpetrate such cruelty? I turn to see

Emily doubled over in pain, and I realize I am viewing more of Chidworth's evil handiwork. She moans, and I take both her arms and half drag her back to her room.

"Get out!" I hear Elizabeth screech at the men. She begins to cough violently.

I keep one ear out, expecting that the men will leave then, but they do not. There is a moment's stillness after Elizabeth's coughing settles, and Mr. Corbyn pipes up once more.

"How the mighty have fallen," he says, and I think he is exiting the room, for his words snake clearly down the short hallway. "What a sight you are. Now that you have lost your beauty, you have nothing, Elizabeth, for no one was ever interested in you for your personality. Not even Sir William. You're no better than Mother Wallace. Though Mother Wallace has one up on you—she, at least, ran her own establishment for a time."

I hear Elizabeth suck her breath in, and I wait to hear what she will say. But she only begins coughing again.

"A thousand pounds." Mr. Corbyn speaks over her coughing. "By the morn."

I must focus on Emily, who is drooping now, heavy in my arms. It is all I can do to shuffle the last few steps and lift her onto her bed, swing her legs up.

It is then that I realize that the smell in the room comes directly from Emily herself.

She is rotting.

"Emily, I—" I begin, but I am interrupted.

Dr. Chidworth and Mr. Corbyn, Emily's debaucher, have entered her chamber.

"Ah, here is the patient," Dr. Chidworth says, approaching the bed.

"Get out." I repeat Elizabeth's words. I fly across the room like a wild animal. "Get out! Get out! Get out!" I begin to scratch at Dr. Chidworth's face with my nails.

He draws back, lifting a hand to his cheek. One of the scratches fills with blood.

Mr. Corbyn laughs. "The little minx!"

"Get out!" I screech one last time, moving toward Mr. Corbyn. But Chidworth grabs me first. He steps forward and heaves me to one side, then pushes me to a wall, pinning me there, one hand at my throat. I cannot speak, nor cry out.

"Both of us may as well have her before we go," he says in a low voice, "for we can't catch what she has."

Mr. Corbyn comes closer, then suddenly gags. He retches, vomiting upon the floor, then wipes his mouth on one of the bed hangings. "Chidworth, I cannot bear the smell a moment longer. Let us depart. I will have to air my clothing after this."

I am let go, coughing, spluttering, my legs shaking.

And then they are gone.

I sink against the wall, sliding to the floor, all the while attempting to catch my breath. Only my eyes can move to Emily, who is so awfully still as she lies upon the bed. I hear Sarah open and close the front door.

Yes, they are truly gone. Though we are not safe. We are never safe in this world.

I hear Sarah's footsteps on the stair, hear her open Elizabeth's door.

She gasps. "Oh! Polly!" Sarah cries out. "Oh!"

Elizabeth begins coughing again. Coughing and coughing and coughing, as if she may well expel her lungs from her very body.

In her chamber, Emily finally shifts and groans.

I have barely enough strength to push myself up. Slowly, one hand gripping a chair, the door, I make my way to the hallway. My free hand wipes at my face as tears spill down my cheeks. What is to be done? I do not know where to start to mend any of this shattered life. How did I so thoroughly lose my way and wind up in this desolate place?

"Miss Eleanor!" Sarah enters the room. "Did they hurt you?"

I shake my head. Wipe my nose. "No. But, oh, *Polly*. What are we to do, Sarah?"

Sarah's face is white, her hands trembling. "I . . ." she starts, but it is clear that she does not know what to do either. There is nothing that can be done. It is too late. "The pessary," she finally says, leaving the room.

I turn to Emily.

She has recovered a little since lying down, and her eyes move to meet mine before closing for a moment or two. When they reopen, they spill over. Tears run down her cheeks that become less full by the day.

"I need you to know . . . Do you remember that morning I disappeared?"

I nod.

"I know you think I spent that remaining money from Sir William on drink, but I did not. It went to Dr. Chidworth. When he examined us, I told him about a sore that I had noticed on my nethers. I did not think much of it—there was only one. I thought he might give me a potion to make it heal quickly. He told me he would not tell Elizabeth of it if I paid him some money, so I did. He gave me the name of a potion I might try to rid myself of it, but I could not have Sarah fetch it, lest she tell my secret to Elizabeth, and that is why I left the town house on my own. I thought that if I could only find a simple cure and get everything put to rights, Elizabeth need never know anything was wrong. But somehow Dr. Chidworth only made things worse."

"What did he give you?" I ask.

"He bade me purchase a potion. That was where I went that morning, when Elizabeth was so angry—I went to buy the concoction. And, oh, how it stung! I thought my insides were on fire! I kept on with the potion, thinking it would help, but soon the smell and the fevers began. And now Sir William's physician says Chidworth is an utter fool and that I have ruined myself, that it may be too late for me. He thinks I caught a disease from Mr. Corbyn, but that the potion has sickened me, poisoned me. Oh, Eleanor, do you not see? We are finished. There will be no *sérail*. Elizabeth cannot come up with a thousand pounds overnight. She is in debt already! By the morn it will be over, for Mr. Corbyn will write that review—you may have no doubt about it—and it will be scathing. Eleanor, please—I beg you for the last time—take what you can carry, and leave. Before the debt collectors return. Before Elizabeth is better. Before the morn."

There is no more talk of paying off debts, of sending for Emily in due course, of her joining me.

A sob comes from deep in my chest. I cover my mouth with my hand.

I am torn. I cannot leave her. Not like this. There is no denying that a part of me wants to run from this crumbling town house, from this sinking ship; to take whatever items of value I can carry, and depart London forever; to make a new life for myself, free of all that has passed. To forget. But I cannot. I *cannot*. For Emily lies there in pain. Her suffering is palpable. The stench of her ordeal lingers in the air, a sickening reminder of all that she has endured. And meanwhile, that vile Mr. Corbyn flits about the city, pleased with himself, reveling in his twisted victory. How can he dine, drink and sleep soundly while Emily suffers? He is wickedness personified. The injustice of it gnaws within me. Oh, how I would like to make him pay.

"Eleanor," Emily whispers, her eyes closing once more, "only a fool would stay."

"Then I am a fool," I say simply. "Call me what you will, but we made a pact. We are our own family—remember? We said we must look out for each other." I do not add the rest of her speech—the words "until the very end" remain stuck in my throat.

Emily turns her head away. "That was a child's game, Eleanor. Fanciful words. I did not mean what I said."

"Yes, you did. *We* did. We made a pact."

"Do not talk to me of childish pacts."

I feel as if she has slapped me in the face. "It's not childish. It's—"

Emily turns to look at me now, her gaze cold and hard and direct. "For goodness' sake, it was only ever a pretty speech. Did you really think that one day we would have a little cottage with roses around the front door?"

No. I did not believe this. But I did think we might, somehow, find a better existence. That, together, we would find a way through this situation. A way out. The freedom to truly be ourselves.

"Oh, Eleanor. Why can you not go? I tire of asking you to do so."

Emily pulls the bedclothes over herself, curling into a tight ball, her back to me. She groans with her efforts. "Go. Fetch Sarah, who may be of some simple use to me with her pessaries and powders. Do you not understand that you were nothing to me but an interesting diversion? A playmate? I have no further use for a playmate—not in my state."

I take a step back from her bedside.

"Away with you! Fetch Sarah, as I have asked you, and close the door as you go."

There is nothing left for me to do but back out into the hall, closing the door behind me.

And there I stand, torn.

How can I leave? I have nothing. No one. No place. No situation. No ... person.

All I have left in this life is Emily.

She is asking me to do the impossible.

She is asking me to go, and leave my heart behind.

ALYS

LONDON, PRESENT DAY

IN A DAZE, I drive the fifty-odd miles needed to get close to my apartment in London, then make my way to the parking garage. I park in the spot that's been allocated to me and sit, trying to decide whether or not to stay in my apartment at all. Catherine knows where I live, of course. I'm half expecting her to turn up on my doorstep to hassle me further, seeing as she's gone from serial pest to properly unhinged now, rocking up at care homes for the aged to scope out people's family situations.

Too nervous to go to my apartment, I end up checking myself into a hotel on Russell Square. Huge. Redbrick. Victorian. I consider paying in cash, but I don't think Catherine has reached the point of hacking my credit card. Yet.

In a suite with soothing eggshell-painted walls, I abandon my suitcase, sit on the bed and give myself a moment. The double-glazed windows mean the room is eerily quiet, so I turn the TV on. A music video channel pops up, and I blankly watch people gyrate for a moment or two before turning it off.

I'm left with a reflection of myself in the blackened TV

screen, and I don't like what I see. A person I barely recognize. A hot mess. Someone on the run. Nervous. Anxious. Fleeing from... where do I even start? Perhaps *ghosts of the past* would cover it nicely.

I run a hand through my now-super-short hair and start in on the old what-ifs. What if I'd stood there at the café and told Catherine the truth about what I planned to do? That I was going to gather the two remaining Venuses and the necklace of hair and burn the lot. What if I'd told her even part of the truth that I know? That the Venuses were no scapegoats, as she thought. That the Venuses were, indeed, cold-blooded murderers.

And worse, that they could do it all again if the conditions were right.

Here's what I haven't told you, Catherine... I could have laid it all out, then and there, in that darling little café, as she ate her scone. *The truth is, the Venuses are bewitched. There is a spell—a strong one—that was cast upon their hair long ago.*

What would she have said to that? Would she have laughed at me?

It is no laughing matter. It is the absolute truth, what I've been hiding—what my predecessors have been hiding too. We are bound together with this curse we must carry for all eternity—unless I put an end to it with the ritual burning I've promised Mrs. Yoon.

I close my eyes and attempt to conjure up the image of Elizabeth I saw at Poulston Park. Even as I'd taken tea with Mrs. Owen, I'd started to doubt myself. What if it had all been in my mind? My imagination racing away with itself, wanting a sign from Emily. Forcing me to see something. To *feel* something.

But no. It was Elizabeth, sure enough. She is here. Returned.

If there was any doubt, it was for myself. Because... oh, because I knew I wasn't enough—smart enough, strong enough.

I would never be enough when it came to Elizabeth.

My heart racing again at the thought of her, I turn my phone back on with shaky hands, and I am flooded with messages.

I ignore them and call Ro, who answers immediately.

"Tell me Elizabeth can't rise," I say straight out of the gate, before Ro can even get a word in. I need to know this much, at least. Maybe if Elizabeth can't rise, I will stand a chance.

Ro hesitates for only a moment. That the Venuses are bewitched is something she knows I don't like to discuss, but now I've brought it up... "What do you want to know exactly?" she says. "She can't rise—not without the necklace. You know that."

That necklace of hair was recovered from the fire that destroyed Emily. The hair has a spell upon it, cast by a terrible witch—a witch who, long ago, belonged to the same coven as Ro and Sorrel. She found a way to control, to force others to do her bidding, until others in the coven stepped in and stopped her in her tracks.

None of that matters now, though. All that matters is that there is another spell, upon the crystal box that the necklace of hair was placed in by the coven. Their spell silences that evil witch's magic. Until that spell is lifted, Elizabeth is stuck and I am safe.

So why don't I feel safe?

Because I live in fear of what Elizabeth would do if she were ever able to rise again—that's why. She wants her freedom, forevermore—to be both mortal and immortal. And because she is both cruel and power hungry, she would stop at nothing to get it. She has murdered before. She has forced others to murder for her. I know what she would do. She would not take me out first. That would be too simple, too easy. No, she would take out the coven first, and make me watch. Then it would be my turn. And when that was done... Well, who knows what she is capable of? She would most likely attempt to take on the world. And there is a good chance she would succeed.

Which is why this must end now.

She *must* burn.

"Alys..." Ro says slowly. "What's going on?"

I take a deep breath, try to calm myself. I'm not sure how much to divulge, which cards to hold close to my chest. Trust is difficult for me, even with Ro. "Catherine happened. She turned up in Hampshire."

"What? No! How did she know where you were?"

"I don't know. But she knows a lot of things—too many things. She went to visit my mother." I leave the rest unsaid.

"Oh God, Alys."

"I know. I didn't know what to say. I bolted, to London." I shift on the bed. There's something I want to ask, something that was in the back of my mind as I spoke to Catherine. "Ro..."

"Yes?"

"What would you do if I told Catherine everything? If I told her the truth?" I've always wondered this. Would I be allowed to come out and tell the truth of the Venuses if I wanted to? It isn't just my story to tell. There are others who know the truth as well, a truth they would prefer to keep covered up, for there is much at stake. Every time I think of airing the Venuses' truth, I am torn in two different directions. If I don't tell their story, who will remember them? Who will speak their names? Warn of the dark? Praise the good, those who go above and beyond, the helpers? But then... oh, then. I imagine the Venuses' story out there in the cold, harsh world. The horrible clickbait headlines on the internet. The public's fear of the unknown. The—literal—witch hunt. Some stories are better off untold.

Ro pauses. "It's always been your choice, Alys. You know that. You do trust us, don't you?"

It's this that breaks me. How can I question Ro's loyalty? I do trust her. I do. Sorrel, Ro—my contacts—they have always wanted the best for me. The ones I have not yet met—such as Jennet, the leader of their coven—I know will be the same. So why do my words stick in my throat? Why can't I tell Ro about Elizabeth? About what I saw at Poulston Park. What I heard at the art-storage facility.

No, I know why. It's because this is my fight. That's why. It was always going to come down to me. And Elizabeth. And I don't want anyone else involved. It's too dangerous. *She's* too dangerous. Even the coven can't help me in this. They can only stand by me and my decision. And this they are already doing.

"Alys? Are you still there? How can I help? Do you want me to come down to you?"

I take a deep breath. I have to move forward. I have to be brave in this moment.

I almost snort at the thought of this. I'm not brave. I've never been brave. I've always been the person who waits for someone else to make the call, to decide what needs to be done. I am not the driver but the passenger. That this—all of this—should fall to me is ridiculous. The universe is laughing at me.

"Alys?"

Do it. Just do it. Say it. Move forward. Forward to the end.

"Can you arrange to transport Eleanor tomorrow?" I say quickly, before I can think twice about it. "To the New Forest. To Jennet's."

"Of course. I'll need to arrange things with Sorrel. I'll get her to call you when she needs the codes. You know the drill."

"I know the drill. But don't move Elizabeth. I don't want her moved until the last moment." I think of her face in front of mine. I have to be careful, so careful. I need to weigh up every move I make.

"Of course. I'll tell Sorrel. Do you want me to come down to London? It's honestly no problem."

"To hold my hand?"

"Yes," Ro says simply. "Because this is hard, Alys. It's really hard. Don't think we don't know that. Don't think we don't think about it every day—think about *you* every day."

"I know. And it is hard. But I'm fine—or as fine as I can be. I'll head to the New Forest tomorrow, after I tidy up a few bits and pieces here."

"Sure. Let me call everyone—Jennet, Sorrel. I'll send you Jennet's address in Burley."

I sigh. "I know Jennet's address. I've driven past it before. Thinking. Wondering."

"I thought you might have. Okay. I'll go call everyone now. But if you need me, or anything, you just call, all right?"

"I will. I'll see you tomorrow."

"Tomorrow."

I hang up. And then I make my next call immediately. I'm informed that a driver can be with me in twenty minutes.

It's time to empty out the bank vault.

I DECLINE THE OFFER of the bank vault's car service. I've never really understood why a vault would use a Rolls-Royce to ferry its customers about as they pick up and drop off their diamond necklaces and so on. Does that not scream *Rob me*? Not that I'll be exiting the establishment with anything like a diamond necklace. If a thief were to shake me down, they would be disappointed with their haul. I grab my satchel, throw a hooded coat on and walk the ten minutes to the vault.

The vault is housed in a Grade II listed 120-year-old Gothic-style mansion not far from the Savoy. It is the most exclusive vault in London, the most expensive. But you get what you pay for. The walls, ceiling and floor are steel lined, to prevent tunneling. Not even Catherine could get in here. Apparently a lot of applicants end up being rejected from vaults such as this because it's difficult to be sure of the origin of their wealth. I am the business they want. I am from a family of very established, very English antiques dealers, which ticks a lot of non-crime boxes for them. If only they knew...

I am greeted by two doormen and discreetly ushered into the clinical facility. Safely locked inside, we begin the lengthy security process, including fingerprint and iris scans. A custodian then guides me to collect my box. I have one of the smallest boxes on offer, because there is not much left to store when it comes to the Venuses—not since the fire.

"Thank you," I say to the custodian, who leaves me in the private room, with my box of—whatever he imagines it might be. He melts from the room as if he were never there in the first place.

I wait until the door closes behind him with a click, and then I open the box. There is only one item inside.

Elizabeth's ledger.

The coven knows that I have it. It is useful for me only inasmuch as it gives me a reminder of what I'm dealing with—*who* I'm dealing with.

I stare at the ledger's weathered leather cover for a moment before lifting the book out and cradling it in my hands. It is substantial. Heavy. Laden with secrets. And lies. A ribbon, once scarlet, now marked by the passage of time, protrudes like a serpent's tongue.

I place the ledger on the bench before me, knowing that the fact that I am here means I'm about to do the unthinkable—the thing I never allow myself to do.

I am going to allow myself to slip back into the past.

Nausea swells at the thought of doing so, and I reach into my pocket for a ginger chew, wondering if I should just take the item and leave, get some air. I continue to eye it warily as my jaw works away.

In my line of business, I know that the ledger should, of course, never be housed here. It should be in a museum, in a temperature-controlled environment, handled only with cotton-gloved hands. But what does that matter when I am about to set it alight?

I open it up, the timeworn spine cracking horribly as I do so, making me flinch.

I turn its brittle pages, my eyes skating over Elizabeth's meticulous writing.

My ungloved finger traces its way down the many columns. Payments for household items. For furniture. To a mantua-maker. For food, candles, a macaw. I pause, and turn to the final page. There I spy a different hand—smaller letters, more rushed. There is a note about some pearls that have been sold. And then . . .

Nothing.

I close the book with a slap.

Tomorrow, if I so choose.

Tomorrow it can all be over.

I pick up the ledger and slide it into the satchel I've brought with me.

As I leave the premises, I arrange the closure of my account. Someone else will take over the box—for their jewels, their medals. Whatever. It will be as if the ledger was never here.

When I'm back on the street, the city is as it ever was, bustling with life. This is what London does—it swallows its secrets.

Needing time to breathe, I walk the streets as the light fades into night, slipping, slipping into the past—into the world of the Venuses.

I walk down the Strand, through St. James's Square, and find myself on King Street.

I stand in front of the white Portland stone terrace house and take in the ironwork, the fine Doric columns. I close my eyes and try to imagine what an onlooker would have seen exiting that front door. Elizabeth. Emily. Eleanor. Such youthful blooms. Such finery. Those matching pearls. Silk gowns fresh from the mantua-maker. Burnished gold. Ice blue. Rose pink. My eyes still closed, I turn my head, following their step as they make their way to St. James's Park.

I jolt and open my eyes as a scooter rushes past me with a whoosh of air.

They are gone. Disappeared.

I take a last look at the town house then—my final look—and turn.

Time for me to do what must be done.

I have just turned out of King Street when the call comes in. It's from Ms. Han—Mrs. Yoon's lawyer. I figure she's checking in on me, wondering if I'm on track for our two-week deadline.

"Ms. Han," I answer, "I—"

"Excuse me," she replies. "There is no time for pleasantries. It is Master Yoon. Geon. His mother had arranged that he go to a retreat on Ulleungdo Island. It is a difficult place to get to—east by train, and then a long ferry journey. During this journey, he managed to slip away from his escort."

"Where is he now?" I ask.

"I'm afraid we do not know. But I thought I should make you aware. Please notify us if you hear from him, or see him. We would be very grateful, as he has not been"—Ms. Han pauses here—"well."

In that pause I suspect she is seeing the same thing in her mind's eye as I am.

Geon Yoon violently banging against the boardroom glass. Wild. Frenzied.

A desperate man.

And his agony is all my doing.

ELEANOR

LONDON, OCTOBER 1769

IN THE HOURS after Dr. Chidworth and Mr. Corbyn leave, Sarah frets, nervously checking and rechecking that the doors and the windows of the town house are locked tight.

"I do not like it, miss," she tells me in whispers. "They must be dangerous men to do such a cruel thing to Polly. What if they come back to do more harm?"

"It will be all right, Sarah." I placate her despite feeling that things will be anything but all right.

Obviously she does not believe me, for by the morning Sarah has fled with her few belongings. She takes with her the money I gave her to purchase food, which is less than what she is owed. I do not blame her for it.

There is little left to eat, and the fireplaces remain unlit, the rooms cold. Some letters arrive, and with no servant to deliver them to Elizabeth, I take them to her myself.

I approach her warily with the letters, and the news about Sarah. I ask for money so that I might go out and buy us something hot to eat—some pies, perhaps.

She sighs on hearing Sarah has gone—as if it was to be expected, simply another misfortune in a long line of misfortunes.

But the letters... On opening them and scanning the pages, she makes a strange guttural noise in her throat. Her jaw tightens.

"Well," she says, slapping them down on the bedclothes beside her. She coughs and spits into her basin. "News does get around. Lord Levehurst retracts his bid." She looks up at me as if remembering that I am present. "Why are you still here? Do you not have anything better to do?" She hurls the letters at me from her bed.

"I thought... you might care for something to eat." I take a couple of steps back.

"Do not be so ridiculous. Unfortunately, I have little energy with which to beat you." She finally reveals her secret hiding place then, directing me to a post at the end of her bed. It is loose, and it lifts up to reveal a cache of money. Emily and I would never have found it.

"Five pounds. It is all I have left to my name. But I will prevail. I always do," she says.

I note that she does not mention the thousand pounds that must be procured this morning. Neither does she ask after Emily, whose health has worsened overnight.

"Pass me Polly's cage," she says as I am about to depart the room as quickly as I can, now that I have enough money for breakfast. I pick up the cage from the floor, barely able to look at it. I am not sure what is worse, the glassy, forever-still eyes of the bird, or the wild ones I will never forget—the ones that searched in vain for their mistress as the bird was dragged from her home. I place the cage on the end of Elizabeth's bed.

"Now I must think," Elizabeth says, her gaze sharpening as it locks onto Polly. I hesitate, my unease growing, calling upon me to retreat. There is something building within Elizabeth that I cannot quite fathom—a kind of intense, almost palpable rage. It emanates from her. She seethes with it, and it seeps from her now, as if she is unable to contain it any longer.

And is it any surprise? After all, she lies abandoned on her deathbed, deserted by the man she thought loved her, who, in the end, cared to see only if he might have the pox.

She has been blackmailed by the very man she blackmailed herself.

Her hopes and dreams of becoming the mistress of a grand *sérail* have been dashed.

Emily lied to her about her health, Elizabeth's "trusted" physician colluding with her charge, who is now so unwell she can do little more than sweat profusely with fever.

And to add one final insult, Polly—whom she must have felt something for, as much as her black heart allowed—has met a tragic end, murdered in cold blood.

I do not wait around to hear what Elizabeth thinks we might do, but I do not doubt for a moment her ability to come up with *something*. For she is as wily and cruel and spiteful as this Mr. Corbyn who is blackmailing *her* now—perhaps even more so.

I return with hot pies and more willow bark, in the hope that it might give Emily some relief.

Emily slumbers, but I remove her chamber pot and the fetid cloths from her undergarments, my heart sinking when I see them.

When I can put it off no longer, I return to Elizabeth with a pie and an apple and some ale.

I am surprised to see that she has summoned the strength to rise and dress herself, though her movements are decidedly slow and deliberate. Illness has inflicted a cruel toll upon her, aging her significantly. Her complexion is pallid, her once-glorious hair lackluster and thin, and her collarbones protrude in an unflattering manner. Polly's cage remains in plain view, and the sight of the bird sees my appetite vanish, my gut rolling over.

Elizabeth takes the food and begins to eat—not because she is hungry, I think, but because she realizes it is the only way in which she might restore herself to her former glory.

"We must move quickly," she tells me. "It is obvious that rumors of my having the pox circulate. And of Emily being ill. But you—you have come out of this unscathed. We still have your maidenhead. And the new edition of *Harris's List* has not yet been published. This means there is hope for us yet. I will claw my way back, despite Mr. Corbyn and his threats. This evening, we will dress in our finest. We will attend the pleasure gardens again. And we will show everyone that it is all mere gossip. Lies. Lies from those serpents who are jealous of our fine new life, of our wonderful *sérail*. We will find another silly lord willing to bid a hundred pounds for your maidenhead, maybe even one smart enough to stump up money for the *sérail* itself. What say you to that?" She pauses to cough.

I stand, silent, unwilling to speak the truth. Does she truly believe any of this is possible?

"Well? Speak up, Eleanor."

"It is a fine idea, but I do not think Emily able to make such a journey."

"Do we not have more willow bark?"

"Yes, but even so . . ."

Elizabeth sighs. "Not the pleasure gardens, then. Perhaps St. James's Park. This afternoon. A short stroll."

I am not sure Emily can manage even that, not even with all the willow bark in the world. But I see the look in Elizabeth's eyes and know better than to say this. Instead, I nod. "I will give her the willow bark and hope that she rouses," I say, already leaving the room.

"Your best dress," Elizabeth calls, with another hacking cough, as I go. "Look your finest."

I do not have the courage to reveal that I have sold my pearls.

I waken Emily to give her the willow bark, and I manage to get her to take a little pie and some ale too. I tell her the news that Sarah has gone from us.

"Good," she says, not meeting my eye. "I am glad to hear it. You should do the same."

"Emily..."

"Leave" is all she will say after this. *"Leave while you still can."*

I want to stay by her side, but with Sarah gone, there is too much to do. I attend to the fireplace in Emily's room, and the one in Elizabeth's. I fetch basins of water for washing, and empty chamber pots.

At one point, I enter Emily's chamber to see her sitting on the side of her bed. She looks much brighter.

"Emily!" I say, overjoyed. I abandon the chamber pot I am carrying and run to her.

"Oh, I had such a sweat," she says, seemingly forgetting that she refuses to speak to me. "And now I feel... much revived. In fact, give me your arm."

I do so, and gingerly, she stands. We look at each other, and she cannot help it—she grins.

There is hope!

"Elizabeth wants us to dress and take a short stroll to St. James's Park. She is attempting to find a way out of this mess. It seems the first step is to have us all appear hale and hearty in public. Do you think you could manage a stroll to the park?" I ask doubtfully.

Emily's expression says no. But "Yes" is her reply. "Perhaps with some more willow bark."

"You have already taken a significant amount. I am not sure how much is allowed," I tell her.

"Help me to dress. I will take more of the medicine at the last moment," she says.

I nod and sit her back down. I then run off to tell Elizabeth the good news, and to fetch everything I require in order to begin the long and involved process of dressing us all for our stroll with no maid in attendance to help.

HOURS LATER, ELIZABETH lines us up in front of the glass, just as she did before our very first outing to St. James's Park.

I attempt to be jolly, but the sad truth of it is that all three of us look second-rate.

Elizabeth's skin is sallow, and her dress gapes after her illness. Emily has wasted also, her cheeks hollowing by the day, while her belly swells due to infection. Her pained gait is mincing and odd.

With lack of good food and with large servings of worry, my collarbones jut, but again I cannot help but notice how my bust strains at my dress. It is not my imagination, for Dr. Chidworth also noticed.

"What a sight we are," Elizabeth says, adding to her cheeks

more rouge than I have ever seen her use before, in order to give them some color—any color. "But I have seen worse. Far worse! Come, let us go and show London we have not been knocked down yet."

Behind Elizabeth's back, Emily's eyes meet mine. There is something aggressive and snappish in Elizabeth's manner, like that of a dog about to lunge and bite. I dare not challenge her.

Outside, Emily takes my arm and we walk as quickly as she is able. I am happy to see that she looks a little brighter after having yet more willow bark.

We catch the eye of quite a few people as we go, but Elizabeth does not stop to talk.

"Let them look. Let them *look*," she tells us, her smile unnatural. "See? We are not done yet. Far from it."

"Of course we are not," I reply, trying hard not to notice that Emily leans on me more heavily by the moment. Her eyes are a little too bright, her breath a little too labored.

As we start down the Mall, Elizabeth spies some acquaintances. She calls out to some, waves to others, but does not receive many greetings in return. One gentleman spies us and quickly turns about, scurrying away, waving at a nonexistent friend. But mostly there is a widening of the eyes in recognition. Whispers. Turning of backs. Only a little white dog is game enough to come to us. And even he is soon called away.

"They are simply jealous of our finery, as usual." Elizabeth ushers us along.

We all know that this is not true.

I pause beside a bench. "Emily must rest," I say to Elizabeth.

Emily protests, but I will not hear it. I force her to sit down. She does so, but soon begins to shift this way and that. She cannot find any comfort, and at one point she even gasps at a stabbing pain. When Elizabeth strolls off, Emily looks up at me, a question in her eyes.

"Eleanor, tell me, what became of Fanny?"

It takes me a moment to realize she is talking about Fanny Hill, from the book we purchased with our money from Sir William. Our merry, carefree outing seems so long ago now.

"Well, Fanny fares very well in the story. She lives a long life and ends up in keeping with an older gentleman who is good to her. He dies and leaves her his fortune, and she marries the man she fell in love with many years before."

"Oh." Emily seems surprised by this. "So it is a happy ending?"

"Yes, it is, I suppose."

She shifts again, stares off into the distance. "I did not expect that. Perhaps there is hope for us yet, then," she says wistfully.

Before I can answer, I turn to see Elizabeth bearing down on us. "You must get up," she hisses at Emily. "People are beginning to stare. You look ill."

"She is ill!" I whisper, and Elizabeth gives me a look that warns me that I should not say anything else.

I am just about to help Emily up when we hear it... a guffaw.

A gaggle of young men has been walking toward us, up the Mall, behind Elizabeth. When they spy us, they stop and move to one side, forming a huddle. They hold something between them, something they seem to find amusing. One by one, their heads pop up to look at us, and down again to whatever it is they hold.

It does not take me long to work out the source of their mirth.

It can be only one thing—the new edition of *Harris's List*.

"What is it?" Elizabeth catches the look upon my face.

I can say naught. She follows my gaze over to the men—boys, really. Her body stiffens as she takes in the scene.

"Eleanor," she says, "go. Go and take it from them."

"But—"

"Do it," she continues. *"Now."*

I run over to the young gentlemen, who notice my approach only at the last moment. "Give it to me," I demand, holding my hand out.

They pass the pamphlet over to me, speechless.

"It is not true," I say. I have no idea what is written in its pages, but it will not be anything good. "None of it is true." I run back to Elizabeth and Emily with the pamphlet.

Elizabeth snatches the paper from my hand. She scours its pages frantically until she finds what she is looking for.

As she reads, her already-pale face loses even more color with every line her eyes devour.

I look on in silence until she is done.

Her eyes close. Her hand droops to her side, the pamphlet loosening in her fingers before sliding to the ground. I catch it just as it begins to drop.

Emily tugs at my dress, indicating that I should sit down next to her so that she can read also.

Silently we take in the listing.

Oh, how the mighty have fallen. Behold! Queen Elizabeth of Covent Garden has lost her crown. Have we not all been captivated by the promise of what was to come? A story of a magical castle—a sumptuous *sérail*—complete with wallpaper that made one believe they had entered a tropical paradise (with a living macaw, no less!). Two princesses lived in the castle's fabled tower—beauties such as our city had never before seen. Watched over by their Queen, they spent their days primping and preening, readying themselves for the day the Queen might allow gentlemen to cross the castle drawbridge and enter their domain. Only the highest bid would admit entry to this palace of pleasure! But alas, the Queen had an uninvited visitor—that wily jester known as the pox. The castle gates were no match for this guest. With no ticket of admittance, he danced his merry jig of disease around the chambers of the castle! How sad for us all that the sumptuous *sérail* has become little more than a domain of decay. For I now hear our Queen and princesses have been slain with one fell *swoop*. One with the pox. One with putrid distemper. One with child. Apparently not even the macaw lives to tell the tale of our beauties three, who shall, no doubt, soon fade into obscurity, their names spoken no more, the castle a crumbling ruin.

Emily's hand lies on my arm as she reads. As we near the end of the listing, her fingernails press into me.
One with the pox.
One with putrid distemper.
One with child.
I stare at the page for a moment or two before my gaze moves up to meet hers.
Only now do I finally admit the truth.
I am with child.
Nicholas's child.
Part of me had known for some time and did not want to acknowledge the truth, not even to myself. My missed courses, my engorged bust, my weak stomach—yes, I had known, I think.

I still, not daring to move a muscle. If I do not move, perhaps the Queen the pamphlet speaks of will overlook me. Perhaps my head will be spared.

We remain in this tableau for I know not how long. Until... a great cry rings out.

Elizabeth.

I jolt, my head whipping up to look at her. It is a noise unlike any I have heard before, a wailing that emerges from the depths of Elizabeth's very soul. It is a sound of bitter, seething torment, a guttural wail that shatters the air around us.

She quivers with absolute and utter fury as she screams, the raw intensity of her anguish echoing through the park. Her voice carries, and it feels as if every person in the park turns to witness her emotional eruption.

As she cries out, nary a bird twitters or a horse whinnies. The little white dog dares not bark.

London has stilled around her.

When she is done, she takes a deep breath. She stares into the distance, unseeing, her jaw rigid. "No one bests me," she says. "No one. I will take them all for this. All of them. Every. Last. One."

Emily and I say nothing.

Now that the screaming is over, the onlookers' whispers begin.

Elizabeth's gaze sharpens, and she looks down at Emily and me. She takes another deep breath.

"I have a plan," she says. "A new plan. And this evening we shall execute it."

I do not blink as I look at her. There is about her expression an intensity that sends a shiver down my spine.

It reminds me of her recklessness at the curricle race.

Danger is coming.

WE RETURN TO the town house, where I help Emily—wilting by the minute—to her chamber. Elizabeth soon informs us that she is going out, though she will not be long.

"Where are you going?" Emily asks boldly.

I am surprised when Elizabeth answers her. She has been behaving oddly since our return from the park. She is in a world of her own. Thinking hard. Pacing. Talking to herself. Seemingly staring straight through us. It is as if she can think only of this plan, whatever it may be. It worries me greatly that she has not mentioned my situation—not once.

"The anatomist's," she says, before taking her leave with rouge-painted cheeks that only highlight her lack of color.

"The anatomist's," Emily whispers to me when Elizabeth has gone. "Surely he will not have us sit for him now. We look a sight."

"Briar did say each model's beauty is able to be heightened," I say doubtfully.

Emily shakes her head. "What does it matter? We cannot continue in this way. The anatomist's fee will not last long. I am ailing, and you are with child. Why did you not say, Eleanor?"

"I was not sure. I thought . . . I have missed my courses many times before when I have not eaten enough, when I have worried. Only now can I see all the signs together. Dr. Chidworth obviously observed the changes in me, however."

Emily sighs, shifting again and again in her bed. She is unable to find any comfort now.

"Is it very painful?" I ask her. "Should I prepare another pessary? A poultice?"

"No," Emily says. She reaches out to take my hand. She grasps it more tightly than she ever has before. "You should leave. That is what you should do. It is all I ask of you, Eleanor. Leave. Leave me. Leave Elizabeth. I beg you. If you cannot leave for yourself, leave for your child. Leave now, while Elizabeth is at the anatomist's."

For a moment, I cannot answer. Each time Emily has pleaded with me to leave, everything inside me has screamed *No. No, I cannot leave. No, I cannot leave you here, in this place, with this woman, to die.* But now . . .

Now something has shifted.

Now I have someone else I must consider.

I have my child.

Everything has changed.

"See?" Emily tightens her grasp upon my hand when I hesitate. "You see the sense in what I am saying now. Please, Eleanor. Please leave. There is little you can do for me, but so much you can do for your baby. Stand now. Turn and go. Take what little there is left and run, before Elizabeth returns."

I stand, my heart beating as if it might hurl itself from my body. I turn, then think better of it. There must be another way. There *must*. "What if . . . what if I sit for the anatomist too? There will be a little more money then. What if I do that and then leave?"

Emily shakes her head, wincing as she does so. "No, Eleanor," she cries. "Just go. Now. While you can. Not later. Now." A tear slips down her cheek, and she wipes it away.

Once again, I find I cannot leave. It is not right—not right to leave her like this. Perhaps with a little money, another physician might . . .

"This is the last I will speak of it." Emily's voice turns cold, her eyes hard. "Do not remain here for me, for I do not ask you to do so. I do not want it. I cannot save you in my condition. I can only ask you to save yourself and your child. It is now over between us. Do you understand? You go against my every wish, and not another word shall pass between us until you do the thing I ask of you. Leave me now. Forever. I am done with you. Do you hear me? *Done*."

"Emily," I entreat. How can she be so cruel? So unfeeling? I want only what is best for her. How can she not see this?

But she only turns her head from me.

GOOD TO HER word, Emily will not respond to me in any way. Elizabeth returns several hours later, but she speaks to us only briefly before shutting herself in her chamber.

"Ready yourselves," she says. "A carriage will arrive for us at six."

I fix Emily's hair in silence. Help her to change her soiled cloths. Give her some more willow bark, and another apple procured from the market. I ready myself as well, though I can eat naught. Now that I know what is wrong with me, my belly can seemingly hold nothing. Whether it is because of the baby or fear, I am not sure. Elizabeth has still passed no comment on my condition, and this does not bode well for me, I feel.

The carriage arrives at six, just as Elizabeth said it would. She bustles us inside while a thin, fine rain begins to fall. I help Emily into her seat, and although she cries out in pain as she sits, she will not look at me, her eyes persistently averted. Elizabeth will not look at either of us.

So I find myself, once again, on my own.

The carriage sets off with a jerk, making Emily gasp and

clutch at her insides. Elizabeth ignores her, resting her head back and closing her eyes. She has brought her ledger with her, though I know not why and do not feel it wise to ask.

"Will it take long?" I ask hesitantly. "Sitting for the anatomist?"

"An eternity," Elizabeth answers.

I do not ask any further questions, lest she guess at my plan—to wait until we have the funds from the anatomist, then to steal them and run. I have been thinking, and I know Emily is right. If I cannot leave for myself, I must leave for the baby. I must find a way to move on to a better life.

The carriage wheels grind to a halt on the damp street, and I glance out of the window to see the figure of Briar, holding up a lamp just as she had done on our first visit. Her face breaks into a toothy smile, which is unsettling in the flickering light. "Our three beauties!" she says as Elizabeth and I alight. It is only as we help Emily from the carriage that her crooked expression falters.

"Ah, she is worse than I thought," she says, looking on as Emily grimaces, trying as best she can to look well.

Elizabeth only waves a hand dismissively at Emily's discomfort, as if it is of no consequence.

"Shall we?" Briar gestures to the open door—the mouth of the black-and-white half-timber building.

We follow her inside the building's gaping maw and ascend the creaking wooden stairs that have seen so many students. As we venture along the long, dark hallway—into the belly of the beast—I hesitate, a foreboding sensation seizing me and whispering in my ear that all is not right. I look to Emily for reassurance, but despite our close proximity as I support her by the waist, yet again she refuses to look at me.

"Emily," I whisper.

She turns her head farther from me.

I exhale, ignore the feeling of dread and continue to help her down the hallway. There is no time to argue. I am not sure how much farther she can go on before she must sit.

We enter that cavernous room filled with the jars housing those pitiful and wretched creatures. To my astonishment, it lies barren of its other occupants. The tables remain, but they have been cleared. There are no shrouded figures to be seen today, and the slow drip of ice has been silenced. A disquieting emptiness remains in its place.

The anatomist is already present, and eager, it seems, to greet us. "So, you have really come." His eyes skate over Emily and me and come to rest upon Elizabeth.

"Did we not agree that I would return this evening?" Elizabeth snaps, placing her ledger upon a table. "Did you not send a carriage?"

I look from one of them to the other. It is an odd exchange. It feels as if something occurred between them during Elizabeth's visit that afternoon. A deal has been made. I suppose that is why she has brought the ledger. I had wondered about it, as I had never seen her take it from the town house before. Perhaps she wishes to write down the terms of their agreement, though why she could not do this at King Street, I do not know.

The anatomist holds up his hands, and I am reminded of how diminutive he is. His students must tower over him.

"Perhaps we should get on with things," Briar says. She is behaving strangely also. Like the anatomist, she does not meet my gaze, speaking only to Elizabeth.

There is something about this that heightens my nervousness. Will they not meet our eye because we are so changed? Because Emily is sick? Will there be less money changing hands now?

"I agree. We should proceed with haste, for this is no social call," Elizabeth says. "Perhaps some wine, to calm our nerves. For while we should be used to a state of undress, we have never been models before."

"Of course," Briar says. "I have prepared a draft."

Emily leans into me. She can stand no longer. "You must sit," I say. I can see no chair, so I help her over to one of the tables where the bodies once lay. I hoist her upon it, her face continually turned from me, as is her wont.

After a few moments, Briar approaches with three glasses on a tray. She passes one to Elizabeth and comes over to deliver the remaining two to Emily and me.

I take a sip. The wine is sweet and delicious, and I hope it will help to alleviate my fears of this place and all its oddities. Of the walls full of the dead. Of Briar. Of the anatomist. Of Elizabeth. Of my situation.

Emily goes to rest her glass upon the table.

"Drink up," Briar tells us, "for we must soon begin."

Emily and I obediently drain our glasses and hand them back to Briar. Elizabeth, however, sips hers slowly as she watches us.

"Would you care for another glass?" Briar inquires, her gaze fixed on me.

"I . . ." I pause, considering the offer, but then a peculiar sensation begins to wash over me. I lick my lips. A bitter taste lingers in my mouth after the initial rush of sweetness, and something feels decidedly wrong. I feel as if I have already drunk too much wine. My lips are tingling and becoming numb. I feel lightheaded.

Beside me, Emily holds a hand to her forehead. "I . . . Something is . . . not right. You, Briar, what was in that wine? That draft?"

"Miss?" Briar says, as if she does not understand the question.

"What potion was that? What was in that draft?" Emily demands.

Briar does not answer this time. She is still unwilling to look at us, to meet our eyes. She looks to the anatomist, who turns his back.

Emily sees it before I do—that something that we are not privy to is going on here.

"Elizabeth," Emily says, "what have you done?"

It is only then that I notice that Elizabeth has not been drinking from her glass at all—she has only been giving the appearance of doing so.

In the eerie, flickering light, Elizabeth makes her way across the room to the table Emily sits upon and I lean against. "What have I done?" she says. "Why, little more than you were willing to do to me, you ungrateful wretch. I may have been lying on my deathbed, but I could hear your every traitorous word. Unwilling to fetch a doctor, hoping I might die by the morn. I am surprised to find myself here, doing you such a favor as this. For now you will live forever. In beauty. Revered."

I try to take her words in as the world darkens around me. I try to understand. What is this "favor" she speaks of? But my sight is murky before me now. I must lie down. "Emily?" I say. Something is wrong. Something is very, very wrong. I need Emily to look at me. Just once. Just once before I sleep. I need her to tell me all is well. That the wine was simply strong. That I will soon wake from my dizzy spell and feel well once more.

"I am here," Emily says. "Hold my hand. Eleanor, hold my hand."

I hear the true Emily in her voice—*my* Emily. She has returned to me. I reach out for her hand, unable to find it as I slump into her lap. But Emily locates my arm and her hand finds mine. She holds it tight. She is with me.

"Look at me," she says, tugging upon my arm. "Eleanor, look at me!"

But it is too late.

Everything has turned to black.

ALYS

LONDON, PRESENT DAY

I DREAM OF EMILY, of course. Running. Forever running. Never turning.

In the soft folds of the hotel bedding, I roll over with a groan. This has to be the fourth time I've woken from the dream tonight. Each time I do, a wave of thoughts floods into my mind. The Venuses. Mrs. Yoon. Geon.

My hand slaps around on the bedside table until I find my phone.

Five twelve a.m.

There's no point in trying to fall asleep again. I know it won't happen. I get up and pad about the room, making myself a cup of tea. I'm not hungry, but I find myself compelled to place an order for some French toast. That done, I drag one of the room's upholstered chairs to the window, steal the duvet from the bed and hole up at the window, overlooking a quiet Russell Square. There I sit, my head resting back, and watch London wake up before my eyes. The city begins to stir. As it has always done. As it always will do.

I take a shower. I'm dressed and beginning to gather my things when my phone rings.

"Hi, Sorrel," I answer.

"Alys. Thank goodness. Is everything all right there?"

I stop packing, my heart seizing up with fear. "Yes. Why? What's going on?"

Sorrel exhales. "There's been trouble overnight, at the storage facility. It's all over the news."

"What sort of trouble? What's happened?"

"It's Geon Yoon. He attempted to break in."

I'd alerted Ro to the fact that Geon was on the run, of course. I'd been worried that he might show up in Whitby, looking for me, but I hadn't thought about the storage facility.

"How is that even possible? How could he have known where Elizabeth was? I didn't say anything to the Yoons about where she would be held."

"I don't know how he knew. He had a knife on him, but he didn't use it, thank goodness. He seemed to think better of it and dropped it. He got away."

"Thank goodness." I breathe a sigh of relief. But then I realize Sorrel is far too quiet.

"Alys, there's something else. The thing is, he had your code."

I take a moment to process this.

"No," I finally say. "No, he can't have. That's impossible. No one has that code. Not even my solicitor. Only me. I changed it when we left the facility."

"I know. And yet Geon Yoon had it, Alys. He did."

We both know it can have come from only one place. From one person.

Elizabeth.

She's managed not just to connect with Geon Yoon; she's

managed to connect with me, without my knowing it. "But . . . how?" I whisper, although, even as I utter the words, I think I know. "Listen, can you send me the footage?" I ask.

"Of course. I'll send it on. I've had security override the code. I'm the only person with it now. Is that all right with you? I thought it was the safest option. We've used some protective spells to ensure that Elizabeth isn't able to connect with me."

"Yes, thanks. You'll need the code anyway, to move both Eleanor and Elizabeth."

I stare out the window. London is in full swing now. Cars and double-decker buses. Pedestrians. Life.

"I should have said—there was a moment," I finally say, "in the storage facility. I thought I heard my name. And then, at Poulston Park, she appeared to me—Elizabeth—as a vision."

"What did she say?" Sorrel asks.

"Nothing at all. It was just her face, a vision. I'd hoped to see Emily. I half believed I imagined the whole thing, that I'd talked myself into it."

"It would seem not. It shouldn't be possible."

"Well, it's Elizabeth, so anything's possible. Still, I think . . . probably best to move quickly now."

Sorrel hesitates for only a moment. "You're coming to Jennet's today?"

"Yes."

Another pause, in which Sorrel clicks her tongue, thinking. "Look, we'll do what we can from our end. I know Jennet will have some ideas on how to keep Elizabeth at bay. But she can't rise, not without that necklace. At least we know that."

"Yes."

"She's getting desperate now that she senses the end is nigh for her. She'll try anything—anything she can."

"My thoughts exactly," I agree.

"Look, I don't want to sound condescending, but you'll have to be strong. And know that we've got your back, that we'll do everything we can to help you."

"I know you will. Thanks. I'll finish packing and I'll be on my way."

"Great. I'll see you at Jennet's. And if there's anything you need, just call. Ro and I will keep our phones right by us."

"I will. Thanks again, Sorrel." I end the call.

Sorrel sends the footage to me within moments, and I watch it carefully, several times over, a lump in my throat. I feel awful. Geon Yoon is no willing participant in this exercise; that much is clear from the footage. His movements are erratic. He approaches the desk at the storage facility, reaching constantly for something inside his jacket, then stopping himself, his hand jerking away. When the staff alerts a security guard, Geon finally grabs the knife and hurls it away from him, as if he's scared of what he might do. It skitters across the floor, making me shiver as I remember another time and place. I squint, trying to get a good look at the knife. Small. Black handled. Nothing special. It hits a skirting board and comes to a stop, and Geon backs away from it, then turns and runs. He's clearly fighting Elizabeth with everything he's got. It's a terrible thing to watch, terrible to see someone controlled by an outside force. I feel for him. I really do. I hope I can help him. I hope his throwing the knife away means he's managed to break free of Elizabeth's chains. I so wish I'd never had to involve him in any of this.

I watch the video again and again, all the while trying to understand. Why did Elizabeth force him to go to the storage facility? What did she want him to do there? It didn't make sense to me. She would need the necklace of hair in order to rise from her waxen form. Did she really think we'd keep it at the storage facility? Surely not. But she must have. Or at least she wanted to check.

I think about this for a while, because it doesn't sit right with me. But I don't come up with anything.

Time to get moving.

I'm racing about the room, packing up my things, when the door chimes. I'd completely forgotten about the breakfast I'd ordered. I go over and look through the peephole to see a staff member in a mask waiting with a trolley. I crack open the door, and as I do so, a fierce wave of nausea rolls over me, out of nowhere. I wrench the door open then, and call out that I'll be just a minute as I race for the bathroom. There I heave into the sink.

How embarrassing.

I clean myself and the sink up as fast as I can and head back out into the room, expecting to have to sign for the breakfast. But the door is just clicking shut behind the staff member. And who can blame her for not wanting to stick around after that performance? I glance at the tray and, at the thought of French toast, almost run to the sink again. Why did I order it? I don't even like French toast.

After this excitement I check the room to see if I've left anything behind. As I do so, a thought floats to the top of my mind. Catherine—she's been awfully quiet.

Sorrel mentioned that Geon Yoon's break-in attempt at the storage facility was all over the news. So why hasn't Catherine called me? Why hasn't she texted? I pick my phone up once more and look at it with narrowed eyes.

Catherine's far too quiet, and that can't be a good thing.

But—let's face it—Catherine is the least of my problems.

Or so I think until I go to leave the room and realize my satchel is nowhere to be found.

My satchel with the ledger in it.

It takes me only a moment to realize what's happened, who has been in my room. That subconscious thought about Catherine was no coincidence. Neither was my ordering of the French toast. I felt that wave of nausea for a reason.

Because of Elizabeth.

And the staff member with the trolley—the one with the uniform and the mask?

That was Catherine herself.

That's why she's been so quiet. She's under Elizabeth's control, just like Geon. Elizabeth sent her to steal whatever it was I'd removed from the vault. Perhaps she thought the vault was where the necklace of hair was located? That would make sense.

I go over to the bed and sink onto it, my face in my hands.

What a fool I am.

I remember Elizabeth's face in front of mine—mocking me, taunting me.

You think you can defeat me? her eyes had said. *Go on, then. Try.*

I close my eyes for a moment. I have no idea how this is going to play out, how I can get the better of her. Look at the tricks she's pulled off already: connecting with Geon Yoon, with Catherine, with *me*. It's as Sorrel said. She'll try anything now—anything she can. I can't help but remember something else Sorrel said, too, something about me.

She said I'll have to be strong.

I open my eyes and push my shirtsleeve up to reveal my left forearm.

I am the mistress of my own fate.

Oh, but I'll have to be strong. And I'll have to be smart. I'll have to come up with a few tricks myself. I guess I have the advantage, being here—in the living world. As things stand, I hold the cards. Sorrel is right. Elizabeth is desperate, grasping at straws, trying to scare me off. I have to take control. I have to know what I'm up against when I finally meet her head-on. I have to believe that I can beat her at her own game.

How do I do that?

Maybe I need to begin by standing up to her, because if she can connect with me, I can connect with her, can't I?

And I know the perfect place to do it in.

I grab my phone again and start texting.

PHOEBE, THE EVER-WONDERFUL Phoebe, welcomes me with a broad grin.

"I'm so glad you could stop by," she says, ushering me through the staff entrance of the Pleasure Gardens Experience an hour before opening time. Phoebe is the curator of the small but popular museum in Vauxhall. It's a wonderful, heady re-creation of the Vauxhall Pleasure Gardens that existed nearby in the eighteenth and nineteenth centuries. Around two years ago, it was low on funds and looking at having to close. An anonymous benefactor provided the funds to keep it running. Unfortunately, I was not able to stay anonymous for long, thanks to my bank, which had accidentally left my name on some paperwork.

"I'm so sorry to spring this on you with zero notice," I reply.

"It's perfect," she says. "This way I've got time to see you before my first meeting. I'm actually pleased you could stop by, because I've been meaning to contact you."

"Oh?" I look up at Phoebe, who towers over me.

"I know you've seen the exhibit since we redressed it, but we've just rotated a few of the objects for conservation reasons, and we've managed to include an absolutely divine dress in the exhibit this time. Really, it's simply stunning. I know I'm not supposed to have favorites, but..."

"It sounds lovely," I tell her as we wind our way between the tall panels that provide museum guests with information on what they are about to see. The panels detail what an evening at the pleasure gardens entailed—from arrival by boat or carriage to the music guests might have listened to, dances they might have danced and food they would have supped upon, as well as other entertainments, such as the cascade waterfall.

"How is everything with you, anyway?" Phoebe continues. "I heard a rumor that you brought one of your wax models back to London."

I nod. "It's true. Elizabeth."

"Oh. The beautiful one with all the hair?"

"That's Elizabeth. The beautiful one with all the hair."

We stand at the entrance to the exhibit, and I brace myself to turn the corner and enter the immersive wonderland that lies beyond. It's an experience that tends to overwhelm me, given my long connection with the Venuses. For the average visitor, I guess it offers a fascinating glimpse into what nightclubbing was like two and a half centuries ago, but I know those three women intimately. To me, the mannequins in the exhibit aren't lifeless figures displaying pretty frocks but individuals with hopes and dreams. Fears and longings. Wishes and desires.

I take a deep breath as we pass under a bower that drips with fake purple wisteria.

And I find myself transported back in time, to the pleasure gardens.

The darkness, necessary to preserve the exhibit's fabrics, enhances the illusion. Behind glass, mannequins are grouped together, engaged in conversation, laughing, listening to the sweet melodies of the stringed music that permeates the space. Wealthy women adorned in intricate gowns, gentlemen in matching patterned coats and waistcoats, middle-class folk in plainer clothes, musicians, waiters... all sorts mill about. Overhead, lanterns twinkle, casting reflections that deceive the viewer into believing the gardens stretch on indefinitely. I feel as if I might be able to stride through the glass, push through the crowd and move on to supper, or perhaps stroll to marvel at the cascade—that wondrous artificial waterfall.

On person-sized screens scattered throughout, actors perform small vignettes. Phoebe and I catch snippets of conversations—gossip about an upcoming marriage; a warning to steer clear of the dangers that can be found on Druid's Walk; a woman's order for food, followed by her sharp criticism of how thinly sliced the ham has become and how steep the prices are.

The past has come to life.

"It's just over here." Phoebe touches my arm, breaking the spell.

"Sorry?" I say before I recall the dress Phoebe wanted to show me. "Oh, of course." I follow her over to the other side of the room. My step falters when I see it. *The dress.* I have to force myself to keep going.

"So, how do you like it?" Phoebe asks when I am silent for too long.

"It's..."

"Exquisite. I know." Phoebe must believe my lack of vocabulary is due to the beauty of the dress alone.

But it's not that.

"Do you know something? I think it would probably fit you," she says. "I don't think I'd get one arm in most of the dresses here, but you're so wonderfully petite, I believe half of the gowns here would fit you." Her phone pings and she pulls it out of her pocket. "Sorry, Alys. I'm going to have to run to that meeting, I'm afraid."

I make myself turn away from the glass. "Of course. Thanks so much for letting me stop by. Do I need to . . . ?" I gesture toward the exit.

Phoebe waves her hands. "Goodness, no. No need to leave. We'll be opening in about twenty minutes, so enjoy the peace and quiet while you can. And please, do let me know whenever you want to come in."

"Thanks." I watch as Phoebe exits the room, and when I'm sure she's gone, I turn back to the dress.

The dress.

The sheen of the shimmering ice-blue silk. The French lace trim. The flounces. The embroidery.

It's not Emily's dress, but it may as well be.

I step up, right up, to the glass. My reflection comes into view and a magical transformation occurs. I become one with the mannequin before me, my features seamlessly transposed onto its blank face. My face is her face. The dress she wears is my dress. We are one.

I close my eyes. All around me, the atmosphere is filled with vibrant chatter, laughter—life. The pleasure gardens are alive once more, and time is meaningless in this enchanting setting.

Which means that when I open my eyes again and spy not my own, not the mannequin's, but Elizabeth's visage, I am not as surprised as I might be.

She smirks that same taunting smirk that I saw at Poulston Park.

"It's Alys, isn't it?" she says.

I square my shoulders. Brace myself.

"You know it is," I reply.

"Are you a sailor? I mean to say . . . all those tattoos . . ."

She is trying to rile me. And I do not let her.

"You had Catherine steal the ledger from me," I say. May as well be up-front about things.

"And what if I did? It's not your ledger, is it? It's mine."

I shake my head. She's always been so attached to that book. But I think there's more to it than the fact that the ledger was hers. I think she believed the necklace of hair might have been stored with the ledger in the vault. I decide to let that go, because I don't want to bring up the topic of the necklace with her. "What were you up to with Geon Yoon? You can't possibly think we'd keep anything but the wax models in that sort of storage. Or are you just trying your luck everywhere? Searching high and low now that you're running out of time?"

A mocking laugh is her reply. "I'm not too concerned as to time. After all, you haven't had it in you to destroy the Venuses yet. Why should you be able to do so with any haste now?"

"Because . . ." I start. And flounder.

"See? You know I'm correct. So much talk of gathering the Venuses, of destroying them, and yet here you are, in London, the Venuses ungathered. You'll never destroy them. You can't. Do you know why? I'll tell you. It's because you'll never be strong enough."

"Geon was strong enough. He resisted you, even if Catherine couldn't."

"Couldn't? Didn't want to, more like it. And why do you care so much about this Geon fellow, anyway? He's nothing, no one. He and his father kept me caged, like a beast. They would have done the same to Eleanor's model given half a chance—locked her up, ogled her."

I shake my head. "Geon Yoon didn't want to be like his father, or those foul men who came before him. It was you. You turned him into one of them."

"Oh? And here I was thinking it was *you* who did that."

My breath sucks in upon hearing this brutal truth. Because Elizabeth is right. She's *right*. I wanted this, to frighten Mrs. Yoon into giving Elizabeth to me.

I'm no better than Elizabeth is. No different. We are cut from the same cloth, the two of us.

"Where is he now? Where's Geon?" She'll have tucked Catherine away somewhere safe, especially if she's a willing participant in Elizabeth's evil antics, but Geon doesn't deserve to be used like this, as Elizabeth's pawn—as my pawn. I have to save him if I can. I owe him that much. I owe myself that much, too, to be redeemed.

"Do you really think I'd tell you where he is?"

No. Of course not. But I had to ask. I'm about to reply when all that Elizabeth has been saying to me sinks in. Her speech—it sounds . . . modern, or at least modern-ish. I realize something horrifying.

She's been awake. She's been awake in her model form for all these years.

Sentient. Scheming. Biding her time.

I can't even begin to fathom how torturous that must have been. Not that she doesn't deserve it, but still . . .

My thoughts come together then. "You convinced Mr. Yoon to steal some of my hair, didn't you? That's how you connected with me. And Geon—he has the hair now, doesn't he?"

"What do you think, Alys?"

I take a moment to collect myself. It doesn't matter what she's done already. It's her next move I have to worry about. I can't let her get to me. I will be strong enough. I can be strong enough.

I am the mistress of my own fate.

"It sounds as if you want me to destroy the Venuses," I finally reply. "As if you *want* me to gather all of them in one place. You believe that will be your big chance, don't you? To obtain the hair necklace, to rise again." Of course, I'd considered burning everything separately—Elizabeth, Eleanor, the necklace of hair. But apparently it's not that simple. There are words that need to be spoken, spells that need to be broken. I know it's best if the ritual burning happens at the home of the coven, at dawn, and that all the materials burn together in their entirety.

"So much talk, Alys. So much talk and so little action."

I don't need to listen to this. I step back and close my mind to her, severing the connection. My choice. The illusion vanishes. My reflection, Elizabeth's face, Emily's dress—all gone. "I guess I'd better get moving, then, and prove you wrong," I declare to the empty air.

Because she *is* wrong.

This time, action will follow, action that I know will lead to the battle of a lifetime. It's just as I thought in the hotel room. I knew it would come down to the two of us. I've always known.

Elizabeth and me.

She believes she has it all figured out. She thinks she knows exactly what she's doing. But what she hasn't accounted for is that she is, as always, desperately, painfully, alone. Meanwhile, I possess the united strength of all those who have come before me—that long line of women stretching back through time. We'll come together, united, in order to defeat Elizabeth. We'll have to merge our knowledge, skills and strengths, leaving our weaknesses behind. But I know Elizabeth hasn't considered this—the fact that it's not just me she's up against but all of us. And, as one, we are poised to push back against her with every ounce of our combined essence.

And, somehow, we will find a way to prevail.

ELEANOR

LONDON, DECEMBER 1769

I AWAKEN CONFUSED. I do not know how it is possible, but I am upright when my eyes flicker open. I am alone, in a room that I find unfamiliar—not the vast studio of the anatomist but a much smaller space. I struggle to recall how I got here, to determine what time of day it is, how much time has passed. I look around me in the dim light and see a lamp resting on a wooden chair, which provides a small puddle of illumination. The door is ajar, as if someone has been in the room to check upon me. I look down and notice my skirts, smoothing my hands down the unfamiliar fabric. I seem to be attired in black, but I do not own a black gown.

Slowly, I begin to recall the trip to the anatomist's. The wine. Emily's hand. The terrifying, all-enveloping dark.

I must have fainted. The wine—the draft—must have been too strong for me. Perhaps I sullied my own gown and had to be dressed in another?

I turn to see a long table in the room, the ominous outline of a body concealed beneath a white sheet. There is no incessant *drip, drip, drip* of melting ice, so I assume it to be a waxen model. This knowledge does nothing to assuage my fears, and a shiver courses through me, a vivid memory of Lavender resurfacing. Lavender, so intensely, ecstatically beautiful, until the eye moves down to see how she is rent, butchered to display organs and entrails, her innards surrounded by grotesque, puckered, wrinkled skin. I do not dare to lift the corner of the sheet. Who knows what horrors I might find underneath?

Bile rises in my throat, and I bring a hand to my mouth. I must leave this place. King Street is no home to me, but anything is better than here.

I peek out the open door. All is quiet and still. It appears to be early morning, a soft gray light filtering through the window I can see at the end of the hallway.

I must have slept the whole night through. I suppose Elizabeth will be angry about this—that I have not had my sitting with the anatomist. Or perhaps he was able to make his sketches and so on while I slept? Either way, I know that the sitting must be completed if he is to pay us. And I need him to pay us his handsome fee in order that I may then steal it and run away. Far, far away.

I tiptoe down the hall, quiet as a mouse, opening this door and that as I go. There is a storeroom, full of metal pans and folded sheets, which gives me the misguided confidence to open the next door. The interior of this room immediately causes me to gag. Deep shelves reveal a mixture of repulsive wax models—a skull cut to reveal a brain; a head tilted back at an odd angle to display a gaping mouth and fleshy tongue; a gruesome half face that seems melted and dripping, as if burned by fire; a baby's torso showing the dark welts of a skin affliction; a severed leg that shows a thick twist of veins.

I quickly close the door behind me.

The next door along the hallway opens to a larger room, its expanse empty save for a few mostly vacant anatomical tables. A scent of decay lingers in the air, a reminder of previous occupants. In the dim half-light, I discern, reclining on a table at the back of the room, a figure left uncovered. As my eyes adjust, I am taken aback to discover that it is Elizabeth, in a deep slumber. She lies with one arm gracefully tucked behind her head, her lustrous golden hair splayed around her, her chest rising and falling in rhythm with her peaceful dreams.

"Elizabeth," I whisper. She does not reply.

My cautious steps echo throughout the room as I approach her. Something nags at my awareness, a disquieting feeling. I stop halfway across the room. Those golden, flowing locks. Her complexion. Elizabeth has been sick. She does not look like this.

No, this is not right.

Slowly, the hairs stand to attention on my arms, rise at the back of my neck.

The figure—it is not Elizabeth at all.

It is a model. A model such as Lavender.

I edge forward, the oppressive silence in the room now punctuated by the uncanny rise and fall of the model's chest. How? How can this be possible? How can it breathe as if it lives? My eyes widen when I reach it, taking it in, one finger hesitantly stretching out to make sure it is not flesh and blood.

It is cold to the touch. Cold and yet . . . so real, the chest forever rising, falling, in a deep, breathy sigh.

It must be clockwork, an automaton like the one Emily spoke of, which struck at the dulcimer—the one with the dull eyes. But this . . . this is no such simple thing. I do not understand. When did Elizabeth sit for the anatomist? Such a model must have taken much time to create. Has she been visiting the anatomist without our knowledge?

Caught up in the vision before me, I do not hear the footsteps until it is too late.

Someone enters the room—a young maid wearing a linen apron, her hair scraped into a cap that a few wayward curls escape from. She gasps when she sees me, a hand flying to her chest. Slowly, the hand rises to bring a finger to her lips, entreating me to be quiet. She places on the floor the pail she has been holding, and swiftly closes the door behind her.

She approaches me hesitantly, her arms outstretched, as if I am a wild animal that might flee. Then, in an odd gesture, she comes to take my hand as if to soothe me. I allow her to guide me over to a corner of the room. As we go, her eyes glance at the closed door.

"My name is Lucy," she says. "We must be quiet. We may only have a moment."

"Elizabeth . . ." I start, in a normal voice.

The finger rises to her lips again. Her eyes search mine, and she squeezes my hand tight. "You do not understand. Your mistress made a deal—a deal with the anatomist and Briar."

I nod. "Yes." I remember to whisper this time. "To sit for him, for wax models to be made in our forms."

The maid shakes her head. "No. I wish this were true, but no. First, you must know it is a great secret that I am here. I have been placed here to help you—you and Emily."

I stare at her blankly, my head still spinning from awakening.

"I am new to this place. Briar will check upon me soon," the maid continues. "She lurks around every corner. Please—you must listen to me." Her tone turns urgent now, her grip on my hand tightening. "Briar is a witch. A terrible, malevolent witch who—"

I take a step back from her, pulling my hand away. This woman has clearly lost her mind. Words that make no sense tumble from her mouth. Malevolent witches? I have never heard such talk! "Where is Emily?" I demand. "Where is Elizabeth?"

"Please, you must listen. Several weeks have passed since you were last awake. Briar has been hard at work, perfecting her evil art. It did not take, you see, the first time—on Lavender."

I frown. "Lavender? Elizabeth said she has gone to Bath."

She shakes her head. "Lavender has not gone to Bath. Lavender has been . . . lost to us. Or trapped, inside her wax model. We do not entirely know. Briar's magic did not take as she wanted it to."

I am starting to become cross with this woman's ridiculous talk. I go to move toward the door, but she catches my arm, forcing me to turn back.

"Where is Emily? Where is Elizabeth?" I ask again.

"They are as you are," Lucy says. "They are wax models now, their souls bewitched, though there are ways in which it is possible for them to rise from that form. Briar struggles with her spell. It is unstable."

A creeping sense of unease washes over me as I remember the sheeted form in the room I found myself in. My breathing quickens. But no. Whatever am I thinking? I can no longer listen to such drivel. I pull away from her. "This is nonsense. Stop with your fanciful tales. Tell me immediately, where is Emily? I must find her, so that we may leave this place. She is unwell and must rest."

"It is best you do not see her. It is not a pleasant sight to behold." She glances away as she speaks.

I take this lapse in her concentration as my opportunity to

run. I bolt from her before she knows what I am doing, streaking across the room toward the door, which I wrench open violently.

"Eleanor!" she blurts out in a half whisper, though there is no point in lowered voices now that the heels of my boots pound as I run across the wooden floor. When I do not stop, she begins to follow, chasing me out the door. I make my way down the hallway, blindly opening doors as I go. It does not take long for me to come across a room with another model—this one without a sheet.

And then I halt, for when my eyes register what lies before me, I can move no farther.

It is the most grotesque, most abhorrent sight I have ever beheld.

It is Emily. Beautiful Emily. My Emily. But here, her beauty is cruelly dashed.

Emily's waxen form lies on the table before me, naked save for a velvet drape that lies across her torso. There are her plump cheeks, smooth brow, wayward curls, strong shoulders, graceful arms that I have watched flourish as she danced. But then... oh, then...

One hand rises to cover my mouth as I take in the interchangeable parts laid out upon the velvet. I cannot help but step forward to inspect them.

They are numbered so that Emily's face and groin may be changed, as if she is nothing more than one of the newfangled puzzles sweeping the city.

A plaque reads *The Stages of Syphilis*.

My hands trembling, I reach out for the first waxen puzzle piece and pick it up.

"The chancre," I whisper, staring at the masklike section of smooth, full lips I know so well, marred by a single angry red lesion. A sob escapes my own lips as I replace the monstrosity upon the velvet and my eye is cast upon what comes . . . next.

An abomination is laid out before me, Emily's beautiful face a gnawing plague of lesions, each mask worse than the next, the lesions slowly eating away at the flesh of her mouth, her nose, until there is no nose left. A grimace sees teeth protrude and a bony jaw revealed. If this model were alive, it would shortly be fit only for the grave.

My sobs cannot be contained, building and racking my chest.

A touch on my shoulder causes me to startle and whirl about. "Emily!" I cry out.

But no. It is only the woman again. The maid. Lucy.

"No," I say. "No." I begin to tremble as my understanding grows. For I can feel it. I knew at once—this is no simple model. It *is* Emily. I can tell that there is truth in what Lucy has told me about bewitchment. Here, before me—still and silent—is Emily. *My Emily.* Always laughing. Always chattering. Always so . . . alive. And yet, here she lies, trapped inside a repellent waxen, diseased beast.

And there is more.

The model—I am kin to it somehow. There is between myself and the figure a pull I cannot deny. A tie. A bond.

It is this . . . this . . . feeling that tells me all I need to know. Something monstrous has occurred here. Something beyond mortal comprehension. Something wicked and devilish and sinful and wrong.

I turn to Lucy, my chest rising and falling far too quickly. "Explain." I step forward, closer to her, and she recoils as if I might hit her. *"Explain."*

"I . . ." She looks as if she does not know where to begin. But then she draws breath, steadies herself. "Briar and the anatomist work together. As I said, Briar is a witch. The anatomist is also a woman, disguised as a man so that she may move in the world of men and practice the art of medicine. I believe she wanted to create some female models that might entice males to study the female form. Instead, men like Dr. Chidworth happily continue to mistreat their patients, and the students drool over the models. And so she and Briar have devised a trap. Any man who views these figures with a lustful eye will pay for doing so."

This cannot be true. It is ludicrous talk. Some silly jape. A farce.

Lucy reaches out, touching me on the arm. I slap her hand away.

And then I scream.

I scream right from the depths of my very soul—if I still have one.

Lucy moves then. Not toward me, but away. Away, down the hallway, as I scream and scream and scream.

They come running then, woken from their slumber.

Briar. The anatomist.

And then Lucy appears once more, as if conjured by a magician. "What is happening?" She plays her part neatly, as if she has not been in attendance of me the entire time.

"Away with you, girl. Leave us," Briar barks as soon as she sees Lucy.

Lucy scuttles away like a beetle.

"How has she awakened?" The anatomist turns on Briar.

I open my mouth to scream once more, and Briar utters some nonsense words as she walks toward me, her hand at her throat.

I cannot scream.

I cannot move.

Emily! I cry out, but only in my mind. How can this be? What is happening here? *Emily!*

My voice is silenced.

I can only look on, helpless, unblinking, as Briar and the anatomist approach me. Briar moves in close to examine me as if I am one of the creatures in the anatomist's glass jars—as if I am not a living, breathing person. I stare at a new piece of jewelry she wears—a necklace of braided hair. It is much like the bracelet she wore when we viewed Lavender, though this one seems to be made of different shades, tightly bound. She fingers it for a moment, then seems to remember herself and tucks it inside the high neck of her dress, out of view.

"This should not be." Briar glances at the anatomist. "She has not been given a task to fulfill. Not yet."

"And yet here she stands," the anatomist says with a sigh. "You assured me it would work this time, that there would be no repeat of what happened with Lavender. I will not have it. Not again. This time it *must* work."

"Yes, yes. Always with your demands," Briar hisses. She begins to speak again, uttering more words that I cannot understand. A long, seemingly unending chant.

No, wait. It is like . . . a cruel lullaby. Like the draft she plied Emily and me with. For I suddenly find the world dimming about me again, as if she has given me another draft. And then I feel, inexplicably, a gliding, pulling sensation, as the light extinguishes around me.

And blackness envelops me once more.

I AM AWAKENED BY the sickening sensation of a finger tracing its way through hidden parts of me. Something is wrong. Very wrong.

"Do you not see? Here, on the right side of the uterus. The tube is distended."

I feel a prodding.

I am exposed, I realize. There is no clothing, nothing down there. My eyes fix on two men standing above me. They are peering down at my body, ignoring me as if I am not present.

I try to recoil, but I am frozen in place, unable to move. I try to cry out, but I am voiceless.

Stop! I call out. *Stop that! Get away from me!* But my pleas reverberate only in my mind. I am imprisoned by an unseen force, held by invisible restraints.

As I lie rigid, the touch continues, the men oblivious to my silent suffering.

"Here and here."

"*Most* interesting."

I can only stare up at my tormentors. I am condemned to endure this nightmare as if I am an unfeeling, unseeing doll in a nursery, something to be played with, its arms bent and twisted.

Emily! I try again. I struggle for a moment to remember the maid's name. Lucy. That was it. *Lucy?* Perhaps she understood the words that Briar uttered, the words that forced me to still, to sleep. But I cannot call out for her. My voice remains trapped. Silenced.

The men's heads are together, their eyes narrowed as they squint and discuss my body as if it is not my own, as if I do not exist. I am reminded of Lord Levehurst and his friends in the park. Of how their eyes did not see me. Of how I was of no consequence to them. I am reminded of Henry, with his hands that fumbled at my dress while I stood, crushed by his weight, unable to move—to think.

If I were able to cry out, would these men even help me? Free me? I have my doubts.

Once again, I am nothing. No one.

I scream in frustration. I wail. I beat my fists that do not move as the men continue to peer down at my nude form as if I am no more than a lump of wax.

And all the time I struggle, there is something warning me that I must be alert, on guard. Something that waits for their touch to become . . . something else. Something more intimate.

This is what it is like to be buried alive. I begin to panic, trapped by the weight of knowing that there is no chance of escape, that this torment may never end.

My heartbeat rises, thudding in my ears, while I am forced to view their faces above me, ever closer. Each whisker. Every blemish to their skin. A little spittle at the corner of a mouth.

The men ignore me, are oblivious of me, and continue their discussion.

"Now, see how the ligament extends to the deep abdominal ring of the inguinal canal, crossing the inferior epigastric vessels?"

"Yes, I see."

The finger creeps along my insides, and warning beats above my terror, forcing me to pay heed. It is crucial that I note his face now, that I know his scent. I must watch. Wait. Be ready to pounce.

"Now, if we move on to this next model, you will notice . . ."

The pair move away.

My hunger abates.

And some unseen force returns me to the dark once more.

MY EYES SNAP open yet again. Another student stands above me. He is alone. He glances up and around before returning his attentions to me.

And then his gaze fixes, changes. He reaches out tentatively and strokes my breast with a light touch. His look is long and lustful.

This time I do not need to question. I *know*. His touch disgusts me to my very core. It is not academic but lecherous. Each stroke is an abomination. There is no learning to be had here. There is only lust, desire.

Hate swells throughout my stiff form.

Oh, but I will have him. *He will be mine.*

I stare up at him. His nose. The curve of his lips. His jaw. I smell his tang.

Tonight, a voice in my head says. *We will meet again tonight.*

I FIND MYSELF STANDING in the dark. I blink. Blink again. It takes some time for my eyes to adjust to the dim light. My heart sinks as I realize that I stand in my dress of black—the dress that is not mine.

But wait. I am moving.

Am I free? Oh, the relief of it!

But no, the relief is only temporary, for it seems my will is not my own. I want to stretch, to bend, to look around myself. To locate Emily.

I cannot.

I am not allowed such liberties.

Instead, I am compelled to move forward. I move like a puppet—an unseen god tugging upon my strings, forcing me to complete a task I have no knowledge of. Silently, I move along the hallway, the black skirts rustling, bile rising inside me with the injustice of it. *Release me!* I cry out to no one with the voice I do not have.

I hear voices behind me.

"Truly amazing," one person says.

The anatomist, I believe.

"Did I not tell you the magic would take this time?"

Briar.

"I expected no less."

Unmistakable.

It is Elizabeth.

Elizabeth.

But how is this possible? I saw her upon that table—a waxen model herself. And yet she is not like me—she speaks as if she is free of Briar's chains. Oh, I do not understand how this works, this monstrous magic. How can it be that we come and go from these lifeless forms? It makes no sense. Such a thing is not possible! And yet, it happens. I am somehow pulled into the model, trapped inside it like an animal in a cage. And the next moment, on Briar's command, I might be standing, dressed, flesh and blood—the model lying on the table behind me. It is a terrible, evil magic of the most sinister sort.

"I will accompany you," Elizabeth says. "I must see the performance with my own eyes."

"No," Briar replies. "It is too great a risk."

"But there is no risk at all," Elizabeth argues.

"You will be noticed in an instant."

"I will wear a hooded cloak. And I *will* come." Elizabeth's voice is firm.

I know she will win. For she always does, somehow.

Briar sighs, defeated. "I will fetch a cloak. But you must stay close by me."

"Happily," Elizabeth purrs.

There are footsteps. A cloak is fetched. The world continues around me, behind me. But I am apart from it. I can only listen in, hope for a hint of what is to come.

Eventually I hear a muttering. Briar.

And then, once again, my body betrays me. It moves ever onward, gliding smoothly from the anatomist's studio, out onto the dark streets of Holborn.

I am forced to walk swiftly through the thick night air, as if drawn to a fated destination. I know not where I go, but dread permeates my bones as it becomes clear I have an objective to fulfill. I have been tasked with a mission, and nothing shall stop my grim march.

Inside this shell of myself I flail and cry and scream, and it is all for naught. I am made to traverse the shadowy streets, as if my will is seemingly my own. And all the time, my mind buzzes with questions. *Where am I going? What am I doing? What is happening to me?* I want to reach out and throw myself upon the mercy of each person I see. *Save me. Help me. Awaken me from this nightmare.*

But I know this is no dream—no nightmare, even. Somehow, it is Elizabeth's doing. It is her revenge. Her revenge against Emily. Against me. Against the world.

Every so often, I catch sight of the black fabric encasing me—black as the night, as my soul.

I catch sight, too, of a lurking Briar, Elizabeth in her hooded cloak. Briar toys with that necklace at her throat again.

Before I know what is happening, I take a sharp right turn.

I am outside a tavern.

I am forced to wait in the shadows of the building's thick, weathered beams. I am as silent and still as when I am forced to lie upon the anatomist's table. Men come and go through the tavern door, some laughing, some stumbling. The hour is obviously late, and the men have had their fill.

And then... I smell him.

That tang.

It is unmistakable. Every fiber of my being is forced to stand to attention.

He exits the tavern with two friends.

The threesome walk along together for some time. One peels off with a drunken wave. My target continues with his associate. On and on they walk, as I slip through the dim light in close pursuit.

Finally, they pause. There is a minute or two of chitchat. Another wave.

And then he is alone.

My lips are forced upward in a garish grimace—something akin to a smile—as he starts off again.

I cross the street toward him, and he hears my footfall and turns. When he sees me, the set of his shoulders relaxes and he continues on his way.

I am no threat to him.

I am just a woman.

I close in on him within moments, all the time wanting to warn him. To call out. To tell him to run, tell him that he has found himself caught up in the devil's work.

But in my silent state I have no hope of this.

There is only my steadfast advance, his impending doom.

"You there, what do you want?" He finally turns to confront me when I am a little too close.

"Why, only the same as you," says a silky voice that is not my own, yet is mine.

"I have no money upon me," he tells me. There is no recognition in his face. He does not remember me. I am no one to him, nothing.

"There is no need for money," I tell him. It is all the enticement he needs. I take his hand and lead him a short distance down a passage. He comes willingly. In the dark and the quiet,

I slip that hand inside my bodice. I let it stroke my breast just as it stroked me earlier this day, as I lay on the anatomist's table, helpless, exposed.

Moments ago, I wanted to cry out, to tell him to run. But when I feel his hand upon my breast once more, it is easy to slip the knife from my skirt. And as the blade flashes silver in the moonlight between us, and as I thrust it detachedly once, twice, thrice, with a newfound strength that shocks me to my very core, I can only think...

You deserve this.

MY RETURN TO the anatomist's studio is swift, Briar and Elizabeth racing along before me. My eyes scan the streets, searching desperately for anyone who might save me, sense my predicament. But no one notices me as I scurry along. I am carried along an enchanted thread, reeled back against my will by a powerful force. Knowing I am being made to return, I struggle to cut the filament that controls me. Moments ago I had the strength of three women. So why can I not find the strength to do this, to free myself from my chains? I want to be anywhere but here. I am appalled at my actions. Appalled at what I felt, what I wanted in that moment. It is abhorrent, this thing I have done. *I* am abhorrent. I am no murderess. And yet I am—I am!—for I have murdered a man. He is now gone from this world. It is a sin. A dreadful sin. Whether it was of my will or not, it was by my hand, and surely I will pay for it. If not in this world, in the next.

I see Elizabeth slip out of the murky shadows and through the door to the anatomist's studio moments before I make my own approach. She pushes past Briar and tips back the hood of her cloak. The light of the moon shows that she is as beautiful as she ever was. It does not seem as if she is under the direction of enchantment at all.

"We are returned," I hear Elizabeth call out. And now that she stands before me in the candlelight of the entry, I see that she has truly been returned to her finest form. She looks as her breathing model looked at repose on the table—in the first flush of youth, not sickened and pale, as she was that night we journeyed to the anatomist's. The version that stands before me is rosy of cheek, her hair thick and lustrous. I do not know how this is possible. How has she been allowed to turn Emily and me into monsters while she is allowed her own free will? And yet I am not surprised at all, because Elizabeth, I see now, will always find a way to get what she wants.

Always.

She will let nothing stand in her path. There is no hesitation in felling any person who stands between her and what she desires, and there is no guilt after she has done so. I had thought it was only gentlemen she despised, but now I see it is anyone who is in her way. Man, woman, beast—none are safe. She thinks only of herself, of her own needs. There is no room for any other in her heart.

Now I recall what she had said when I'd drunk Briar's draft, right before the world darkened around me forever. Elizabeth had repeated Emily's words—the conversation she had overheard as she lay, feverish and dying, at the town house.

I could hear your every traitorous word. Unwilling to fetch a doctor, hoping I might die by the morn.

Yes, Elizabeth always finds a way to get what she wants. And what she desires now is to be as beautiful as she once was. Oh, and to exact revenge on those whom she perceives to have wronged her. Let us not forget that.

In this hell I am now trapped in, Briar approaches me.

Again she touches that odd necklace of braided hair that lies at her neck.

"The spell has taken," she croons. "It works."

"So it would seem." Elizabeth sounds pleased with herself.

"I have done it," Briar says.

"*We* have done it," Elizabeth corrects her.

"You have done well." The anatomist sweeps in to join the pair, while I can only stand there, mute, forever silenced. "It is fine work. I have watched that student for many months. How he sickened me. You have made her sense the indelicate touch, the lustful gaze, and she has arisen to right the wrong. One by one, we will hunt them down, these vermin. Oh, how they will pay for it! How they shall get what they deserve!"

Gagged, I can say naught, do naught. Internally, my fists beat against the cage I am locked inside as they celebrate. *Let me out!* I cry over and over. And I am reminded of Polly—poor Polly—her wings beating futiley against the bars of *her* cage. I am no different. My actual limbs lie deadened and useless to me. What can I do? While I remain conscious, I try valiantly to recall all that Lucy the maid had told me. If only I had better understood the information she had been attempting to impart... for I have so many questions now. Perhaps there is a way out of this jail? Something I might do? Some... incantation I might speak? That muttering that emanates from Briar's lips—it must mean something. That necklace of hair—it is important. I know it is.

I recall Lucy saying that the models were a trap. That the anatomist had a hidden agenda—revenge against the men who did not deserve to practice medicine. She has hidden herself in plain sight, disguising herself as a man, so that she might cull their ranks herself. Elizabeth is a contemptible creature, but I see the anatomist as worse. She wishes to gain revenge against those who would suppress her knowledge and skill, but she will use another woman to enact that revenge. The thought of it sickens me—that a woman might use another in such a way. What else might she make me do? What skills does Briar possess that might enable this trio of wickedness to coerce me into even more unspeakable acts?

Also, this Lucy who promised me so much—where has she gone? Have they found her out while I have slumbered? She said she was stationed in the house to help me, but she is now nowhere to be seen. I see no hope for myself if they have discovered her.

"What now, Briar?" the anatomist asks.

"We must clean her up," Briar answers. "For when she rises again, it will be in this same state. That is not what I aim for. There is more work to do on the magic. Far more. I must find a way to make multiples—multiple versions, renewed afresh each time. I want a number of her to rise at my command, so that I may call upon ten Eleanors in a row that might do my bidding. And when I have done that, I will attempt to place her within different objects—small objects, portable objects."

For a moment, I forget my hate and despair and try desperately to follow the conversation. Multiple versions? Ten Eleanors? And different objects . . . What can she mean?

"For now, you must focus on this task alone," the anatomist reminds her. "For you have not yet fulfilled our agreement."

"That is true," Elizabeth replies.

I know then that there is more, that I will be called upon to do more. My heart fills with dread at the thought of it.

"Yes, yes." Briar brushes their comments away. "But for now we must tidy her up."

"Clever of you to put her in a black dress." Elizabeth rounds on me, eyeing my form.

Now I understand. Black. Blood cannot be seen easily upon a black dress.

Briar mutters some words and I am forced to stagger forward. This time, to my table. I stand beside my other form, a sheet covering my model to protect it. I have not yet seen what lies beneath, what I look like in waxen form. I think of Emily—of Emily and her interchangeable parts—the horror of her beautiful face eaten away, and I wonder if it is better if I do not know what horrors Elizabeth's anger has fashioned for me.

My arms are lifted. I am sponged. My sullied skin and dress are cleansed.

But my soul shall not be cleansed, I know it. It is as black as my garb now, and the stains will never be erased. If I could tremble in fear, I would do so. In the knowledge of what I have done. In fear of what is to come. I am both desperate to be returned to the dark, so I might forget, and terrified to be, because I know it means I will soon be awakened again, and each awakening brings not hope now, but terror.

After my limbs have been wiped clean, Elizabeth approaches. She skirts the bowl upon the floor, a bloody pool of freezing cold water swirling within it, and stands back, inspecting me.

"Oh, do not give me that look," she says, as if I have any control over my expression at all. "What hope was there for you before this? Before me? What did you think would become of you when you ran away to the city? Even before you started, you were finished. There was always going to be a price to pay, Eleanor."

Even before you started, you were finished. How her words

sting. How they burn. There was never any hope for me. For Emily. She is right, too, that there was a price to pay. It could not have been higher. And Elizabeth has made sure that Emily and I paid it for her.

Briar mutters more words, touches the necklace of hair. There is that strange pull, and I am returned to my living sarcophagus.

I lie, staring upward, unblinking, on the table.

"Until tomorrow." Elizabeth's golden hair falls over me. She bends down to gaze into my fixed eyes. She knows full well that I cannot move to sit up—to spit on her, which is what I would like to do. "Yes, tomorrow we shall awaken you both. And tomorrow you shall kill together."

Before I can take this information in, I am falling, once more, into the dark abyss.

I OPEN MY EYES to a darkened room.

As soon as I awaken—as soon as I am aware—I long to be returned to the shadows. For I know that if I have been summoned, the nightmare will truly begin. There is no freedom to be found in being allowed movement. There is only the knowledge of what I will be forced to do with it.

The next thing I know, there is that pull I cannot reject, and I find myself standing, waiting in the entryway of the anatomist's studio. I know this much already—this evening I seek two men. There is a strange sensation building inside me, an insatiable hunger. I cannot name them. I cannot see their faces in my mind's eye. But I *know* them, can feel them, am drawn to them. The beast that inhabits me can smell them, will hunt them to the end of time.

I hear a shuffling beside me and catch a glimpse of someone out of the corner of my eye. There is a swish of familiar black skirts. But wait. They are not my skirts, but Emily's. *Emily!* I can feel her warmth. I long to reach out to her, to speak to her. But we are both shackled by magic.

Briar circles us, muttering, her hand clasping that braided necklace of hair. Three strands bound tightly together. Mine. Emily's. Elizabeth's. I had not understood at first, had pondered the different colors. The bracelet she wore at the pleasure gardens had been fashioned out of rich, dark hair—Lavender's, I see now. It has now disappeared, as has Lavender—and talk of her. Has Briar disposed of her somehow? It does not bear thinking about.

Footsteps. The anatomist appears beside Briar. "Will Elizabeth not be accompanying you this evening?"

"I have instructed her to return to her model."

"I thought she could come and go as she pleased, unlike the other two. I thought the spell upon the hair enabled her to do so. Was that not the deal?"

"It was. And she can. I told her I am working on my spell, strengthening it, and that all three souls must be housed within their models for me to do so, but the truth is simply that she tires me with her endless demands. I wish to see if the pair can carry out their task independent of me. I do not need Elizabeth demanding to attend, or watching over my shoulder, all opinions and gibes."

"She will be furious when she awakes."

Briar shrugs. "Then I will deal with her fury when she awakes. She won't dare awaken until I tell her it is safe to do so, for she fears being lost like Lavender."

If I could gasp, I would do so. If only Elizabeth could hear Briar now. She would be livid to hear how the witch speaks of her! Oh, but this is good. This is very good indeed. I attempt in vain to turn my head, to catch Emily's eye. She is standing slightly behind me, just out of sight. I take heart in her presence, though. She is with me. We are together. And she will have heard Briar's words concerning Elizabeth as well.

Only moments later, we are commanded to move forward, to exit the dingy entry of the anatomist's studio. We are coerced into marching via an unseen force, into parading the cold streets, side by side, set on a destination that we do not know. If only my will were my own, so that I might turn to Emily. Speak to her. Take her hand and run with her. Run away from this place. From these fiends that have enslaved us. Instead, silent as death, Emily and I stalk the streets. Every so often, I catch a glimpse of her out of the corner of my eye. As do I, she has a black shawl draped over her head and shoulders. Any passerby will think our shawls are for warmth, the black for mourning. Only we know the shawls are for privacy; the black for mourning our old lives, for disguising spilled blood.

After some time, I realize Emily is hunched slightly and looks to be in pain. I guess that she has been offered no relief in this hellish new form she has been given. Elizabeth may have risen fresh and new, but Emily has been given no reprieve from her sickness. She is being made to march across the city in her deathly ill state. As for myself, I have noticed the old churning in my belly from time to time. But I do not know what it means. Am I still with child? My model might have told me, but fearful of the horrors I would surely see, I did not dare to look at it when I might have. Oh, what has Briar done to us? Are we alive? Are we dead? Can we escape these forms somehow, or is there no hope for us? Perhaps this is a purgatory of some description. If only I could go back in time and ask Lucy these questions.

I think back to Emily's constant pleading with me to run.

How I wish I had listened to her from the start. But then... perhaps I would not change so very much of the past few months, given the chance. For if I had not met Elizabeth, I would never have met Emily. Even now I could not run, given the opportunity, for I could never abandon Emily to suffer this cruel fate alone. Just as I know she could not—would not—leave me.

So we march on, unwilling soldiers.

Though I do not know where we are headed this evening, my body could find my targets anywhere. They cannot hide from me. It is inevitable that this evening will end in their deaths. They are blissfully unaware that they are drawing their final breaths, eating their final meals, that I am on the way to extinguish the flame of life.

A newsboy attempts to press some papers upon us as we pass by. He cries out about the grisly murders of some students of medicine, and I strain to hear. Does this mean that there has been more than one murder? Is it not just I who have been sent out to prey upon the anatomist's students over the past dark nights? Has Emily been sent out as well, even though I have not seen her before tonight? I doubt Elizabeth is sullying her hands. It cannot be Lavender behind the killings, for with that bracelet of Briar's gone from sight, I am convinced that Lavender is now useless to the wicked trio. What were the words Lucy had used? "Lost to us," I believe.

As I march on, I wonder if Lavender's fate will be our own. To be trapped forever in our models—that end would be a fate worse than death. What truly troubles me, however, is that I do not understand how this hunting can continue. For surely we cannot be sent out onto the streets of London to kill night after night. Someone will see us. We will be found out. And then they will be discovered—the anatomist and Briar.

Or will they?

Perhaps this is a more clever ruse than I thought, for just as the anatomist has found a way to disappear in plain sight, in the man's disguise she wears, so the anatomist, Briar and Elizabeth have found a way for their murderers to disappear in plain sight. I may be recognized upon the street, but I can easily be made to disappear into waxen form. As such, I cannot be tried or hanged. There is little use in stringing up a wax model. And the anatomist's, Briar's and Elizabeth's hands are clean of actual blood.

And Elizabeth herself? How will she fare in all of this? Unlike Emily and me, she has bargained her way to a better position, as she seems to be always able to do. She is as slippery as an eel. Her looks and health have been restored to her. She is not confined to a waxen prison but seemingly can come and go as she pleases. And I suppose she shall have the revenge she spoke of. *I will take them all for this* she had said on reading Mr. Corbyn's entry in *Harris's List. Every. Last. One.* She chose to have her revenge at any cost—perhaps even at the cost of her soul. But I take heart in Briar's words that I overheard. Briar can trick Elizabeth into retreating into her model. Perhaps she can even force her to stay there. This weakens Elizabeth, makes her vulnerable, especially as Briar and Elizabeth argue. Emily and I have that much. Even if it is little, it is something.

I am forced to take a sharp right. The smell of them is stronger now. We are getting close. A group of men amble down the quiet street, and Emily and I must make way for them as the passage narrows. She is forced in front of me, close enough to touch now. How I long to stretch out my hand to her, to speak to her.

The men pass, and she drops back by my side once more.

Another turn. And another.

And then we have arrived.

It is another tavern. And, oh, the stench of them... Above the ale. The wine. The rum. The cheap but filling food. Everything inside me quivers with the thought of my faceless quarry being extinguished. It must be done. I follow Emily inside, and we glide ever upward, taking some stairs to a private dining room. There, a group of men are gathered. They talk and laugh in the dim light, some shrouded by shadows in the corners of the room. Emily and I instinctively evade the servants who furnish them with food and drink. I sniff out my prey. *There. There!* I finally catch sight of the pair we have been sent to hunt.

And I see it is two men who are familiar to me.

It is Dr. Chidworth and Mr. Corbyn.

I feel a smile lift the corner of my lips, as it has done before. But this time I wonder at being allowed the expression, for tonight it aligns with my true feelings. It is as if I have smiled of my own accord. Here are two men who do not deserve to walk the face of this earth, or breathe its air. Now I know I truly will go to hell, for on this outing I will not struggle against my task. Instead, I will relish it. Relish the murder of Mr. Corbyn, who debauched Emily. Who thrust upon her some terrible disease. And Dr. Chidworth, who worsened it. Who sealed her fate with his "cure" that left her belly distended and putrid, fever racking her body.

I feel Emily close in beside me, and while I cannot see her face, I imagine a predatory smile on her lips also.

Yes. Finally, these men will get what they deserve. We will make sure of it. *Together.*

When the time is right, I lower my shawl, as Emily lowers hers beside me. We are revealed to Dr. Chidworth, appearing in the doorway in his line of sight. He pauses, stares at us as if he has seen a ghost, then turns to speak to Mr. Corbyn, on his right. Mr. Corbyn laughs loudly with a friend, raucous and drunk. But when he hears what Chidworth has to say, he sobers quickly and his dark eyes flick up to the doorway.

But I am already gone, Emily following in my wake.

Along a hallway, then a pause at the end. Are they following? We wait until we are sure of it.

"Hey!" a voice calls out. Mr. Corbyn's, I think. "You there! Come back here."

We ascend another flight of stairs, always remaining just out of sight. It is quiet up here. We are made to pause once more. And then we are off again, to the end of the present hallway and to an empty room.

Yet another pause, in the doorway as they close in.

Quick footsteps. Searching.

I reach for the pearl-handled knife tucked into my bodice.

I must be at the ready.

Voices. They are almost upon us now.

Or, as it turns out, we are almost upon *them*.

OUR ATTACK IS vicious.

We work together. Easily, as if this is a dance we have rehearsed many times, preparing ourselves for our grand performance. We have learned our steps by heart. Readied ourselves, drawn breath. Entered with aplomb. And now here we are, on the stage.

A curtsy to the awaiting audience, and we shall begin.

Or Emily shall, for it should be her time to shine. I want this to be her thrilling victory, want her to squeeze every last drop of enjoyment from the vanquishing of our enemy.

I step to one side so that she might reach Mr. Corbyn first. Back at King Street, I had railed at the thought of him—wickedness personified. Well, he had no idea of the true wickedness in the world, and now it has gathered like a storm cloud and shall rain down upon him. I had wanted to make him pay, and I have gotten my wish. There is not a doubt in my mind that he must die this evening, and that he must die by Emily's hand.

I watch as Emily advances, her pearl-handled knife—the sister to mine—gripped tightly in her hand. She takes him from behind, slitting his throat as easily as slicing through butter. Despite the affliction that makes her stoop with pain, she finds spell-given strength to do now what she has so long dreamed of. There is a short, sharp squeal such as I have heard the swine make in Spitalfields Market. Blood sprays her face, her gown, but she does not seem unhappy about it. And I take delight in that small smile, rigid upon her lips as she watches him slump to the floor, a thick pool of scarlet soon surrounding him.

Dr. Chidworth attempts to run, of course. To scream. To cry out. But he cannot. For I have pinned him to a wall. In this moment I am thankful for Briar's despicable magic, for I would not have had the strength to hold him back in such a way in my previous life. I keep one hand firmly at his throat, just as he pinned me in Emily's chamber.

Both of us may as well have her, he had said.

And now both of us have him, which seems only fair.

His eyes bulge, and I care not. *I care not.* I would not stop—could not stop—even if Briar's magic fell away. And I see in his eyes what must have appeared in my own that day—that day he pinned me in the selfsame position. Surprise. Fear. Shock.

Oh, but it would be something to slice his throat such as Emily has just done with Mr. Corbyn.

But I will not.

For, as I said, the pleasure should be all Emily's.

So I wait for her to be done with Mr. Corbyn. I wait for her to take her fill of enjoyment.

And this she does. For she does not stop with Mr. Corbyn's throat but moves on to swiftly disrobe him. She cleaves open his belly, such as we had seen on viewing Lavender, and with a newfound knowledge of anatomy, she proceeds to display some of his organs for good measure.

I make sure I angle Dr. Chidworth so that he may have a full view. He is a man of medicine, after all. Surely he will be interested. He may even learn something!

And all the time, Dr. Chidworth writhes and protests under my tight grasp, his eyes bulging farther and farther until I believe they may exit his very head.

Finally, Emily is done.

With Mr. Corbyn, that is. For Dr. Chidworth's trial is just about to begin.

I pass him into her care and stand back so that I might have a better view.

Her attack is frenzied. Not an easy slit to the throat this time but a feverish, frenetic stabbing, so quick that it is barely perceptible to the eye. His belly. His groin. I see that she focuses on those areas that gave her so much pain—pain provided by Dr. Chidworth, who was meant to heal her. When he slumps, life draining from him, I push him upward so that Emily may continue. Only when she has decided that she is finished with him do I let him thump to the floor.

And the sound is sweet to my ears.

BACK AT THE anatomist's studio, Emily is removed from my presence, from my line of sight. I can hear Briar attending to her, sponging her. Elizabeth is awakened now, and the trio chatter excitedly as they work on Emily, pleased with what they have done.

With what *we* have done.

I try desperately to turn my thoughts to anything other than the slumped forms that we left behind in the attic room, for now that the thrill of it all has passed, I am torn. The delight I had felt as I watched Emily exact her revenge. The sweet sound of those men hitting the floor, devoid of life, as still as our waxen forms. The relief of knowing that they could not hurt us, or others, ever again. But then... oh, then... The ever-widening pool of blood seeping into the boards. The realization of what had occurred at our hands. Of course I had wanted Dr. Chidworth and Mr. Corbyn removed from this world—had wanted them to suffer—but now that those moments are over, I am not so sure as to my feelings. I take no delight now in having their blood on my hands, having the vision of their final moments seared into my memory. I had looked on with such glee, but now I feel only horror at what we have done—what we have been made to do. Their actions in life showed who they were, but my actions are not my own. I refuse to believe it. My actions reveal only who Elizabeth is, what she had Briar turn me into.

I am, once again, Elizabeth's puppet.

I am not a murderer. I am not. I would not have murdered these men had I not been made to, however real my hate for them was.

And Emily—that smile that had played on her lips—was it real? How much of what we feel is because of Elizabeth's doing? How much is because of Briar's magic? I do not know and cannot tell. When we were returned to the anatomist's studio this evening, there was no wicked grin upon Emily's face. Instead, tears had stained her cheeks.

I am afraid that if this continues much longer, we will lose ourselves—our true selves—for I find it increasingly difficult to remember who I am. In vain, I attempt to recall who I was in happier times. I cling to any carefree memories I can find. I recall falling asleep as my father read to me. Being released by my stepmother to run an errand in the village on a sunny day. Curling up in bed with Emily to read another amusing, lurid passage about Fanny Hill's adventures. But each time, the memory fades and the vision returns. The men. The blood. I cannot escape the thought of it. I will go mad, trapped as I am, with only these memories to keep me company. So I cling to the remembrance of Emily, of our connection. That is more real to me now than who I once was—and, I feel, truer.

My attention is finally caught by the conversation in the anatomist's studio as it turns to Emily herself.

"Her body is not strong," Briar says. "Perhaps she is not of as much use to us as we thought she would be."

What does that mean? I think of Lavender, lost Lavender. What will they do with Emily?

There is a noise upon the wooden stairs.

Briar, the anatomist and Elizabeth gather together.

"Lucy! Go back to bed immediately." The anatomist steps into the doorway, blocking Lucy's view of the scene.

"Sorry, sir. I heard voices. I thought you might need something."

"I do not require assistance. You are to return to bed now."

"Yes, sir."

Lucy. Lucy is still here.

She has not been discovered, or sent away.

My heart swells with hope. Perhaps she will find a way to help us, to release us, before Emily . . .

The anatomist closes the door, and Briar comes over to begin her fierce scrubbing of my hands.

Elizabeth, in her golden dress, moves between Emily and me. Day to our night. Life to our death. Free.

"Do not look at me so. Are you not happy?" she says to me, as if I might be allowed to reply. "Those vile men—they got everything they deserved," she says. She circles me, basking in the glory of what she has achieved. She has triumphed against them. "Do you not see? We have had our revenge. There will be no repercussions. It could not be more perfect. What fools they were to cross me. I am only sorry I did not bear witness to it."

I have never hated Elizabeth as much as I hate her in this moment. *Happy? No repercussions? It could not be more perfect?* Emily has been sent out on the streets in pain. We have been forced to murder. We are trapped.

But I only stare at her, unblinking, unable to reply. And all the time I think, *How can she not see that this cannot last?* You do not make deals with the devil and win.

But perhaps I had not banked on the devil being Elizabeth herself.

I DO NOT KNOW how many nights pass. I know only when I am awakened—by another student's errant touch, a lustful gaze—and then I must hunt again, for my hunger is deep and strong and pulses through my veins.

I hunt alone.

I have not seen Elizabeth for some time, and I live in hope that she and Briar bicker even more than before, that Briar has told her some lie and bidden her to enter her pretty tomb.

But Emily—I worry for her. Where is she? Have they discarded her, as I am sure they have discarded Lavender?

I do not know. I can only hope, which feels futile. What is left to hope for? Our pretty cottage, with its roses by the front door?

But my feelings do not matter. I am naught but a hollowed-out husk of a person. There is nothing inside. I am only this shell that is made to move, to perform.

To kill.

Sometimes there is a clue as to who I will meet in the dark of the coming night. He will touch me by day. My eyes will flicker open, and I will know he has a date with destiny. Other times I have no clue as to who I will be forced to slaughter. Sometimes Briar whispers a name in my ear, puts a piece of clothing under my nose to inhale a scent, shows me a drawing of a face.

But I always find him, my mark.

Always.

Briar's malevolent magic finds a way to make this happen.

They blend into one, those faceless men. They are nothing to me, just as I was nothing to them. I am that automaton, forever hammering at the dulcimer. Feeling nothing. Awakening, rising, murdering.

On the streets, the newspaperboys are in a frenzy. They do not need to thrust their papers in the faces of people who pass by, for the people are now queuing in order to purchase them. Everyone wants to know about the terrible medical murders gripping the city. There is much speculation as to who the Bow Street Runners think the killer might be. I hear the newsboys cry out about revenge—how such frenzied attacks can mean only that the murderer is consumed by revenge, perhaps after the loss of a loved one at a doctor's hands. They are half-right, I suppose. The anatomist is consumed by revenge—angry about being shut out of the world of medicine while men such as Dr. Chidworth effectively murdered their patients, and her students of anatomy drool over her models. Elizabeth was set on revenge after being blackmailed by Mr. Corbyn, turned against by Dr. Chidworth. And she had gotten her revenge too. But Briar? The reasons for her involvement with the anatomist and

Elizabeth have not, as yet, been revealed to me, though I often ruminate on her talk of copies, versions. What did she mean by those words? What is she planning? Whatever it is, I know it goes beyond the anatomist's studio. Her vision is broader than these small rooms, and I doubt it can be contained.

That gaunt, skeletal hand of Death slips its cold fingers into mine night after night, and leads me to a new haunt. One evening I am prepared for yet another journey. I am standing in the hall, awaiting my imminent departure. Speechless. Motionless. Briar fusses as she always does before I am ordered to leave. She adjusts the shawl that she uses to hide my appearance as I walk the streets, checks the knife that is tucked into my bodice. I am interested to note that she always checks the knife out of my sight. Why does she do this? When she checks my knife this evening, she calls out to the anatomist that there is a problem.

"I sharpened it myself," the anatomist replies.

"It is not that," Briar says. "Fetch Elizabeth's. Eleanor can use her knife this evening. Elizabeth will not be needing it anyway, not if I can help it. Did you know I have had her in that model for two days straight now? She has no idea."

The anatomist snorts. "She will not be pleased when she arises."

"She is not pleased about many things, which is why I keep her in her model."

I am glad to hear that Elizabeth and Briar continue to bicker. This is good. Facing the wall, I cannot see who comes and goes, but I hear footsteps upon the stair. Behind me, Briar toys with my knife. At least that is what I believe she is doing as I listen in. She taps again and again upon the small hallway table.

Eventually the anatomist brings Elizabeth's knife. Briar

takes both knives away and returns after some time. The pair whisper under their breath.

"That should suffice," Briar finally says, tucking a knife—Elizabeth's, I suppose—into my bodice.

Briar's detestable muttering begins once more, and I am whirled about and ejected into the cold night air, the door to the studio slamming shut behind me. Panicked, I attempt to clear my mind, not to dwell upon what I am about to do—be made to do—but it is no use. Of course I can think of nothing but this. And of Emily. Will she be made to stalk the streets as I do this evening? Or is she now too ill to do so? I am not sure which is worse.

I am made to walk farther than ever before. A man's scent guides me to a chophouse. I am made to stand and wait by its window. I can see them inside—a group of young men. I am made to hold off, something in me sensing that the hour is too early, the men too sober. I stand, waiting, in the shadows. When a few of the men look out the window and catch my eye, I am forced to draw back farther into the shadows.

I do not know how long I wait in the freezing cold. Minutes. Hours. What does it matter now? Time has become meaningless to me, and my comfort is nothing to my captors.

And then the man gets up, perhaps to relieve himself.

I am forced to attention.

Now. *Now.*

My shawl is drawn up. I enter the chophouse, following him. Past the other patrons. Down a hallway.

I am closing in.

Just as we are about to exit the building, he turns unexpectedly and lunges at me, whipping the shawl from my head. "You were outside," he says. "I saw you watching us." But then his gaze narrows. "Those eyes. I knew I recognized them. I know you..."

Now. *Now.*

No, a flicker of something inside me wells up in reply.

No, I will not.

I reach for the knife in my bodice—Elizabeth's knife—and to my great surprise, I am able to hurl it away from me.

"What do you think you're—" The man sees the weapon and cries out, realizing I had meant to use it upon him. He makes a grab for the knife as it clatters to the floor and skitters, the mother-of-pearl handle loosening and detaching as it goes. I see that it is stuffed with a clump of wiry material, which flies out of the handle. For weight, I suppose.

What does this mean? I have managed an action of my own accord, of some free will. What else might I be able to do?

But no. I jolt, jerk. Something is wrong. The unseen hand that controls me struggles, but I am forced to take a step closer to the student, who brandishes the knife now. He has put it back together. Another step closer. I am made to pause again. And then a swell. My limbs twitch against my will. I can fight the spell no longer.

I am turned about and made to run.

"You! Stop!" he calls out.

But I am already out the door, past the privies, down a lane and gone.

I am guided through dim alleys and quiet streets until, finally, what feels like an eternity later, I reach the anatomist's studio yet again. The force becomes stronger as I close in. I could not overwhelm it again, however hard I tried.

I hurl myself at the door, which soon opens. They all appear in the entry—the anatomist, Briar and, I am surprised to see, Elizabeth.

"What has occurred, girl? Speak," Briar says. She looks spent, and her fingers are tightly entwined in the necklace of hair at her throat.

And then I find I *can* speak. I want to ask where Emily is, but I am not allowed this. I choke on those words. I may only answer her question. "He recognized me. There was a tussle." My voice is husky through lack of use. "He has the knife. Elizabeth's knife."

"What were you thinking?" Elizabeth screeches at Briar. "Giving her my knife! How dare you? And now look what has happened!"

Briar ignores her.

"Where is the other girl?" the anatomist asks Briar.

She grunts. "Still hunting. I have called her back. This one went too far. I could not control her properly. They must remain close by, or I must accompany them on their travels."

"Perhaps your spell is too weak," Elizabeth hisses. "Perhaps you are not the witch you believe you are. I begin to doubt your skills, Briar, but I hope you can perfect your work soon, for I wish for my strength to be beyond belief before I take on Sir William myself, as per our bargain."

I can only look on, silent and still, taking all of this in. That Emily lives (if one may call this living) gladdens my heart, though I worry for her having been sent to hunt. It does not surprise me to hear of Elizabeth's bargain with Briar—that she wants to have her revenge on Sir William.

"Were you followed?" Elizabeth approaches, her gaze intent upon me.

I cannot answer her.

Elizabeth turns to Briar. "Ask her," she demands.

Briar stills for a moment. "Were you followed?" She repeats Elizabeth's question, and this time I find I must reply.

"I could not say," I tell her. I am glad to see that Elizabeth looks annoyed that I have responded to Briar and not to her.

The anatomist paces. "This is not good. If she has been recognized, the student will come here—and soon, no doubt."

"To what end?" Elizabeth scoffs. "To view a wax model? What does it matter if he comes here?"

"It matters because it ties her to us," the anatomist barks. "There are too many now, too many men who have perished who had ties to this establishment."

"And whose fault is that?" Elizabeth argues. Then she turns from the anatomist and focuses in on Briar. "The knife. We must get it back." A knowing look passes between them.

"The knife does not matter. We will simply purchase another," the anatomist says, waving a hand. "Now, quickly, we must—"

"Quiet," Elizabeth snaps. She grabs Briar and drags her into a corner. They argue in heated tones.

I look on, not understanding. Why is the knife so important to Elizabeth? What are they not sharing with the anatomist?

A banging on the door sees everyone startle.

"They are here already," the anatomist exclaims. "Away with you both."

"I will do as I please," Elizabeth retorts. But I notice that she leaves the scene as requested.

"I cannot force the other one back into her model until it is close," Briar says under her breath. She begins to mutter, and the pulling sensation floods my body once more.

I am returned to my model self.

But surprisingly, the darkness does not envelop me. An oversight on Briar's part? Or was she too hurried to complete her mutterings? I am not sure. But I can see. I can hear. Perhaps she wants me this way.

There is more banging. The door is opened.

"Yes?" I hear the anatomist say. "What is it? Whatever can you want at this late hour?"

"This is the place. In here," a voice says. I know who is at the door even before he speaks. It is the student from the chophouse, my mark. I can smell him. A group bursts inside, and I hear heavy footsteps pound across the floor, perhaps those of four or five people.

"This way! Here she is. This one." He appears above me, breathing heavily from exertion.

Several men join him.

"What is this?" one of them says. I see a familiar flash of blue coat. He is a Bow Street Runner, I think. Elizabeth had pointed them out to me on the streets of London before—men who are paid to patrol and keep the peace.

Another blue-coated man speaks. "Are you drunk, young man? We did not come here to be shown a doll. We are supposed to be out hunting murderers."

"I am not drunk. It is a model. Do you not understand? It is as I told you on the way here—they are modeled on *real women*. The anatomist is always saying so. He has commissioned four now, from an Italian master, but they have all been fashioned upon living, breathing women. They are not dolls, as you say."

"Is that so?" the first Bow Street Runner says.

"That is correct," the anatomist replies. "My models are modeled on real women, but that is where our connection ends, for after the models sit for me, I have no further contact with them. I believe one has gone on to Bath. The three others live just off St. James's Square, on King Street, from what I recall. They have a place of... work there. Or they said they were setting one up when they modeled for me, months ago."

Oh, if only I could cry out. *I am here, good sirs! I am imprisoned!*

Save me! But I cannot. I can only watch. And wait. And hope. Where is Lucy? Why does she not come and tell the Bow Street Runner what is truly happening here? Of course, this is not possible. Just as the Bow Street Runner is annoyed at the student for bringing him to see a "doll," he would only brush away Lucy's tale of witches and sorcery and revenge, and I could not blame him for doing so.

"And you, madam? What is your business here? Why do you mutter so?"

"It is an affliction, sir. I cannot help it. You must excuse me. I work here, sir, assisting the anatomist. It is a busy studio, with many students, and thus there is much to do."

Another knock comes on the front door.

"And who do we have now? This is like something you see upon the stage." The second Bow Street Runner crosses the floor to inspect the new entry to the scene.

I cannot see what is happening, so I must listen closely.

"This is Emily, one of our servants," the anatomist says. "She was sent out on an errand."

"Bit late to be out. There is a murderer crawling the streets."

If I could laugh at this I would. If only he knew. If only he could stop us. I hope Emily was called back before she could find what she was sent out to destroy this evening.

"Lucy!" the anatomist calls out.

I hear a light footstep upon the stair.

"Yes, sir?"

"Lucy, take Emily to the kitchen. Give her something warm to drink, for it is cold outside."

Lucy.

I listen carefully as Lucy leads Emily away.

This is good. This is very good.

Lucy has been left alone with Emily, while the anatomist

and Briar are busy with the Bow Street Runners. And I suppose Elizabeth has safely retreated to her waxen form. Perhaps this will be the chance Lucy needs to help Emily. To break the spell. To enable her escape. Perhaps I can allow myself to hope. Just a little. For one of us, at least.

"This is all a waste of our time," the second Bow Street Runner says. "We're not after a woman. We're looking for a man. Large. Strong. Maybe even two men."

The student speaks up. "I am telling you, it was her. I recognized her face. She attempted to stab me. She was waiting outside the chophouse, watching us. I *saw* her. Perhaps she is after money and knows the students are easy pickings. You must do something about this. We lose students night after night. If these models reside together, the others are most likely in on it too. They work together, surely."

"We are investigating," the first Bow Street Runner says.

"Well, you are investigating too slowly!" the student cries out excitedly. "For there is a fox in the henhouse, sir. And the fox gets away with murder each night you do not act!"

"A fox in the henhouse!" the anatomist scoffs.

"Perhaps you yourself are part of it all," the student continues. "For everything points to your establishment. I'll not be back here—that much is certain."

This riles the anatomist, who steps up to the student, seething with rage. "And good riddance, for you are not welcome here, sir. I have seen your lackluster attempts to learn. My time is wasted on the likes of you and your friends. You will make neither a decent physician nor a decent surgeon. And now you dare to come here in the middle of the night and tell drunken tales of being robbed by women, as if my fine studio has something to do with that? Next you will be saying the model arose through bewitchment and hunted you down with a knife! And so she should have, given your disgraceful treatment of her in my studio. You, with your wandering hands—you should be ashamed of yourself. Be gone with you and your ridiculous student capers."

The Bow Street Runners step between the pair.

"We will attempt to track this woman down," one of them says. "And we will be back for more information if we cannot find her."

"Of course," the anatomist replies.

The student eyes the anatomist with distaste. "There has always been something odd about this place. Everyone speaks of it. Now this. This studio has far too many connections with the murdered. And now talk of bewitchment crosses your lips? It is too much. I will spread the word, and you will soon lose all your students, you will see." He struggles, but the Bow Street Runners have him firmly by the arm now and are ushering him outside.

The group exits the room and I can no longer understand what they are saying, though their voices continue to rise and fall in the entryway to the studio.

I stare my fixed stare upward, trying to hear something—anything—wondering how Emily fares in the kitchen, whether Lucy has managed to work magic of her own.

And then I hear footsteps. Light footsteps. A familiar tread.

"Eleanor." Lucy appears before my eyes. She touches my face gently with her hands. She begins to mutter some words I do not understand. They do not sound like Briar's mutterings to me. Instead, they are sweet to my ears. She closes her eyes for a moment, then opens them to stare into mine intently. "Yes, I believe you can hear me."

I can. I can hear you, I think. Oh, to be able to talk, to have a voice. I have so much to say to her. So many questions to ask.

"I am sorry I have been so absent. The anatomist and Briar do not like me being near the wax models. I am kept busy with the house." She pauses a moment and glances toward the door, as if listening for their voices. "I could not explain all the last time we spoke, but I am sure you now understand much of what Briar has put in place. I am not like Briar. I am part of a coven of good witches. Briar once belonged to the coven, too, many years ago, but the darkness called to her. The coven is intent on stopping her, which is why I have been sent."

Go on, I say with my eyes. *Tell me more. I am listening now. I am ready to hear what you have to say.* And perhaps Lucy senses what I am thinking, because she then continues.

"We believe we have found a way to separate your mortal body from the wax model. But once you and Emily are freed, we must burn all three of the models together."

Yes. Yes. Please do it, I think. *Please. Save me. Save Emily. Release us from this torment.*

"May I have a lock of your hair?" Lucy asks. "I will need it for the spell to release you."

Take it. Take it, please! I beg her. Oh, to be asked! She is asking me if she might touch me, might handle me. I am safe with Lucy. Emily and I are safe. We will be saved.

Lucy nods and quickly snips a lock of my hair, then places it in a pocket.

"Eleanor, you must expect a fire. You will be called upon to rise, but this time it will be different—it will be your choice to do so. And you will be free. When you are called to rise, you must accept, rise and leave this place as quickly as you can. Do not stop for anything—not even for each other. My friends will be waiting. They will meet you and help you to escape and lead a new life away from all of this."

The front door opens and the voices trail off. It closes again with a bang. I think the Bow Street Runners and the student have finally gone.

"I must depart," Lucy whispers. She touches my face once more, and as she slips from the room, her kindness toward me makes me weep invisible tears, as does that small heartbeat of hope that flutters against my chest. There is hope. *There is hope.* All is not lost. Emily and I may yet be free.

I keep listening. There is hushed talk—the anatomist and Briar's, I think—then footsteps. Elizabeth joins the conversation—Briar must have had her arise from her model again. The voices become raised—the three of them are arguing fiercely now.

"How could you be so careless?" I hear Elizabeth say. "To actually speak of what we are doing here! To tell them outright the truth of what is going on!"

"It is so far-fetched, no one would ever believe it," the anatomist blusters. "It is the perfect foil."

"The student will repeat your words," Briar disagrees. "The tale will spread. It was a foolish move on your part."

The anatomist reminds them both to quiet down, and the voices lower again, though the arguing continues.

After some time, the voices cease. Footsteps ascend the stairs. For a while, I hear nothing. Then another light step enters the studio. Lucy again? *Oh, please, let it be her.*

But it is Elizabeth who comes to lean over me. I hear more footsteps, and Briar appears.

"We must find that knife," Elizabeth says.

"It is of no matter."

Elizabeth grabs her by the arm. "It is of matter to me. *It is mine, and it will be returned to me.*"

Briar pushes her off. "The knife is useless to anyone else

now. Let me be. I must focus on the loss of control that happened this evening. The spell must be strengthened."

She turns from Elizabeth and roughly tugs my hair. I cannot see what she is doing, but there is a snipping sound. *Scissors.* She holds up a long, thin lock of hair.

It is obvious now that our hair is the key to how Briar's despicable magic works. I think back to that bracelet of hair Briar had worn when we viewed Lavender at the pleasure gardens—the bracelet that has since disappeared, as has Lavender. Other things come to me too. The strange way Briar had plucked a stray hair from Elizabeth's clothing that same evening at the gardens. The way she had stroked Lavender's locks. And then the braided necklace of hair that she is forever touching, with its three woven strands—the gold of Elizabeth's, the deep black of Emily's and my burnished brown. I believe that is what she had in mind this evening when she was speaking about my going too far. It sounded as if the spell does not work when I stray too far from that necklace she wears.

If only I can obtain that necklace somehow, destroy it . . .

A hiss draws my attention. Briar hovers above me. "She hears us. Foolish of me to forget, but with all the fuss . . ."

She begins to mutter words that make no sense.

And, once again, I fall into darkness. Down and down and down.

MY EYES FLICKER open, and I am immediately on guard. The white sheet over me lifts, and a student leers. He is in a group of three males, and as their faces jostle above me, I recognize them. One of them is the student I attempted to attack in the chophouse.

What is he doing here? What are *they* doing here?

"That's the one," the student says. "I will never forget her face."

"Let's take it," another one of the students says. "It will only burn."

Burn? But how do they know of Lucy's plan? Of the fire?

"We can only carry one," the third student says. "We should take the one that breathes first. She will be far more valuable, with that clockwork mechanism. She's kept upstairs. If there is time, we can come back for this one."

The three look at one another and nod in agreement before tossing the sheet back. It falls upon me, covering one of my eyes.

They rush off.

And, the threat to my waxen form gone, my one uncovered eye loses all sight as I return to the murky depths of nothingness.

ARISE, ELEANOR. ARISE. Arise.

I am awoken gently from rest, someone stirring me with hushed tones. At first I believe I am at home—back in my village, in my bed.

But then my eyes open. One sees naught but white cloth, and the other catches sight of Lucy, who gently peels the sheet back from my face. In one hand, she holds a twist of braided hair identical to the one that Briar wears at her neck. It must be the lock of hair Lucy so kindly requested to snip from my head.

Again, she mutters words I cannot understand—nonsense—until I realize they are repeated in my head, and that they seem to make sense after all.

Arise, Eleanor. Arise if you will. The voice in my head is calm and firm.

The choice is all mine.

I must accept. That is what Lucy had said. This time there is no force, no wrenching or pulling.

Yes. Yes, I will arise, I reply.

And just like that, I am not pulled but assisted upward, stood up.

And I am free.

I turn back to see the white cloth over my form, my own face. I have not seen my model in its entirety. My hand reaches out (I am incredulous at the action), but Lucy catches it.

"No," she says. "You should not. It is not you."

"Emily," I say, and then cough. The air seems to be smoky. I cough again.

Expect a fire.

Lucy takes my hands. "Eleanor, all has not gone to plan. The fire has taken hold, and some of the anatomist's students have learned of it. They have come from a nearby tavern. Listen carefully. You must run now, out the back entrance. Do not be seen by anyone. My friends wait for you. They will help you, take you far away from here."

"But Emily..."

Lucy hesitates. She looks upward. "Emily is free."

I cover my mouth with my hand, hardly able to take in the news. She is free. Emily is free.

"You must run now," Lucy repeats as two women I do not know enter the room. I pull away, and Lucy reassures me. "It is all right. They are here to help." She grasps my hand one more time. "I must go. I must help. And you must run. Promise me you will run." Lucy turns to the women. "Take this waxen form to safety, to our sisters."

And then she is gone. Without a backward glance, and coughing as she goes, she streaks from the room as if the very devil is at her heels.

The two women begin to wrestle with the wax model. With a groan, they lift it, and the cloth upon it slips slightly. They shield the model from my sight.

"The back entrance," one of them reminds me. "Go. Now."

I want to quiz her—the models are meant to burn—but then I remember what I have been told.

Emily is free.

And I am free.

I must leave and join her while I am able.

I am in the doorway when a loud thumping begins on the stair. Someone is coming down.

"Quickly," one of the women says. "Close the door behind you and go!"

But it is too late. The students are almost at the bottom of the stairs now, and I will be seen. There is time only to close the door and cross the hallway to the space under the stairs. I hide in the shadows.

"Be careful with it," a voice says. It sounds like one of the students is speaking again.

"*You* be careful with it," another snarls. "For I see you are not carrying your share of the weight but a useless ledger."

"I doubt it is useless, for it lay directly beside her. I believe it is significant. It must carry details on the use of her mechanism or some such."

"Perhaps. So take it, but hurry." Another thump. A bang.

"Come this way. The back entrance."

"Ugh, why must the confounded beast of a model be so heavy?"

They round the corner and I push myself farther into the shadows. I cannot be seen, for the student from the chophouse would surely recognize me. I look on as they half drag, half carry Elizabeth's form. Her hair is trailing, her dress dragging, stepped upon and torn by one of them.

A banging sees them pause in their step.

"See? Did I not tell you? There it is again," one of the students says. "The banging upon the door. Do you think someone is trapped?"

"If they are, let them burn," the student from the chophouse says. "I told you there is something evil here. I told you they spoke of witchcraft."

And then a bursting sound. A roar. The building creaks and groans.

Fire.

"Hurry!" all three cry out. They stagger toward the back of the building.

I wait a moment before emerging from the shadows. I cross the hallway and open the door once more. "The students are gone," I tell the two waiting women.

"And now you must go too," one says.

"We will attend to everything here. We will help Lucy. Run."

And, with one last glance upstairs, that is exactly what I do. I turn and I run. I run from this place as fast as my feet will take me—my feet that are free and will lead me to Emily.

Outside the studio, two women lurk in the shadows in the alley that leads away from the back entrance.

"Eleanor?" one says.

I draw back, wary.

"Do not fear," the other says. "You are safe now—safe with us."

I nod. Lucy told me they would be waiting. I must trust them. I let them wrap me in a cloak, pulling up the hood so I will not be seen.

I pause as we are about to turn the corner onto the street, allowing the cloak's hood to fall back from my head. The smoke rises now, and I can see a flame licking at the sky.

"Come now. This way."

I let myself be led from that terrible place.

And I go willingly, for I know Emily is waiting for me.

ALYS

BURLEY, THE NEW FOREST, PRESENT DAY

As soon as I step out of my car and onto the gravel drive of Jennet's house, I ask myself why I didn't come here sooner. I'd only peered at the house from the driveway before, stared at it on satellite maps, wondering. I'd been afraid of it, of what would happen here. But, strangely, now that I'm here, I feel only peace.

The house squats on the very edge of the forest, and beyond it is a sea of tranquility. I gaze up at the crooked character of the chocolate box cottage with its thick thatch—like something out of a fairy tale—and feel that I've somehow come home. There are even roses climbing around the front door.

Rose Cottage, I think to myself, the world stilling around me for a moment.

"Alys." A woman trots out from the side of the house, her arms outstretched. "I've been keeping an ear out for you all morning." She comes to take my hands.

"You must be Jennet," I say, holding back tears of relief.

She smiles warmly. "But of course I am."

I take in a deep lungful of cold, fresh air. "Why didn't I come years ago?"

"Because it wasn't the right time," she replies, as if it's as simple as that.

And perhaps it is.

"Come. Let's get your things. Ro's making us some afternoon tea."

"Oh," I say. Ro isn't exactly known for her baking skills. Or she is, but not in a good way.

Jennet chuckles.

"How is everything?" I ask. "There hasn't been any more trouble?" I think of Geon Yoon, how desperate to escape Elizabeth's clutches he'd seemed in that video. And I think of Catherine, too, completely under Elizabeth's control. The long silence from Sorrel when I'd called her from my hotel room to tell her about Catherine stealing the ledger right from under my nose— I knew then just how unsure the coven was about what would happen here at the coven home, despite all their precautions.

But if Jennet's worried, she hides it well.

"Everything's gone very smoothly. Eleanor's wax model has been moved here. She's in the summerhouse. The hair necklace is here—still heavily protected, I assure you—and Elizabeth will be brought in just before dawn. There's been no sign of Geon or Catherine, I'm happy to say."

"Good." I breathe a sigh of relief.

"Sorrel's out in the garden. Ro's here, as I mentioned. That's three members of the coven, and there are only five of us now. We need a majority to break the spell we need to break. The others are nearby in case we need them, and they will come before dawn, with Elizabeth's model. We didn't want to overwhelm you with too many people."

I nod. I don't ask about the other arrangements, the bonfire.

There are things it's best not to know about, to dwell upon.

"Come, now," Jennet says softly. "Let's get you settled in."

I fetch my things from the car and follow her.

"Now, I'm sorry not to take you in through the front," Jennet tells me as our footsteps crunch on the gravel, "but we never really use it, as is the way around here. And anyway, you're family to us."

We head down the side of the house and enter via a functional mudroom with a long bench seat. Jennet kicks her shoes off, and they come to rest beside several other pairs. I take my boots off.

Jennet inspects my feet. "Good. You've warm socks on. I've always spare slippers, in case you need them." She takes my bag from me and opens the door that leads into the house proper. We walk through a pretty little sage and cream utility room, with a standard washer and dryer and a large farmhouse sink. And then we're in the kitchen.

"You're here!" Ro stands from her seat at the island bench.

"I'm actually wondering why it took me so long," I tell her. The kitchen is gorgeous, with its large, warm oven and its rustic wood-topped island complete with stools just begging to be perched upon while tea is drunk or wine is sipped as someone stirs a pot on the stove.

"We would have had you," Ro says.

"I know. That's the worst bit. It really is . . . lovely." I have to choke out the last word.

Ro rounds the island in a second, her expression only of concern. "Hug?"

"Sure." It's not a thing for us. For me. Hugging. But look at me now. I'm not even flinching.

After exactly the right amount of time, Ro pulls away. "Now. Tea and cake. Special cake, actually."

I eye her dubiously. "Special cake? That sounds . . . ominous."

"Rude. You'll see. Take a seat."

I do as I'm told, taking a seat on one of the stools. Sorrel appears to greet me (another hug!) and settles in next to me. Jennet helps with a large teapot.

She places it on the table before me.

"I hope you're not wanting me to turn it clockwise a certain number of times or something," I say. They all know how I feel about anything superstitious; talk that even comes close to being borderline supernatural is out-of-bounds with me.

"Feel free, but there are tea bags in there," Ro tells me as she unboxes a cake. "We're, like, modern witches."

I laugh.

"Now, the cake might come as a bit of a shock," Ro says.

I eye the store-bought box. "It should be okay."

She gives me a look. "Again, rude." She comes over to place it before me. "I know you don't do birthdays, but happy birthday. For last week." She puts a hand on my shoulder.

The cake looks delicious—a vanilla confection with creamy icing and a scattering of pretty dried flowers.

There are also numerals on top.

Three, to be precise.

273

Ro takes a deep breath. "I figured we're discussing it now," she says.

A long silence follows, which I know I'll have to break eventually.

"You couldn't fit two hundred and seventy-three candles on top?" I finally say.

Ro is right. Now that I'm here, how can we not discuss it? All of it.

That I am not only Alys.

I am also Eleanor.

I have also been Bridget, my "mother," and Gwen, my "grandmother," and back and back and back. Always disguising myself, moving, changing personae when needed as the years pass. No wonder Catherine thought my family's documents were dubious. No wonder poor Mrs. Owen (already confused, thanks to the coven's work) mixed up my name; she had known Bridget, who had also visited Emily's portrait at Poulston Park.

I guess I'm not the only person present to have a tricky situation when it comes to relations, because Jennet, Sorrel and Ro do too. They're all related to coven members who helped free Eleanor from the confines of her wax model in 1769. Briar was part of that coven once, Briar who turned against them— against the very world—seduced by the power that evil offered her. After Briar left their fold, the coven kept track of her over the years, worried about how she would use what they had taught her as a base upon which to build her malevolent ways. They tracked her to the anatomist's studio. Sadly, it was too late for them to intervene and save Lavender, whose model—along with her very soul—had been destroyed, but they knew they could help Emily and Eleanor. All they needed to do was get one of their own into the house.

This was where Lucy came in.

Lucy was part of that coven. She was their youngest member, unknown to Briar. Lucy sacrificed herself so that I might be free.

On that darkest of nights, nothing went to plan.

Expect a fire, Lucy had told me. And the following evening, it came.

Lucy had been busy listening at doors, listening to Briar's mutterings. When she was sure Briar had once again lied to Elizabeth to get her into her waxen form, Lucy plied the anatomist and Briar with Briar's own sleeping draft. And then Lucy uttered the spell she had learned to release both Emily and Eleanor from their waxen forms if they so wished.

Members of the coven were admitted into the building. They quickly spread lamp oil throughout the premises.

The plan was for Emily and Eleanor to flee, leaving their wax models behind, and for those models, Elizabeth, Briar and the anatomist to burn.

But that plan was never to be.

We will never know what really occurred in the anatomist's studio that night, but we believe we have an idea of how the scene played out in its entirety.

And what of me?

Well, I fled.

For Lucy had told me that Emily was free.

I believed her to be safe.

Members of the coven were waiting for me. I was wrapped in a cloak and ferried away.

I could not believe my luck. I was free. Truly free! No longer was I held captive, my body bound rigid by bewitchment. Lucy had assured me that Emily was free, and I knew that soon we would be reunited and leave London forever.

I was taken to a fine house—a coven member's, I think. Hours passed. I was given brandy, plied with food.

I waited for Emily.

But she did not come.

Members of the coven came and went, some reeking of smoke, their faces smudged with ash. My waxen form, covered with a now-sooty sheet, was brought to the house.

They had not let it burn.

It began to become clear that things had gone badly indeed. No one would answer my questions about Emily. No one dared look me in the eye.

In the early hours, there was a gathering of the entire coven—or what was left of it. And those who were left shared what they knew.

Elizabeth had been separated from her model—for a time. Briar had released her, perhaps because she wished to overpower the students in the building. But then, somehow, Elizabeth had turned on Briar. She had locked her in the room that Emily's form was kept in.

She had locked her in there to burn.

Surely so she would be free of her captor forever.

How things played out from there, we can only guess. Briar had the advantage in that she had her necklace of hair to control Elizabeth with. That must have been how she forced Elizabeth back into her wax model, which the students then stole not long before the building collapsed, taking so many people with it.

The anatomist. Briar. Emily's model. Several of the witches.

Including Lucy.

A private fire brigade had finally arrived, located their company insignia upon the building, and brought the fire under control.

The witches had told me their tale, and I had sat and listened to it. But they had left out the most important part.

"And Emily?" I cried out at the remains of the coven. "Tell me, what of Emily?"

The truth was, I already knew. I had already felt it, but I had not wanted to acknowledge it. I could feel a connection with Elizabeth's model, but the connection with Emily was severed now.

She was gone.

She was *free*.

This was the word Lucy had used. And she had not lied to me.

"I am sorry," one of the witches had said—Sybil, I think her name was. "Emily initially refused the call to rise. It was . . . what she wanted."

And it *was* what Emily had wanted, wasn't it? To be free of that life. To be free of Elizabeth. To be free of her diseased body. At one point she had even told me that she wanted to be free of me, that I was only an interesting diversion. And, oh, I see that coldness for what it was now. Emily was simply trying to distance herself from me so that *I* might be free. The moment we both realized something was wrong in the anatomist's studio—that Briar had drugged us—that we were in danger. The way Emily had grasped for my hand. Entreated me to look at her. Her artifice had dissolved in an instant. I had known, deep down in my very soul, that we were each other's person—until the end, as we had both vowed.

But then I recalled the witch's exact words.

"What do you mean, Emily *initially* refused the call to rise?"

The witches had looked at one another. "Something occurred in that locked room. Between Briar and Emily."

Of course it did, I had thought. Because Emily would have done anything to save me. To see Elizabeth trapped. And Briar burned. The anatomist too.

She would have wanted them all to go down in flames.

She would have wanted to make sure that I was safe, that I would go on and that I would finally be free.

She knew I would have to go on in a world without her. But she also knew it would be in a world without Elizabeth and Briar and the anatomist. And that would be enough for her.

Sybil had crouched before me. "Emily left this for you." She held out a glass vial with a stopper.

Inside was Briar's necklace of hair.

"Take it away from me." I hurled myself backward, almost toppling off the upholstered stool I was sitting on.

"It is not what you think," Sybil said. "The necklace is not what it once was. No longer does it control you. The spell has been changed, and another was placed upon it in order that the vial might survive the fire."

I stared at the vial dubiously. Was this simply another of Elizabeth and Briar's tricks?

"We believe the vial might have been Emily's doing, for it rested upon the remains of her wax model."

Emily. Was that why she had risen? Had she somehow convinced Briar to change the spell upon the necklace of hair? But how? And why would Briar agree to do so?

"I will lift the spell upon the vial now." Sybil began to mutter those words that always seemed so foreign to my ears.

My hand had been outstretched in that moment, waiting to take the hair—waiting to take all that was left of Emily in this world. But almost as soon as Sybil began speaking, I had recoiled in horror as the hair's siren song began to swirl about me.

"Take it away," I had said immediately, hurling the stool from beneath me, clambering backward. "Get it away from me."

"Eleanor."

"*Get it away from me!*" I had screamed, covering my ears with my hands. "I want no more to do with your ways. Do you hear me? *No more.*" The hair called out to Elizabeth too. I could hear it. And I could not bear to feel that connection—not without the strength of Emily by my side.

"Sybil." Another of the witches had placed a hand on her

shoulder. "Later, perhaps. Eleanor may want the keepsake in time, but not now. It is too much for her."

I could still hear it, whispering away in Briar's tones. "Make it stop." I had rocked back and forth. *"Make it stop!"*

The witches had removed the hair from my presence. They had huddled together. Words were uttered. And then, just like that, I could hear the charm upon the hair no more. They told me they would keep the hair safe.

I knew I would never want it.

It might have been all that existed of Emily in this world, but it was not enough. A lock of bewitched hair would never be enough.

How could they not understand that?

Over the coming days, there was more bad news. The witches told me that Briar's spells were more complicated than they had expected, that while they had managed to invite me to arise from my wax model, not all was as straightforward as they had thought. I was not, perhaps, entirely . . . mortal.

And, oh, I was angry.

Why had they not simply let me burn too? Why had they not let me burn alongside Emily? Why did they not chase down those students who stole Elizabeth's model? Why had they not taken her model back by force and burned everything together?

I told the witches that from that day forth, I wanted no part of their world.

Ever again.

I wanted nothing to do with their magic. Nothing at all. I had no need for their complicated explanations of what they thought I was. What good would it do for me to know how Briar had created the models? How they worked. The ins and outs of her sorcery. No. The terrible deed was done. All I could do now was leave my old life behind me. Become someone completely new.

They respected my wishes.

I was given a new life, away from the coven. It did not take long for it to become clear that they were correct—I was forever changed. I was not aging. There were other things, too, things I had to be careful that others never found out about. I could be hurt—I would bleed—but I would heal within minutes. I did not get sick, though my nausea would come and go—a cruel reminder of a child who could never be born. If I cut my hair, it would not grow back. My nails did not grow. A scratch would heal, but a tattoo would remain. The witches could not explain the rules to me, for they had not made them. They could only guess at what Briar had put in place for me.

I ran from my past. Initially I worked as a governess, and after a few iterations, established myself in the antiques business. Despite myself, I was always drawn to the familiar past. And I lived day to day. So many days. So many years. Always moving. Always changing. Always longing for things I could not have. Mortality. Normalcy. *Emily.*

Oh, and I was always wary too. Let's not forget that. Everyone was kept at arm's length, because I had learned the hard way that the devil walks among us, that no one is to be trusted—not even oneself. If I was a murderer, anyone might be. All it took to be a murderer was circumstance. Timing. A chance meeting.

The coven had seen it as their duty to watch over me in all my iterations. They kept their distance. Provided me with one or two contacts. Stored Eleanor. Briar's necklace was placed in a beautiful crystal box to keep it safe. And they kept it under lock and key, and charmed always, its whisperings silenced for me.

The coven had always made it known that it was my choice how my never-ending life should play out, what my fate should be. They sat back. They gave me space. They respected my need to pretend I had no past, that each new persona I took on was a person born anew. But they were always there if I had a question—if I needed them.

And, for the most part, I didn't.

In time, I was able to separate myself from my past. I became practiced at not looking back, at dulling that feeling of connection with Elizabeth. I was able to tell myself what had occurred was simply a fanciful story, that it had all happened to someone else—a distant relative called Eleanor.

And then . . . Alys.

I don't know why it was Alys who was prepared to push back. Perhaps I was simply ready. I had had enough of disguising myself. Changing. Explaining. But it was Alys right from the start. Pursuing that opportunity with the Yoons. And then the tattoos that could never be removed. The short hair that would never grow back. I knew Alys would be the one to return Elizabeth to London.

To end it all.

Alys would be the mistress of our shared destiny.

In the kitchen, Ro places something in front of me.

"Don't open it," she says. "It's not really a birthday present."

It is a beautiful round crystal jewelry box with a hinged lid embellished with a band of rose-cut Bohemian garnets. As the coven has always told me, it is heavily protected with a series of spells, for the box contains the last piece of enchanted hair that would allow the remaining two Venuses to come and go from their waxen forms.

It contains Briar's necklace.

Burning it is the only way to truly vanquish Elizabeth forever.

I know it's this final item that Elizabeth wants. And she must have it if she is to rise again.

I'm sure this is why she goaded me in the vision at the Pleasure Gardens Experience. She wants everything to converge here, at the coven home. She knows the necklace of hair will be here, because we will have made sure everything is here, ready to burn.

And when it's here, she'll make her final move to steal it from us.

I stare at the necklace of hair, remembering when it had been around Briar's neck. How her fingers had toyed with it. How she had muttered. Used us. Forced us to become murderers.

Emily's hunched body as she walked the streets in pain.

My nausea. The baby who would never be.

The stench of those men.

My hunger for Dr. Chidworth. Mr. Corbyn. How I had stepped aside to let Emily take her fill of enjoyment.

The blood.

Oh God. The blood. Their final cries. Their blank gazes.

But then I remember our own blank gazes. The feeling of being entombed as men did what they wished with us in the name of science.

I cannot say those men deserved their grisly ends, but I understand a grain of the anatomist's anger; I do.

I wonder at the anatomist's grisly end too. Did she slumber on, drugged, as smoke filled her lungs? Somehow that seems too peaceful an end—too easy compared with the struggle Briar and Emily surely had. What truly happened between them remains a mystery to us all. How had Emily convinced Briar to change the spell upon the hair? Had she threatened her? Or maybe told her that I would seek revenge against Elizabeth? I wish I knew.

Tentatively, I reach out and pick up the jewelry box.

It lies heavy in my palm, and inside, the necklace of hair remains quiet, thanks to the coven's charm.

Again, Ro rests her warm, solid hand on my shoulder.

"Thank you," I say, "for keeping it safe all this time."

"Thank you for trusting us," Ro replies, glancing at Sorrel and Jennet. Their hands come to rest on my other shoulder, my back.

I do trust them. I do.

I trust the coven. With this.

The end.

After a moment or two, I exhale and look to Ro with watery eyes. "There's only one thing..."

"What's that?"

"I mean, not having candles is bad enough, but the present? A necklace I can't even wear? Come on, now..."

WE EAT CAKE and drink tea and surprisingly, given the circumstances, laugh about many things. Or perhaps that is all you can do when you're faced with the gallows.

When we're done, I know what I need to do next.

"Do you think I could go and see Eleanor?" I ask.

"Of course," Jennet replies. "Why don't you take Alys out to the summerhouse, Ro?"

I begin to collect a few plates and cups, but Sorrel shoos me away. "Off with you. We've got this. We'll start the roast soon. It's all about the food when we gather here."

"If you'd told me about the food years ago, I really would

have been here much more speedily," I tell Ro as we leave the kitchen.

She turns back to give me a "you said it, not me" lift of the eyebrows. "I sort of wish you had, because there's this sofa we've been wanting to move upstairs for a while."

I give her a small shove. "Stop it." This isn't the first time Ro has joked about my being unusually strong. Briar's spell had a few small benefits. I recall the jar lid that Marco had needed help with. If only he knew the truth about my "knack." But he'll never know. He won't even remember me after Ro helps him to forget.

"This evening we're having roast beef, a fine selection of roast vegetables, Yorkshire pudding and a good-sized dollop of crème fraîche with fresh horseradish and a sprinkling of chives. Just saying," Ro tells me as we exit the house, perhaps sensing that I'm spiraling. She takes my arm.

"And pudding?" I say weakly, already dreading what's coming for me in the summerhouse. I'm not sure I'm ready for this, even though it's been more than a hundred years since I've seen her. I feel sick to my stomach at the thought of it. Or maybe that's too much cake. Or my nausea returning. Or all of that smashed together.

"Have you ever known me to skip pudding?"

That's a hard no.

I'm still holding the crystal box carefully in my hand. "How long does it take to remove the charms?" I ask Ro. "I'm just wondering about timing—about Elizabeth's model arriving, and so on. Is it a lengthy process?"

Ro shakes her head. "No. But we need three of our five coven members present in order to break the spell upon it."

"Yes. Jennet said."

"There's a collective spell, and we each have our own spell upon it too."

"And when all the spells are lifted, the hair will begin to sing once more?" I remember its singing like I'd heard it yesterday. Calling to me. Giving me the choice to return to my model or arise from it. I suppress a shiver thinking about it.

"Yes."

We snake our way along a gravel path toward an outbuilding that looks a little like a converted barn. And then, beyond, past the green of the garden, a vast expanse of forest and heath—a mosaic of heather and woods and, in the far distance, a group of ponies.

"Oh, Ro."

"I know. It's beautiful here. There are badgers. Deer. A goshawk. It's like another world, really."

"It's like the past," I say. Sometimes I forget what it was like to live in a village, to be surrounded by nature, quiet. But I try not to romanticize history. It's far too easy to gloss over the poverty, disease, hunger, cold.

Ro unlocks a set of French doors and opens them wide so I can step inside. The summerhouse seems to be a simple affair of two large rooms. The first is complete with some comfy furniture, a small wood-burning stove, a bathroom and a galley-style kitchen. The other, I suppose, houses Eleanor.

"Do you want me to come with you?" Ro asks.

"Yes. I'm not sure I can do this alone. Can you . . . go first? Is she uncovered?" I take a deep breath as my stomach rolls over.

Ro gives my arm a squeeze. "Of course I can. And you've got this. Give me a second. And don't run away."

"You know me too well." I'm a bolter, a runner. I have form in this area. I have, after all, been running for centuries.

With a snort, Ro disappears through a door into the next

room, leaving me to stare out of the large windows into the beauty of the heath with its bracken and gorse beyond.

"Okay," she finally calls out. "Anytime you want to come in."

I pause for just a moment before taking the few steps required to enter the room that the crate is in, sitting on top of a couple of pallets.

I note a case that lies close to it. It looks important, and I'm about to ask what it is when I realize it's something I've asked Ro to prepare. I go over and rest the crystal box atop it. Ro sees me looking at it and nods.

"Now, are you sure you want to see Eleanor?" she asks.

My mouth opens and closes, but my reply catches in my throat. Yes, I want to see Eleanor. I want to be reminded of what Elizabeth did to me.

I want to be angry.

I try not to look until I am standing over her. I don't want to catch only a glimpse. I want to see her in her entirety.

And then I do.

There she is.

Eleanor.

Breathe. Just breathe.

She is a surreal, sadistic nightmare of a thing—female misogyny personified, crafted to mock womanhood. She is a macabre, anxiety-inducing monstrosity, so far removed from Elizabeth's sleeping, golden-haired creation that it is hard to believe both came from the same mind.

This version of Eleanor is a gynecological model—Elizabeth's final cruel jab. She is not like Emily—there are no interchangeable parts to be found here. Her horror is of a different sort, and it is merciless. Her arms are bound with strips of white fabric and tethered to the surface she rests upon. Her legs are bound also, tied together tightly at the ankles so that her lifeless form might not move during medical examination. Her eyes are open, fixed and unblinking, giving the appearance of consciousness as she succumbs to her fate. She wears a fine white nightgown—so innocent, so pure—unbuttoned down the front to expose all, including those milky-white breasts that led several students of medicine to their wretched ruin.

And then down we go, down, down to the climax of this demented vision—down to the abdominal incision. It is skillfully yet savagely made, revealing a fetus for onlookers who would like to peer inside voyeuristically. Elizabeth's masterpiece is a deep, malevolent twist of the scalpel, a final, sadistic slash.

But Elizabeth did not stop there. Of course she did not, for that would not have been enough.

Hovering above it all, cunningly attached to Eleanor's sides, the attachments hidden by the nightgown, four hands are displayed. They are attached with wire, but they appear as if out of the ether—four ghostly appendages that perform a cesarean section with finesse. Two hold sponges; one has a scalpel; one retracts the uterus masterfully. And all of them have neat nails. White cuffs. The beginnings of black suit sleeves. As if their owners might have a fine dinner to attend when the procedure is complete.

Oh, and Elizabeth made it clear that the baby is a girl—just in case I was wondering.

"What an absolute bitch," Ro says, breaking the silence. "I'm so, so sorry, Alys. It's an abomination."

I can only nod as I stare at her—at myself. "Have you been told much about Emily's model?" I finally ask. "What she was turned into?"

"Yes. It sounds equally awful."

"It was. Because to see her in life . . . well, she was glorious. She was beautiful, of course, but that was nothing in the grand scheme of everything she was. She was so alive. Oh, she had such a spark to her. She was endlessly amusing too. And caring. I wish you could have met her. You would have adored her."

"I wish I could have met her too."

"You know I try not to look back—it's too painful—but every now and again I allow myself to pretend that, um . . ." I have to take a moment and a long, shuddery breath as everything comes flooding back and my worlds collide, finally melding in my mind. Eleanor and I are one. The same. "That I had listened to Emily's warnings, left London. That Emily had followed, got better. That I'd had the baby. And that the three of us had carved out some kind of existence in a village somewhere. What a ridiculous fantasy! The reality was that I would have died in childbirth, or of some infection shortly after. If the baby had survived birth, it would have soon died of something or other too. And Emily—what chance would she ever have had of going undiscovered? The newspapers were already on the hunt for women fitting our descriptions, and—let's face it—there weren't many mixed-race women living a simple village life in those days."

"It's not ridiculous. It's only what you deserved," Ro says simply. "All three of you. To be safe. To be happy. To be free."

I nod. "Emily so deserved some happiness after her terrible upbringing. You know, we had made a pact—to be family to each other until the end. And Emily kept her side of the bargain by making sure I received Briar's necklace safely. I know she must have fought for me until the end. All she cared about was that I go on, that I have a chance at freedom. I just feel like . . . I've always felt like . . . I failed her. Like Emily kept up her end of the bargain, but I didn't keep up mine."

"But was there really anything you could have done? From

what I understand, Emily would have already been sick before you met Elizabeth."

I nod. It's true. But still, if only... if only... The longer you live, the more "if onlys" you have, I suppose. "I guess I'm just desperately ashamed of how long it's taken me to come to grips with what happened to me. And all the time, the coven has been here for me, patient and kind. You, Sorrel, Jennet and all the others before you—right back to Lucy. Poor Lucy. She was so young."

"As were you," Ro says. "What were you? Seventeen?"

"Eighteen. Just."

Ro shakes her head.

"Do you know how long it took me to understand that I was groomed? I'm embarrassed to say. Oh, I was so foolish. So weak. I believed Elizabeth's lies, and then excused them. All because of the abuse she suffered herself."

Ro speaks up quickly. "You weren't foolish. You were trusting, and that's something else entirely. And whatever happened in Elizabeth's past doesn't excuse what she did to you."

"I know. I just wish I'd listened to Emily. She warned me, you know. Right from that first day. As soon as she could, she entreated me to run. And then, at the end, when she knew there was no hope for her and that her illness would only progress, she tried so desperately to get me to leave. She obviously thought there was hope for me—and, perhaps, for my baby. I've always thought..." I've never told anyone this before. But I know Ro will understand. "The baby—I would have called her Lucy."

"Oh, Alys," Ro says. "That's beautiful."

We stand in silence for some time, staring at Eleanor—and Lucy—until I can stand it no longer.

Enough.

"Let's go outside," I say.

Attached to the summerhouse, there's a small terrace with two chairs that overlook the forest. I go out and take a seat in one of them, and Ro fixes us a couple drinks—a gin and tonic for her, and an elderflower cordial for me. I still find it difficult to accept food or drink from other people. I haven't touched a drop of alcohol since drinking that wine given to me by Briar, the wine with the draft in it. I can taste the bitter dregs of it still, and the stench of alcohol will somehow always remain in my nose from those taverns—those taverns where I was made to hunt, to kill.

This is why I don't look back.

But seeing Eleanor again has given me the fuel I need: an injection of fury, of righteous indignation. The Venuses and everything to do with them will burn now. I will make sure of it. Elizabeth must *never* be given the chance to rise again. She's simply too dangerous. Given the chance, she would take me out, take the coven out. Geon and Catherine too. And she wouldn't stop there. She is a power-hungry demon, with no scruples, who will eviscerate everything and everyone in her path. I can only imagine the sort of life she might carve out for herself here, in the future, the havoc she'd wreak if she gained access to modern technology. I could see her as a far-right politician, or the host of some sort of diabolical reality TV show—a real-life *The Hunger Games*.

Ro comes out of the summerhouse's small kitchen with our two drinks and takes a seat beside me.

"I am very, *very* nervous about bringing Elizabeth's model here," I tell her. "It really will be at the last moment, won't it?"

Ro nods. "Yes. The absolute last moment. Just before dawn."

"I get the feeling she's going to use her connection with me to get to the necklace. I don't know how, but she'll come up with something. You can't let her." I look Ro dead in the eye. "Look how she managed to steal the ledger. She'll use me somehow, or she'll send Geon, or Catherine, or both of them. Whatever happens, we have to do everything we can to stop her, anything it takes." My gaze doesn't budge.

"We know that too. We know it's what you want."

"Good." I think for a moment. "You know, I still can't understand exactly how Elizabeth managed to connect with Geon Yoon. Catherine, I understand—the Venuses are her life—but Geon wanted nothing to do with his father's obsession."

"Don't forget that we've always thought her model—her hair—was enchanted in a different way than yours. That's why men are so taken with her. And you mentioned that Mr. Yoon stole a few strands of your hair. That can't be a coincidence. She engineered that. I think she's used your hair as a bridge to strengthen her connection with you."

I nod. I had spent centuries dulling my connection with Elizabeth—pushing it away—but I suspect she spent those years building on hers with me. And she had Mr. Yoon steal some of my hair to strengthen it even further. Elizabeth's model was obviously different from Emily's and mine—and she was always supposed to be allowed to come and go from her waxen figure as she pleased. When she was outside her waxen form, she didn't appear as Emily and I had—she hadn't suffered from any of the afflictions that had recently plagued her in life. She was special, and she wouldn't have had it any other way. There was still so much both the coven and I didn't really understand about the ins and outs of what Briar had put in place with her evil words.

"I hope we can break Elizabeth's connection with Geon, for his sake. She really has used him terribly," Ro continues. "Just like she used you."

I take a deep breath. "But I used him too. I can't deny it."

"You didn't want things to turn out like this," Ro replies.

"But they have. And I feel awful about it. I don't want to be like Elizabeth. All my life, I've wanted anything but that." How could I have done to another human being what Elizabeth did to me?

Ro sighs. "Maybe we can help him to break free and forget. There's still hope. After all, Elizabeth can't rise without Briar's necklace."

This is true. Elizabeth might have found a way to connect with people telepathically, but there is no way for her to rise again in bodily form without that necklace of hair. Briar's necklace is her only hope of getting what she wants.

"You haven't wanted to talk about it all before. But is there anything you want to discuss now?" Ro says. "Before . . ." She trails off.

"There is one thing I wanted to see if you know," I say.

"What's that?"

"I know why the anatomist wanted revenge, why Elizabeth wanted to kill the men she had us murder, but Briar—what was she doing? What was her plan? Does the coven know?"

"Only a little. From what we understand, she had some pretty grand plans. It seems she left the coven after a leadership dispute, and she truly turned to evil magic after that—to show the coven how important she was, how powerful, how they had been wrong to choose someone else over her. She became both money and power hungry, and it seems that she stumbled onto the idea of creating armies—creating multiple versions of one person, containing them in an object to be brought forth whenever she desired. To be able to control them from a distance—you can see how it would be ideal. They could be easily moved around. They wouldn't need to eat, to sleep . . ."

I sit on this for a moment. "I recall her talking about it once. She said she wanted to find a way to make multiples, multiple versions, renewed afresh each time. 'Ten Eleanors in a row,' she said."

"It's a horrific concept. Thank goodness you stopped her, and she didn't get any further."

I shake my head. "No. Emily stopped her. It was all Emily."

"Yes, I suppose it was, back then. But now it's you, Alys."

We sit in silence for a while, staring at the idyllic wilderness beyond.

"So, do you have doubts? About tomorrow, I mean," Ro says tentatively.

"Not about burning the Venuses. But about taking on Elizabeth, yes. She'll stop at nothing. *Nothing*. But, also, I can't think of anything else I can do to prepare. So now we wait. All I'm saying is, we have to remain vigilant."

Ro nods. "Of course. That's what we're here for." And with that, she leans over and tips her gin and tonic out onto the grass. "Best stay sober."

I look on, impressed. "Wow," I tell her. "Now I really believe you've got my back. I wonder what else you'd do for me. Can I have your share of pudding?"

Ro gives me a withering glance. "Look, I've got your back, but that doesn't extend to pudding. Sorry."

DINNER IS DELICIOUS, of course, and Ro actually offers me her pudding (albeit with sad eyes), which makes me laugh.

After dinner, we head into the snug. The fire is stoked, and we play Scrabble.

"Is this what you usually do here?" I ask.

"No," Ro replies. "Usually we get the cauldron out, dance around it naked, fly about on our broomsticks..."

"Hilarious as ever," I tell her.

Ro and I stay up talking and watching TV.

Sorrel and Jennet eventually peel off, Jennet asking if she can take the crystal jewelry box with her, which is fine by me. It's better that way, safer, especially if I suspect that Elizabeth will somehow try to use her connection with me to obtain it.

Around midnight, Ro stifles a yawn.

"Go to bed," I tell her, standing. "I'm exhausted too."

"I can stay up," Ro says valiantly.

"I'll have a lie-down even if I can't sleep." We make our way upstairs to the bedrooms.

"Call out if you need anything," Ro tells me as I brush my teeth. "Jennet's already secured the house."

"Okay. Will do."

In my bedroom, I close the door behind me.

I'm alone.

I run my hand over the lovely handmade quilt, and then I take the few steps to look out the room's small window. The wind has picked up outside, and the house creaks and groans as if it's talking to me, telling me secrets.

I don't get changed. Let's face it: I won't be doing any sleeping.

But I do lie down on the bed and attempt to calm myself.

What will Elizabeth try next? Will she send Geon Yoon or Catherine here, as I suspect? Maybe both?

There is always a part of me waiting for Elizabeth. Even now. I don't think it's ever stopped. Sometimes I think she is only one person. She was once flesh and blood, just like me—mortal. I know this for a fact—I've seen her on death's very door. She is no god. Why, then, do I allow her to be one to me?

Even on the brightest of days, she manages to block out the sun in my sky.

I take a deep breath and think about this stopping—ending.

I think about finally being at peace.

It's hard to fathom.

I'm not sure if I doze off or not, but I jolt into full alertness when I hear some footsteps. Someone's in the hallway. But then there's a flush of a toilet, water from a tap, more footsteps, a return to bed.

I close my eyes again.

They soon flicker open once more, with the dull feeling that something is not right. I lie, staring upward at the ceiling, for some time, but I don't hear anything except the wind at the window.

Inside the house, all is still.

Except for me.

I shift this way and that, but it's no use. There will be no more rest.

As silently as I can, I rise and make my way down to the kitchen. I put the kettle on to make myself a cup of tea.

A step on the stairs sees me whirl about.

"Everything all right?" Ro says, bleary-eyed.

I exhale. "It's fine. I'm fine. Go back to bed, even if it's just for another hour."

"No, I'll—"

"Ro, *please*. Really," I say firmly, hopefully giving the impression that I'd rather be alone.

"All right. But if you need anything..."

"I know."

The footsteps retreat.

I make a cup of chamomile tea and take a seat at the island bench. From where I sit, I can see out the window to the dark shadows of trees, their branches swaying along the drive. I sit for a few minutes, but I can't settle, and soon I get up to mooch about the small downstairs rooms. The dining room. The snug. I cross back through the kitchen and pass by the dark utility room.

And then I pause.

The feeling of everything not being right intensifies.

I stand very still for a moment or two, looking into the dark. I reach a hand into the utility room and feel for the light switch. I flick it on.

There is nothing, of course.

Just the washer, the dryer.

I flick the light off.

It's only then that I notice the light beyond that.

The light moving around in the summerhouse.

FOR A MOMENT I consider waking the others. But no. It's as I've always thought.

This is my fight.

And now I'm going to fight it—fight whoever it is Elizabeth has been able to connect with, using every fiber of her being to do the impossible. Geon. Catherine. Maybe even someone else entirely, someone she should never have been able to connect with in the first place.

I exit the house and wait a moment for my eyes to grow accustomed to the dark of the garden and the forest beyond. When they do, I assess the area around me. I don't want any surprises.

I can't see anything, anyone.

I cross the garden toward the summerhouse, keeping my eyes on the windows in the second room, where a low light continues to move about.

Someone is searching for something.

The light pauses. Moves on. Moves back again.

What are they looking for? There is only Eleanor in there. Surely Elizabeth would never think Briar's necklace would be left unguarded.

I creep around the side of the summerhouse and attempt to look in through the window, but I can see only the dark outline of a person.

No, wait. Two people.

There are two people in there.

Geon and Catherine, surely.

The French doors stand ajar—an invitation, or perhaps a dare. I slide inside and cross the first room of the summerhouse quietly, each step calculated. The mysterious light continues to move about, casting fleeting shadows. With a sense of dread pooling in my gut, I make my way to the doorway to the second room and peer inside.

I can see only a partial section of the room, but instantly I see that I was right. Geon Yoon is here. Moonlight from the room's skylight shines down upon him. He sits in a chair as if someone has placed him there, and he looks terrible—pale and drawn, gaunt and dazed. His arms tremble as they rest awkwardly upon his thighs. He hunches over slightly, as if in pain, and his posture reminds me of someone long ago—someone else who suffered at Elizabeth's hand.

It reminds me of Emily.

The light continues to move about in another section of the room. It pauses a moment, and I catch sight of something on the floor. Elizabeth's ledger. Half of the spine is ripped off of it for some reason. The light sweeps again.

Catherine.

It must be.

And there's no point in holding back now, so I reach my hand around the doorway and search for the switch. I find it, flick it on, and light floods the room, revealing every corner, every crevice.

A movement. Someone steps out.

"Catherine," I say.

Except it's not Catherine.

It's Elizabeth.

It's Elizabeth herself.

Time slows. For a brief but eternal moment, I stand frozen, believing myself to be paralyzed again, back in my waxen form, helpless—as helpless as Geon.

Reality cracks at the edges as my mind attempts to come to grips with her resurrection.

It's not possible.

And yet here she is. In the flesh. Not an illusion. Not a figment of my imagination, not some ghostly apparition but a corporeal presence, as solid and real as the ground I'm standing on.

She is risen. Somehow she's managed it. It was, I see now, inevitable. Of course she has. How did I ever doubt her ability to do the impossible?

It's the strangest thing, seeing her again—in modern clothes, no less. She wears a beautifully fitted power suit of muted gold brocade—a nod to the gown her waxen form wears. For a moment, my brain can't quite compute. It's as if we are returned to 1769. As if everything that happened then was only yesterday. As if we've just been sauntering around the pleasure gardens, drinking champagne and eating delicately sliced ham. Strolling in St. James's Park. Sipping tea in the wonderfully wallpapered sitting room of the *sérail*. And so many other things come flooding back—visions of the past. I see Polly's wild, beseeching eyes. I see Elizabeth pushing Emily, knocking her head. I see her hovering above me after the curricle accident. I see her conspiring with Briar at the anatomist's, giving us the draft that would entrap Emily and me forever.

"Well," Elizabeth says, giving me a long once-over. "I was wondering when you'd show up."

The shock of seeing her has made me stupid. I can't think. "But how did you—"

"If you think I'm going to stand here and deliver some monologue, divulging all my secrets, you're sorely mistaken."

"I—"

I hear footsteps behind me, at the door. I whirl around and jump sideways. Is it Ro? Does she know I've come out here? Did she hear me?

"I can't see her anywhere," someone says, entering the summerhouse. "No one seems to be awake in the cottage."

Catherine.

"Oh," she says, spying me. For a moment she looks guilty, but then her expression turns triumphant. "I knew you were hiding something. But never in a million years did I guess it might be this." She glances from me to Elizabeth and back again. She speaks too quickly, her words tripping over one another. She seems overexcited and feverish, her cheeks highly colored. For a moment I doubt that she's under Elizabeth's spell at all, wonder whether it's plain old Catherine, finally getting what she's always wanted. I stare at her, incredulous. I suppose she doesn't know Elizabeth, but if she thinks Elizabeth is going to let her write this tale—publish it in a book—she couldn't be more wrong. Elizabeth has got what she wanted. And now Catherine will be discarded. There won't be any book, because Catherine won't be leaving here alive.

"I always knew my knife was special," Catherine gloats,

beaming. "So did my ancestor. The ledger too. I knew there was more to it all."

My gaze moves to the ledger, still lying on the floor with its spine ripped. Why have they ruined it?

Elizabeth snorts. "The knife was special! Don't be stupid. Your ancestor was an idiot. The only thing he thought was special about that knife was the quick buck he could make out of it, touring the country and telling the tale of how he'd been attacked—which he richly deserved to be, the pervert."

Catherine looks a little hurt by Elizabeth's words. "But he was right, wasn't he?" Even now she can't let this go, can't help arguing her point. She glances from Elizabeth back to me. "Anyway, I knew there was a missing piece. But it wasn't your mother, was it, Alys? It was my knife. All along, it was my knife."

That knife.

My gut turns over as I remember my own, remember what I did with it.

The stomachs I slid it into. The throats I slit with it.

I have to push the thoughts from my mind. *That wasn't me.*

I did those things because I was made to. Not because I wanted to.

Never because I wanted to.

My gaze turns to Geon, sitting, shivering. "You need to let him go," I tell Elizabeth. Whatever his purpose was, he's useless to her now, surely—now that she's managed to rise. I don't think he has much fight left in him. How I hate myself for seeing him like this. His fate is all my doing.

Elizabeth gives me a look that tells me all I need to know. "You can't really think I'd let him leave. He's with me now. I'll need a few willing people to do my bidding, to get me started." She looks over at Catherine. "Catherine here wasn't difficult to persuade."

I'll bet.

I don't ask what Elizabeth's plans are. She won't tell me, and it doesn't matter anyway. All that matters is that I have to stop her from enacting any of them.

It's just going to be a little harder than I thought.

What I really don't understand is why she's come here—to the coven home. If she's risen, if she's got what she wanted, why bother? Why hasn't she run far, far away, where the coven and I could never find her?

It simply doesn't make any sense.

"What do you want?" I ask her bluntly. "If you're risen, why are you even here?"

Elizabeth nods. "A good question. I knew you'd get to it eventually. All I want is the necklace—Briar's necklace—and I'll be on my way. See how accommodating I am? I don't even want my wax model. Just the necklace, and I'll be off. No one needs to get hurt."

I glance at Geon.

"What are you looking at him for? He would have happily locked up both our models for all eternity given half a chance."

That's true, but again, he would have done this only because of Elizabeth. Because of the Venuses. The bewitchment. And my involvement of him. Not because it was in his nature. Not because he wanted to. He never wanted to. I'd seen that in his eyes the first time I'd met him.

"Honestly, you're boring me already, with your sniveling sentimentality. You should be thanking me. I scraped you off the streets of London. If it weren't for me, you would have been that creature we discussed when we first met—a miserable, toothless old hag riddled with disease, rutting against some lecherous old fool in a dark corner of Covent Garden." Elizabeth flicks a hand. "It's difficult to believe that you haven't grown up in two hundred and fifty-odd years, but here we are. I *saved* you. Gave you immortality. You were the lucky one."

Incredible. She wants me to thank her. For grooming me. For drugging me. For taking my life away, and my unborn child's. For stealing my future, Emily's future, what we might have had. And yet I'm not surprised at all by this. Elizabeth always thinks only of herself—can think only of herself. She is the ultimate narcissist.

"Catherine," Elizabeth barks, "go to the cottage and fetch the necklace of hair. Break in if you must. Stab a few people if you need to." She bends down and slides something across the floor. It skitters as it goes, and for a moment I remember Geon's black-handled knife doing the same thing in the storage facility. But this knife is different—pearl handled. As I watch it go, I'm taken further back. Much further back. To that chophouse. To my last outing. To standing outside in the freezing cold. To following the student—Catherine's ancestor—who had eyed me so lasciviously as I lay in my waxen form earlier that day. To the tussle, the knife clattering over the floorboards, the handle loosening and detaching.

And something falling out.

I had thought the handle had been stuffed for weight.

But now I remember the wiriness of the material inside.

"Oh." I exhale as Catherine stops the knife with her foot. How could I have missed this? I can't believe I didn't understand what I'd seen back in the chophouse all those years ago. "The knife handles were stuffed with hair. That's how Briar controlled us from afar."

Now I understand perfectly how Elizabeth has risen. Just as Ro mentioned this afternoon, Elizabeth's hair always had different properties than mine and Emily's. It was bewitched in a different way. That was the deal, wasn't it? That she be allowed to come and go as she pleased. When the knives had been stuffed with our hair, hers had sung out a different song.

The night that I'd attacked Catherine's ancestor in the chophouse—I'd had Elizabeth's knife, not mine. When Briar had taken the two knives out of my sight, she must have stuffed my hair into the handle of Elizabeth's knife, along with Elizabeth's own hair.

That's why Elizabeth behaved so oddly when the knife had been lost in the chophouse. She didn't want her hair—her bewitched hair—out of her presence. And it's why she's come here. She wants all the remaining pieces of her hair. She wants to make sure that she has all the control, that no stone has been left unturned.

It's very Elizabeth.

Suddenly the ledger's ripped spine makes a whole lot more sense. I eye it on the floor once more.

"Added security," Elizabeth says, looking pleased with herself. "I managed to store some hair in the spine of the ledger as well—just in case."

Which explains why she had Catherine steal it from me as soon as she could.

Elizabeth really is too much. My eyes narrow as I stare at her. "You never knew, but Briar lied to you. Often. She used to tell you to return to your wax model so she could work on her spell. But she wasn't doing that at all. She was just sick of you and your demands."

Elizabeth scoffs. "You think this is news to me? I suspected as much. Why do you think I locked her up to burn when I got the chance?" She turns. "Are you still here, Catherine? I thought I told you to go and get the necklace."

Catherine has picked up the knife now. She looks at it nervously as she holds it in her hand. "I didn't . . . I didn't agree to stab anyone," she says to Elizabeth, though it seems difficult for her to form the words.

Elizabeth takes a deep breath. "Catherine, come here."

Catherine hesitates for only a moment before crossing the floor.

When Catherine reaches her, Elizabeth takes her hands. She positions them so that Catherine's palms face upward, the knife resting gently on them. "Look into my eyes," she says.

Again, Catherine does what she's told. I doubt she has much choice.

"You are going to go into the cottage. You are going to locate the necklace of hair. I think it will be with the coven leader, whose name is Jennet. You will kill whoever gets in your way. Return here with the necklace immediately, but do not open the vessel it is kept in. Do you understand?"

Catherine stares at Elizabeth, mesmerized. She nods. "Yes."

"Good. Now go and—"

"Alys . . ." A voice interrupts from the doorway. "How . . . ?"

Ro. I turn to see her, ashen faced as she stands staring at Elizabeth and Catherine before spotting Geon Yoon as well.

"There was hair," I explain, "stuffed into both the handle of Catherine's knife and the ledger. Our hair must have been in all the knives originally. It's how Briar controlled us from afar."

"Oh no."

Elizabeth sighs. "What timing. The cavalry's arrived. Well, Catherine, you may kill her too. Just as long as we get that necklace of hair."

Catherine immediately moves forward, but her expression reads as if she's shocked to find herself doing so. I'd doubted her being firmly under Elizabeth's control before, but now it's clear who is in command. She grips the knife in one outstretched hand and begins to wave it about erratically.

"Catherine, put the knife down," I say, still hopeful I can get through to her. "You don't know what you're doing."

She doesn't put the knife down. But she doesn't move forward again either. Her mouth opens and closes, a line of spittle trailing in between her lips.

"Elizabeth," I hiss, "stop it. Just stop it. She's not part of this. It's got nothing to do with her." I might not like Catherine, but I remember what it is to be under Elizabeth's control, trapped, with nowhere to turn. I can't see that happen to another living soul. Not to Geon, and not to Catherine either. I won't stand by and let it happen. I won't.

"I wouldn't feel sorry for her if I were you," Elizabeth tells me. "Did you know she attached a little device to your car? To track you, so she'd know where you were at all times."

So that's how Catherine tracked me down in Hampshire. But as I look at her, holding that knife, nervous and trembling, her gaze flicking between me and Ro, I see that she's panting, almost frothing at the mouth, and I can't find it in myself to take my anger out on her. No one deserves Elizabeth.

No one.

"Catherine. The necklace," Elizabeth demands.

Catherine's hand stretches out farther. She takes another shuffling step, waves the knife again. She'll have to get past Ro and me to get to the door.

"Ro . . ." I'm about to tell her to step aside when she pushes past me and makes a run for Catherine. "Ro, no!" I try to grab her, but she weaves from my grasp.

"*Stop her.*" Elizabeth's voice is firm.

Catherine shivers involuntarily at the command, and lunges out as Ro reaches her. Ro makes a grab for the knife as I run over to her. I'm stronger. It should be me taking Catherine on, not Ro. I manage to grasp Ro's shirt and hurl her to one side.

But as she flies backward, Catherine lashes out. The blade glints silver in the light and I watch as it catches Ro's upper arm.

Ro gasps as she staggers back toward the summerhouse window, hitting the frame with a thump. The movement—the sound—sees me flash back to Emily hitting the doorframe in the *sérail*. That sickening thud. Her dizziness. The blood.

Ro looks down at her arm just as blood begins to seep through the fresh cut in her shirt.

"Ro!" I cry out as Catherine looks on, horrified at what she's done.

"Fetch. The. Necklace," Elizabeth repeats to her charge.

Catherine's eyes flick wildly, anxiously. I can see she's trying to resist Elizabeth's orders. "I—she—" she stutters.

In the corner, Geon groans, hunching farther forward.

Blood seeps between Ro's fingers, clamped around her arm.

I can't bear it any longer.

"Stop. Just stop. No more. You can have it. You can have the necklace."

"Alys, no!" Ro cries out.

I shake my head. I'm not going to stand here while Ro bleeds, watch Catherine walk into the cottage and stab whoever gets in her way. I just can't. I can't let that happen.

There has to be another way.

"It's not worth it, Ro." I glance over at her for a second before turning my attention back to Catherine and Elizabeth. "It's just not. She's not worth it."

"Right, then. That's sorted. Off you go and fetch it," Elizabeth says—not to Catherine but to Ro.

"She's bleeding," I tell Elizabeth.

"Well, she's hardly bleeding to death, is she? Go and get the necklace, and don't—" She halts here. She looks from Ro to me and back again, with that calculating gaze that she has. I can see that she's assessing, planning, scheming. How will she find a way to triumph? To get what she wants?

Then, as I watch, I'm surprised to see something else in her expression—a flicker of something I've rarely seen.

Fear.

Elizabeth's worried.

What had she been about to say? She'd pulled herself up as if she'd been about to say something she shouldn't.

As if she'd been about to give something away.

I frown, a thought ticking over in the back of my mind. It takes a moment or two for it to come to me. But when it does, the world around me slows. Stills.

I force myself not to look at Elizabeth.

I can't give myself away.

Because I've just realized what she's worried about.

I think I've worked out why Elizabeth's really here. It's not just to leave no stone unturned. It's not just to gather every last strand of her precious hair. No. She's guessed the same thing I've just guessed.

Oh, how I hope I'm correct.

Even if I am, to get this to play out right will be difficult. It's like I'd thought back in London—I'll have to be strong. And I'll have to be smart.

"Ro, are you okay to get the necklace?" I ask.

For a split second, Ro's eyes beseech me to ask her to do anything but that, but then she nods. It's always been my choice how this would all end, and I know she'll do whatever I tell her to. She pushes herself away from the window and starts for the door, still clutching her arm. As she passes by me, I give her a look, trying to let her know that it's all right.

That it's going to be all right.

At least, I hope so.

"No tricks," Elizabeth says. "Everyone else stays inside the house. Everyone."

"You can wake Jennet and Sorrel. Tell them who's here, what's happened. But don't bring them out with you," I tell Ro.

Wake them, I try to have my gaze tell her. *Tell them what's happened. And maybe one of you will come to the same conclusion I have.*

I watch Ro go. She's out the door and running down the side of the summerhouse in a moment, and I can only hope that she begins to put everything together, all the pieces of the jigsaw puzzle. Elizabeth rising. But coming here anyway. For the necklace.

Come on, Ro. Come on.

Think. Think hard.

The problem is, I'm not sure whether Ro heard Elizabeth's instruction to Catherine. Those words were uttered just before Ro arrived at the summerhouse, but was Ro already there? Watching? Listening? Maybe she was. I try to recall Elizabeth's exact wording.

You are going to go into the cottage.

You are going to locate the necklace of hair.

You will kill whoever gets in your way.

Return here with the necklace.

But do not open the vessel it is kept in. That's what Elizabeth had stopped herself from saying to Ro. She'd stopped herself just before she could tell her not to open the box.

I bite my lip, my gaze moving to Elizabeth. I can't give anything away. I have to pretend she's about to get everything she wants on a silver platter. "Where will you go?" I ask her. "After this."

"Well, I'm hardly going to tell you, am I?" she scoffs. She moves over to grab the knife off Catherine. "Give that to me," she snaps. "Sit down there. Next to him. On the floor."

Tears are streaming down Catherine's face now, though she doesn't make a sound. Elizabeth gives her a shove and she sits down upon the floor next to Geon Yoon. His whole body is shaking now, his legs twitching uncontrollably.

"Outside." Elizabeth points the knife at me.

I almost laugh.

We are both as strong as each other. The fight would be epic. But also pointless. Our bodies would only repair themselves in a moment.

No, I'm not going to fight her.

But I *am* going to stand up to her.

"He needs a blanket," I tell her, my gaze shifting to Geon.

"You can't be serious."

"I'm going to give them both blankets. And then we're going to go outside. And then you can have the necklace and you can go. But Catherine and Geon stay here."

Elizabeth glances at the pair, Geon on his chair, Catherine on the floor. "Fine. In this state they'll only hold me back anyway." It's clear that she doesn't think they're worth her time.

I'm reminded of Emily again, her body racked with pain. *Perhaps she is not of as much use to us as we thought she would be,* Briar had said.

And it's Emily I think of as Elizabeth moves toward the door. As I fetch two blankets from the chest in the room. As I wrap one tightly around Geon, who stares fixedly at the floor, practically catatonic now. The other goes around Catherine. As I wrap it around her, she looks up at me as if she's hoping I can wake her from this nightmare, a feeling I remember all too well.

"I didn't mean to . . ." she says.

"It's all right. Everything's going to be all right," I tell her.

Please let it be all right.

Please let Ro work it out.

S HE'S CERTAINLY TAKING her time," Elizabeth says.

We're standing on the wide expanse of lawn, staring up at the cottage, where the first bedroom light has just flicked on inside.

"Probably because you had Catherine stab her," I reply.

"Yes, I suppose so," she says, feigning boredom.

But she doesn't fool me for a moment. Elizabeth is tense. Ready to spring into action at a moment's notice, like a cat waiting to pounce.

I stare at her. At this creature. This complicated creature. This devil. Will I ever understand her? I don't think so. And perhaps it's best that I don't, or can't. That something inside me will always refuse to. I could never be like her. Not in a hundred years. Not in a thousand.

"You once told me that you wanted the *sérail* to be a place of companionship, of protection, a fair establishment, unlike Mother Wallace's. You said you wanted it to be like a family. You could have had such a place. You could have had all those things if you hadn't got in your own way."

Her eyes flick to mine. "Could I? One of you was diseased, and the other pregnant."

So that's how it's going to be. If she's learned anything, she won't admit it.

"Don't you ever feel guilty?" I can't help but prod further. Is there anything there? Any feeling at all? There must be something. "Guilty for what you did? To Emily. To me."

She stares back at me incredulously. "Guilty? No. No, I don't. And I'll tell you why. Only the strongest survive. If you couldn't survive what I threw at you, then you didn't deserve to go on. I didn't make you run away to the city. I didn't get you pregnant.

And yet you looked to me, expected me, the strong one—the survivor—to save you from the mess you had made, to find a way, to carry you. That's why I don't feel guilty. Because if you can't find your own way out of a situation, you don't deserve to go on. You need to step aside and make way for those who can, those who are stronger. At least Emily could see that much, staying in her model, waiting and wanting to burn."

I shake my head. She thinks Emily was weak, pitiful. That she didn't have the courage, or the strength of mind, to go on.

How little she understands.

Emily was the strongest of us all. She had wanted to use the little strength she had left to push me forward so that *I* might survive, so that I might have a chance to go on. My baby too.

But I'm not going to argue with Elizabeth. There's no point. And I don't want to give away the fact that I think I know what Emily did—her final, triumphant act, her final act of love for me.

"Well, I'm glad we got that sorted," I tell her.

The bottom line is, Elizabeth isn't worth my time. She never was. If there was a part of her that wanted that equitable establishment—and I think that, deep down, she might have believed in that concept—there was also a sharper, meaner, bleaker part of her that would never have been able to execute it. She would always feel the need to come out on top of everyone else. Perhaps Sir William had sensed this in her when he had abandoned her—that she was a lost cause, that she was rotten to the very core.

We stand in silence as the windows of the cottage begin to light up. I think I see Sorrel at a window. Jennet. The moon shines down brightly on us, and I'm glad there's still some time until dawn.

I take a deep breath. Look up at Jennet, at Sorrel. I know they are here for me. And for Emily.

And then Ro appears at the back door of the cottage.

I know it as soon as I lay eyes on her.

She's worked it out. Or Jennet or Sorrel has.

A swell of relief almost overwhelms me.

Let both of us be right. Let all of us be right.

Elizabeth moves away from me. She's wary, I think, that I'll try something. She knows I'm the only person here strong enough to take her on. But I know her well enough to see, once again, that she's nervous. Her jaw is hard now, set. Her gaze flicks quickly this way and that.

She's terrified.

She wants that crystal jewelry box with Briar's necklace inside, and she wants out of here.

"No tricks," she calls out, to no one in particular. She motions to the center of the lawn with the knife. "Leave it there. And then step away."

"Go on, Ro," I say. "It's okay. She'll leave then. She'll go."

Ro nods, and her poker face is good, believable. Oh, but I hope that's what it is, because Ro has always had a terrible poker face. She's the absolute worst at keeping secrets.

"Stay away from her with that knife," I say to Elizabeth.

She ignores me, doesn't even give me a second glance, her eyes never leaving the crystal jewelry box.

She's done with me. Again. I have been discarded. Again.

And I'm glad of it. It's good. Because I think . . . I think she actually believes she's going to get away. Which is all I care about now.

"There. Leave it there," Elizabeth barks at Ro.

Ro bends down, places the crystal jewelry box, with its beautiful garnets shimmering in the moonlight, carefully upon the ground, nestled in the grass. The twist of braided hair lies in the box's depths, silent and still.

"Good," Elizabeth says, still holding the knife out, just as she had made Catherine do. And, like Catherine's, Elizabeth's hand has a tremor to it. The smallest tremor, but it's there. I see it. The fear is real. "Now go," she says. There is an insouciant flick of her hair, that glorious, bewitching red-gold hair.

She thinks she's won.

No one bests me, she had said in St. James's Park, in that moment when she had decided what our fates would be. *No one.*

Ro begins to rise. But as her fingers leave the box, they flip the hinged lid open.

And, as one, the coven chants, lifting the spell.

My eyes close involuntarily as the hair immediately sings out to me. Whispering. Calling. Giving the choice to come and go from my waxen form.

It sings to Elizabeth, too, but, the words not being meant for me, I can't understand what that song says. I know that it once would have allowed her to come and go from her model as she pleased, as she and Briar had agreed. That was a choice that had been afforded to Elizabeth when all was well between her and Briar. So that is what the hair encased in her knife allowed her to do.

But the hair in Briar's necklace was different, wasn't it? I had forgotten that. Unable to cope with my grief, my loss, I had pushed it away as soon as it had been offered to me after the fire. And then I had not wanted to think on it again, that necklace, that terrible object that had lain at Briar's throat, that abomination that forced us to march, to hunt, to kill.

I shake my head, breaking free of the sound, and open my eyes once more. I'm met with the sight of Elizabeth, her own eyes widening in dawning horror of what Ro has just done, and I know instantly that I was right in my guess in the summerhouse. Elizabeth does not hear the same song I hear—inquiring as to whether I would like to enter my model or be released from it. Her mouth gapes open in incredulity. She drops the knife, her hands reaching up to cover her ears.

No, I do not know what she hears. But I know what it is.

It is Briar's final spell. Her final revenge.

Against Elizabeth.

How perfect that Elizabeth's final plan—locking Briar in that room to burn alive—had been her very undoing.

I think that what Elizabeth didn't bank on was that Briar could change the spell upon her necklace. On realizing Elizabeth had locked her in the room at the anatomist's burning studio, Briar must have quickly forced Elizabeth to return to her model. Then she had changed the spell upon the necklace entirely, changed it to a spell that would trap Elizabeth in her model forever if she ever managed to rise again. That was when Emily had risen and somehow convinced the witch to change the spell upon my hair in the necklace too. I don't know how she did it. Surely there would have been some sort of struggle, for Briar could have used Emily's strength to release them both from the room. No, I don't know how Emily succeeded in having Briar change the spell and in making sure she burned. But I know she did it. Somehow.

It's as I thought before, what Elizabeth didn't understand.

Emily was the strongest of us all.

Whether Elizabeth utters any final words, I'll never know, because as that inexorable darkness swirls around her, grabbing at her and dragging her away into that lavish, beautiful sarcophagus that will be her final resting place—if only for a few hours, before I burn it—I'm already speaking over her. "I would hazard a guess that we are both here for the same thing,"

I call out. They were her first words to me, and they will be my last to her.

Because I realize that maybe I do understand her after all. Looking back, I think she did love Sir William, in her own way. Or she came as close as she could come to something like love. At the very least, she considered him hers. And when her beloved toy was taken away from her, she could not stand for it. She had to find a way to triumph, to show him he was wrong. And she would have done anything to do so, would have gone to any lengths.

Which she did.

How confusing love is. How disorienting. It had led me a merry dance to London when I thought I had found it in Nicholas, but I could not have been more wrong.

How lucky I had been, then, that it had found me.

I blink, the hair still singing in my ears, Emily's final act of love stretching out across the centuries.

And when I open my eyes, Elizabeth is gone.

WE WORK QUICKLY then. Ro hunts in the left-behind pile of Elizabeth's nonmagical clothes to find the knife and the plait of hair from the ledger. She struggles to open the knife handle, and, slightly dazed, I race over to her. I use my strength to wrench it apart, catching the hair as it falls out. Ro takes a box of matches from her pocket.

"I'll let you do the honors," she says, passing it to me.

I take the hair over to some nearby pavers and light it, the acrid smell instantly filling my nostrils and making me cough. And then I stand, Ro beside me. She takes my hand, and we watch the hair burn in silence.

Only when it is gone does she dare close the crystal jewelry box. She holds it gently in both hands and utters some words that silence the singing for me. I know it's fine for her to do so. Briar would have made sure that final spell trumped all others when it came to trapping Elizabeth inside her model forever.

"You did it, Alys" are Ro's next words to me. "You really did it!" She envelops me in another of those hugs that I could definitely get used to, though she winces with pain as she pulls back.

"Is your arm okay?" I inspect it through the cut in her T-shirt.

"I don't think it's big. It's stopped bleeding." She shakes her head. "You really had me going. I thought you were actually going to give her the necklace. It was only when I got inside the cottage that I realized it didn't make sense—why would she be here if she'd already managed to rise?"

"It took me a while too. I think it was because of the shock of seeing her standing there when it shouldn't have been possible."

Hearing a sound, we both turn to see Jennet and Sorrel exiting the cottage.

As she crosses the lawn, Jennet is on the phone—I'm guessing with the final two members of the coven, letting them know what has happened.

I imagine them opening up the truck where Elizabeth waits, trapped inside her waxen form in the crate, hopefully screaming with rage. But I know that she'll remain there now, thanks to Briar's spell.

And then, in just a few hours' time, she will be gone.

We concentrate on looking after Catherine and Geon now. They're ferried into the warmth of the cottage's snug, and given hot tea and toast. They're both dazed and confused—Geon more so than Catherine. I keep away from them both, knowing my presence is probably triggering for them. Instead, I hide out with Ro and her bandaged arm in the kitchen, peering around the doorway every so often at the pair's blanket-covered backs.

"What are we going to do with them?" I ask her. "How can we explain this away?"

"It won't be easy, but it's possible. I think the connection with Geon will be quite easily broken. Once Elizabeth's hair has all been destroyed, his interest will probably wane. We can return him to his mother. And before we do so, we'll help him to remember in a different way what has happened. Have him believe that Elizabeth was his father's obsession, never his. That he had a hand in destroying her so she can't ruin anyone's life ever again."

I nod. I can see Geon remembering everything in a foggy fashion, just like Mrs. Owen. "But what about Catherine? She's always fought through those spells. Her obsession is next-level. There's the book she's writing. She has an agent. She'll be surrounded by research, papers, files. The Venuses are her whole life."

"That will be harder. I think the best we can do is to give her back the knife, and maybe have her believe you've moved overseas with the Venuses. That her line of research into you came to a dead end. It's not like we can make the myth of the Venuses disappear. They're too well-known."

I peek around the corner to see Catherine sipping from a mug of tea. "I'd like to feel sorry for her, but apparently she has a tracking device on my car."

Ro sighs. "That really doesn't surprise me at all. Because . . . Catherine."

I give Ro a look. "I can't say I'll miss her. But . . ." I think of the few people whom I will miss and think will miss me too.

"Marco. Mrs. Owen. Phoebe." I can't really find the words. So few friends for someone who has lived so long.

Ro reaches for my hand. "I know. We'll help them to remember things differently."

"Good." I glance out the kitchen window. "I think it will be dawn soon."

"Yes," Ro replies.

"Do you think we can . . . Is there still time?" I know the truck has arrived now, that Elizabeth's waxen model is here.

There's a long silence, filled with so many emotions: sorrow, relief.

When Ro speaks again, her voice is full of concern, her expression grave. "You don't have to go, Alys," she says. "You're safe now. Everyone's safe now. From Elizabeth."

"I know," I tell her. "But the thing is . . . I want to go. It's . . . time."

AS DAWN BREAKS, Ro, Jennet, Sorrel and I get ready to burn the wax model of Elizabeth. I'd imagined a ritual bonfire on the lawn, so when I'm led to the industrial-waste incinerator that the coven has purchased, I stop in my tracks. "Couldn't be bothered with a pyre?"

"Environmental regulations," Ro replies with a grimace.

"I thought it was a pizza oven," I tell her. And I can't help it—I start laughing. As they say, if I couldn't laugh, I'd cry.

"We did stump up extra for the black version," Ro tells me. "You know, to make it a little more . . . witchy."

This only makes me laugh harder. I'm going to miss Ro so very much. Only Ro could have brought me out of my shell, made me be able to trust someone again.

When I'm finally done, I have to wipe the tears from my eyes. "Environmental regulations. This modern world..." I say. "A girl can't even have a good old-fashioned witch burning these days. No offense."

"None taken," Jennet replies for them all.

Elizabeth's wax model lies, covered with a sheet, just outside my line of sight. It's ready and waiting to be rolled over on a trolley and placed inside the incinerator.

"Will it... hurt?" I ask. "Will she be sentient?"

"She might know," Jennet says, reluctantly. "But I don't believe it will hurt."

I nod. Despite all the pain Elizabeth has caused, I'm not sure I could burn her model if I knew that I was inflicting pain. There's been enough pain, enough suffering.

I stand back and look on, detached, as the coven goes through the motions of destroying Elizabeth. I have often wondered whether, having got to this moment, I would feel that thrill of exhilaration that overcame me on my seeing Dr. Chidworth and Mr. Corbyn meet their maker. Or if I would feel the sickening sense of shame that came... after.

But I feel nothing as Elizabeth's model goes up in flames. I'm numb as I try to grapple with the fact that she is truly gone, our connection severed forever.

I feel it lift and float away.

And just like that, I'm alone.

I don't feel triumphant, for I know I haven't won.

There are no winners in Elizabeth's game.

"Alys?" Ro comes over to touch my arm. "The ledger next?"

Sorrel has kindly brought it out, along with a small wooden table. The ledger, with its haphazardly torn spine, rests on the table. There is also the crystal jewelry box with Briar's necklace in it, and the small case that had been in the summerhouse—

the one I'd asked Ro to prepare. I reach for the case now, and I open it up. Inside lies a beautiful vintage fountain pen.

I hadn't wanted the ledger because I'd known about the hair inside it—I'd never guessed that it was there.

No, I'd wanted it for this moment.

I pick the fountain pen out of its case. "It's really special, Ro," I say, holding it carefully. I know she would have looked at hundreds before choosing this one. She would have wanted it to be just right.

She wrinkles her nose, not speaking because, I think, she's fighting back tears. She sniffs and helps me to find the correct page in the ledger, that old spine cracking as we turn the pages.

I make my way to Elizabeth's final entries, the ones where she totted up what Emily and I owed her.

And then, beside these figures, I uncap the pen and write.

Debt settled in full.

We owe Elizabeth nothing. She took more from us than we could ever have imagined. She stole our very selves. Any future we might have had. Any happiness. My child. But it is over now.

We are done.

I re-cap the pen, put it back in its box and pass it to Ro. "It's yours," I tell her. I know she'll keep it as long as she lives. And I hope that is a very long, happy time. I've already made sure everything I own is in her name, or is accessible to her—including Mrs. Yoon's money, and our business in Whitby. And I know Ro will be okay. This was always on the cards. From the very first day I met her, she knew what I was, what would happen. Eventually. Yes, she'll be okay. In time.

We burn the ledger then.

Which means there is only the necklace left.

The necklace and Eleanor's model.

I can't bring myself to think of it as me, because it's not. That ugly piece of wax—that horror show—is not me, is not my baby. It never was. It was Elizabeth's revenge; that's all. It remains in the summerhouse. I simply need to accept the call to join it once more. Then the coven will bring it out and it will burn.

No one speaks for some time. Not Jennet. Not Sorrel. Not Ro. They wait for me.

It's beautiful to stand there with them in the dawn, in the ancient woodland of the New Forest, birds filling the silence.

"I suppose it's time," I say at last, my words heavy with finality. This is truly it, the closing chapter in what seemed an unending saga. "You know I'm not one for pretty speeches, or grand declarations. But you also know how I feel about all of you, the depth of my gratitude for everything you've done for me. Thank you all. So much. For everything. For standing by me. Through... well, through it all." I can barely look at them. I'm already breaking away. Leaving. But I know they will understand. They have always understood me, seen me for who I really am, not what I once was.

Jennet steps forward, her expression grave. "Alys," she says, "I must ask if you're absolutely certain about this. Elizabeth is gone. You are safe."

Her words hang in the charged air, and I cut them down with my quick reply.

"I'm sure," I say. And I am, just as I told Ro.

I take the crystal jewelry box and open it for the final time. The necklace begins to sing to me. I may come or go from my model as I please. The choice is mine.

And I know that when I make my reply I won't be afraid to return to my model—not this time—because it will be my choice. I will finally reclaim my body, myself.

Finally—*finally*—I am the mistress of my own destiny.

"There isn't a doubt in my mind," I tell my friends—my true and trusted friends.

I squeeze Ro's hand. Quickly. And then I let go.

I close my eyes and ask to be returned.

And then, blackness.

But there is no fear, for I know that soon I will dream again.

And that this time Emily, forever running, will have stopped.

She will have turned. Her arms will be outstretched.

Emily is waiting for me.

AUTHOR'S NOTE

The initial idea for *Slashed Beauties* came after I saw an anatomical Venus in a museum in Vienna. I could immediately see that, just like Elizabeth, she was a complicated creature. With her long, luscious hair; dewy, waxen skin; lustrous pearls; erotic expression; and... entrails, I wasn't entirely sure what to make of this uncanny collision of art and science, violence and beauty, but I knew I was transfixed. I began researching the models, and I spent hours gazing at the illustrations and photographs in Joanna Ebenstein's wonderful *The Anatomical Venus*, delighting and sickening myself at the same time. I knew I would have to write a book about these amazing creations one day, but I also knew that meant waiting until they spoke to me and told me their tale.

A number of years later, I found myself reading volume after volume of *Harris's List of Covent-Garden Ladies*—an annual directory of London sex workers that was published from 1757 to 1795. These incredible, bestselling compendiums, some of which can be downloaded for free from Project Gutenberg, are well worth reading for their casts of characters and glimpses into the past, even if they are to be taken with a grain of salt. It was during this reading that the characters of Eleanor and Emily came to me. And they were soon joined by Elizabeth. And poor Polly. The cast grew and grew, and I found myself busily plotting away.

Readers have asked me where they might see an anatomical Venus in the flesh (so to speak) for themselves. Some of the finest examples can be seen at La Specola in Florence, but there are also some to be found at the Semmelweis Medical Museum in Budapest, at the Josephinum Medical Museum in Vienna, and at the Museo di Palazzo Poggi in Bologna.

ACKNOWLEDGMENTS

It most definitely needs to be acknowledged that however worthy an idea might be and however wonderfully it might be executed, there is much luck and timing involved in publishing. I've been extremely lucky with all the help *Slashed Beauties* has had along the way to make it the story it has become, and I am supremely grateful for everyone's assistance.

First and foremost, thank you to my agent Edwina, for spotting the tiny little gem amongst all the rubble, for taking me on board and for supervising all the rigorous rounds of polishing. Thank you also to agent Jason for finding the book the perfect home in the US. Thank you to agent Annabel for knowing it was all going to be too difficult and encouraging me onward anyway.

Thank you to all at Verve Books, particularly Jenna and Demi, for seeing what could be and for further polishing assistance, and to Ellie for finding even more perfect homes overseas.

Thank you to Annie and the team at Berkley and to Rachael and the team at HQ for their genuine enthusiasm and so many kind words.

Thank you to all my literate guinea pigs who have read along the way—Mum, Dad, David, Nilly. Thank you to Allison and

Megan for listening to me moan (writers love to moan, but we keep writing anyway).

Thanks to Harry for accompanying me on plotting walks. And no thanks at all to Titus, who most likely asked to be fed 1,658 times and danced upon the keyboard while I was trying to write this book.